God Shuffled His Feet

Mark Ellenbogen

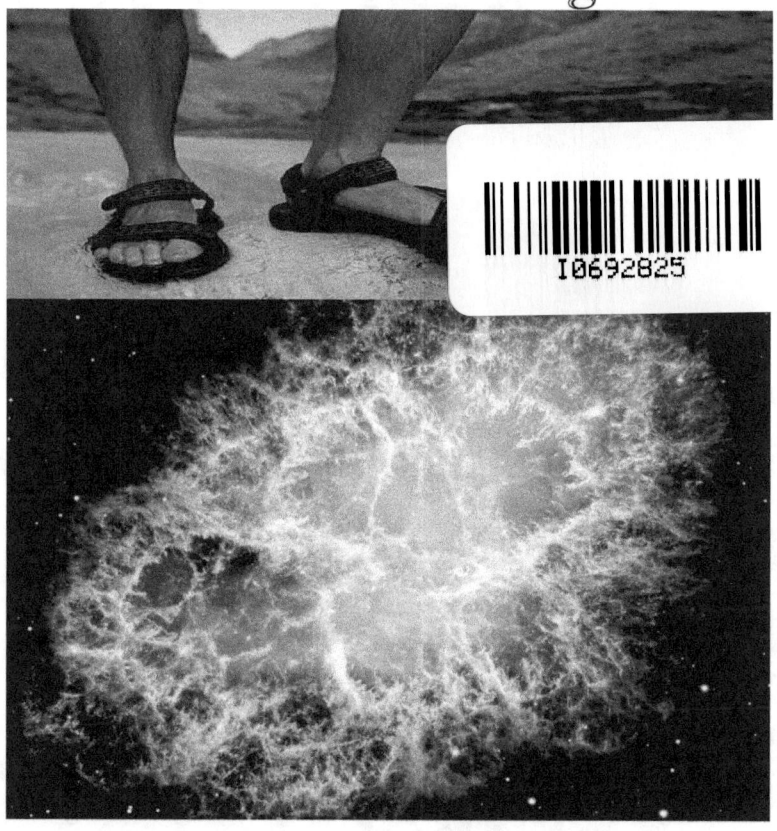

I0692825

A Book of some facts, Science Fiction and Opinion

GOD SHUFFLED HIS FEET

A Book of Science Fiction, Fact and Opinion

Written by

Mark Ellenbogen

This is a work of fiction and science fiction.

Though some of the characters and events in this book are real, most are fictional, as are all of the events that make up the storyline. Any similarity to real people, either living or dead, is coincidence. Other than direct historical facts, the celebrities mentioned and their participation in this story is fictional and is not to be mistaken as fact. Mr. Elon Musk, Jon Stewart, Andersen Cooper and Wolf Blitzer are individuals that I hold in the highest regard. I hope that the portrayal of them in this work of fiction brings a smile to their faces as I have made every attempt to portray them in a positive light.

*GOD SHUFFLED HIS FEET

ISBN-10: 0985386614 ISBN-13:978-0-9853866-1-0-print copy
ISBN-10:0985386606-ISBN-13:978-0-9853866-0-3-ebook Amazon kindle

*Special thanks to the Crash Test Dummies for the title song of the same name.

ABOUT THE AUTHOR

People have called the Author many things other than an author. Don't take him too seriously, he surely doesn't.

Surfer, skier, man, waterless cookware salesman, dry cleaner, delivery man, laborer, auto-mechanic, racer, patient, carpenter, FOS, cabinet-maker, furniture builder, student, architect, home builder, real estate developer, husband, brother, son, father, fly fisherman, scuba diver, lover of books, music and art, mushroom hunter, gardener, chef, white water rafter, jokester, authority, fool, hiker, hunter, farmer, traveler. FOS yes, philosopher and author, never before now.

Mark Ellenbogen makes his home in New Jersey with his wife Alyssa, five kids who roll in and out; two dogs, a cat, a rabbit, lots of tropical fish and two Guinea Pigs. He enjoys doing a little bit of everything from the list above and tries to learn something new to add to it every single day. He's been known to try anything, at least once; some things too much. He's annoying at times. He never knows what he might want to do tomorrow. He likes it that way. If you call him, he won't answer, and if you write him, he probably won't respond.

INTRODUCTION

This book was a test, only a test. The test was to write a novel in ninety days just to see if I could do it; stick to eighty-thousand words and get as close to four hundred pages; why, because the internet told me so. That was the only goal and I passed the test. I'd never done it before and it seemed like the thing to try that day.

This is a book about the immensity, power and mystery of our Universe and God as I understand them to be. This is a work of some actual facts, some fiction and some science fiction. It is meant to entertain and have a little fun. Though it may offend some; no offense is meant.

This is a book about my opinion of religion and man. My opinion is not intended as fact----it is just an opinion and opinions should only be tolerated, sometimes respected and never, ever, taken as Gospel. Well, that's my opinion.

Mark Ellenbogen
Phoenix Hill Farm
Pennington, New Jersey
March—2012

DEDICATION

This work is dedicated first, to Stanley my father, my mentor and my friend; I will love, cherish and miss him always. To Doris, my dear Mother, without you nothing would have been possible for me----go figure.

To Lyss--my love, my Princess, my beshert.

To all the E's and B.E's. All five of you-- give me purpose, joy and love, with a daily challenge too boot.

To my siblings M, M and P; better friends a man could not want. You all indulge me, tolerate me at times, and inspire me. I can't wait for how much humbling I will take about this book from the three of you. Bring it on! Marcia you are welcome to check the facts.

To Eli, Benny and Rex; God never made more perfect creatures. Thanks for your unconditional love.

To the folks in that hall, in that town, that took me in and saved my mind, body and soul through no original thoughts of their own. Thank you; thank you all, from the very bottom of my heart for sharing what you have with me.

In the Land of The Blind the One Eyed-Man is King.
Unknown Author

PROLOGUE

The Hubble Space Telescope is positioned 353 miles above the surface of the earth. Cruising at a speed of just under 5 miles per second, Hubble moves through a synchronized orbit that completes it circuit of our planet every 97 minutes

On April 24, 1990, Hubble finally launched into orbit aboard the Space Shuttle Discovery. The telescope carried five instruments: The Wide Field/Planetary Camera, the Goddard High Resolution Spectrograph, the Faint Object Camera, the Faint Object Spectrograph and the High Speed Photometer. The Hubble Space Telescope and all its cool hardware opened up the heavens and made them visible to man in a way never before experienced.

Members of the Astronomy and Space Science community bid for time on the Hubble by submitting requests to the Flight Operations Team at the Goddard Space Flight Center in Greenbelt, Md. Of the 1000 annual requests for time on the Telescope only 200 requests are selected each year. Being awarded time on the Hubble is considered a coup by any Astronomer or Space Science authority.

BOOK I

CHAPTER 1

Northwestern Coast of California-
December 1, 2011

Situated on a Pacific Coast bluff just outside of McKinleyville California, sits a small planetary observatory run by the science department of Humboldt State University. Inside, surrounded by glowing LED screens, chart recorders and planetary mapping gear, sat Dr. E J Camlala. Camlala, forty-three, is professor of planetary science and astronomy, and director, of the Humboldt Space Observatory. Dr. Camlala was quite respected in the academic world having made a few significant discoveries over the years. A small Pulsar situated near the descending cusp of Gemini was his first eventful claim; quickly followed by a radical approach to separating the distortion in radio wave transmissions known as the Camlala Filtering Formula. His name popped up in the astronomy community as an expert in his field, and as a regular publishing contributor for Astronomy Today magazine. Not a widely read publication, but in his circle, it did carry some weight.

Dr. E. J Camlala took a big hit off the joint in his hand and handed it to the two graduate students across the table from him. Ravi Najir and Sam Klein, both twenty-two years old, and both third year astronomy doctoral grunts, graciously accepted the bone and passed it between them.

Pulling off the rubber band, Dr. Camlala went through the evening delivery from the U.S. Postal service. The sweet smell of fine Humboldt County mountain-grown sinsamellia wafted about the domed observatory control room while a bootleg recording of Umphrey's "Conduit" played in the background. Partying in the Observatory was not the normal protocol; typically, it was the business of observing and mapping the heavens. On a regularly scheduled observation evening, the posted crew would be charting the heavens, taking measurements and communicating globally with their counterparts situated around the Earth. That being said, tonight, with finals having just ended that day and the Christmas break about to begin, the team was letting its hair down for this evening's rotation.

Camlala, with brow scrunched and glasses on the tip of his nose, shuffled through the pile of circulars, robo mail and bills. The pile dropped from his hand to the table leaving one envelope anxiously clutched in his hand—with a wave in the air, he let out a whooping scream.

"Whoo--Hoo!" "This is too much!!" "No Shit! We did it!" A vibrating Camlala shouted out.

Camlala jumped up from the table and danced around the room waving the letter in his hand. He swooped in on his two stoned cohorts, taunting them with the letter as they unsuccessfully tried to snatch it out of his hands. Feinting to the left, Camlala landed a safe distance from Ravi and Sam's reach and proceeded to enlighten them as to the content and cause of his celebration.

"We got the grant! And---we got a slot on Hubble for 2012!" "Do you two Bozos have any idea how big this is?" A breathless and finger pointing E.J. rhetorically demanded of his team.

Najir and Klein looked at E.J.--each other, and burst out laughing. It was their assigned summer study project to file a grant request and observation proposal to the Hubble Observation Committee at Goddard Space Flight Center in Maryland. Both young men were incredibly academically gifted, somewhat geekish in nature, and both shared a twisted sense of humor. In exercising their practical humor; as a joke, they had applied it thickly while they formulated their idea for their thesis. Their concept blossomed into full bloom over summer break as they worked their way across the country. None of the three expected the letter held in Camlala's hand to be the outcome.

The young duo followed the annual music festival season from coast to coast all summer long. As they made their way across the country, they received regular prompting from Professor Camlala for updates on their summer study progress. The summer wore on, and the boys were woefully delinquent in getting the thesis paper work done. A recipe for an ugly cram event loomed as procrastination firmed its foothold. On the final evening of their summer travels, at a weekend gathering at Red Rocks Canyon in Colorado, the boys completed the drafting of their thesis while sitting around a campfire. Their epiphany came well into the inspiring third set of Umphrey's Mghee. The plan formed, a thesis was named and pen went to paper. As the boys furiously scribed their work, Umphreys was shredding the soundwaves; unbeknownst to the band, providing the role of muse for Ravi and Sam's creation.

The serendipity of winning that $250,000 grant, and a yearlong opportunity to view the cosmos from the comfort of their little observatory, was beyond belief. Even better, was the fact that their thesis request was for the, *'Intermittent monitoring of gamma-ray activity in the 4th quadrant of the Crab Nebula for the purpose of verifying the galactic construction of new solar systems'*, a study formulated after much festival enhanced late-night debauchery; a study pulled directly out of their butts. A thesis named with the sole intent of making it sound as impossibly complex and incomprehensible as possible.

When an expectant Camlala had arrived on the morning of the last day of the Red Rocks festival, the final draft had been proudly presented as a goof. Camlala read through it once giving both men a twisted smirk. While Ravi and Sam hovered about waiting for feedback Camlala made for a large boulder to perch upon and finish his reading. The professor read it again and then tossed it down with a chuckle. He looked at the two and said:

"You know what? I like it!"

Camlala, over time, had shared with the two grad students his tireless, yet failed efforts, to gain time on Hubble since 1993. While still a doctoral student at Cal Poly, Camlala sent Hubble requests in on an annual basis. And, on an annual basis, he received one rejection letter after another. Frustrated, he had all but given up his attempts to access the super star-gazing machine.

The three left Colorado with the thesis accepted and their summer study complete. With minor re-writing the request was sent off to Maryland and Hubble for review. The trio had figured 'what the

11

hell'; it was as good a shot as any Camlala had tried over the years. They submitted the request, expecting to hear nothing back short of a rejection.

With wide grins and disbelief in their eyes Ravi and Sam lunged and grabbed the letter out of Camlala's hand. Both boys settled back and read the document. They both turned to Dr. Camlala looked up and in unison said,

"Awesome!" "Fucking-Awesome!"

The two young grads collapsed in a bout of uncontrolled laughter and coughing.

The three Humboldt academics circled back to the table to discuss their good fortune. With excited enthusiasm, they started making plans for what would surely prove to be a pay bonus and possible tenure for Camlala; and for Klein and Najir, a fast track to completion of their doctoral thesis and early graduation.

Un-known to the trio, 6300 light-years away, deep on the far side of the fourth quadrant of the Crab Nebula, a small burst of gamma radiation and static chaos started to emit from a previously unmapped proto-planetary disc. A power beyond their comprehension had made plans of its own and was in the process of fully implementing them. Like a cosmic Lava Lamp on steroids, an amalgam of star and planetary matter, both light and dark energy, was excited and in motion manipulated by some force yet unknown. This pulsating mass of energy was about to redefine the lives of these three Humboldt scientists. Ultimately, the unfolding event would redefine the lives of all Earthlings as well. What a night it was turning out to be!

CHAPTER 2

Macedonia Hills-Roman Empire
C.E. 1054

High in the hills of Macedonia above a well-traveled road stood four solemn figures looking down on the spectacle below. The four observers were dutifully in attendance at the request of their employer. Mandatory attendance was more accurate. Their mission was to observe and take notes. There was every likelihood that there would be a test.

Headed eastward toward Rome marched a Roman legion in full battle dress chanting in cadence with torches held high. Among the group were three Papal Legates of Pope Leo IX. (Three recently excommunicated Papal Legates that is). Legates—for those wanting to know—were entrusted foreign ambassadors of the Pope used to communicate the Church's decrees to all corners of the empire. Having these divine mouthpieces escorted by a fully armed Roman legion just seemed to emphasize the importance of the message more forcefully when presented to the receiving party. The Pope, from his Papal suite in Rome, had just dispatched this group to carry his message of a divine decree as to how the Catholic Church and its rituals were to be properly performed to his Eastern counterpart. The Pope insisted that he had direct divine input on how to achieve salvation, and his methods were not to be trifled with. A most unpleasant visit to Constantinople had just occurred. These Legates had just left the court of Michael Cerularius the Patriarch of the Eastern Roman Catholic Church who had quickly excommunicated the Legates after they had excommunicated him. Apparently, neither group liked what the other side had to say. The source of the medieval pissing match was over whether to use leavened or unleavened bread in the Eucharist. A most critical issue to say the least. The Great Schism separating the Eastern Orthdox Church and the Roman Catholic Church was now final, the lines drawn in the sand, the centuries of blood-letting about to begin. Yet another opportunity lost to unify God's children.

From atop their panoramic perch, the eldest of the four observers leaned in on his staff and turned to his companion.

"Well Yeshua, he's going to be pissed about this now, I guess I see why he wanted us to see this. Not exactly the 'subtle' approach. "

Yeshua sighed and looked at the two younger members of the team.

"Yep, looks like we missed the mark and blew it again. But you know, free will is his policy, not ours. I really thought we had it right this time. We got the message out, widely distributed, unifying and easy to read, for the most part. It was spreading as planned, more and more were embracing the message. I don't know Moshe, maybe Moh and S.G. have a chance to right the cart before he comes down and takes matters into his own hands."

The two younger men nodded in agreement and looked apologetically, with a tinge of condescension, at the senior members of their team.

Moh offered his ascent and smiled confidently,

"I think the Koran as a guidebook, and the Mullahs as messengers are on the right track this time. We have a great chance of molding the order of things—to become a shining example of good orderly direction for mankind. Yes my brothers, have faith, things are moving well and coming together nicely among my people."

Moshe and S.G. were jointly perusing a piece of scrolled parchment, punctuating the air with tsk-tsk sounds while occasionally nodding their heads as Moh rambled on. Moshe looked up from his reading and said:

"What about this? Did you see this memo he sent out? The one about the Caliph vs. Iman issue? Looks like a problem to me, and from the memo, it looks like it has the boss's attention as well."

"A minor set-back. We're sidetracked a bit and have a little dissension in the ranks with regard to management style. My brother-in-law's management system differs from my original plan for uniting and governing all the faithful. That issue aside, we're spreading the good word and managing the needs of the people. We're working through this Sunni-Shiia issue very nicely indeed. It's a little rocky right now, but I don't think that will last. God willing, there will be a consensus soon and the enlightenment can begin anew in peace. It shouldn't be a problem at all. Surely not as drastic as this!" Indicating with his hand, he pointed and nodded towards the retreating army below.

S. G. as was his nature said very little. He shook his head in disgust and gathered his robes about him, being assured that there was no living creature beneath him that might suffer being smashed by his mass; he lowered himself to the ground. Once comfortably situated, he shut his eyes and began to contemplate the suffering of man. The other three looked down as he settled, each rolled their eyes as Moshe said,

"When you have all of eternity to meditate who needs to act? Good luck with that, S.G. and let me know how you make out; I'm going to check in with the Big Guy and see what he has planned for us next."

Yeshuah looked toward the heavens and said,

"Uh-Oh, I think he already has a plan."

It was July 4th, 1054 C.E. and high in the evening sky, deep inside of the constellation of Taurus; a bright light appeared and expanded outward in an amazing light show. The cosmic explosion was observed and recorded simultaneously, by ancient astronomers the world over. From Japan to China, Arabia to Africa, to the Mayan and Inca, recordings and drawings were made; dates were affixed, calculations started. The Crab Nebula had formed; the message clear. God was pissed; and he had a plan.

The three standing members of the team gazed at the procession moving through the valley; shaking their heads as they took one last look at the torches, men and animals marching below. Moh took out a brace of Kat put a wad in his mouth and offered it around. All waved it away graciously declined. After a quick but respectful look at billowing flash of light filling the night sky, they mumbled good-byes to S. G., who sat comfortably and quietly on the ground. With that, they walked their separate ways into the gathering night.

CHAPTER 3

McKinleyville California

December 1, 2011

Ravi Najir and Sam Klein hiked up the hill to the Humboldt Space Observatory with their heads down while deep in thought. It was now two weeks since having been awarded their grant and Hubble observation time. The two young men were still in amazement that no one had called them out on their bluff. Having taken a swipe at the grant with utter bullshit, they had still received everything they had requested. No one, as of yet, raised the first question as to their totally un-proveable and far-reaching dissertation title. So far, the ' *Intermittent monitoring of gamma-ray activity in the 4th quadrant of the Crab Nebula for the purpose of verifying the galactic construction of new solar systems'* held its ground as just the right combination of psycho-pseudo-science-speak that its provenance defined.

The cash strapped California education system had reduced the budget for the Humboldt State Astronomy and Space Science program to a mere trickle; for that, their boon won them accolades among their peers, both students and faculty. The Humboldt Observatory Team was enjoying its newly elevated status to no end, basking in glory and riding the wave. The University President, Roland P. Skinner threw a cocktail party for all the faculty and grad students from the department in celebration. Klein and Najir were paraded on the podium to receive a plaque and hold a giant prop check for $250,000, made out to the Humboldt State Astronomy and Space program. E. J. Camlala stood behind them during the ceremony, beaming in fatherly pride with an ear to ear smile created by the finest of strains grown in the area. Now with the celebrations behind them, the reality had set in that they were counted on to produce and make good on their dissertation's focus of study. Not only were results in demand, they would be expected to publish! Shit!

Camlala weighed in blandly assuring them,

"Guys, Its cool, don't worry about it. It's all good." As their senior advisor he always had all the right answers.

The week earlier they sent the initial target coordinates to the Hubble team at the Goddard Space Center. Over an evening of light drinks and green weed, they had conferred with EJ Camlala and two other members on the faculty to come up with a grouping of four coordinates. The learned team, settled on a position to the northwest of the star Tau, in the constellation Taurus. As an extra measure of fine tuning, further defined by being focused upon the back left quadrant of the Crab Nebula. The team sent the information via an email to their assigned counterpart at Goddard. They had been expecting a quick call back accusing them of being the poser's that they only knew too well they were. No call came, and the two were much relieved and confused as to how far they had been able to play this.

Tonight was to be the first night that Hubble would be swung into orbit and directed to their target. Tonight was the night that they both knew they were to be exposed; and tomorrow would be the day that their academic and future employment hopes would be dashed to earth. Neither said a word as Sam put his hand to the control room door and opened it wide to the path that he was assured would lead to their mutual punishment.

E J sat at his usual seat at the control table. The Disco Biscuits were playing in the background, loudly pounding from the speakers strategically placed around the room. Camlala exclaimed,

"Well boys, tonight is the night!"

Both boys waived him off and went about checking the settings on the observatory refracting telescope.

Camlala said, "Suit yourself but I'm staying tuned in, plugged in and ready for the fireworks show. It's just seven minutes and fifteen seconds until we're on-line with the Hubble. The show is about to begin."

Ravi said, "Knock it off, E. J., we're all very screwed in exactly seven minutes and fifteen seconds. You included."

Sam chimed in, "The best we can hope for is kicking the can for another thirty days by saying our coordinates were off by two or three light years; then, send out another set of bullshit coordinates, after that, I say we high tail it out of town."

Camlala turned to his two miserable charges, and with a look of sage intelligence pontificated. "No one knows what the hell is up there until you look."

"Your choice of coordinates may have been pulled out of your behinds, but your focus direction is going into the thick of some of the most active energy soup in the near galaxy. Maybe something is there, maybe not, but we won't know a thing until they look. So, my suggestion is that you turn the music up, have a glass of wine, and wait for the chart recorders and pictures to come flowing in. Until then...it's all good."

The three desk-top LED screens pinged in recognition that they were now network connected to Goddard, prompting the live feed to start uploading data direct from Hubble. The boys turned on the chart recorders and checked them for paper.

On the far wall was a 50" inch monitor that displayed the view generated by the traditional ground-based mirror reflecting telescope housed at the Humboldt Observatory. Though old and somewhat arcane in technology; the Humboldt ground-based telescope still worked reasonably well. The technology challenged unit was vulnerable to the distortion of the earth's atmosphere, and any direct observation would have to be morphed and adjusted to accomplish the most accurate picture of the object under observation. The Hubble, fully free of the Earth's atmosphere, was not subject to this distortion, and therefore, could portray real time, clear, high- resolution photos of the target object in view.

All four monitors filled with a display of the outer west corner of the Crab Nebula. Following direction the focus started to move away, up and to the left into what was typically dark space. As each increment of adjustment and focus ratcheted in staccato synchronization, the screen began to fill with a rolling, boiling ball of gas, fire and rotating debris. A cosmic fire ball that wasn't supposed to be there and hadn't been there 30 days prior.

"What the heck is that?!" E J exclaimed.

Sam and Ravi stood gaping at the screen, with their jaws dropped in awe. All three were frozen in place when the phone started to ring, and emails started to ping. No one moved. No one breathed. The group totally transfixed, stared at the monitors in disbelief. Ravi broke the spell and grabbed the phone just as the chart readers started to gauge and graph gamma, x-ray and radio waves emitting from the target area. The incoming data was displayed in signature waves that were beyond any graphing parameters on the form chart paper in the machines.

"Hu- Hu –Hello," Ravi stammered, putting the phone to his ear.

Barking from the phone came, "What the hell did you guys find and how the hell did you know it was there?" demanded the special positioning tech from Goddard.

Ravi said, "Look dude, give us a minute here to review the data, can we call you right back? Whatever you do, don't lose your lock on this setting when the orbit trajectory starts to change. Lock it and load it, if we start to lose it, we need to get another fix for the next 97- minute pass."

The tech said, "I'm keeping a fix and transmitting the image and coordinates all over the place right now. My phone is ringing off the hook; my supervisor is jumping up and down waving at me from the observation booth in his pajamas. Call back quick and have a name for this thing. Naming rights goes to the discoverer. Whatever you call it; it's going to be plastered across the news tomorrow. Give me something to put in this stupid report."

Ravi looked around the room, nudged the baggie on the table, shrugged his shoulders at E J and Sam and said, "Let's just call it----the Master Kush formation."

"Works for me," said the Goddard tech.

Ravi hung up the phone and fell into the seat just staring at the monitors with his two dumbstruck colleagues.

CHAPTER 4

News of the celestial discovery of the now famous Master Kush Formation bounced around the science world like a neutron in a mega collider. Every available institutional ground-based telescope—whether operated by seasoned scientists, or by star gazing hobbyists—was locked on tight with the heavens around the Crab Nebula. For six long days astronomers observed and took notes as each new stage of the discovery unfolded. CNN, BBC and al Jazeera ran continual feeds on the event complete with signature music to match the theme. Music choices ranged from the alien bar band scene on Tatooine, to the themes from ET and Star Wars. Network commercial breaks were subtly announced by the mono-tonal five-bar chimes from Close Encounters.

The parade of academics vying for their fifteen minutes of fame in front of the camera; was causing a producer's nightmare of who to put on next. Competition was stiff for commanding the time slot that would generate the most advertiser interest. Madison Avenue spin doctors monitored the Nielsen data around the clock. Bidding pits for ad time were set up in their lobbies. Frantic chaos ensued for auctioning minutes of advertising airtime for millions per minute. It was a veritable information technology orgy in full obscene swing.

Those that couldn't make national TV were relegated to the internet. The internet was abuzz with opinions and comments from all areas of the globe. Mavens of astonomy, astrophysics and space science from every country and center of learning, weighed in with their two cent analysis of the rapidly changing character of the formation.

Google, Facebook and Twitter, along with Wikipaedia, had to bring in extra staff to try to reduce the search engine hits that kept directing people to glossy photos of very green and red hairy buds of the other kind of Master Kush. Curious patrons of astronomy were being mistakenly treated to pictures of illicit crops rather than the targeted celestial display causing the hubbub.

Parents the world over were filing complaints with the FCC while Internet censorship support groups were having a field day. The agenda driven groups were hard at work forcing erroneous horticultural hits by typing the combination of 'Master' and 'Kush' in to search engines. Every mistaken pictorial display of California illicit agrarian effort lent justification and support to their censorship cause.

Conspiracy theorists swore it was a government hoax and doomsday soothsayers came out in droves. The fanatics started to predict the end of days according to their unique understanding of the data at hand. Everyone had a forum. Everyone had a soapbox.

The presses were stopped; the previously committee-approved cover stories pulled in editing rooms everywhere. The covers of every science journal, as well as Time, Newsweek and People, now featured a Hubble generated full glossy layout of the Master Kush Formation. Below, or to the side on each cover, was a caption photo of Sam and Ravi. The two students—and to a lesser degree, their academic advisor Dr. E.J. Camlala—were praised for their monumental discovery and their incredible contribution to the world of science and astronomy. The two graduate students were an instant overnight hit on the talk-show circuit, and they rocketed to immediate fame.

While the media frenzy rocked on, in the back rooms of Space Science centers the world over, fresh calculations were made for distance, spatial alignments and spectral quality of the unknown astronomical mass. Comparisons to existing stars were made and the rotation and orbit of the new cosmic mass were estimated. The object remained observable at intervals that pulsated with intense light at times, and seemed cloaked in darkness at others.

On the third day following the discovery, a plume formed at the center of the formation. Over the next two days, the plume expanded and thickened. The mix of gas, debris and space dust; started to envelope and obscure the increasingly violent cosmic activity at the center. And finally, by the end of six days, a gaseous cloud was expelled from the stellar region and obscured all further clear observations.

The floodgates of opinion opened from every direction as new theories and hypothesis were proffered; very few agreed as to what exactly might be going on behind the veil that formed in the night sky. While the curtain of gas and cosmic debris dropped over the display, the ball of gas, space dust and proto-planetary matter began a slow rotation about its axis.

The motion took on a rhythm that was hauntingly familiar to the last observers to record the event.

CHAPTER 5

"Trenton New Jersey!! You have to be kidding me! "

"Nope, I'm serious," said Yeshua.

"Why Trenton? What did we do wrong to earn that posting??" Moshe asked.

"He says they have a decent planetarium and we won't draw too much attention. He also said to stop arguing about it."

"Did you call S. G. and Moh?" Moshe asked.

"Yep, already done. They get into Philly on Wednesday and said they wanted to take the train into Trenton on Friday when we're supposed to meet. There's a Marriot in town and we're supposed to rendezvous in the lobby Wednesday night at 10 pm for further instructions."

"Did he say what we were doing there?"

"Nope, all I got was the usual 'Mandatory observation'. He expects all of us to be there." Yeshua responded.

"I guess that settles it—I'll see you there."

Trenton, New Jersey

Two days later……..

"I'm not wearing this get-up," said S G. as he tried to push away the pile of clothes being offered to him.

"You will and you are." said Moh.

S.G. angrily snatched the uniform duds off the flip down baby changing station and grumbled as he removed his robe.

Moh and S G angrily looked over at Yeshua and Moshe as those two finished dressing. Both were looking dapper with their hair cleanly tucked under their green and red ServPro logo bill caps. Both were proudly wearing the familiar uniforms with 'Jesse' and 'Moses' respectively displayed on their neatly pressed shirts.

"Is this really necessary?" asked S G to no one in particular.

"I mean really— we're meeting in the men's room of the Trenton Marriot and disguising ourselves as a specialty clean-up and water remeditation crew—really!?"

"Look, he wants all of us at the planetarium, in our seats after hours—and he doesn't want us drawing any attention to ourselves. I guess he thought the ServPro cover was clever and that we wouldn't mind." responded Yeshua.

Donning the uniforms and caps, Moh and S G reluctantly conformed to the orders at hand. Tucking their civi clothes into their travel gear, they signaled they were ready to Moshe.

"Ok, let's roll—follow me to the parking garage." Moshe said.

With a last check once-over in the men's room mirror, Moshe surveyed the team's disguises and nodded his approval. He picked up his shiny metal clipboard box and headed the entourage out of the men's room and across the lobby hall to the parking garage of the Marriot. With an authoritative swagger the four made for the brightly painted ServPro van, all played their parts to the hilt.

"I'll drive." said Yeshua. "I'm a little rusty but I think I can handle it. It's only four blocks."

Moshe consulted his clipboard and said: "It says here that we're supposed to park in back at the maintenance and service entrance. He says the door will be open and the alarm off. We're supposed to go take a seat and get comfortable in the observatory area."

The van pulled cautiously into the service entrance of the building and Yeshua backed into the parking space next to the heavy-metal door at the rear of the building. Glancing around the area, the four exited the van and made their way in to the science building. The soft glow of the safety lighting guided their way as they shuffled through the massive auditorium and found their way to their seats. They all settled in and tilted back with no expectation as to what was next.

Within moments, the ceiling lit up with a giant real time HDTV-like window that displayed the recent events at the Humboldt Observatory. Ravi, Sam and EJ appeared in perfect visual, sound and detail as the discovery of the Kush Formation was played out for the benefit of the limited audience of four. As the evening wore on the presentation moved forward in time, split into dual screens and provided the four a glimpse of events currently unfolding and to come. The celestial activity marched across the planetarium ceiling followed by intermittent segues into the events on earth.

The group watched in wonder as the projected display walked them through their first encounter with the Crab Nebula on that faitful evening in 1054. to the progression of events that were unfolding today.

"I wish we had some popcorn" Moshe said.

"I'll share my SnowCaps with you." offered S G as he shook the box in Moshe's direction.

"Shhh-Shhh" hissed the other two.

"We're trying to pay attention here. You know he is going to test us on this sometime soon. "

All four settled back in their seats and watched attentively, all were trying to gather as much information as they could. Not really knowing what the message was, but fully aware that something of huge import had demanded their presence here this evening. They knew as a group that more was to be revealed in the months to come. They resigned themselves to a long evening of entertainment and information with no clear direction yet as to what they were to do with it. Past experience dictated that they would soon be called into action, given further instructions and delivered some impossible task to attend to. It wasn't worth it to try to guess ahead as to what that may be. Second guessing was out of the question when God Almighty worked his wonders for all to see.

CHAPTER 6

Our Universe has sometimes been described as the totality of all that exists. That's a pretty bold statement in itself. Our known universe contains all the galaxies, stars, planets, matter and energy that we are aware of. What we know about it, its purpose and how it works, amounts to be very little. Based on the work done today by Hubble it is estimated that our observable Universe contains between 125 to 170 billion galaxies. That's a lot. That's only what we can 'observe'. Beyond the observable limit it can be assumed that the Universe continues on in infinity.

Our solar system is part of the galaxy known as the Milky Way. The Milky Way is a Spiral Galaxy. Since it is closest to home and part of our observable Universe; we've estimated that the Milky Way contains some 200 billion stars. That's really a lot.

We have a neighboring galaxy to us called the Andromeda Galaxy. Andromeda is a bit bigger than the MilkyWay and contains over a trillion stars. That is mind boggling.

Elliptical galaxies are even bigger still. Inside the Abell 2029 cluster of Galaxies is the largest observed galaxy to date. This single galaxy alone is estimated to contain 100 trillion stars. Combining the entire above, all you have to do is the math to determine how many stars there are in the Universe. Do the math---RIGHT? Got a calculator?

In addition to the Hubble Space Telescope, NASA, launched the Kepler Spacecraft Photometric Telescope into orbit above the Earth in March of 2009. The Kepler differs from the Hubble in that rather than producing high resolution photographic images; Kepler records the intensity and spectral quality of the light produced by a source target. The sole purpose of the Kepler Mission is to map some 100,000 of the 200 billion stars in our galaxy. NASA is using Kepler to search for habitable planets in our galaxy. Kepler's task is to look for stars akin to our sun, that have planets in a solar orbit at a similar distance to that of the Earth. Based on the limited data received to date from Kepler, it appears that there may be over 1 billion planets in our galaxy alone. With what we found out from the above information provided---100 billion planets multiplied by, 170 billion galaxies, is a very big number of planets. Do the math. Get your calculator.

Though we Earthlings occupy only a small corner of our known Universe we go about our lives assuming a unique and superior dominion over the stars, the galaxies and all that lies therein. Our sun is a simple star, one of many just like it in the cosmos. It would be foolhardy for us; in fact, downright small minded of us, to believe that we're the only habitable planet and intelligent life forms out there.

If you do the math, the numbers are— astronomical.

With all those planets at various stages of development and all those life forms moving through the evolutionary process, being alone in the Universe is not an option. With multiple worlds progressing from a primordial soup of carbon and amino acids; to amoeba, to cold blooded, then hot blooded, to mammal, primate and on up in the food chain; the Universe is a busy place indeed.

God has his hands full on any given day. It's a managerial nightmare at best—more likely it's a time management impossibility. Even with an iPad it can't be done. There's no App developed so far for managing the Universe.

Get on it. Everyone will have to have one.

"God shuffled his feet and looked around……"

-The Crash Test Dummies

CHAPTER 7

Space the final frontier

God breathed a sigh of relief and dusted off his coveralls. He looked down at the dirt on his sandals and shuffled his feet. He stood back to look at his handiwork and saw that it was good. He chuckled to himself and looked backward towards the spinning, blue-green Earth. The planet was currently shrouded by the celestial remodeling curtain that he had carefully placed to separate his construction efforts from prying eyes.

"Well, that's that." He said to him self.

It had been a grueling six days and he was tired and felt like a beer and a nap. It had been a long time since he had done one of these marathon 6-day creation jobs, and he felt a great sense of satisfaction that he still had it in him.

Contrary to the last six days of intense effort; gradual, methodical world creation was the current norm—and—God's preference. Slow-and-easy allowed him time to focus his energies in more places at once; it gave him more time to monitor progress. God liked to tweak and adjust; avoid, or correct errors, as the Genesis progressed throughout the universe. However, the shift back to the Big Bang methods of his younger years, still had a nostalgic effect on him. God felt an invigorating fresh satisfaction for a job well done, and well done quickly at that. God the Almighty, God the All-knowing and God the All-Present was just a bit exhausted today.

God chuckled as he thought of the mental dilemma that was about to face the inhabitants of the Earth. When faced with the unexplainable, man usually botched the assumptions and came to erroneous conclusions. Explaining this one was going to be a doozy.

Two, fully evolved, celestial objects appearing in the sky were going to give the creationists a field day, and God was sure they would come up with all the wrong answers and reasons behind it. The same would be equally true for the evolutionist camp. The Earthling schools of thought were already fractured into Creationist and Evolutionist. Both camps took to thumping books, quoting scriptures and punching numbers on calculators to argue their case. In doing so, they sought converts from either side in the belief that with the right number of human adherents embracing their theories, it would make all that they said and believed fact. The reality is that both camps were partially right-----and partially wrong in their beliefs.

The biggest problem they faced in the search for the truth is that all of their reference and religious documents were written by humans. All The numbers, the formulas, the rituals and the stories were generated from the limited and narrow viewpoint of the human psyche. All subject to the one guaranteed constant; humans were fallible creatures—very fallible indeed.

God was frustrated by the human Earthlings. The Earthlings were so headstrong, always thought they were right and never seemed to learn from their mistakes. For the most part, they couldn't get past their egos long enough to conclude that there may be a multitude of correct answers. In obdurate intellectual folly, they insisted in promoting their subjective conclusions as the ONLY right answer, and then owning and defending it to the death. Man consistently confused opinions with facts. If ever there was a situation where the inmates were running the asylum the Earth was it.

Evolutionists were right; they could correctly radiocarbon date until the cows came home and get accurate answers. Sure they could register a reasonably accurate 300 million-year Earth age for a fossil or mineral. What they were lacking, the science they didn't have access to or the ability to even come close to achieving was the physics of God. Man's reference point and perspective were narrowed and limited to his known condition. All of his science started from a little blue and green planet spinning on its axis for a 24-hour day and orbiting around its Sun for a 365-day year.

God had no such limitations on his perspective, however. God could bend and shape time and dimension. He could slow it down, speed it up and move an object, a world, a galaxy through multiple phases of folding space and bending time. God was not limited to an X, Y, or Z axis on a piece of graph paper. Every world passed through the evolutionary path, the process of evolution was the same. It was the point of reference and observation that was confusing the Earthlings.

Objects in God's Universe could age 5 billion Earth years in one reality, and only appear to have aged one Earth day in another. These concepts were not something humans had a great chance of grasping or writing a formula for. Good luck coming up with a formula for that one guys, there are much more advanced lifeforms in the Universe that concluded there's no reason or benefit to pursuing the exercise further. It wasn't meant to be understood. The lesson it delivered is that there's much we don't or can't understand, and that's Ok. It is humbling and good to know that there's a power greater than one's self. It keeps the ego in its place where it belongs.

The Creationists are just too rigid, God thought. Sure, evolution happened just as the evolutionists said it did. Why in their infinite faith did the creationist not just accept that God set evolution into motion and tended it from time to time? Why was it so hard to fathom that God was improving on the program as he saw fit or felt the inhabitants might benefit?

Their biggest problem was Creationists were so hung up trying to prove that every word in one book was right and indisputable. Subsequently, they blinded themselves. Pride of authorship was blinding and then killing the world. Sure they had some of God's story right, and just as much of it wrong. What could one expect? All the events were seen through the eyes of humans! Humans were imperfect by nature, full of ulterior motives and seeking to control all of their brothers. And if they couldn't control them, then shun them, hate them, and then kill them.

The monkey was good, the chimp and ape better; Australopithecus ugly and the Neanderthal somewhat of a mistake. The current evolution of homo-sapiens was a work in progress. God kept it all moving in a better direction tending his garden and watering and fertilizing when his travels brought him back this way. They just couldn't get it, and that was OK. Creation depended on evolution as equally as evolution depended on creation. It was all one and the same. It was Creative Evolution.

No one appreciated the magnitude of his efforts or the expanse of his works. Oh they tried to grasp it. Some even falsely pretended that they had direct knowledge and contact allowing them access to the information. They blabbed away on Earth and elsewhere in the universe by promising to share their knowledge with the faithful. They promised to allow a poor soul a brush with their exclusive, yet elusive line of direct communication to God's ear. For a swipe of a credit card, a fat check, an endowment of their entire life's earnings, salvation and eternal life could be bought. God had seen it all. The banners rolled across the TV monitor screens with a call-in number or email address, while some Brill-Creamed–holier-than-thou loudmouth sold the lies of salvation. They encouraged people to transfer their hard-earned savings across the airwaves with the net result to enrich yet another false prophet's pocket book. It all just turned God's stomach.

He saw it again and again on multiple worlds and multiple points in time. The tendering of the first born for sacrifice, the delivery of virgin daughters to the priests, the selling of absolution to the masses, on to the rolling request for electronic payment; it was all more of the same and it disgusted him.

In spite of all of his powers, the one thing God wished he could take back, was the rule that even he did not breach. It was the quirk in the works, the elusive ghost in the machine and the continual dropped stitch that could unravel the very fabric of the universe; and, his best laid plans. Free will-Self will. Free will was a universal constant that all of God's higher creatures enjoyed and it was the bane of all that he created. It was a powerful tool that invariably landed in the wrong hands. It made them interesting to observe, no doubt, but it screwed the soup at every turn.

He had tried to keep it simple for every world, and intelligent (loosely applied), creature he had created. The Golden rule, the Ten Commandments; how much simpler could you get?! They all were signed up to the same basic plan with their deal. Love each other, don't kill anyone, feed everyone, keep your hands off the other guy's wife, be tolerant and courteous, take care of your planet; and while you're at it, throw your creator a bone and show some respect. Just do these simple things, and your worlds are your oysters.

How hard was it? But before you knew it, the message grew from a single simple sentence to 10 lines, and then off to the races and out of control. Ego and self-will in sentient creatures ran rampant. Opinions fueled by the latter, started the ball rolling, and before long the scrolls were scribed, the tomes of opinion being produced. In no time at all (at least by God's reference), multiple gospels, Talmud, Midrash, this Bible and that bible, Korans and Vedas and even books you needed magic glasses to read. It went on and on to no end.

Like the Childs game of "Telephone" or "Rumor," what came in at one end rarely came out the same on the other. Lending new meaning to "Babel" or 'lost in translation', the words were converted from their original Hebrew to Aramaic, then to Greek, Latin and on through the languages of the world. Each iteration open to new meanings and interpretations; and, with each interpreter willing to defend their version to the death.

The talking heads and self-righteous control freaks produced like flies. This one had to have leavened wafers, that one un-leavened; consume a pig or not; we came from monkeys WE didn't (hello, who made the damn monkeys?); drink wine or no wine; rubbers or no rubbers. Before you know it, they all start killing each other in the name of God and salvation.

Contrary to the teachings of the so-called "Organized" religions of the world; it was God's policy to hand over the tools, suggest the path, and put it all in motion; but that was it. God created; God set in motion, God loved and maintained. But after that it was all on man to make the choices. Free will out of control, or try to understand and follow God's plan in all aspects of their lives. Few made the right choice.

The heads of the organized religions hijacked the message. In their own self interest, whether for ego, riches or just plain crowd control; they promised 'Eternal Life', '72 virgins', whatever it took in reward. In the end with mankind, it came down to the promise of reward in the future; rather than just doing the next right thing and being satisfied in the here and now.

Oh when he could, God heard the prayers. Praying was good, but all the answers were already right there; right inside the lines of the Golden Rule and the Ten Commandments. They really didn't need anything else. But man sought to complicate the simple.

Man sought answers, power over others and control. They all wanted to circumcise the gnat and dissect the Big Mac before they took a bite. Did they really need to check each time to see if-- *Two all-beef patties, special sauce, lettuce, cheese, pickles, onions - all on a sesame seed bun* were all there, or, just bite into it with the spiritual faith and conviction that all was good without their further meddling? How much better was the dissected Big Mac than the one consumed in total faith. Not at all.

God had no intention of meddling in the individual affairs of Man. They either got it or didn't. God was principally a gardener by nature; he pulled the weeds and culled the inferior shoots and seedlings. God watered, fertilized and tended. All green shoots got an equal chance to flourish, all got what they needed, but in the end all would not survive.

CHAPTER 8

At the center of the Crab Nebula are two faint stars, one of which is the star responsible for the existence of the nebula. SN-1054 is the Super Nova star that started the whole mess. The other is the Crab Pulsar, the source of much of the energy emitting from the area.

The region around the star was found to be a strong source of radio waves and X-rays. In addition, it was identified as one of the most prolific objects in the sky in production of gamma rays. The radiation emitting from the Crab Nebula is in rapid pulses, making it one of the first pulsars to be discovered.

Pulsars are sources of powerful electromagnetic radiation; emitted in short and extremely regular pulses, many times a second. They were a great mystery when discovered in 1967, and the team that identified the first one, considered the possibility that it could be a signal from an advanced civilization. The pulsar's extreme energy output creates an unusually dynamic region at the center of the Crab Nebula.

While most astronomical objects evolve so slowly that changes are visible only over times scales of many years; the inner parts of the Crab, show changes over time scales of only a few days. A significant problem in studies of the Crab Nebula is that the combined mass of the nebula, and the pulsar, add up to considerably less than the predicted mass of the progenitor star. The question of where the 'missing mass' has gotten off to, remains unresolved. No one knows for sure where the missing mass and energy are. Do the math.

CHAPTER 9

Arcata California

Three months to the day after the initial sighting and subsequent naming of the Master Kush Formation phenomena, Sam Klein and Ravi Najir were pushing their way to the front of the line at the Arcata Taco Bell. Both were famished and were anxiously awaiting their opportunity to order. Sam went for the double stuffed steak chalupa and Ravi ordered his usual; a #4 Mexican pizza and two Taco Supremes—vegetarian style of course, just out of respect for his body and his mom.

Grabbing their 64-ounce to-go cups they headed over to the ice and soda machine. The boys topped their tumblers with ice and started to spray a mixed cocktail of multi-colored sodas and juices into their cups. Satisfied that they had the proper measured formulas in hand; they headed for their seats facing the parking lot.

"#264", screamed a loud voice.

Sam popped up from the table, "I got ya covered" and walked to the counter, handed over his receipt to the medusa-headed, dreadlocked server (who was losing the battle of hairnet vs. dreads), and grabbed his tray. Sam dug into the bin of salsa packets selecting only "Fire" and "Hot". In a flurry of bacchanlian waste, he grabbed a fistful of napkins that would have lasted a family of four for a month and then made his way back to his seat.

Settling in, the two started the ritual unpacking of specialty boxes and undoing of wrappers to expose the culinary treats. Once the meal was made ready to accept the salsa, they commenced with the ripping open of salsa packets with their incisors. Mushing the goo around, they applied the requisite condiments to personalize their meals.

"What I was trying to say," said Sam, "is it can't be a coincidence that we picked that particular Nebula, that particular quadrant of the sky, at that specific time and distance to observe."

Ravi said. "Oh right! It was fate! A fucking miracle, divine intervention and the hand of God all rolled into one." "You my friend, smoke too much dope."

"That's not what I'm saying" Sam retorted. "This is too big and too weird to just be a coincidence. Maybe we're meant to do something big with this. Maybe we have some purpose or plan we should try to understand and follow."

Ravi set his spork down on the tray and looked at his friend in confusion. "Right. Like Ravi and Sam save the world?"

"Give me a break, would you"

"You don't get it do you?" We just lucked out, is all. Fate had nothing to do with it. It's like winning the lottery or getting to go home with the hottest chick at the bar." It's luck."

47

Sam screwed up his face in thought, and said, "I don't think so Ravi, I think there's more to this than just dumb luck. I think something big is going on behind that cosmic dust cloud. And, I think it has more meaning for us than you're willing to admit."

Ravi said. "Listen, we've made it to something big. We have a little over $3 million bucks in the bank from speaking engagements and selling our story to Rolling Stone, People and High Times. We have a South Park episode about us that we'll get royalties from. We have endorsement contracts with Taco Bell, Facebook and Google that will keep us set for life. We have Leno, Letterman, John Stewart and Saturday Night Live in the next 60 days. Let's not screw this up by reading more in to it than it is. Let it go Sam. Why can't you just be happy? Let's milk this shit for all its worth. 'Cause a year from now when the Kush melts back into space, burns out, blows up or whatever it's going to do; no one is going to remember us. We're going to be a flash in the pan. I'd like to flash in the pan while rolling in the dough."

"I hear you, but it's gnawing at me in a really weird way. Somehow, I feel that much of what you and I have been questioning since we were kids is tied to this event."

Ravi said, "I'm done. Let's get out of here. This is getting way too serious for me. Tonight's our Hubble pass for this month, and I want to see what the status of the gas shroud is out at the Kush site."

The young men gathered their tray and dumped their debris in the can. Both went back to the ice and soda station for their requisite 64-ounce-free refills for the road. As they got into their car, they high-fived each other as they looked up at the vinyl poster in the taco bell window. Plastered across the glass was a picture of the two of them superimposed over the now-classic Hubble generated photo of the Master Kush Formation. Above the photo was printed, 'Ravi and Sam Think Outside of the Box--- You can too! ---Eat More Taco Bell'.

CHAPTER 10

Afghanistan- March 2001

The sounds of drills and hydraulic hammers played a droning staccato beat, upsetting the normal quiet and serenity of the lower Bamiyan Valley with their annoying din. The valley floor was littered with earth-moving equipment and sweat-soaked Afghanis toiling in the heat of the Afghan summer. The men were busy doing God's work, or so they had been told, and so they believed.

A caravan of Toyota pick-ups and Land Cruisers made its way through the valley traveling swiftly the 140 miles from Kabul directly into the Hindu Kush Mountains. The road from Kabul followed the Silk Road route that had connected China with the west from the time when BCE had rolled over to CE. Much to Toyota marketing's dismay, the vehicles were festooned with Taliban flags, 50-caliber machine guns and a Type-63 bed-mounted multi-barreled mobile rocket-launcher. That the Toyota had become the signature transportation of choice for one of the most regressive and repressive Islamic regimes to roll around in some time, was the source of much embarrassment and dismay in the Toyota boardroom.

The valley roadway was cut deeply through the buff-hued mountains of the Hindu-Kush. The ancient evidence of man's hand print on the landscape was obvious in all directions. The sheer walls of the Hindu-Kush rose up on either side of the lush date palm valley; the vertical cliff walls were peppered with alcoves and man-made caves in all directions. The ubiquitous cave dwellings formerly housed monks and aesthetics of many ancient faiths; now occupied by the hungry and homeless displaced by the violence and war plaguing each corner of the region.

The current condition of Bamiyan belied its prior glory as an enlightened center of learning. In its heyday, Bamiyan had been a multi-cultural melting pot where Slavs from the North, Arabs and Jews from the south, Romans and Europeans from the West and Indians and Asians from the East, could all come together and share their wares, their cultures, their knowledge and their faiths. At one point in time God's plan for man was practiced and evident on these ancient grounds. Not today, though.

Carved into the sheer walls of the cliff and central to the multiple cave dwelling openings, were two massive alcoves. Standing proudly, in each alcove, stood the two largest surviving statues on Earth dedicated to Siddharta Guatama Buddha, the enlightened one. Standing 180 and 121 feet tall, the two Buddhas towered over the valley floor and welcomed all who sojourned there in peace. The greatness of man's broad devotion to faith, and the manifest expression of the art form expressing that faith, was about to be destroyed. The magnificent Bamiyan Buddhas were about to be lost to the world by the narrow-minded actions of a group that had simply lost touch with the message and missed its meaning by a long shot.

Quiet descended in the valley; all the equipment shut down. A mullah with an eye patch over one eye held a megaphone in his hand and began a loud recitation from the Koran. Wagging an angry finger in the direction of the statues; his voice raised in an ever building emotional appeal to the heavens. The charismatic mullah called upon the faithful to denounce the two massive effigies symbolizing the heretic blasphemy. The two Buddahs were an insult, a curse, provided by the infidels that did not adhere to his beliefs.

Positioned with an un-obstructed view of the unfolding event, and just a bit to the West of the Mullahs truck bed podium, was parked a Taliban style Toyota Land Cruiser sporting all the symbols, flags and trappings of the Taliban regime. It was not, however, associated in any way with the Taliban. Leaning against the hood and the front quarter panels of the cruiser were four men dressed in traditional Pashtun garb defined by baggy pantaloons draped over with light linen jackets called a shalwar kameez, all topped with Kandahari caps for decoration. The only additions to their wardrobe were their stylish Maui Jim sunglasses guarding against the brilliance of the noon Afghani sun. Three of the men had the traditional scraggly full beards of the faithful and one was unusually clean-shaven and devoid of hair. The men stood enthralled by the spectacle in front of them.

As the Mullah started a chant of "Allah Akbar" one of the men winced and scrunched down into his shoulders. "Oh I hate when they do that in this context." Why do they have to do that, it is so wrong and embarrassing?"

The youngest of the three observers placed his hand on his companion's shoulder and squeezed gently. "It's not your fault, Moh. This wasn't your doing. All will be forgiven in the end."

As the last "Allah Akbar" was screamed out in unison by the throng; a massive explosion rocked the valley floor and all of those in attendance vibrated with the force of the blast. The Buddhas came crashing down and were reduced to a pile of rubble at the foot of their prior perch. Ululations and AK47 chatter filled the air as the mass of faithful danced in elation.

The four observers stood and watched in disgust. The beardless—and noticeably rotund member of the observation committee—wiped tears from his face and turned to the others with a look of painful nostalgia plastered on his face.

"Why does He keep insisting that we visit these events? Each one is more painful than the next. He won't let us intercede. He watches it happen but does nothing to stop it! It's like some kind of cruel punishment."

The oldest member of the group stroked his long white beard and shifted his balloon pants aside to access his pocket and handed his friend a handkerchief.

"I know how you feel my friend, Bonaparte and the Grand Armee outside Moscow, living human skeletons at Auschwitz, Dresden, St. Petersburg, Tianamen, Darfur, Biafra and Rhwanda. I agree; it's all so bad. He even made Yeshua and I stand five paces away from Titus during the sacking of Jerusalem and the last destruction of his house. The meetings are mandatory; we all got the memo. It's not for us to decide. I'm tired of arguing with Him, after all guys, when have you ever known Him not to have a plan? Whether we agree, like it or not, he always has a plan."

Unfortunately, outside of the "plan" and unknown to the four; in a large compound just south and east from where they currently stood, a group of Saudi and Egyptian fundamentalists were formulating a plan of their own. The plan that was taking form included the old tried and true Palestinian fear platform of the high jacked jetliner, only with a new twist. That event was just 6 months away. September couldn't come quick enough for the fire eyed fanatics sitting around the fire in Tora Bora.

The four ersatz Talibani took one last look at the Buddha rubble littering the valley floor. With heads hanging low they settled back into the Land Cruiser and set the GPS for Karachi.

"Imagine there's no heaven, it's easy if you try"

-John Lennon

CHAPTER 11

Somewhere in the clouds

God just couldn't figure out why they couldn't get it.

What a mess. When Moshe raised the issue that the multitudes were un-educated and that more would follow the Word if it was mass produced, he had bought into the plan. He hadn't been so sure about the idea of sticking the Good Word into little leather boxes and painfully strapping them on to the foreheads and hands of his test Chosen people; it seemed a bit cruel and excessive at the time; but in the end, he deferred to Moshe. Moshe insisted that his rabble was so stubborn and pig headed, that the only way to get the message across was to strap it to their bodies as a constant reminder, or they would just forget it.

God thought the prayer binding ritual a bit of overkill; frankly, the little prayer box nailed to the door posts of the house seemed to be working fine. In the end, God figured Moshe was still pissed about the golden calf event and hadn't gotten over it. There was a good reason vengeance was his and not Moshe's.

It all seemed to have worked for a while, but it still always came back full circle to free will misapplied, and the bad choices that resulted. Before long, they were killing each other, or looking for others deemed not quite enough like them to kill.

At one time, God thought that maybe the problem was the invention of ink, paper and the printing press put into the wrong hands. On the third planet from the sun known as Ceti Hidalgo, near the Horned Nebula; solely, in an attempt to try to avoid the anticipated and inevitable manipulation of the Good Word—God had even created a race of globular plasmic mass with no arms or legs (that would keep them out of trouble, he had thought).

The creatures of this planet propelled their way through the pea soup atmosphere of their world by an undulating cilia transportation system; like some mammoth Paramecium on steroids. Even with the challenge, they had put their two cents in. In and effort to get their bastardized version of the Message out, they developed a voice and thought activated recording and typing software. He had finally dispatched the whole flagellating, flatulent race in a global fireball to correct his error and started over. The inhabitants had been most unpleasant and very hard on the eyes anyway. He didn't miss them.

As far as the people of Earth went, God's first thought was; if they only knew how close they had come to destruction just a few short months prior, they would be shaking in their boots. The fact that Reverend Dr. Harold Camping was batshit crazy and had loaded up his coffers with the life savings of so many innocents; was all that had saved them this last time. Over the years, Camping had incorrectly predicted the "End Times" on many occasions.

Camping loved to promote his predictions with much media exposure and fan fare through his books, radio talk show and the internet. Camping, much to his own, and to his follower's frustration, had to revise the date a third and fourth time when he found not only himself, but the world still intact the day after each erroneously predicted end date. The fact that Camping and Family Radio had somehow finally hit on the right date of October 21st 2011 for his next planned world destruction event, was a stroke of sheer luck. By coincidence, God actually picked this date at one time, as a potential date to cleanse the Earth of man and his folly. As far as God was concerned the rest of Harold's teachings were the ramblings of a defective mind run rampant, a wiring defect in a product he produced in his own image.

Just out of principle and as a personal joke, God was changing the date for cleansing his mistake to December 21, 2012. He liked the idea of it coinciding with the presumed Mayan date of destruction. The reason being, one, to close the protocol leak that caused the Camping algorithmic biblical math problem in the first place; and two, to make sure he didn't lend any credence to a bunch of wing nuts like Camping and his followers.

God always suspected Moshe of the original biblical algorithm leak and considered it as payback for God having denied him access to the land of milk and honey. He and Moshe had regularly come to loggerheads—stiff necked was an understatement. The guy navigated like shit on top of that. How do you get lost for 40 years on a little strip of land with large bodies of water on both sides? Seriously, ten years maybe------but 40?

The Mayan astronomers of ancient times properly applied their science to the heavens; and for what it was worth, had correctly estimated and mapped December 2012 as an eventful future occurrence. The date had been based on information a Mayan astronomy student had put together while studying abroad in the Amazon. The young man came to his conclusions by deciphering ancient temple paintings and hieroglyphs deep in the Amazon in what was the glorious lost city of "Z" (still lost to his day along with El Dorado and, the Fountain of Youth). The young Mayan was able to get the proper coordinates and locations for the return of a multiphase four headed comet that travels between multiple galaxies on a 20,000 year orbit period. This comet, though unique and massive in size, color and quality of scientific value, would never have posed any significant danger to the safety of the Earth. The comet would produce a glorious light show yes, destruction no.

Once the young Mayan had deciphered the information and graphed his proofs, he returned to the Yucatan from the deep reaches of the Amazon and submitted his report to his Master Astronomer. The Master Astronomer in turn, shared his new-found information with the high priest and asked him if he would be so kind as to have one of the priestly scribes illuminate the report so that it was suitable for presentation to the King. The King preferred his official reports with lots of screaming jaguars, anacondas and Quetzcoatles adorning them.

The Priest, never one to miss an opportunity to better his personal condition, had the Astronomer and his student arrested, imprisoned in his pyramid dungeon, and, for good measure, their tongues immediately excised from their mouths. Once silenced, he was then free to inform the Great Mayan King that the world was going to end December 2012; and that the priest through his direct contact with the God and the heavens, knew this to be a certain fact. God, mind you, had never spoken a word to the man.

After having extracted a fortune in gold and jewels from the King and all the noble families of the region, the Priest set about with the appropriate dogma and ceremonial fanfare to ensure that all those that had ponied up with the cash and jewels would receive eternal life; and a further guarantee of safety from the ravages of the destruction of the Earth. For added benefit and effect, he took the hottest virgin daughters from the aristocracy and sacrificed 22 of them, along with the young astronomer and his master as extra insurance. As an aside, he kept four of the best-looking gals for himself as priestly wives. Waste not, want not. Free will run rampant. God found it even more ironic that the direct descendants of the high priest had eventually settled in Medellin, and today, made up the core of the current Cartel wreaking havoc in the region on both sides of the border.

All of this misinformation could have been avoided had it not been for the incredibly efficient work of Cortez, Pizzaro and the Catholic Church in obliterating the combined knowledge of the highly advanced civilizations of the South American continent. God had no intent of ever seeing that repeated.

The search for perfection, and the hope that one day he would get it right, kept God at the game. God could create; God could enlighten, and God could teach; God could destroy, but God could not breach the rules of self-will. Like a virus in the software, the system always seemed to crash. Before God was ready to load a new version of the operating system though, he thought the best plan was to re-format the disk.

What God had just created out of the neutron soup of the Crab Nebula, was his remote, resident, Earth back-up system. A storage place in the "Cloud" so to speak.

So December 2012 was the Earth's new real date with destiny, and God felt it only appropriate to call his Earth management team together to tell them his plan and give them a chance to respond. After all, he was a benevolent deity and believed in the democratic process.

He snapped his fingers in four directions around his head and in a blast of light and energy was gone. The summons was heard in four remote locations around the Universe.

CHAPTER 12

About 39 light-years away from Earth and orbiting the star Er Rai in the constellation Cepheus, rotated a rocky mountainous world bisected and criss-crossed with a system of verdant serpentine valleys, centered about wide clear blue rivers.

It was the planet Kazaria. Both banks of the rivers were green with expansive hardwood forests interspersed with grass carpeted meadows, which rolled for miles up toward the lower slopes of the barren mountains. The air was sweet and filled with the scent of wildflowers; colorful birds flitted from tree to tree or soared high above the peaks and crags of the mountain range. The high flying flock was banking gracefully in the thermals thrown off by the heat of Er Rai.

From space, it was clear to see that the source of the rivers came from high in the mountains and cascaded from that source on a meandering course that carved its way through the face of the planet. Each of the rivers converged into a confluence that terminated in a massive delta on the shores of the solitary sizeable body of water on the planet; an ocean about as large as the Atlantic of Earth. The rivers flowed along a path from the top mountains to the river delta; clocking a little over 8000 earth miles in length; or, about twice the length of either the Amazon or Nile rivers.

Stretching as far as the eye could see along the banks of the largest river, was an encampment set up with 1000's of multi-colored tents surrounded by a bustling activity of grazing animals. The herd looked related to, but different from, sheep and cows. The only truly common characteristics of the creatures were their distinctively cloven hooves, and their propensity for continually masticating great wads of their pasture fodder. With much burping and farting, the herds moved about the meadows regurgitating their feed on a regular basis. They alternated between up-chucking and re-swallowing the cud; then transferring it into another one of the multiple chambers in their ample well fed bellies; only to start the noisy process all over again.

The animals were nudged and herded along by what appeared to be furry black, brown, and white canines of some sort. With a set of eyes both fore and aft, six legs and small stubby horns on their heads, the Kazarian border collies seemed to keep order and direction among the munching herd. They all seemed quite content.

The encampment stretched for miles in every direction but was amazingly organized; neat and free of the chaos that one would assume would follow along with a mass of people of this magnitude. There was no crowding evident, as there was plenty of space to stake a claim of the adjoining gently sloping land, without infringing on any neighbor. Handsome men, woman and children worked and played, while the sounds of soft music, conversation and laughter mixed with the surrounding babble of the river and cadence of the forest. The kids played tag with the Kazarian canines but were out classed by the fact that it was hard to fool a dog that saw just as well in front or behind.

Along the banks of the river, a group of men and woman hitched a net to two row boats and fed the seine across a slowly moving pool; taking turns and pulling it to shore. Gutted and seasoned fish hung on poles drying in the warmth of the Kazarian sun as they were flavored by the well tended smokey fires set about the base of the drying racks.

A symphony of mouth watering aromas wafted out of the tents and settled over the encampment as the noon meal was prepared from every hearth. Each whiff of air delivered a rich tease of what lay in store for those getting ready to partake of the afternoon feast. The cooking was performed like a work of art portraying the eclectic culinary skills of the locals; then presented as a testament of the inhabitants respect for the bounty their planet provided.

The tents were a colorful canvas fabric that had been dyed in unique color patterns. Each area of the encampment seemed to be segregated into groups of ten. The locations separated by a signature color code, and flying a distinctive flag with its own individual coat of arms portrayed on its face.

At the center of the host stood a large community tent boldly striped in a multi-colored pattern that was blended from all of the ten colors portrayed throughout the community of tents.

Fixed to the supporting perimeter frame of this prominent pavillion, flew the individual coat of arms banners that were unique to each homogenous group making up the community encampments. High at the apex of the structure, waving quietly in the breeze, was a large blue and white flag. With each puff of wind, the flag alternately furled and unfurled in the gentle wash of air. Inside, sat 11 men deep in serious discussion. The men lounged about on the floor, supported by substantial overstuffed pillows and bolsters of varying sizes and shapes. A great platter of indigenous fruits, nuts and berries served as refreshments. The food was receiving some attention as the men chatted while munching away.

The tent was divided into two chambers. At the rear stood a curtained veil and raised platform separated from the main gathering area. Leaning against the wall of the tent, and outside of the veiled area, rested two long poles which were covered in gold plate. Inside the alcove chamber and sitting on the platform, sat a gold box about 42 inches long, by 24's wide, and about the same in height. The box seemed to have some significance to the group as it was beautifully decorated with gold, and sported two little naked cast-gold winged creatures plopped on the lid.

As the discussion around the tent got more heated, the men started to single out the eldest member of the group. All were looking down at a large map and gesticulating with emphasis. The man known as Dan raised his eyebrows and frowned at the older man; "Really Moshe, is it that hard? I mean really, you just follow the freaking river and it should get us to the sea!"

Napthali piped in with his own two shekels, "I mean really guys, what were we thinking--there's more than a little history here that it might be a problem having Moshe guide the way?"

The man called Asher reflected, "Well, Moshe is the only one that has seen the sea, he kinda was the logical choice by default. We've been going on his word that it's there, but none of us get to travel that high to get the overview from space."

Moshe replied in exasperation, "It's there, I know is there, I've seen it with my own eyes. It's a long hike! 8000 twisty miles doesn't get done overnight when you have 1 million people and twice that in livestock and pets to move through the forest. On top of that these women take SOO long to pack and get ready! Their hair, their shoes. I've never seen anything like it. Give me a break. Its only been 6 years since we started moving again; not even close to 40 years and I resent Reuben's insinuation last night. Rueben, I repeat! I am not LOST! I repeat I am not LOST! If you want wandering I'll show you wandering. Wandering I know from!"

A humming vibration and a harmonic resonance started to fill the room. Everyone turned as the box in the back of the room started to glow with a yellow shimmer. Zebulon called from the back of the tent.

"Hey Moshe, It's for you."

CHAPTER 13

In another part of the Milky Way, about 2000 light-years from our Sun and near the constellation Virgo, is a star blandly named and known as PSR 1257+12 (really we can do better than that!). In orbit around that star and along a similar elliptical path about its sun, is a planet comparable to Earth, but much more arid.

It was 3 am., and the surface of Jann-1 was already starting to heat up. Moh stretched out his frame on his bed and sighed in satisfaction. Next to him lay the two favorite of his 72 wives. Both gals were fast asleep with a look of placid serenety upon their faces.

He gathered his robe about himself, put on his ceremonial dagger and prepared for the journey ahead. Looking out the window, he surveyed the windswept dunes lit by the two crescent moons glowing in the early-morning sky of Jann-1. He looked over the stars in the sky and couldn't help wondering if he had only settled closer to Earth, that he could have headed off some of what had become. There had been other choices for a place to rest his head but he had been swayed by Virgo's relationship to the rewards of heaven, and the similar quality of Jann-1's surface to his earthly home. There was no looking back now.

He gently leaned over and kissed the two young angels asleep on the bed, steeling himself for the difficult travel and even more aduous task that he knew lay ahead. With a grunt, he walked out of the sleeping chamber and headed downstairs.

It had been three short days since he got the message from the Old man and subsequent follow up call from Moshe. He was ready. Stopping in the kitchen just long enough to grab a hand full of dates and a loaf of pita, he headed out the door and over to the stables.

At the stables, he began rifling through the tack room; he found a bridle that met with his pleasure and made his way back through the stalls. He stopped in front of the largest one, which was set apart from the rest. Whinnying and snorting loudly, the magnificent white stallion greeted his master with enthusiasm. The beautiful beast nuzzled against Moh's shoulder as Moh palmed a couple of dates into the horse's mouth. Affixing the bridle, he opened the stall and coaxed the stallion out into the walkway and toward the double doors.

Stepping out into the moonlit morning, he stroked the mane of the horse to calm his jitters. With a gentle push downward, he lowered the horse's wide feathered wing and leapt upon his back.

With a gentle whisper Moh said, "Alright, Barak, it's your show."

With a throw of his long head and shake of his mane, the white horse spread his wings and flew off into the sky. The horse and rider scorched the morning sky in a blaze of white, leaving a trail of fire and lightning marking their path through the night sky."

By sunrise, the call to prayer was sounding from the top of minarets all over Jann-1 as the call to the faithful began. The mullahs, and all the peaceful inhabitants of this world, knew that today was a special one. Praise to Allah the Almighty and blessings on his prophet were offered, as all people on Jann-1 faced the direction of the eastern heavens and the small blue dot of a planet 2000 light-years from their own. They were a tolerant, content and observant people that lived their lives with the loving kindness found in the teachings of the Koran. Five times daily, their souls were soothed by the interruption of their day for the call to prayer.

Many had seen Moh taking off into the heavens last night, and each said a silent prayer of hope. Hope that he would be safe and successful in turning their brothers on Earth back towards the way of peace and tolerance as the Koran had dictated. None of them wanted to think about the alternative.

CHAPTER 14

If in autumn one is standing on the surface of Earth, feet planted in the northern hemisphere and gazing high into the northern night sky, the constellation Pegasus, the winged horse of the gods, presents in full view. Within Pegasus is a single bright object known as 51-PEG (Oh, we definitely need to do better with the names). 51-PEG is almost a perfect match to our Sun in spectral quality and intensity. 51- PEG is about 50.9 light-years away from the Earth. That is very far, but, not nearly as far as PSR 1257+12, in Virgo, at 2000 light-years and only a bit farther than Er Rai in Cepheus at 39 light years. Considering that a single light year computes to a distance of just under 10 trillion kilometers, or for those of you that don't own a calculator, or further, don't want to "do the math", about 6 trillion miles.

Needless to say, even if you grab the calculator and start mashing numbers and calculating how far the three celestial bodies in discussion are from the Earth; the result probably won't display on your key pads anyway. Are you really that anal? Put the calculator down and read.

Orbiting around 51-PEG is a planet damn near identical to our Earth. Gradis-2 forms an elliptical path around 51-PEG making its circuit about every 365 days, and rotates on its axis every 22 hours. The 2 hour reduction in rotation helps to keep the inhabitants of Gradis-2 more grounded, down to Gradis so to speak, and with their feet more firmly planted in today; much more so than Earthlings. Even if it is ever so slight, the additional centripetal force and its benefits are noticeable on the populace.

Gradis-2 is a blue and green planet lush with oceans, lakes, rivers and forests galore. The desert areas are broken up with many oases' that are close enough together to afford ease of travel to cross the expanse of the sandy dunes.

Power for comfort, vehicles and convenience is provided by Hydrogen fusion reactors and supplied at a minimal charge to the populace; considering that the raw source for the hydrogen molecules are cracked from the ample supplies of water on the planet. There are no hydrocarbon gasses in the atmosphere of Gradis-2, except for those produced by flatulence or decay.

Twenty years prior to the present, a young Gradisian named Chen Li Goldsmith had been tinkering in his garage and was able to develop a simple and inexpensive Mag-Lev drive that had proven to be very planet friendly. Since everyone needed one, everyone bought one, which had made Chen Li enormously wealthy in the process.

The Mag-Lev drive excites the electrons on the underside of the vehicle while producing an opposing excitement to the surface directly below the vehicle; this allows for hover travel at great speeds while producing no surface contact or friction with the planet's face, except when parked.

As transportation and recreational vehicles were being converted to Mag-Lev, Gradis-2 wide, the parks and recreation areas enjoyed a huge drop in the cost of maintenance. The planet's vast and convenient network of roadways, rails and bridges which had cost a fortune to build and maintain due to design standards for vehicle impact loads, were now free of the typical wear and tear.

Replacement structures were now designed and built with the lightest available materials and constructed more for pedestrian traffic than for heavy traffic loads. All the benefits of the Mag-Lev, combined, had allowed such a huge budget surplus that the workweek was reduced to just four seven-hour days, all health care was made free and the planetary income tax reduced to a 2% flat tax (with no loop holes). Even with the global healthcare system in place, Doctors were given a large government stipend that kept them very rich and able to play golf on Wednesdays. It was found that happy docs kept you alive longer than did the ones who were worried about the next paycheck.

Life is good on Gradis-2 and life is fun on Gradis-2.

Yeshua lived on the outskirts of a medium-sized village on the lush southern continent of Gradis-2. The town, known as Galil, depended on fishing for its primary industry. Commercial fishing and recreational use of the large deepwater lake that was the main natural feature of the town, had proven to be sustainable due to the high quality of the regional water, incredibly rapid reproductive cycle of the local fish and a little enhancement from time to time from the town's most famous resident. He definitely had a way with fish propagation.

At the end of Tiberius Avenue was a medium-sized home of about 1800 square feet with four bedrooms, 2-1/2 baths, a two-car garage and a white picket fence. The house sat on 5 acres of land, four of which had been converted to pasture for his small herd of sheep. Adjacent to the garage was Yeshua's cabinet shop and over the front door was a sign in the shape of a fish that displayed:

J. of N. Woodworks est. 1 AD.

Inside the shop, Yeshua stood over two large pieces of wood as the high-pitch scream of his Makita biscuit jointer whined down. He placed the tool on the workbench and ran his hand across the face of the joint in the top of the table he was crafting. A natural occurring book-matched pattern, simulated the shape of giant butterfly wings as it radiated from the center of where the two crotch-cut olive tree flitches had been re-sawn and matched. He picked up his orbital sander, turned on the switch for the cyclone dust collector and started sanding away.

James, his youngest son, came running in screaming "Dad, come out to the pasture, Mom needs you now!"

Yeshua dusted off his bib, turned off the equipment and paused at the door to put the "be back in 10" sign in the window, and followed behind his son. Mary stood in the back of the pasture in front of a massive group of boulders surrounded by a small patch of blue berry bushes. Sheep milled around as a large black-and-white border collie named Elijah, tried to keep them at bay. Mary waved him over toward her and hollered across the field.

"I think you need to come over here. It's for you."

Yeshua walked over to where she stood. Behind the boulder was a blue berry bush burning with blue fire, though no heat or smoke was coming from it. The summons understood and completely acknowledged, Yeshua turned to Mary and said.

"I guess I better pack my bag. I'll try and get back as soon as I can."

CHAPTER 15

Back on planet Earth, high in the Indian border region of the Himalaya Mountains, is a group of sub ranges known as the Dhauladhar. Of particular note to the reader is the mile-high city of Dharmasala that is nestled in the heart of the scenic Kangra Valley. The name Dharmasala, loosely translates into English as "Spiritual Sanctuary," a sensible translation as the most recognized resident of the town is one Tenzin Gyatso, better known as the 14th Dalai Lama.

Mr. Gyatso and the Tibetan Government in exile, have called Dharmasalla home since 1959 when the Chinese government decided it was time to take over the sovereign nation of Tibet by force, kick out the Dalai Lama and cleanse its people of the 'opiate of the masses'. 'Opiate of the masses', by the way, is the label that all good practicing followers of Marx, Lenin and Engles, use to describe a healthy spiritual connection and constant contact with one's God. In the case of the displaced Tibetans, Buddhism practiced the Tibetan way.

The Himalayan wind blew across the Kangra Valley; the silence was broken by the tinkling of the wind chimes and the muted luffing sound of snapping prayer flags. The pot of incense had long ago burned to ash as the gently featured Buddhist monk's eyes fluttered, returning his conscious state to his present surroundings.

Sitting comfortably on his cushion with perfect postural alignment in the Lotus position, Tenzin Gyatso, the 14th Dalai Lama hardly looked close to his 76 years. Almost simultaneously, as if the two communicated wordlessly in full spiritual synchronization, his meditative companion smiled and with eyes still shut said,

"It is good to share time and space with you again, Tenzin." His companion was none other than the Earthly form of S. G.-Siddhartha Guatama Buddha-the enlightened one.

Tenzin smiled "And with you, Master. What news do you bring me? "

The Great Buddha shifted his girth about and settled deeper into the cushion below him. He furled his brow and reached side to side and squeezed the two corners, released, and squeezed again. The silk covered padded matt returned immediately to its original thickness in his hand. He raised his behind up and down as the cushion formed and reformed to meet his every move.

"Tell me Tenzin, this is the most comfortable meditation matt I've ever had the pleasure of sitting on. What have you stuffed it with; it's so much more relaxed and supportive than buckwheat hulls?"

"Ah, Master, they call it 'Memory Foam'. I picked it up at the Sharper Image Store while I was attending the World Peace Conference in New York last year. Isn't it wonderful?" I couldn't resist a product with a name so in tune with its purpose!"

"Ah, the news then."

S. G. paused, took a deep breath and then began, "I've pled your case to the Old Man on a regular basis. You know He's always hesitant to intervene in the affairs of man, but he does see your plight as unique, due to your direct involvement in it." I believe I am making headway, and that he may be willing to create a scenario whereby Tibet may be free once again. I have no guarantee yet, but he was more than receptive the last time I was summoned."

"Frankly, Tenzin, He's appreciative of your efforts on his behalf here. In fact, he told all four of us that you're the only one that 'gets it' down here. He is ready to take action, and I mean BIG ACTION. We've never seen him so fed up with conditions on Earth."

"Unfortunately, His plate is full. He's so swamped and distracted I'm concerned that he's going to be reactive and do something hasty."

Gongs began to sound in a wide cacophony of ranges as the Radongs, the Tibetan Temple Horns, started moaning their dissonant yet sonorous sub-sonic moan. The room around the two companions vibrated as the incense pot started to spew smoke and ash. Tenzin chuckled and looked over at S.G.,

"I think it's for you; do you want some privacy?"

CHAPTER 16

Abu Dabai--U. A. E.--December 24 2011

Palm Island Jumeira Grand Hotel

The gilded elevator doors opened with a gentle 'ding' as the number '30' lit on the panel above the door. With a hydraulic whisper the doors separated revealing a hand woven Arabian carpet hallway inlaid with marble and brass. Stepping out on to the 30th floor hallway was a short and somewhat rotund, gentleman of indeterminate age, Asian ethnicity and calmness of features and mannerisms.

Gazing all around while taking in the interior décor he vocalized a resounding tsk-tsk while shaking his head in disgust at the bold bourgoise display. He brushed his hands over his belly and adjusted his robes; cinching the wide silk belt he headed down the hallway following the hand carved and ivory inlaid signs that guided his way to room 3666. As he reached the door of suite 3666, he chuckled to himself at the ethereal glow emitting from under the door sweep lighting the floor at the entrance. With two swift taps at the door, he entered the room.

"S.G. how wonderful of you to make it," said a deep voice turning to receive him in an embrace.

"Moshe, you look well. Have you lost weight?"

"Come, Come S. G. the others are waiting on the terrace."

The two walked together through the expansive suite adorned in plush hand woven carpets and frescoed desert scenes of camel caravans and date palm oasis' on the walls. The ceilings were painted sky blue, and wisps of clouds were scattered across the surfaces to simulate the expanse of the desert sky.

The men passed through the living room fitted with a large central table and surrounded by plush silk pillows. On the walls were two large-screen TV's, one tuned to CNN and the other to Al Jazeera. News of the world was blasting at high volume, as Wolf Blitzer competed with Ayman Mohyeldin for first place in placing fear in the viewers via the airwaves. Molotovs flew and burned in the streets of Greece; Occupy Wall Street protesters choked on tear gas in Los Angeles; blood and gore spewed across the screen in Homs and Damascus.

Moshe reached over to the coffee table and picked up one of the five remotes resting there, each with a different array of buttons and each with a different manufacturer label affixed to its face. He pointed with one at the set featuring the moving maw of Wolf Blitzer and mashed the button. Nothing happened. He picked up two more remotes, one in each hand, and started pressing buttons with the same null effect. Finally tossing the two remotes onto the ample throw pillows on the floor, he walked over to the two displays and pressed each "power off" switch; silence and a sigh filled the room.

S.G. shrugged and said, "I never held much faith, or found any use in modern human technology. It just serves to create frustration and further suffering."

Resuming their progress, the duo moved toward a wall of glass opening on to a wrap-around balcony. The expansive opening looked out onto a breathtaking view of the cerulean blue of the sunlit Persian Gulf.

S. G. and Moshe stepped out on to the terrace to find Yeshua and Moh lounging comfortably on two cushioned chaise chairs while deep in conversation. Both men rose in unison and heartily embraced and welcomed S. G..

To look at the two men observantly, they could have been brothers born of the same mother. They were distinctly similar with their sharply angular Semitic features, close dark beards, and swarthy complexions. If it were not for the slight straightness of Yeshua's hair and the auburn tint to the same, one might assume that they had been twins separated at birth and reunited at present.

Moshe and Yeshua were dressed in basic casual western wear with white cotton linen slacks, Che Guevara shirts and leather sandals. Moh had chosen to don the traditional local garb of the white thobe, sans the keffiyah and aghal headgear, as he found it restrictive when lounging around the suite.

Moshe was taller than all three and had aged to the appearance of a man well in to his seventies, with long white hair and full beard. His hair was pulled tightly back and was fixed into a pony tail at his back. S. G. appeared to be of comparable age to Moshe and was devoid of any hair at all, either facial or upon his shiny, oiled, nut-brown pate.

The four made small-talk for a few minutes while leaning over the railing of the balcony and taking in the view of the man made, palm-shaped island of Jumeira.

"You know that the lower level of the hotel is starting to take on water and is sinking at 5 mm per year into the substrate," stated Moshe. "The Dubai government pumped over 13 billion dollars into this white elephant, shipped in over 40,000 Asian workers to live in squalor and, displaced almost a 100,000,000 cubic meters of the Old Man's sea bed. All they have accomplished is a bunch of pissed off oysters and clams and a temporary eyesore that's slowly sinking back into the sea. In the big picture, I don't think it matters much anyway with what HE told me he has planned for this place next December."

S.G. nodded in agreement and looked over at Moshe and asked how he and Yeshua made out traveling together to the UAE.

"Oh, that went reeaaaal—welll," said Moshe cynically. "We both had to travel on Aussie passports as Moe Bullrush and Jon Baptiste. I don't think the immigration, and customs officer bought our atheist/non- affiliated story. I thought he was going to check if we were circumcised before he was going to let us enter the country. We both had prior Israeli stamps on our passports, and that started all the trouble at the gate."

The others smiled knowingly in unison.

S.G. contemplated the view below as he spoke, "It never ceases to amaze me at the ego and arrogance of mankind. It is appalling that a country that cannot house, educate or feed half its people, stuck in a region with no fresh water or arable land, would put so much treasure and engineering energy into trying to sculpt a palm tree out of the sea bed. The fact that they stuck a bunch of condos and luxury hotels on it, only to have the sea reclaim it at rate that's faster than they can sell the real estate, seems such a waste. Even if we could save their asses, The Old one will take it back into the sea before the next real estate boom comes around."

Moh looked down below with a face full of true emotional pain and turned his countenance toward the crowded work camps on the mainland. "You know, for a while there I thought they were getting it. The traditions of Zakah and Saddach, obligatory and voluntary charity, were being practiced everywhere. The poor were being cared for; schools were being built, both sons and daughters were being educated; woman were being respected as equals both wives and partners, Jewish and Muslim scholars, Asian and European scholars were all working together sharing their hearts and minds together in enlightened learning. Where did it all go wrong? Shia, Sunni and Wahabi are all fighting in His name. We blew it when we tried to take over Spain and all of southern Europe. Next thing you know, the enlightenment goes out the door and we're killing each other, brother against brother. Maybe the Old Man is right. We're all hopeless."

Moh turned to the three,

"This is all too depressing. I don't know about you guys, but l want to take in the sites as long as we're here. A little gaming, a show maybe? I hear Barry Manilow is playing across the bay at the new concert hall on 'World Island'."

The other three begged off and settled into the living room pillows. Moshe picked up a fistful of remotes and pointed them at the two screens on the wall pushing multiple buttons in frustrating sequence.

Yeshua turned to Moh and said, "Hey, be sure you're back by 6 am sharp tomorrow; the Big Guy expects us to be on time up there at his new playground in the sky-- all bright-eyed and bushy tailed."

Moh flipped the peace sign their way and headed out the door whistling Copacabana as the three cringed in painful recognition.

CHAPTER 17

Humboldt Space Science Observatory
McKinnleyville California

With a sound like the mating call of a bull alligator, Ravi produced a Taco Supreme-induced burp that seemed to start from the depths of his ascending colon as it made the journey out of his head. The belch resonated obnoxiously through the Giant Sequoia surrounded glen that the Humboldt Observatory called home. Sam slapped him on the back with a "Good One!" as he attempted to better his friend's musical efforts.

It was just a few minutes past seven pm. and the students were preparing for their next scheduled Hubble observation opportunity of the Master Kush Formation. For all intents and purposes, every nation on the planet, every university and centre for learning and every sky gazing hobbyist who had a piece of equipment capable, was locked on to the area of the Master Kush to monitor the activity daily. Unfortunately, except for the well-documented initial collection of pictures that had circled the globe from the first three days after the discovery, nothing but conjecture could be offered as to what was occurring up in the Crab Nebula now.

With the Master Kush Formation cloaked in darkness behind its shroud of cosmic gas, all was a mystery. News had been floating in all day from the world over that during the last two days, there appeared to be some shifting and movement of the cloud cover. Some even claimed to have measured a quantifiable reduction in density around the right side; but to date, it was all unsubstantiated.

The boys figured tonight would just be routine and deliver more of the same occluded view with the added Hubble advantage of better pictures of a celestial mystery shrouded in darkness. Camlala was away for the week in Hawaii. The professor had scored a speaking engagement at the University of Honolulu scamming for honorarium dollars and getting a little surfing time in. The observatory was all theirs tonight.

Ravi and Sam entered the control room flipping on lights and equipment as they made their way through the room. Ravi headed over to the entertainment system, patched in his iPod to the AV connector and hit the button on the amp.

"What's your pleasure?" he asked."

Sam looked up and said, "Let's do the Concert for Bangladesh tonight for some 'old school' effect. After that, shift to the Bonnaroo collection '06 to '09 to smooth it out."

"Good choice, good choice." Ravi scrolled his finger around the circular touch pad to pick the appropriate Playlists; dipped into his top pocket and pulled out a joint and looked questionably at Sam for a co-sign.

Sam shook his head, "Nah-you go ahead" I've cut back since the discovery and all. Check this out, I even went to one NA and a AA meeting last week just to see what's up. Kind of made me think I want to keep a clearer head for now with all this stuff going on."

"No-Way!" Ravi said. AA? NA? Where? How'd you find it?"

"I looked it up on the internet. There's a meeting every day at seven in the morning and five-thirty at night over the top of the Umpqua Bank in Eureka. I walked in to a very interesting bunch of people in attendance and more familiar faces than I ever assumed. You're welcome to come any time."

Ravi, with the buzz opportunity tainted, shrugged his shoulders and dropped the bone back into his shirt pocket.

"Oh great, now I will have to contend with your 'higher-power' weighing in on academic arguments. How am I supposed to win against that kind of super-juice?" Ravi turned up the volume as George Harrison and band kicked in to Wah-Wah.

The two sat down at the control table and started typing furiously, entering the now familiar log-in information, reaching out to their new-found buddy at the Goddard Space Flight Center. On the right hand coast of the US map, their recent good pal, Perry Stanton, Special Hubble Positioning Technician, grinned as he saw his two west coast pals log on. Both monitors pinged in unison as the handshake completed and the network connected Humboldt to Goddard in Maryland. The trio of young scientists logged on to their Skype accounts and their faces all popped up in boxes on the large 50" monitor mounted up high against the wall of the observatory.

"Hey guys, what's up!" blasted Perry's voice from the speakers.

Perry leaned back in his chair with his feet up on the table, a soda can and crumpled bag of Doritos was next to the keyboard.

"I got some good news for you guys tonight! The guys at the University of Moscow had to give up their Hubble time tonight. They said something about a riot outside the school over election fraud or something and their offices are locked down and off limits. I checked with my supervisor, and he agreed we could double up on your Master Kush observations. With positioning, we should get two 20 minute continual views out of 194 minutes of orbit time."

"Awesome!"

Ravi faced the screen, "Hey Perry, have you heard anything about those reports about the shroud dissipating?"

Perry's face lit up, "I was getting to that. We've been monitoring the reports here, and we did pick up at least some consensus data here using our big ground based unit. The big news is that last night I was setting up the Pleiades viewing for NASA, and the left side onthe screen was pretty clear. The shroud has been obscuring that one corner of the Pleiades shots since it formed, so we may be in for a treat tonight, at least something reportable."

"Hey, I read that you guys have been cleaning up the cash out there. How about sliding a little green my way? I saw you guys on Good Morning America and almost lost my lunch laughing. When you told them how you two had spent a year running calculations and researching fifty years of physical data to come up with the Master Kush coordinates, I almost choked it. Your secret is my secret!"

Perry dropped his feet and plopped forward with both feet on the floor,

"Listen guys I have to sign off and get you set up. Let's check back after the first pass and re-group. They all signed off of Skype and turned back to their desktops to start the evenings work.

Sam and Ravi watched the clock as it rolled towards eight o'clock Pacific Time, which was when their pass was to start. Bob Dylan's voice was nasally crooning "Blowin' in the Wind" and the boys joined along with their best Bob Dylan impersonations.

The monitor screens blinked blue and then reset with the familiar Goddard and Hubble logos in the corners. As the staccato ratchet sound of the Hubble equipment started to emit from the computer, the screen filled first with the view of Zeta Tauri, the star making up the northwest corner of Taurus; and then, over again toward the northwest to the Crab Nebula and the Master Kush Formation.

Perry locked on to the area, hyper focusing on the upper left side on the screen, drawing the image in increments down and into the center of the focus, until the screens filled with the Master Kush area.

Instinctively, the boys leaned forward to take in what was on the large monitors. The swirling mass of the shroud was both reduced in size and density, and at the center of the cloud area was a bright yellow object that could just barely be seen through the reducing swirl of dust. The tell-tale outline of the Crab Nebula was no longer discernable in its distinctive shape and color spectrum.

For the next ten minutes of their twenty-minute viewing window, Ravi, Sam and Perry conversed via direct computer link, as well as by voice over the speaker phone.

Sam said to Perry,

"Perry pull in tight on the center, as if you were searching the Crab Pulsar, OK good, now hold it there."

Perry said, "Oh wow, the Crab Pulsar is gone! Check out that star, and look at the chart data!"

Perry continued to pull in as the massive yellow orb filled the screen.

All three began alternating between staring at the high resolution picture on the screens, and reading over the data coming through from the High Resolution Spectrograph, the Faint Object Spectrograph and the High Speed Photometer. All Hubble data sources were posting to tables on their monitors; and simultaneously, downloading and printing onto the hard ink chart recorders which chattered away excitedly in the Observatory control room.

Ravi had been crunching numbers on his calculator as he pulled numbers off the tables being generated on his screen. He paused and said,

"Ok, Perry can you expand the focus and just try and pull in closer toward coordinate G-7 where Master Kush formed at first?"

"Roger, got it." The camera panned G-7:1, G-7:2, …G-7:6.6 and locked as it pinged a hit. The young men looked hard at the screen, and both Ravi and Sam screamed,

"Magnify! Magnify!!"

As Perry furiously pounded his key board in response, the monitors started to close in on the pale dot at the center of the new coordinates. Perry yelled out,

" 15 seconds to 'dark out', we're almost out of orbit range! Shit!"

Magnification was increasing at a slower rate than the telescope was losing its lock on to the object. Just before the object moved away from view, they all had a glimpse of what was an unmistakably a blue and green planet being lit by a yellow sun. They all slammed their heads to their desks and stamped their feet as the Hubble flew along its orbit, leaving them to deal with what would be the most agonizing 97-minutes of their young lives.

As they settled in for the wait of their lifetime, Billy Preston's soulful voice was all they heard as he sang "That's the way-- God planned it, That's the way-- God wants it to be…….." Sam turned up the volume.

CHAPTER 18

Humboldt Space Science Observatory

McKinleyville California

The clock ticked away the minutes in an audible torture that had the room on edge. An insanity of anxious activity surrounded glancing at the clock and answereing the never ending stream of phone calls coming in from outside. Sam, Perry and Ravi barely kept up with the cell phones and direct lines as they tried to field calls from colleagues, news agency science desks, and family that had seen the special news reports that were interrupting their evening prime time shows. Sam's dad was particularly pissed that his CSI New York episode had been cut off at a critical point.

"Sam, I am happy for you and I am interested; I'm just pissed that I'm going to have to watch it on my computer tomorrow. I almost had the case solved from my Barcalounger, I know who the killer is."

Ravi was on the phone to Hawaii filling Camlala in on what they saw. Camlala was frantically checking for flights home on his laptop, leaning over and crushing the scantily clad Polynesian beauty in his hotel bed.

After a good half hour of unwanted interruption with no let up, it became clear what they needed to do. The team decided to pull the plug on the phone riot that was going on. With only an hour to re-group before the next pass, they needed time to think and plan as to what their next steps were to be. The direct lines got pulled out of the hardwired phones and the cell phones were all turned of. As DROOOOIIID and SIRI electronically bitched their vocal frustration at sign off, the room was thankfully silenced. The Bonnaroo playlist had picked up on the stereo and the Disco Biscuits were doing a cover of Pink Floyd's Dark Side of the Moon.

The team switched back to Skype communication and Ravi and Sam saw the screen fill with Perry's face. Perry was sitting upright in his chair and kept taking both hands and running them flat through his hair, slicking it back from his sweat soaked forehead.

Perry's supervisor was walking back and forth in the backg round, talking heatedly in to his cell phone. It was obvious that whoever he was talking to was displeased, being duplicated by the displeasure pasted on the supervisors face.

The supervisor could be overheard saying,

"I don't give a damn that we're government funded! We're not part of the military budget and I don't care what your committee thinks about what people should or shouldn't have access to. We're a public access facility and program damnit! Come on! Your Homeland Security Senator, this is a trillion miles from the homeland and UP IN THE FREAKING sky! I didn't hear anything about you being Galatic

Security; let's leave that to George Lucas and Dreamworks for now can't we?"

"I'm not going to stop the feeds and wait for twenty bureaucrats to decide whether looking up in the sky at the stars is dangerous for the public welfare and the security of the nation! How about this Senator, you go ahead with your threat of having some jarheads with guns come shut me down; and I'll go ahead with my threat to have CNN and Michael Moore here with their cameras! That should help with re-election, right? Now I have to go Senator, Anderson Cooper is on the other line, should I tell him you said, hi?"

The Supervisor threw the phone on the table shouting

"AHHGG--- fucking politicians!"

"Look Perry, I have to go try and straighten this out. You stay on task and coordinate the next pass with Ravi and Sam. Record the event and send a flash stream to my Arlington office computer so I can monitor it while I deal with these idiots." The supervisor stormed from the room and headed toward the exit.

"Wow, I've never seen him that pissed. I think someones hornet nest got agitated, ya think."

"Ok guys lets get down to work here we have twenty minutes til I can lock on again."

Sam said, "Let's review what we know:

-SN-1054 is gone.

-the Crab Pulsar is gone.

-the Crab Nebula is gone.

-There's a G2V yellow dwarf star in their place.

-There appears to be a satellite orbiting around the G2V.

And, in 15 minutes we get our next chance to peek at the biggest discovery since Columbus figured out the world wasn't flat—or was that the Vikings and Chinese?"

Ravi brought it back on task.

"Let's do this. Perry, can you call the guys over at Kepler and see if they'll realign to focus on the G2V?"

"Yeah I know the night tech pretty well and he's been following Master Kush pretty close and calling me for updates. I'll text him now and follow up with an email with the exact coordinates."

"Good, if they can do that, we can just focus on the satellite and study it for the full twenty minute observation window," said Ravi.

Sam said, "I'm going to work distances and trajectory from the tables. Ravi, if you can do surface mapping and features, we could probably have a damn quick picture to put together of what we have here. Perry, you're going to be busy enough with panning and focus to not really be able to do much else. The Kepler guy will handle the spectral analysis and free us up for what we have to do." All agreed that it sounded like a plan.

They set about adjusting their equipment and getting ready for the sky show. Down to just minutes they resumed their positions, not wishing to miss one second of viewing time. Ravi walked back over to the stereo and hit play again, waiting to make sure that the Bonaroo Festival playlist was still cued in. Railroad

Earth's fine acoustical picking kicked in as the lead into Mighty River soothed everyone's nerves.

Perry, still connected via Skype, raised his hand and with five fingers in the air started counting down.

"Five, four, three, two---it's Kushshooowwtiiime!"

The screens went to blue and blinked back up with the dual Goddard-Hubble logo on the screens again. The brilliance of the new sun immediately filled the screen. Perry had panned back into the viewing quadrant with the magnification already cranked up in anticipation, bringing the new planet in to view as large as he could when he locked on.

The G2V shimmered and pulsated in the screen with Hydrogen generated solar flares erupting off of the corona. The panning of the Hubble continued on the same ratcheting path towards the new space body. Within seconds, the blue hue of the planet centered itself on the monitors.

While Perry locked, magnified and focused, Ravi called out coordinates and angles as the two went through mapping the surface of the planet. Sam overlaid the planet and sun on a split screen, and measured distances between the two bodies and surrounding, previously gauged data. By the time 20 minutes were drawing to a close; the trio were satisfied that they were as well prepared as they could be to face the grilling that they expected tomorrow.

Perry announced over the speaker,

"Ten seconds guys and then we lose it."

Sam, "I'm done with everything I can get from this side."

"Ive got all I can get," said Ravi.

"OK say goodnight, boys" said Perry as the planet slid further and further off the monitors and the ebony void started to fill the screen. "It's a take" said Perry.

The three maximized the Skype icons and looked at each others disheveled appearance. The twenty minutes of tense, full scramble pace had definitely taken its toll on all of three of them.

Ravi said "Ok let's name 'em first, cause we found 'em, so the rule is we get to pick the names."

"Well you can't just call it Master Kush anymore - -you have two bodies to name." Perry said.

"Four", said Ravi. "I picked up two small moons while we were panning, they may not be big but if any naming is going on I want first dibs."

After much debate and discussion about potential names and with Sam acting as scribe, Ravi brought over an empty coffee can and a pair of scissors. Sam grabbed the scissors and cut the names off the notebook paper and stuffed them into the can.

Ravi said, "Hey Perry, you're gonna' have to trust us to be fair, we're going to have to pull the names."

Perry said, "Oh this is great, coordinates out of your asses and names out of a coffee can, your guys scientific protocol is untouchable in its professionalism." Ravi and Sam flipped a bird in the direction of the monitor.

"Alright, here goes for Planet we have---drum roll please—Kush! Sam wins!" He threw three more slips in the can and shook it around. "And, for the star of the night we have---more drums please----Genesis! Perry you win."

"Perry, I think we should give the two moons to Ravi since we won out on the big ones." voiced Sam.

"Agreed" said Perry.

"That's an easy one," said Ravi. "Gentlemen meet Copernicus and Galileo without whom none of this would have been possible."

"Hey, I just got an email from the Kepler dude and he said he's still locked on and downloading the spectral analysis. Says we'll have it in the next hour or so but he says the star, I mean Genesis, that is, sure looks like a G2V main sequence star with a Hydrogen to Helium fusion furnace core running the show.

Tell me what you guys found, cause I only got visual while you guys were crunching numbers and yelling coordinates to me."

Sam said, "Alright here's what I have on Genesis:

-The star is about a billion miles across the face so it's a little bigger than the Sun's 875 million.

-Its about 110 million miles from Kush as opposed to the Earths 93 mil from the Sun.

-Here's the kicker-Its only 50 light years away from earth.

"So, in conclusion as to Genesis, we have a Sun-type star based on size, spectral quality and distance to its satellite, which is fully formed as a yellow dwarf; which means it jumped forward about 5 billion years in its evolutionary cycle."

"Here's what I have on Kush

`   -Kush is about 20 thousand miles at is equator which is a bit smaller than Earth's 25 thousand.

-Kush is about 19 thousand miles pole to pole.

-The difference in the longitude vs. latitude makes sense as the sphere is spinning faster than Earth so, I'd predict about a 20 hour day at best. There's a 7 degree tilt away from true north about its axis as well.

- The highest elevation I could get a reading on was a mountain range of about 30,000 feet above sea level which is about 9000 taller than the Himalayas."

"That's all I could crunch guys. It's going to take a while to determine sizes of land masses vs. the two oceans I can see on this side."

Perry said, "Ok Ravi, how about you on physical feautures?"

"Well this is mostly visible observation; I was typing as fast as I saw it."

-Lots of large bodies of land locked water and, lots of snow feeding rivers all over the place.

-There seems to be only two big land masses and only one Island big enough to see from our level of magnification.

-There's a white condensate cloud cover that seems to be moving around and changing in just the 20 minutes we had to observe. I'd say based on the liquid bodies that it's pretty stormy with a good bit of precipitation going on.

-The confusing thing is the green. How the hell is there green on a new planet?

"You need erosion to make soil, eons of erosion. You need plant matter to make soil, eons of plant material. So to add to Sam's statement about the advanced stage of Genesis as having a spectral age range of 5 billion years; I'd have to surmise that we're looking at a planet, that didn't exist three months ago, that's fully formed and fully evolved; with at the minimum, plant life and surface conditions that took over 4.5 billion years to produce."

All three paused as the magnitude of what had just been said settled in.

"We've witnessed something that I can only term as an unexplainable miracle, unless someone can guide me to the physics that explains it." Sam exclaimed.

"Physics! This shit defies explanation!"Perry added shaking his head as he gestured toward the monitors.

"Perry, Ravi and I are scheduled to be in New York and Washington all next week to tape a couple of shows. Let's talk tomorrow when Camlala is back and try and make some sense of this. Let's plan on getting together in Maryland after our trip to Washington."

As they were talking, they saw Perry turn his head toward the observation booth of his control arena with a look of alarm on his face. Ravi and Sam stared at the big LED screen on the wall as they saw two armed figures with official looking badges on their black baseball caps heading towards Perry at his monitor. As they started to speak into the mike, a hand came over the screen and the connection blinked off.

"Hey!" was all that Ravi got off before the door to the Humboldt Observatory slammed against the wall. Standing in the doorway were four mountain sized, similarly attired line backers heading right for them.

CHAPTER 19

It was spring on Kush and the meadow was in full bloom. God set up a big picnic table in the middle of a grass field in anticipation of his guests' arrival. There was still much to do. For the meeting today God rushed to get the lawn in and a few species of fish and lower mammals started. He had hoped to get to some hardwood forest and a few more beneficial insects to help the plants along and feed the fish.

Unfortunately, events elsewhere pulled him away to supervise a phase shift on another world at the other end of the Universe. The other project world was on the gradual genesis path, as opposed to the fast track that Kush was on. The phase change in question was similar to ending a dinosaur era and transitioning towards a mammalian population. God always tried to guide and set in motion a few things when he hit that particular transition point.

God's attentive presence had been distracted away under similar circumstances at points in time during Earth's development. This periodic lack of attention had caused a few interesting errors, some which had grown on him over time. The Galapagos Islands and their resident population for one, as well as the duck billed platypus, were two that came to mind. He had been planning for some time to eliminate the sea urchin until the Japanese built such a strong affinity for eating their privates.

Allowing the house cat to survive was his one big concession. He never intended for any creature to function with such ego and self will, but when the humans decided to tame and domesticate them, he felt they were a perfect match for each other. Cats fooled humans in to thinking that they like them, when actually God knew, that cats despised humans. Cats just liked the food without the inconvenience or danger of foraging, as well as, being scratched where they couldn't comfortably reach themselves. Personally, he would never own one. If people ever became able to read cats minds; that would be the end of the relationship for good.

Dogs on the other hand, were another story. Here was an animal that depended completely on being socially connected with their own kind in the wild. They did everything together, and they did it in a totally successful social structure. Introduce the human, and the dog forsakes its own kind in a heartbeat to devote its' entire life to unconditionally loving their human. God liked dogs a lot and owned many of them.

Walking across the field from different directions strode four figures; God smiled in recognition and stood to greet his management team for this area of the Universe.

"Welcome, welcome, it is so good to see you all again. I know we get to speak often but nothing quite beats getting together in body as well as mind for some 'face time'. You all look well and rested, I see. I hope you've already eaten as you well know I don't do lunch."

The four hungry guests looked at each other wishing they had a couple of Power-Bars to split.

"From the mandatory assignments I've given you, I'm sure you can guess why I've brought you here today. Though you guys have put forth your best efforts, and, I appreciate the challenges of the management program; I'm sorry to say that I am incredibly dissatisfied with the results."

Each of the four started to fidget with their clothes, grind their sandles in the new grass and roll their eyes a bit. Moshe started to make a grunting sound that sounded like a feeble attempt to remove phlegm from his throat.

"Yes I know you didn't have much to work with as far as raw materials. Those Earthlings are trouble to manage, but in every production program there comes a time to reevaluate, and when necessary, cut your losses and return to the drawing board."

"I've made great advances in other areas of the Universe and the four of you have done a marvelous job with your individual planet populations. That being said, Earth is a disaster. I'll tell you, long before your times, just before Noah finally retired; I was in a similar position and frame of mind. I told Noah just animals and his immediate family. As far as man went in Noah's time, they were a despicable lot and hardly worth the effort."

"I'm prepared to listen to your pleas, but I'm inclined to wipe away the Earth of all people and everything they have constructed, on their calendar date of December 21st, 2012."

"I've decided to keep the majority of the animal population intact, as they have done a pretty fair job all in all. As a benefit to the lower mammals, I intend to rework the insect population to reduce a bit of their suffering. Tics, flies and mosquitoes, along with a couple of fresh and salt water parasites,are definitely out, but I have to finish my analysis of the balancing effect before I make my final decision.

As far as Earth and Earthlings go, at this point I don't see much of anything worth saving. Other than Tenzin Gyatzo and his followers, and those folks that that fellow from Ohio, Bill Wilson, motivated; I don't see anything moving in the right direction.

No need to blame yourselves guys, you gave it the old college try and then some. I know it's been painful, but I've tried to make those mandatory meetings that you complained so much about, get the message across to you and try to get you prepared for what needs to be done."

"Questions anyone?"

"Issues and challenges?"

"Feel free to weigh in and we can discuss it."

"Anyone, anyone?"

Yeshua glanced at his peers and signaled he would lead off with a raise his hand, "Father, I hear what you are saying but there are so many backsliders that have been confessing their sins and reforming their lives. Can't we save them? Surely you don't want to slay the innocent along with the guilty do you."

"Look Yeshua, I hear what you are saying, but the folks that hijacked your message from the start, have been making a promise that they can't keep and only I can deliver on. They've mucked the message up so bad that even the faithful can't get it right. I'm inclined to burn them all and start over." He raised his eyebrows and looked downward at Yeshua as if to punctuate that the matter was settled before moving on.

"Next" His gaze passed toward Moh and locked on.

Moh started nervously clearing his throat and frantically fondling the string of beads at his waiste, "Uh, Uh, Oh Great and merciful Allah, I'd like to say something. I think this approach is just a bit harsh. Of course we all surely will defer to any decision you make. However, I believe I've made significant inroads in many peaceful communities and I'm just now beginning to see the fruits of my efforts. Given time I'm positive that these efforts will pay off and we can right the ship— so to speak."

"Right"--"Next"

"Yaweh, we've been down this road many times together," said Moshe. I know that I can count on you to honor our little agreement that has stood the test of time. We made a deal in good faith, and your word is your bond. We're the Chosen people and have suffered much. I'm sure you've taken this under consideration in your decision and will surely spare us this fate."

"Moshe, I am a fair and benevolent God but I'm also practical. No contract lasts forever. If you had read the fine print you would have seen that either party could get out of the contract in the event of a default by the other. There was a requirement to produce a Messiah by the year 2000 and you guys have failed to do so to my satisfaction. With that, I'm comfortably within my rights to get out of the contract."

With a dismissive shift of his present body and quick turn of his head, the Lord moved on to the next victim objector.

"Next"

Buddha, pressed both hands together and pushed them up and away from his body and said,

"Lord if I may, you've said yourself that there are some righteous among the Earthlings that you've observed. We all know your time is limited for focusing on matters such as these on the minute level. Tenzin Gyatzo and those that follow his interpretation of your will are just such a group. May I suggest that he be allowed, with our help, to establish a colony that may please you and set in motion a path to a better solution? I believe if he were able to return to his home in Tibet he could better focus on the issues at hand and serve all of our purposes." Buddha bowed and remained silent.

And God said, "Gentlemen I've heard your suggestions and I have the following comments:

Siddhartha's words are well taken and I fully understand all of your positions and am sympathetic to most. Let's do this; it is now February on Earth. I will give you 30 days to come up with a plan that everyone can agree on. I will consider saving a few of the 7 billion, but only according to some very stringent guidelines and pre-qualifications. I'll agree to the colony in Tibet. I like what that Tenzin fellow is doing. Oh, do me a favor and if you're going to save some of the folks down there, please make sure some of those Bill Wilson people make it on board.

I'm fully prepared to start over from scratch here on Earth. I have some concerns about the colony on Earth idea though. As you can see I built this new world below your feet on the fast track as I'm anxious to get a fresh start. I was so worried about what might be the problem down on Earth that I built this place as a fresh platform for new beings. With the way things have gone on Earth I can only assume that their must be something wrong with the water. If it is the water as I suspect, then I'd hate to start over down there after I cleanse it, only to have the population deteriorate as it has in the past. We tried everything else—right?— so it must be the water."

"Let's give Tenzin a chance and, if this colony idea works, maybe we can try some test populating back on Earth in the future. That is, if we're able to rule out the water issue."

"I expect your reports in my hands in 30 days."

"Have a great day gentlemen." And with that the meeting was adjourned."

All four looked at each other and said,

"Good meeting;" Yes, "Good meeting;" Very good meeting:" Good meeting."

And with that they were gone.

CHAPTER 20

New York, New York. "The Big Apple"

Ravi opened the door of the cab and stepped to the curb while Sam fumbled with the crumpled wad of cash he had pulled from his jeans pocket. He fished out a five and handed it to the cabbie who acknowledged it with a grunt. The cabbie flipped his meter to 'on duty' as Sam slid across the body-oiled seat and checked his pants for residue as he exited the cab. The cab pulled away in a flash of yellow and blaring horns.

The two stood outside the white building on the west side of Manhattan and looked up at the marquee, 'The Daily Show—With Jon Stewart'.

Ravi said, "Looks like we found the right place."

Sam turned to Ravi and said in his best diva-superstar voice, "You remembered to tell them no green M & M's and separate dressing rooms, right? I absolutely refuse to go on stage if they screwed it up."

Ravi punched him in the arm as they walked into the Comedy Central studio doors.

Inside, Jon Stewart had just finished his opening monologue to rolling applause and laughter from the audience and had moved on to the news of the day. A spoofed newsreel ran of Mahmoud Ahmadinejad, President of Iran hosting his fifth annual International Holocaust Denial Convention. The scene switched to Ahmadinejad sitting at a computer monitor surrounded by the media and convention attendees. Ahmadinejad was explaining to all, how the Zionist-controlled media had deceived the world with photo-shopped and fully faked photographs of emaciated skeletal Jewish prisoners at Auschwitz.

Ahmadinejad sat down in front of the computer monitor to demonstate and prove his point. Hitting the key board as the pictures progressively morphed and de-morphed from well fed, full cheeked prisoners, to the skeletal remnants of human suffering that the world had come to know all too well. Each time he hit the key to repeat the process; his group nodded and shook their heads in disgust. The attendees then clapped and stamped their feet as the pudgy healthy prisoners appeared on the screen. The camera kept cutting back to 'The Daily Show" interviewer peppering Ahmadinejad from off screen with questions about what version of Photo Shop the Allies had in 1944, as he tried to coax an answer out of the diminutive troll.

Stewart finished up and turned to the audience and announced,

"We have a great show tonight folks, our next two guests have been in high demand lately and we were lucky to pull them away from their busy schedules. You may have seen them this weekend when they hosted Saturday Night Live. Tonight, from the Humboldt Space Science Observatory in California, we have Dr. Ravi Najir and Dr. Sam Klein, the discoverers of the biggest science discovery of quite some time, the two additions to our night sky, Genesis and Kush. Please welcome Drs. Najir and Klein!"

As the applause crackled through the room, Sam and Ravi jogged out of the wings and up on to the stage to be greeted by Stewart. The two scientists settled into their chairs as Stewart regained his seat at the desk..

Stewart put his hands together and said, "Ok let's get the important stuff out of the way first. Were you guys as crushed as I was when Kyle and Kenny blew up in their space ship over Kush?"

Stewart looked at the audience and said, "I mean, seriously this is important, Cartman got his landing pod off just in time and now he's stranded on Kush!"

"We're not too worried, Jon," Sam said. "Kenny has a way of popping up alive and well for the next episode, so maybe Kyle will have the same luck. Cartman should be fine; there are a lot worse places in the Universe to be stranded than Kush. The writers are not sharing the story line with us in advance; so we'll have to wait just like everyone else to find out."

Stewart lead in, "You know, I got an advance note from my producer to introduce you two as Doctors; last time we spoke, I understood you guys had about a year to go until you graduated, what gives?"

"I'll field that one," Ravi said. "It's pretty cool, actually. Over the course of last summer, while Sam and I were on summer break, we were attending a series of seminars and symposiums for the purpose of expanding our consciousness and creativity. During our travels around to these events, Sam and I were hard at work on our thesis, the '*Intermittent monitoring of gamma ray activity in the 4th quadrant of the Crab Nebula for the purpose of verifying the galactic construction of new solar systems'.* Since our senior advisor, Dr. EJ Camlala, regularly attends these events as well, we were able to get full lecture credits for the summer." Ravi eyeballed Sam as he continued on his roll. "Once our thesis was proven by the recent events, the Dean of the School of Astronomy and Space Science decided to accept our oral and written reports around the Genesis and Kush discovery as satisfying our dissertations and accelerated us to graduation. Not bad, and we owe it to the Kush."

"Wow, what a story", said Stewart. "Now I just heard that there's some controversy around your ongoing work with Hubble and the Observatory. I heard the other day that the whole program was put on hold until further notice. What's up with that?"

Sam leaned forward and said, "I think 'controversy' is a little light, Jon. We're shut down completely and don't know when or if we can resume the study. About two weeks ago, on February 24th during our last scheduled Hubble observation session, a group of very large Homeland Security officers entered the Humboldt and Goddard control rooms as we were wrapping up our work. They shut us down and sealed both our facility and the Hubble facility in Maryland. Right now, we don't have any way to produce any more information or get access to our data, except for what was previously published, which isn't that much."

"No-way!" said Stewart.

"Way" said both boys in synch.

"How can they do that?" said Stewart, "This is the biggest discovery of the 21st century, isnt this public information?"

"Well from what we can gather Homeland Security under authority of the Patriot Act, can by-pass the Freedom of Information Act, and due process."

Sam paused for a moment. "That's one of the reasons we're on the East Coast this week. We were lucky enough to have a colleague on the President's Science and Technology Advisory Council—or PCAST—who was able to get us a hearing in Washington on Thursday. So that's where we're headed from here to try and get things back on track."

A quiet tinkle of chimes sounded from off stage and Stewart turned toward the monitor and announced "We'll be back with Drs. Ravi and Klein after a few sponsor messages. Don't touch that dial—there's more to come."

A dull murmur started in the room as the audience started to recap with their companions and seating neighbors, what they had just participated in. Stewart and the two scientists were in quiet discussion.

"Guys this is some scary shit. Having the government come in and shut down your operation is just the kind of thing that needs to get out there in the public forum. You need to be able to depend on, and use the media to hold these guys accountable and expose them whenever possible. I'll tell you what, when we finish up I'm going to give you my cell number and some folks I know over at CNN and the New York Times. Use them; this is right up their alley. OK. Yeh were ready." said Stewart as the director gave Stewart the countdown to the end of the break.

"Were back again with Doctors Ravi Najir and Sam Klein of the Humboldt Space Science Observatory in California." Stewart turned back towards his guests.

"Ok gentlemen lets get to your discovery. Please tell us all about it."

Ravi and Sam took turns giving their best lay explanation of their findings and walked the audience through each of a series of the Hubble generated photos of the Crab Nebula, on through the Master Kush Formation, the cosmic shroud, and the limited couple of photos that they had been able to download and distribute of Kush and Genesis from the first twenty minute Hubble pass of two weeks prior.

The studio audience, home viewing audiences, Stewart and the Daily Show engineering staff, all watched mesmerized as each amazing photo appeared on the giant monitors staged about the studio. The room alternated between 'oooohh' and 'ahhhh' coupled with a low murmur as the slide show presentation went on.

Finishing up with the last shot of a blue and green Kush with whisps of white rolling across its face, the interview resumed.

"So let me get this right," said Stewart. "We have a newly formed planet and star that have replaced the area in space normally occupied by the Crab Nebula. The star is the same size and type as our Sun, and the planet is just a little smaller than the Earth, and, it looks like it's a habitable planet."

Stewart looked at them for any correction. Seeing none he continued. "To top it off the planet and the sun are fully evolved to a point of about 4 to 5 billion years in age. Do you two have any explanation for this?"

"None whatsoever," said Sam. "We're witnessing something that we have no science for. We can probe it, test it and dissect it all we want, but, there's no explanation for how they got here; or, the advanced stage of development of these two bodies. Since we don't have access to our last batch of information, we can't establish yet definitively whether the planet surface is safe for humans; but yes, all the conditions to support life of some kind appear to be there."

"Wow, this just blows me away!" said Stewart. "I know I will be glued to the news as this story unfolds. Well I want to thank you two for your amazing contribution to science and wish you the best of luck in Washington this week. I know that all the people in this audience, as well as myself aren't going to stand being denied getting all the information we can on this historical event."

With that Stewart stood and shook their hands as they exited the stage and returned to their respective dressing rooms.

"I have finally found a way to live----in the presence of the Lord"
                              -Blind Faith

CHAPTER 21

God pondered the conundrum. The decision to end man's tenancy on Earth was not a conclusion that he took lightly. God had not proceeded in haste with this final destructive solution. He re-played the tape backward in time and reviewed his mental notes as he thought over his plan. Man had been tested and re-tested over the course of his history. God's Prophets had worked hard at guiding humanity. The end result was just totally unsatisfactory to him. God sat down and reflected on many of man's failures and locked on to the damage of man's intolerance as a seminal key in hastening the destruction of Earth.

God wasn't fooling around when he sent the original Genesis message of 'God created man in his own image'. There was no qualification of creed, color or culture in God's delivery. Those qualifications were applied by the feeble mind of man. Those qualifications and the destruction delivered in their pursuit was part and parcel of man's downfall.

God reflected for a moment on how his Prophets had tried to communicate tolerance for each other and the various cultures of the world. Looking for a flaw, he found very few. Why couldn't man have just embraced his diversity and drawn from the experience? What an opportunity lost and misunderstood. Each of the Prophets had tried like hell in the language of their day to get the point across. Some 'got it', not enough to sway God's rath; it was too little, too late at this point.

Man's intolerance of each other was damning him to destruction. No matter how many times the horse was lead to the water; the life giving drink was spat back on to the dusty ground. For a moment in time they might gargle with it; swish it around; wet their palate, but in the end they could not swallow the drought and gain the nourishment it offered. God hated to admit it but man seemed clueless as to the global benefits of tolerant acceptance of his fellow man.

The intolerance of man, bred through ego and self centered will, dashed His message in to the dust, stomped it into a grotesquely deformed shape and format that no longer had any connection to God's original intent. It was frustrating and was pissing Him off.

God tallied the many failed efforts. He ticked off in his head the work of each Prophet He sent to Earth to lead the errant human pack to the water. The Prophets, loaded with His message, tried to get the masses to drink and drink deepley of the importance of being tolerant of their fellow man.

Moshe, Isaiha, Micah gave it whirl on multiple occasions:

" …..nation shall not lift up a sword against nation, neither shall they learn war any more. But they shall sit every man under his vine and under his fig tree."

Yeshua tried from the steps of the temple in Jerusalem, as did his apostles and desciples as they carried the message forward:

".....Let not him who eats despise him who does not eat, and let not him who does not eat judge him who eats; for God has received him...One person esteems one day above another; another esteems every day alike. Let each be fully convinced in his own mind.....for they are all of God."

More recently, Mohammed could not have put it more concisely in chapter 109 of the Quaran:

"....I worship not that which ye worship nor will ye worship that which I worship. And I will not worship that which ye have been wont to worship nor will ye worship that which I worship. To you be your Way, and to me mine. Unto you, your religion; and unto me, my religion. You shall have your religion and I shall have my religion."

And the Great Buddha called all to separate oneself from myopic adherence. He taught that one should never blindly accept following a creed, without staying focused on the 'message'. Calling on man to recognize the simplicity of just doing the next right thing; he offered the 'Four Reliances':

First, rely on the spirit and meaning of the teachings, not on the words;

Second, rely on the teachings, not on the personality of the teacher;

Third, rely on real wisdom, not superficial interpretation; and,

Fourth, rely on the essence of your pure mind and thought, not on judgmental perceptions.

Even with all the enlightened souls that God had sent to man to act as guides, Earthlings had proven to be completely intolerant of each other and the Earth suffered for it.

The people of Earth had stunted their development; handicapped their progress, by adhering to a thought, an opinion, or a creed. Once embraced, and then applying that belief, as a test of value against all beings that they encountered. They twisted the message and formulated beliefs around their fears. Once formulated, they applied their new twisted belief to their neighbor; and, God help him if he didn't pass the test. Earthlings had missed the boat on this one. This was not his plan.

Tolerance had such a calming and curative affect on his creations. Planets that 'got it' flourished in every aspect of their existence. Tolerance was the glue that bound the inhabitants of a planet together; encouraged them to apply their efforts towards the common goals of all the residents. Through tolerance, both the planet and the inhabitants thrived; free to share their advances in social, ecological, technological and spiritual endeavors without fear of threats.

Yes, the multitude of the Earthly 'horse' had been lead to the waters by many, and they had at times put the liquid into their mouths. God was even more convinced as to his conclusion that the waters themselves must be part of the problem here on Earth.

It appeared to be a serious chemistry problem with the drinking water. God didn't like the thought of giving up on man but he was a realist in all of his affairs. A cleansing planet wide destruction and a start over was deffinately warranted and in order to set things right.

CHAPTER 22

Dharmasala, India

An autumn breeze gently pushed puffs of dust off their sandals and into the air as they leaned into the steep slope of the well-worn pathway. As the two made the next bend, the path straightened as it led up to the steps of the magnificent monastery situated high on the side of the hill. The day was glorious, with blue skies and wispy cirrus clouds soared above the peaks of the Himalayas. The two travelers had just arrived in Dharmasala few hours prior, and strolled through town to observe the inhabitants at work and play. The general serenity of the populace was evident in everyone they encountered, which was a welcome change from their last two visits to this world.

S G. and Moshe arrived at the door to the monastery. Moshe raised a long knobby olive wood staff to the door and started to rap. He got off one good lick, and raised it for a second, when the top of the staff went soft in his hand and appeared to shimmer with scales. In a serpentine undulation, the staff started to flop around on its end. Moshe slapped his hand on the side of the pole and shook it furiously, as he turned to S. G. and said, "I hate when that happens. I must be getting old and rusty." The staff firmed back up to its original rigid form, and Moshe completed his taps on the massive teak and wrought-iron door.

A soft-featured young monk in saffron robes opened the door, bowed low and said, "Welcome, the Master is expecting you. Come, I will guide you to his study."

The two prophets followed one step behind the young monk as he guided their way through the maze of rooms and corridors.

The walls were painted in vivid frescoes of mountain and pastoral scenes of Tibetan life that seemed to come alive and jump from the walls. Widely spaced wooden columns rose to the underside of the large beams and girders which in turn supported the structure of the building. Each column was carved with the skill of master woodworkers and then illuminated with red, yellow and blue paint. The finer details were outlined and enhanced by gold-leaf applied with a fine hand, making the impact that much more bold. Sandalwood and teak hinged room panels separated the spaces; each one as intricately carved as the next, with no two exactly the same. The level of hand craftsmanship was so striking, that any example could have been displayed as individual pieces of fine art; at home in a museum, in place of their utile application within the building. The windows were large and numerous; all placed in a fashion to maximize the natural imposing panorama of the Himalayan range beyond.

The monk stopped in front of a double door over eight feet in height, bowing as he stepped to the side and indicated that the two gentlemen were to enter on their own. S. G. led the way through the door to see his good friend Tenzin Gyatzo, the 14h Dalai Lama, rising off of his wood and silk covered memory foam padded settee to greet them, a wide smile upon his face.

"Welcome. Welcome, please come in and I will fix you some tea."

"Please sit here," he said indicating two more benches similar in construction to his own; both situated around a low, stone slab table. Reaching for three cups and the steaming pot resting on a hand tooled silver platter, he pulled the sleeve of his robe back with his left hand; and poured three cups of aromatic brew.

S.G. settled into his seat and shifted back and forth a couple of times. Looking over at Moshe, he nodded at his bench with a knowing look, "memory foam." Moshe craned his neck down and to the left, then looked down at his bottom, shifted left and right as he had seen S. G. do, and smiled. He alternated, pressing firmly on either side of his cushion with the flat of his palm, watched it deform in the shape of his hand, and gently return to its original flat surface. Cool.

The Dalai Lama looked over at Moshe and said, "I'm so honored to be in your presence great Moses. I've spent many years studying the accounts of your life on Earth, and the subsequent interpretations and analysis by the learned rabbis and teachers of your faith."

Moshe sighed and smiled at the Dalai Lama and answered, "As am I in your presence Tenzin. I suggest, however, that for both our parts, it is wise that we don't believe everything we read. Caution is the best policy, as to how we interpret the written words of man. It is a slippery slope to guide our way through what is true, and of valid value, within the pages passed down through the ages."

"Wise advice, and well taken," responded the Dalai Lama.

"So, what news do you good men bring to this simple monk? S. G.'s letter had a tone of urgency and concern."

S. G. said, "Tenzin, the Lord has heard your prayer and has agreed to deliver you and your people back to Tibet, but, dear friend,"—he paused—"there is a serious catch."

"The Big Guy has every intent of destroying mankind; of cleansing the world of not only the human race, but all that they have made. Not a trace is to remain except for a small chosen few, and you will be expected to participate in the selection and hosting of the colony that survives."

S. G. paused; he waited for his words to sink in before he continued. "Further, your time in Tibet will be short—for once you've stabilized the few and organized them, transportation is to start to the new world that he has formed; a planet, out in the galaxy near the constellation of Taurus. I am sure you've been following the news reports. Kush is to be your new home, and the sun that will shine on the face of you and your people, will be Genesis."

The Dalai Lama let the words wash over him; he timed his response carefully chosing his words with precision. "My purpose in the Universe unfolds on a daily basis; for only one day at a time. I try and live my life daily, first, by trying to understand God's will as best I can, and second, by reaching out with the knowledge of that will to help other human beings. I do not question God's will, nor do I try to insert my will into the process. I've found this path to be the one that brings the most peace to me, and to those that I touch. So, I take your words with pleasure, for one of my life's struggles will be fully satisfied by my return to Tibet, and from there, the next purpose for my life will unfold. As I perform God's will as you've told me I'm expected to do, I will be fulfilled. What more can a simple monk ask of life?"

S. G. smiled and turned to Moshe, "I knew we had the right guy!"

Moshe looked firmly in the Dalai Lamas eyes and said, "Tenzin, if you'll have me, I'll stay and help you with the move and the selection process. This is something that I have great experience in and it's hard on the head and heart. I was faced with the pain of the selection process as I left Egypt, and twice again in the dessert as we reached the Promised land. In the end, I was able to only negotiate ten families to take with me, and had to leave the rest. Please, allow me to be your guide."

The Dalai Lama reflected in quiet for some time before responding, "I'd be honored Moses, and I thank you for your offer of help. I fear I will need much council in all aspects of the selection and management of a people in transit. With no insult intended however, I'd like to suggest that in consideration of the short time we have to accomplish our goal, it may be better to use my Sherpas as guides, rather than yourself. I wouldn't want to risk a wrong turn, causing us to wander aimlessly from our desired direction."

"No offense taken"

S. G. said, "That settles it then. Yeshua and Moh are in China as we speak, taking care of laying some ground work for the return of Tibet to our Sovereign control by the end of next week. I don't know how they are doing it but supposedly they have worked it out with the Chinese. I understand they made them a deal they could not refuse. We have a lot to do, and not much time, so let's get to work."

CHAPTER 23

Peoples Republic of China

The little white ball slammed back and forth across the green table top at blinding speeds. Thousands of spectator heads, all in synch, yanked on their necks, right-left, right-left, in a dizzying coordinated attempt to follow the ball. The two contestants smacked their soft faced paddles against the ball with reflexes born of years of practice, never seeming to miss a stroke.

The volley went on for minutes, neither player willing to give any quarter. Both warriors were bathed in sweat which sprayed across those seated closest to the action. The contestants danced and dove across the concrete stadium floor to keep the ball in play. One, was dressed in red, with the star of China on his uniform; the other in saffron yellow and maroon.

In a row of seats directly in front of the action sat Moh and Yeshuah. Seated next to them, were all the members of the Central Committee of the CPC. Each of the Central Committee members was dressed in the traditional drab, olive-green uniforms, replete with medals and ribbons won in their defense of the

Proletariat. Except for the two prophets, all were chain-smoking filterless Chinese cigarettes so strong they could have choked the strongest horse.

Their heads cracked right-left, right-left; then as a moan rose from one side and cheers from the other, the ball flew past the end of the table, and bounced un-returned into the stands. The crowd jumped to their feet.

Filing from the room in single file, the two prophets followed the trail of dense cigarette smoke and olive uniforms heading into designated meeting room.

Standing ceremoniously in front of the table; Central Committee members on one side and the two prophets on the other, the group looked down at the three documents before them.

"Let's be clear, we won the ping pong match and as agreed, it's our rules. The wager is complete as agreed. We get the deed now, and a guarantee, all troops and equipment out by end of the month. Your two deeds get held in escrow, with no disclosure to the world until December 25th, 2012."

In a display of coughing and smoke, the committee acknowledged the terms. Moh and Yeshuah picked up the ceremonial pens on the table and signed their individual documents, as each committee member in turn, initialed theirs. Hand shakes and bows were passed around the room. The two prophets picked up their single document and held it up. In their hand was the deed to Tibet.

The CPC committee members, feeling they had gotten the better deal, picked up their deeds to Pakistan and South Korea. Though the terms had been bizarre in nature—winner takes all in a ping-pong match in trade for the deeds to three nations—the CPC knew these guys were able to provide whatever they promised.

They had done business with the duo one time before, and it had worked well. Working in the background, the two had quietly delivered the British deed to Hong Kong as trade for the Chinese to stop selling arms in sub-Saharan Africa. Granted, the Chinese had to wait the British out until 1997, but it was still a great deal. These two interesting westerners had some serious pull. The Chinese negotiators had no idea how they got it done, and they weren't going to question it this time. It was on pretty good authority that these two had been instrumental in pushing the British to leave India, and even making sure that Argentina kept the Falklands. Where these two went deals got done, governments moved borders and political goals were met without bloodshed.

After all, Tibet was just a thorn in China's side; a thorn with limited resources, and not much value. That fact, coupled with the bad press that occupying Tibet had cost the Chinese Governement, made the deal that much better. With Pakistan, they got control of the nukes, and with Korea, they could shut up the little troublemaker to the North. Not a bad day's work. They all lit cigarettes and walked out of the room in a blue cloud of nicotine laden smoke.

CHAPTER 24

Washington DC

The black SUV's and limos pulled in under the canopy. One after another the business-suited men and women exited their rides. The uniformed doormen guided the guests directly into the hands of Sherman P. Oakley, Director of Special Events for the Watergate Hotel. Oakley, beaming from ear to ear and with hand extended, greeted them each in turn with sycophantic glee as he fauned over each new arrival. As he counted out-loud and tallied the head count, Oakley tried to calculate the fat commission he would earn today—each arrival created a mental— CHAACHIINGG—into his virtual cash register.

Congressmen and Senators from both Houses, and both sides of the aisle, floated in looking all too important with their young staffers buzzing like bees around them; each staffer vying for a coveted chance at their ears. The three Cabinet members that sat on PCAST, the Secretaries of Defense, Homeland Security and Department of Energy, arrived in a show of support for the White House's dedication to the scientific community.

The Nixon ballroom was set up with tables and chairs and decorated to the nines. The rear wall of the room was made up of glass panels with magnificent views of the terrace below. The Potomac River was clearly visable as it wended its way through and along the D.C and Virginia boundary. On a large banner above the podium was plastered, 'Welcome PCAST', with the Presidential Seal of 'the United States lending pomp to the acronym.

Oakley mentally patted himself on the back for his coup. In this economy, he had landed the proverbial 'Big One'. At one thousand dollars per plate, the three thousand in attendance were about to dump a clean 300k into his personal coffers. His house in foreclosure, having been refinanced four times during the course of the real estate boom, Oakley was up to his eyeballs in debt. Working on fifty percent commission, plus a salary that no one could live on in the D.C metro area; Oakley, like millions of others across the country, had tapped the ever growing equity in his home to survive the lean years. It seemed to make sense at the time. The equity dwindled to the negative, and the bank came calling.

The lean years used to come in short cycles. This time however, the lean year that started in 2006 was fully extended to the present. No bookings, no commissions and starving on his salary, this was the first big event he had booked in four years.

Today's event was a gala Washington dinner to promote to all Americans and the world, this Administration's forward thinking policies; and the United States, as the center for advancements in clean energy, science and technology. Ironically, only two of the government vehicles that arrived, ran on fuels other than gas or diesel. After all, it was politics as usual, and this was Washington DC.

Where Washington went, the money followed. The room was full of CEO's and their lobbyists for every major oil and energy-company, auto makers, venture capitalists and green energy providers. The Senators and Congressmen were dispersed around the room, kowtowing to their special interest group of choice, while brokering deals that would enhance their power in Washington. Each politician hoped to line his or her pockets without being set up for an internal senate or congressional ethics investigation.

The senior government members were pulling aside CEO's that had supported them over the years, and gently reminding them of their efforts on their behalf; as well as, their retirement plans for the near future. Hints were dropped as to how delighted they would be to offer their Washington expertise, and what a benefit that would be to the bottom line of the CEO's company. Donations for campaign efforts were solicited with both subtle (and not too subtle) warnings; that it was always better to deal with the devil they knew, as opposed to the alternative.

The Cabinet members had their own agenda; lobbying just as hard as the private sector, they worked the congressional and senate staff to push their individual department budgets, seeking avoidance of reductions in money or staff. It was an orgy of promotion and self-interest; A veritable ass-kissing Olympics of the highest caliber if you will.

Off to one side, was an area of particularly bustling activity. In the far corner of the room, situated around a free standing bar, was a grouping of five tables. Both seated and milling around, were men and woman engaged in heated negotiations. The venture capitalist's group was in high attendance; they were bouncing back and forth between the tables like billiard balls.

At the table closest to the bar, the CEO and Science director of a small California green-energy start-up company was explaining to the two men to his left, the product he was trying to get off the ground. The CEO dumped his entire life savings into his development of a new highly efficient, low-cost coating for photovoltaic panels designed to produce heat and electricity from the sun. The product prototype had proven to be so effective; it could possibly revolutionize the solar power industry once introduced to the market; some said, by cutting costs over two thirds on panel production.

Down to his last nickel, and with zero prospects of a loan in the current economy, he was one step away from the finish line, and also, one step from bankruptcy. The two men, one, a venture capitalist and the other the CEO of a major oil company, were listening intently.

"Listen, your entrepreneurial effort is to be commended. Don't you think you've taken this as far as you can go? Wouldn't you like to have your life back? Golf, fish take the wife and kids on a vacation. Hell, with our offer you can buy a yacht and a small island somewhere."

"But this is my baby! I want to see it brought to market, and think of the benefit to the nation. I want to be remembered as the guy that changed the solar industry, and did something good for the world."

"Oh don't you worry, well bring it to market. We have the money and marketing machine, and we're already in this space. Take the offer. You owe it to yourself. Well keep the name and keep the staff. There just isn't room for two CEO's."

"Maybe I can sweeten the deal. We'll offer you a fully staffed lab in our facility that you can use whenever you want. The only hitch is that we own the intellectual property. That's not a big concession." said the oil-company exec.

After a few more minutes of contemplation, the Cali CEO/Scientist/Inventor nodded his head in agreement.

The venture capital guy leaned in and said,

"Ok, here is how it works. It's like Uncle Sam is going to be our partner. We borrow $3 billion from the fed at 0% interest under the Clean Energy Job Creation fund..........."

Another great idea would never see the light of day. Mission accomplished, the oil company exec got up and shook his new acquisition's hand. He turned, and went over to the bar. Acquiring technology and innovation away from the public had become as important to maintaining the oil company's bottom line as internal research and development. By ensuring that new ways to reduce energy, cut costs and promote alternative fuels never came to market, the oil company guaranteed continued market share and control of its profit margins.

At the bar, the successful negotiator ran into two of his colleagues', one from a major auto maker, and the other from a natural-gas supplier.

"Hey, Bert how did you make out with the solar guy."

"I got it! I think I can hold on to it for a good fifteen years before we have to play a little of it out t the market. We can start with some trumped-up production or technology delays, but I think I can keep it under wraps for at least a good fifteen."

"Good job, I picked up a real promising battery company, and a small turbine guy out of Mexico. We can quash the technology and protect our margins. Same deal."

"Hey, Roger, how did you do?"

"I crapped out. I tried like hell to get Elon Musk to sell me the patent and technology on his new Space Mag-lev but he won't budge. That guy is like a one man wrecking crew for the fossil fuel business. We need to stop him now."

"Ouch" "Ouch" chimed the other two.

CHAPTER 25

Ravi and Sam arrived at the Watergate in a platinum grey Tesla Roadster Sport. Even though they could now easily afford one, they had lucked out. They had just picked up the electric Tesla Sport on Wednesday as a gift from Elon Musk, President and CEO of Tesla. The two had been the featured speakers, as well as the guests of honor, at the Space X victory dinner held in Washington the night before.

Space X, another Elon Musk venture, was celebrating the announcement of their Mag-Lev space drive, which was still early in its development stages. Space X, under the guidance and genius of Musk, used their ability to think outside the box. Space X hoped to be the first to bring commercially viable, private space flight, to the public.

Space X was already leaps and bounds ahead of the worldwide competition, as well as the government sponsored programs. The company had developed unique methods of delivering rocket-propelled satellite hardware into space. Their efforts were opening wide the doors for private industry to participate with peaceful governments in commercial space applications. NASA, in frustration, had recently partnered with Space X finally accepting that if you can't beat 'em, join 'em.

Sam and Ravi ran the Tesla through its paces all day, beating the 3.7-second, 0 to 60 on two occasions, taking turns alternating between manning the stop watch and being test drivers. They had hit the road hard, blasting up the Baltimore Washington Parkway, pushing the electric screamer to its limit. Finally, they had been pulled over by a Maryland State Trooper, ticketed and proudly clocked on Radar at 128 mph (3 MPH over the advertised performance!) The trooper took sympathy, delayed the ticket process as he admired the sleek and sexy Lotus-inspired body style and opulent interior of the car. Recognizing the two, even before pulling their license and registration, he reduced the tickets for 'those Kush guys by 40 MPH to lower the fine. Back at the station he was the hero of the day and laminated and framed the ticket for his wall at home.

Sam and Ravi jumped back in the car to head to the late-afternoon event at the Watergate and meet up with Perry Stanton from the Goddard center. They pushed the car further until they exceeded the 245-mile range. Both were surprised that the extra mileage was gained after the harsh tests they had run it through. They had succeeded in blasting well past the limited battery life suggested by the contested BBC road test.

As they pulled into the Watergate and under the canopy, Sam reached around the back compartment to find the 240V adapter to charge the vehicle. The Valet car park attendant eyeballed the car with envy, practically drooling in anticipation at the parking opportunity. Sam and Ravi took one look at the guy, looked at each other, shook their heads and said,

"Ferris Bueller!" They hopped back in and sped over to the 'self-park' lot.

Inside the Watergate, the Navy band was heating up; the cocktails, canapés and and hoers d'ouerves were making their way around the room on platters carried by starched tuxedoed servers. Oakley flitted from table to stations shaking hands and giving unsolicited and unwanted guidance to servers and the technicians setting up the AV equipment at the head table.

Both of the young doctors walked into the soirée looking pretty dapper, dressed in rented tuxes with collector series Nike Airforce-1's for footwear. Scanning the room, they keyed in on a grinning Perry and his now-familiar supervisor, sitting at a table a couple rows back from the raised head table. The two navigated the crowd over to that side of the room, grabbing a couple of coconut shrimp and a puffed brie pastry on the way.

"I'm going to go get a beer; you want anything?" asked Ravi.

"Grab me a coke and a lime," said Sam.

Sam headed over and hugged Perry the guy way. Perry introduced his supervisor: Dr. Brisbane Brown, Senior Director of Operations at the Goddard Space Flight Center in Maryland. The men shook hands, as Ravi returned with the drinks, and the introductions continued. They talked at length about the incredible paths that all of their lives had taken from the initial impact of the first Master Kush sighting, to where they were now. Bris Brown smiled at the three sitting there,

"You know, Perry and I have some interesting news. I had Perry download in real time, all the data and pictures from the Hubble to my home office in

Arlington. While I was arguing with that jerkwater senator on the Homeland Security team, all the data transferred before they had a chance to seal it. I have a full complete set from both sessions! On top of that, the Kepler Data was sent to me as well. So, we got it all regardless of what these government knuckleheads do. "

"No way" the boys responded in tandom.

"Yep"

"That means we can complete the surface temp, atmospheric and water vapor analysis to figure out whether this place is fit for humans. Ravi can finish his surface mapping and the land mass to water analysis. This is awesome. Right now, we're stuck with ground based viewing data, which sucks, by the way, and no indication whether we can do another view from space on Genesis or Kush," Sam said.

Bris Brown looked over to his left and casually acknowledged a man in uniform talking to the Senator from Pennsylvania, and the Director of Homeland Security.

"There's my buddy, Jefferson Blake, he has the skinny on the Homeland Security idiots. And, that's the idiot from PA that I was screaming at on the phone the other night. You can be sure he's the one that pushed for the Kush shut down."

The uniformed man begged off from the other two and slowly made his way over to Bris and the three young scientists. Bris offered introductions around, and they all resumed their seats.

"I'm really glad to meet you guys. I've watched and read everything I can on the Genesis/Kush discovery. I was trained as an astronaut originally, and somehow ended up here as a political liason and paper pusher! My heart is still in space flight. Bris and I go way back and when he called, I tried to find out all I could."

"The way I see it, there's some concern in the administration that some amount of public unrest might stem from the discovery. I don't think they're focused enough on the issue, being it's an election year. The big problem is the Director of Homeland and that idiot sidekick of his. Ever since they popped Bin Laden, and we started bringing troops home from Afghanistan and Iraq, they've been scrambling to keep the fear level high. There've been talks of budget cuts and repealing the Patriot Act; they're more interested in protecting their cash-cow than protecting the country. These guys are running scared, covering their asses and trying to keep their jobs. Its politics, not protection."

"What can we do?" asked Sam.

"Not a thing, yet. I don't think they will get any further support to quash information, but with no one listening at the Administration level, you're going to get bounced around for months. I think you just have to sit back and wait it out."

"Wait it out" Ravi said, popping his hand on the table. "You're kidding me. We're sitting on the most significant scientific finding of all history, and we're supposed to 'wait it out'. That's bullshit!"

"I don't know what else to tell you. It's about votes. Unless you can get the President's ear, or gain enough publicity in the media to make it seem like a threat to the election, then it's going to sit."

Ravi and Sam were totally disgusted and dismayed by the information they had just received.

As the first speaker was walking to the podium, the group settled into what was going to be a very boring dinner; a dinner poisoned by the bad news surrounding their discovey. They couldn't wait to get out of there.

"All the way down to the bottom-All the way down to the fire-All the way down to the devil-Beelzebub-To the bottom of the pit, now."

-moe

CHAPTER 26

The first Televangelist to latch on to the Genesis/Kush bandwagon was the Reverend Roger P. Hortley of the 'Family Faith and Gospel Hour'.

The reverend had done well for him self over the years. The millions of dollars in contributions given in search of salvation that funded the organization had produced many treasures for Hortley on Earth. A University, a television station, a radio station, a couple of private schools; a church and retreat campus, a faith healing center, all under his wing. As an added bonus, the good Reverend lived in a 20,000 square foot house provided by the ministry. Hortley spent a decent amount of time traveling between Branson Missouri and Nashville; catching the latest acts, and offering free tickets and rides on his Gulfstream to the wealthiest members of the faithful. For, after all, doing God's work was costly, and the Reverend was all about God's work. That was until last year.

The good Rev. Hortley was recently back from "Reprogramming" from the shameful backsliding and slipping that he had admitted to the year earlier. Hortley was arrested in a Mobile Alabama hotel room with three under-aged male prostitutes, a quantity of illicit drugs, and a goat.

Hortley first tried to claim that he thought they were girls. When that didn't work, he said he was trying to save them from Hell and Damnation; that he was conducting an intervention with them. That didn't work either. The faitful tithers just weren't buying it. As a last resort Hortley figured his best approach was to fall back on the leniency of the damned, and cried on national TV: 'I am a sinner under the control of Satan.' That one seemed to work.

Over the next month, after televised scenes of his pleas to God for forgiveness broadcast into every living room, combined with a flurry of interviews with his generous and forgiving wife and family on the religious networks; he announced his decision to enter a faith-based De-Programming/Re Programming facility in Colorado. He was now back in the saddle.

His wife was less inclined to buy into the Satan thing, and was none too pleased with her wandering kinky spouse of thirty-years. She was not however, about to give up the Louis Vitton and Caribbean resort hopping she enjoyed. Between televised trips to Haiti, or the slums of Sao Paolo, Mrs. Hortley enjoyed a jet-set lifestyle funded by the faithful. She was quite the fund-raiser in her own right, parading through refugee centers of dysentery-afflicted and bloated stomach converts, while explaining to the television viewers, that just for a quarter a day, little Juana would not only be fed, but accept God in her life and be saved.

It all was drilled into the faithful watchers' heads, that giving to the Hortley Ministries—the chances of salvation increased exponentially for them as well. Always on the screen, the rolling banner displayed the large bold font call-in-number, while the 'voiceover' droned on about the ten different easy payment plans that one could choose from. The last time anyone checked, the breakdown of charity delivered to the dollar received, was in the range of six cents to the sick and starving, and ninety-four to the Hortley's to run the show. Not bad margins if you can get them. Yes, God was great and God was good, and the business of God was expensive to run.

Hortley latched on to the Genesis Kush thing like a tick to a dog. Hortley told his riveted TV audience that while in re-programming, God had come to him and informed him that Kush was for the faithful and the faithful only. God was preparing the heavens to receive all the True Believers. True-Believers, as opposed to the Non-Believers, was a definition that Hortley felt fully confident in his ability to disseminate as God's designated, consummate authority. Loosely defined, if you believed the crap that emanated from Hortley's pie-hole, you were a True Believer. And, if you gave and gave generously, you were golden. His viewers assumed that Hortley was cured and worthy of forgiveness. Viewer rate's sky rocketed; pockets were laid open and then laid bare. The cash came rolling in.

As Hortley's colleagues in the business of salvation saw the incredible resurrection of their backsliding compatriot, they jumped on the band wagon one by one. From television evangelism the virus spread, engulfing all and forcing competition in the ranks. At the risk of losing market share, one by one the infection rolled across the world until every major organized religion had signed on to the deal. Every one of them sure in their conviction, that they, and only they, owned the exclusive rights to the formula that would gain a seat in heaven.

The end of the world was coming. There was a new opportunity in the sky. Genesis and Kush were going to save the world. If you want to board the Kush bus, you better sign up, pay up and follow the rules to a tee. If not, you were going to be left off at the first stop. The end of the World was nigh, and each had their own idea of 'when'; each had their own idea of what 'the rules' were.

CHAPTER 27

Dahrmsala to Lhasa

A caravan of color moved carefully from West to East on its way through the Himalayas. If nothing else the Tibetan people were brightly adorned and one couldn't miss them in their brilliant contrast against the surrounding countryside. With multi-colored Tibetan prayer flags mounted on standards and flying in the mountain wind, the convoy transporting the people and possessions of the Tibetan Diaspora were traveling from Dharmasala India toward their mountain paradise home of Tibet. The procession formed a ten mile long serpent of gold, maroon, blue, red and saffron as the stream of humanity moved eastward. It was almost 53 years in coming, but was still sweet with the fresh nectar of victory.

His Holiness, the Dalai Lama, with a smile fixed across his peaceful face, a dream fulfilled; rode at the head of the procession in the lead transport. As colorful as the Tibetan column presented itself, the opposite was true of the dusty drab olive of the military convoy carrying the remnants of the abusive occupation force of the Chinese Peoples Liberation Army. The green column was moving out of the

Himalayas and heading down toward Beijing. While light, peace and prosperity came in from the West; the darkness of tanks, guns and armed uniforms exited on the East. It was a portentous picture. The prayers of 'Free Tibet!' had been heard and fulfilled.

Moshe was bouncing around uncomfortably in his seat, next to His Holiness. He did not share the smile and calm countenance of his traveling partner.

"I hate these things; it's like riding a camel with no saddle. I prefer to hike regardless of how long it takes to get there." Moshe blared over the rumble of the trucks as he tried to regain a purchase on the seat.

"We're almost there Moshe, five more miles. The monks have already cleaned out the Chinese debris.

As the convoy entered the city of Lhasa, the people danced in the streets in full traditional holiday attire. The streets and foot paths were strewn with lotus petals as the people welcomed home their spiritual and government leaders. The Dalai Lama stepped down from the truck, and the crowd erupted in cheers and tears.

Turning to Moshe, he said, "I cannot thank you enough for this moment. Come, we have much to discuss and plan at the monastery."

They made their way through the crowd and up the steps to the Norbilunkga Palace, the Dalai Lama's summer palace residence. The more opulent and larger Potala palace, about two-miles away, was still being washed of the stench of the Chinese occupation. Potala would not be ready until the winter for the Dalai Lama and his entourage. Following through a pathway lined with monks, all with their heads bowed low in reverence of his Holiness' homecoming; the two entered a back room for some quiet conversation. As promised, God had delivered the Dalai Lama to his home.

CHAPTER 28

The four Prophets had just left God's presence. He thoughtfully accepted their plan; even accepted it a day late. So be it, they wanted to try to save a sample of humanity; he wasn't going to make it a walk in the park to get it done. He had given in a little on the Tibet colony, and how long they could stay before transfer to Kush began. He was not going to budge on the criteria for salvation though.

Left to his thoughts----He pondered his creation of man. He picked a booger of cosmic dust from his nose and flicked it away; he shuffled from his right foot to his left and cogitated about man and his beleifs.

Miracle or Science. Was it one, or the other, or, could it be both? Science was man's tool to try and explain the unexplainable. What was a miracle at one point in time could become grade school science later. It was all just a matter of time. A Bic lighter in a caveman's hand would make him a magical God of Fire among his peers. A Bic lighter in a woman's hand in Salem Massachusetts in the 1600's would have her burned at the stake. It was a miracle one day, boring fact of science and technology the next. The only difference was time.

But man's time was always limited. As man crawled out of his caves, he trembled in fear over everything he encountered that he could not simply explain or control. Light, Dark, Fire, Water, Wind and Rain---scared shitless he ran back to the protection of his caves. The Earth trembled and spewed lava, fire, smoke and ash. The skies struck back at the Earth with lightening, killing anything it touched. Calm, life-giving waters, rose in anger and engulfed everything in its path. Shit fell from the sky and slammed into the Earth. With all this going on, it was a miracle in itself that man ever left the caves to begin with.

The natural elements were tangible forces that produced the fears and emanated from a direction. Those forces came from either the ground below his feet, or, from the heavens above. So man had a place of direction to focus his fears. He had a few portents to read and could build an avoidance and warning plan of sorts. This helped to calm Man to some level, but not nearly enough to quiet the consuming fear.

Oh, man is a fearful creature in general. But the greatest fear of all was------Death.

Man saw death and didn't like what he saw. Death came at him from every direction. If one of the unexplainable natural elements didn't get him, then he still had it coming from every other direction. Animals ate you; tasty berries killed you, one wrong step on the trail, and you were plastered on the rocks below. Come back from hunting saber-tooth tigers and your whole village is burned to the ground with your women and children gutted and displayed on pikes in a circle. And even if you managed to escape all that---death still got you in the end. The finality of death, the void of death was the scariest place to go. Man just couldn't deal with it.

To try to deal with the fears, man tried appeasing the sources. Maybe by showing enough deference and devotion it would please the gods; maybe they would back off and give him some space to live. Man tried worshiping the Sun, moon, stars and planets. He tried Mother Earth, and each of the scary elements of Wind, Rain, Fire and Water. He even tried worshiping the guys who gutted and posted his family on a pike. None of it sufficed in full. The fears could not be reconciled with. The fears could not be put to bed. And where there was fear, you had the entire perfect framework for a religion. And where you had religion you had a framework for control.

God had been an astute observer and student of his creation. He tended his crop and checked in from time to time. He tested the water and perused Man's progress—or lack therof. He scanned the publications and tuned in to the news. God had been taking the temperature of Man for sometime and didn't like what he saw on the guage. He chuckled at Man's idea of the World Religions and their feeble attempts to define his 'word' in subjective terms.

Man had created religion out of fear and control and spread it under the guise of faith, devotion and spirituality. By way of Man's definitions, religion had drifted far away from the anchor of a healthy spiritual connection to God's plan. Modern dictionary definitions in the English language are somewhat limited. For those speaking the English language, the words used, and the context they are used in, have been defined by Judeo-Christian heritage. Peeling the English language etymological onion further back to the core, the observer can get closer to why the root word popped up in the first place.

Take the word 'Spiritual', for example. Miriam Webster denotes for its first and second definitions: '...belonging to the church' and "Clergy" ,respectively. However in Hebrew, the language of the bible—the root for 'spirituality' closest to its source, is the word 'nephesh', the inner breath and connection to life. Spirituality is a far 'breath' from religion. Spirituality is a breath, a connection to that essence which one can worship with devotion, respect and love.

Religion, very loosely defined, is a system of beliefs and practices created and used by man to display devotion to a superhuman controlling force. Man seeks to show this devotion through worship. Man believes that through worship, he may seek reward, comfort, sustenance, and an answer to life and death. Religion in of itself is not a bad thing by any means. Man has unfortunately and repeatedly, used it badly. Religion is great crowd control, and man liked power over crowds.

Religion, by way of its definition, is a construct of man. Man in all his wisdom, or lack thereof. Man with all his defects of character. Man with all his agendas. Man with all of his prejudices. Man is not infallible. It would take more than a leap to accept any single religion as infallible. Religion is simply opinion. Opinion is not fact. Man, even when inspired by God, is still nothing more than------- a man.

The "Systems, beliefs and practices", leave themselves open to prescriptive critical methods, --- dogma and ritual if you will. Spirituality is personal, and transcends prescriptive methods; it's pristine in its amorphous state. Spirituality requires no dogma to practice; just a breath of conscience and belief in a power greater than yourself. Where Spirituality sought to be free of ego and will, just as we don't need to think to breath; religion sought to control man's will, using the strength and ego of the powerful to allay man's natural fears.

Spirituality fit well it to God's plan. Religion, on the other hand, much better served man's plan. The two were not one in the same. The difference between the two, and the resulting actions, was why God planned to be busy on December 21 2012.

CHAPTER 29

Las Vegas Nevada

The long black limo drove through the legs of the great Sphinx, the long black limo circled into the grand entrance of the Pyramid shaped Luxor hotel. Laughter was heard coming from the back passenger area as scantily-clad doormen, dressed like they had stepped right off the set of 'Ben Hur', reached and opened the double rear doors. The laughing got louder and out from the limo ejected a scowling elderly gentleman with a neatly combed grey beard. Looking pissed; he shook out his long grey hair and then pulled it back tightly in a ponytail. The doormen wondered, 'high-roller', maybe even 'whale'?

The laughing members of the entourage were a group of three, two dark and Arabic, and the last, a rotund gentleman of Asian descent. They were trying to stifle their mirth.

"Oh, come on Moshe it was just a joke. We thought it would be funny to stay here. You'll have the run of the floor and the respect of the natives."

"Very funny. It's not like I had any fond parting memories. You guys are about as insensitive as you can get, you'd think with what is going on, you bozos would be a hell of a lot more serious. You just don't know when to quit."

"Do you want to stay somewhere else or what? I mean Caesars might have the same effect on Yeshua, and it's the only other place that could have accommodated us" Said a chastised Moh.

"No, I'll stay. At least I won against these guys and didn't get caught. Which is more, I might add, than I can say for you and the Romans, Yeshua. As for all of you, you're lucky I didn't turn around and just go back to Tibet."

The driver had finished loading their bags on the Bell cart and they headed into the lobby to check in. Manning the Hotel check-in counter stood a smiling young lady gaudily dressed up as Cleopatra. The four guests sauntered up to the counter and S G. addressed the young lady with the name tag that said, 'Alyssa—New Jersey'.

Hello, Alyssa—reservation for four, adjoining suites—the name is Patel— Sid G. Patel.

"Oh yes Mr. Patel, I have your res-ah-vation right heeahh. As you guys requested, there-ahh four large bot'l's of watah in your room, and the room-service guide is in the drawah' of the desk if you gentlemen want to order anything. Just call down to the front here and ask for me if you need anything else." The men got the gist in spite of the strong North Jersey accent.

"Here you ah' gentlemen, I've given you two room keys each. The gold one will allow you access to the Penthouse elevators and I booked adjoining Temple Suites for you. The other key will gain you access to the upp'ah-level spa and wellness cent'ah'. You are already registered at the high stake gaming table area. Please follow the Bellman to your rooms."

As Moshe softened to the idea of being stuck in his own idea of hell for a weekend, they all followed their bags to the Penthouse elevators. They rode high into the upper levels of the Great Pyramid.

With the connecting double doors open, the four prophets surveyed their living quarters for the weekend. The four eyed the designer furniture selected in a gaudy interpretation of Cleopatra meets Bollywood; they started to enjoy the campy décor. Moshe went over to the coffee table and picked up a remote. He hesitated for a moment and then handed it to S. G. to save him the pain. S. G. clicked the button, and the TV turned right in with Andeson Cooper and CNN blaring on the screen.

"Wolf, the only bright point of the day is in Lhasa Tibet; the Dalai Lama held prayer vigils and celebrations in commemoration of his recent return to Tibet. The streets were filled with celebrants. The peaceful return of the Tibetan government and the un-accounted for change in China's policies towards Tibet is a welcome relief from the world news to follow."

"In Provo Utah, Police had to be called in today to break up a riot at a college football game. The Brigham Young vs. Loyola game ended in 147 arrests and twenty injuries; three of the hospitalized were Provo Utah police officers. The fight broke out over an argument when two Loyola players taunted the

Mormon team as being Non Christians and surely to burn in hell."

"In Israel today, right-wing ultra-orthodox fanatics stormed the Temple Mount and insisted that the "Dome of the Rock" was sitting on their only access to the Holy of Holy's, and they refused to leave the mosque. The Jews held fifteen Muslim tourists from Detroit, Michigan hostage, until a joint Palestinian Police and IDF task force was able to free the hostages and arrest the trespassers."

"In response to the Temple Mount incident, Muslims in Detroit held what started as a peaceful vigil outside three synagogues that later erupted into a brawl when Jewish worshippers arrived. Muslims in Europe rioted in Denmark, France and England. In Iraq, a twenty four year old Shia suicide bomber blew himself up in the center of a Sunni neighborhood outdoor market. The bomber left behind a video saying that it was the responsibility of all Shia to take out as many Sunni Non-believers as possible, before the end of days, to ensure purity of the faith in the new world of Kush. The bomber went on to say that Kush was being prepared by God to accept the faithful followers of Sunni Islam. He was looking forward to a new world with 72 virgins for him and free of western devils and the impure non-believers. Back to you, Wolf"

Wolf Blitzer appeared on the screen.

"Thanks, Andersen. Today the head of Homeland Security Frank Stinchcomb, said that there was still no decision about the release of the Genesis and Kush program information or a date as to when it may continue. Stinchcomb stated that the NSA and Homeland Security were still analyzing the background noise of the recordings for suspected Al-

Quaeida embedded messages. When asked to explain their position further, Stinchcomb responded. 'Just look at your TV and tell me that some message hasn't gotten out in the Muslim world'. He further stated that if 'They weren't already inside our borders now, that they were surely knocking on the door'."

Moshe said, "S.G. turn it off please; I can't take any more. I can't wait to get back to Lhasa."

S. G. punched the clicker and Wolf and Andersen were silenced.

CHAPTER 30

The platinum Tesla Roadster Sport hummed its way through the legs of the giant Sphinx. Sam and Ravi asked the Egyptian Palace guards where the Self–Park lot was. Sam parked the Tesla in the remotest empty area of the lot on an angle, taking up two spaces on the end of the row, ensuring that no one would find it convenient to park next to them. The men pulled their bags from the car and repeated together:

"What happens in Vegas, Stays in Vegas!" a double high five as they rolled their bags towards the Pharaoh's Garden and the rear entrance to the Luxor hotel.

"We booked two premium rooms on Expedia, what do you mean our names are not on the list!" I have the confirmation right here," insisted Ravi.

"But I don't understand," said the Egyptian princess at the counter. It keeps coming back that all of the rooms are taken. If you'd like, I'll check another hotel for you. Hey, aren't you those Kush guys? Her mascara laden eyelashes started batting as they fluttered with excitement as she recognized her two celebrity guests.

"Yep, that's us. Can we speak to your manager please?"

The flustered front desk agent flicked her long Cleopatra black tresses off her shoulders as she leaned in and said.

"Be right back, I'll go get him." Sam paid much too much attention to her retreating Egyptian mini-skirt.

A few minutes passed, and the manager's office door opened. With the coy front desk clerk following behind, the Front Desk manager came walking forward with a look of apologetic embarrassment on his face.

"Drs. Klein and Najir, I'm so sorry for the misunderstanding. I apologize for the mistake. I believe the problem is with the booking agent. I have only one room left, but it is a two-bedroom suite on the Penthouse floor. We'll upgrade you at no additional cost."

Both Najir and Klein looked skeptical as they both thought---"SCORE"

The young gal at the counter went through the multi-colored card system and ran through the list of Hotel amenities.

"There's a couple of large bot'l's of watah in your room, a couple of bibles and the room-service guide is in the dra'h'aw' of the desk if you gentlemen want to order anything, or get some light reading in."

Ravi said, "Draw?"

Alyssa: "Yeah, the things that you pull out of a dress'ah? Keep your undies and socks in----THE DRAW!"

Ravi: "The drawer?"

Alyssa considered the consequences of being fired or reprimanded for mistreating a handicapped guest---"Right.... the draw."

She handed them the keys and pressed a card into Sam's hand; she let hers fingers linger on his for an extra moment. As they walked towards the Penthouse elevators, Sam looked down at the card. In a fine handwriting was written—"Alyssa-cell' 721-555-1126—I get off at 6---call me!" Signed with a smiley face, he could swear it smelled faintly perfumed. Sam thought—Double Score! Ravi tried to snatch the card out of his hand. Sam pulled away with the card and shoved Ravi in to the elevator as the doors to the car opened. Dejected, Ravi punched the button to the Penthouse as they made their ascent.

"Let me see it", said Ravi holding out his hand to Sam for the card.

"Bite me," said Sam.

They reached the top floor of the Pyramid and walked down the hallway to their room, as they went to pass the card key through the electronic lock, a chubby little Asian man stepped from the door of the room across the hallway carrying an empty ice bucket. The pleasant man stopped and smiled at them with the warmest of silent greetings. Ravi turned the knob and the door opened into the living room of the coolest hotel room they had ever seen.

"WOW! This is awesome, Sam. For a minute there I thought we were screwed and were going to be bouncing all over town for a room. We're way lucky."

"Nah, I had faith it would work out. What more could we ask for. A weekend in Las Vegas, fat rolls of cash in our pockets, and I have a girl---oh oh sorry Ravi—who did she give the card to—who's birthday is it?"

"OK. Mark Antony, settle down we have to stay focused. We're here to win and win big. Let's relax a few minutes. I'm going to go get naked and lounge in that pulsating steam shower and sauna in there to loosen up before we hit the casino floor. I suggest you do the same in yours, but take a cold one."

Sam flipped him one and headed to his bedroom. They had a big night planned, and he was ready.

CHAPTER 31

Luxor Hotel Casino-Las Vegas Nevada

A little before four in the afternoon, fully rested and showered, Sam and Ravi headed down to the Casino floor. With dollar signs in their eyes and thousands in media frenzy generated dollars to burn in their pockets; they were two young men riding high on life.

The energy on the floor was captivating. Screams erupted from the direction of the Craps tables of "Yo-11!", followed by clapping and whoops from around the pit. Scantily clad princesses of Egypt, some dressed like 'Nephretiti," over there a "Cleopatra," across the way a couple of harem girls all walking around with trays saying, "Drinks---Drinks". The girls had a challenge just navigating their way through the crowd, dodging scooters and pedestrians as the wagering masses moved from station to station around the Casino floor. Players from the floor reached for free beverages flipping a white chip here, and from time to time, some color for the service.

From the slot areas came a cacophony of bells, jingles and theme songs, punctuated by an occasional choral   of—'Wheel---of----FOOORTUUNE!'

Unmistakable, was the strobe-blinking red beacon, along with sound of distinctive clanging, as a jackpot was hit. A jumble of mesmerized players gathered around to see what the Lucky-One had won, all wishing it had been them, and with renewed hope that they were next, they resumed the frenzy of feeding quarters and dollars into the machines.

Navigating the zoo of humanity, the two docs headed toward the table games. They did their best at avoiding the crowds teaming around the electronic gaming areas. Being mathematically inclined, and sporting the kind of memories that made them dangerous for a Casino's bottom line, they naturally gravitated to the Blackjack tables. Not that they intended to 'count cards' intentionally, per se, but they did have a God given natural talent at their disposal.

The boys chose a ten dollar table with a pretty dealer with long wavy brunette hair, with a nametag that said 'Jordan'. Seated at the table were two older men, both with healthy stacks of chips nestled in the carrier slots behind their cards. Ravi looked over in recognition at the gentleman seated to his right; it was the chubby, pleasant-faced Asian man who was their neighbor from across the hall. Seated next to him was a tall older man with a neatly combed white beard, a Trenton Thunder baseball cap, and a full length gray pony tail flowing down his back.

The two young men greeted their playing companions, tossing five Benjamins each on the table while 'Jordan' announced,

"$500 in chips each for the new players---Good luck gentlemen," Jordan smiled at Sam and slid his stack of chips to him. Sam noticed the small gold "chai" charm dangling from a fine chain around Jordan's neck.

Sam leaned into Ravi and said, "That's one safe to bring home to my Mom."

The older man with the cap said, "Don't you boys want to give her your 'Luxor Player Cards' so you can get credits?"

The pudgy Asian man added, "I used mine at the Pyramid Café Buffet, stuffed myself to the gills!"

"Thanks---we forgot about that," said Sam. Both young men tossed their cards to Jordan, so she could swipe them for credit.

The gray haired man leaned over and extended his hand to the two boys and introduced himself as Moshe, and his friend next to his left as S.G..

Sam said, "Pretty cool that we're on the same floor and across the hall and just happen to find ourselves at the same table. Maybe we'll all get lucky!" The men shook hands and settled into play.

Gracefully swiping her finger across the betting line, Jordan indicated that it was time to put their bets up. All complied, and after a second palm down sweep of the table, Jordan began to deal the cards. Jordan dealt a 10 and 2 to the older gentleman; a Jack and 10 to the neighbor from across the hall; a natural black jack to Ravi, and a King and 9 to Sam. Jordan rolled her buried card over to reveal the Ace of Hearts.

"Insurance?" Jordan asked.

Ravi slid half his bet in front of his hand as the other three shook their heads. The gray haired man indicated he would hold, and the neighbor from across the hall tapped the table indicating a hit. Jordan dealt the man a 9 and he smiled in satisfaction. Sam halted his hand over his cards and indicated he would hold with his King and 9.

All eyes were on Jordan as she rolled a King and cleaned away the others bets and paid Ravi for his smart move. It was one of the few hands Jordan would win for the Luxor with the table crew currently seated at her station.

Using their best mathematical and observation skills, Ravi and Sam cleaned house over a two-hour period while the two elderly gentlemen just barely held their own. With their chip carriers stuffed nice and full, the two elderly gentlemen stood to leave. The pony tailed gentleman looked over at Ravi and Sam and said,

"You know if you two are feeling up to it, my friend S G and I would like to invite you two to a small private poker game later this evening. It starts at 9 pm over in the high-stakes table area. I need to warn you that Luxor requires a $1,000 dollar minimum, not our rules, but the house's. There'll be two other gentlemen joining us if that's OK with you guys?"

Ravi looked at his watch, it was just before 6 pm, both boys shrugged and Sam said,

"Sure, sounds good we'll see you then."

They all rose up, each flipping a $100 dollar chip to Jordan, who beamed at her good luck and said,

"Wow thanks—guys!"

Sam said, "Hey Ravi, I'm going to go see if I can find that Alyssa girl from the front desk."

"Ok Romeo, I'm going to go sit in on a Texas Hold'em table and bone up to whip your butt tonight. Text me and let me know what's up."

The four waved good-bye and blended into the jumble of casino patrons as they headed their separate ways.

CHAPTER 32

Sam held the hotel business card with the pretty desk clerk's number on it in his left hand, while he deftly dialed his cell with the thumb of his right.

"Hello, who's this?" A sweet voice said.

"Hi, it's the better looking 'Kush' guy!" said Sam.

"Ya, right. I can't believe you called. I just got off work. Did you guys have any luck at the tables?"

"Yep, we did alright so far. This place is great. Hey, thanks for hooking us up with the room!"

"Oh, man, you guys lucked out. That's one of the best High Roller rooms in the building. You guys got the double master with twin steam saunas. So, what's up?"

"Well, Ravi and I met a couple of cool old guys that we played Blackjack with. They invited us to a high- stakes poker game at nine; so I have a few hours and wanted to see if you wanted to get together."

"Ya, that sounds good. I'm still in this dumb uniform, but if you give me a few minutes, I'll meet you out in the Pharaoh's Garden in the back, maybe 6:30. I can't stay though, I have to study tonight, its finals week at UNLV and I have a class tomorrow morning early."

"No problem, sounds like a plan. See you soon."

Sam went back out through the casino floor area to make his way to the rear of the Luxor. Looking around the table game area, he finally spotted Ravi. He stopped by the table where Ravi was playing at a 15/30 Texas Hold 'Em table. Ravi appeared to be up quite a bit and was wearing his goofy 'no-tell' sunglasses.

"Take the glasses off; I can't talk to you with those California-trooper-Ray Bans on your face. You look like a douche-bag."

Ravi turned toward him with a big grin and dropped the shades down the tip of his nose. Looking over the top he said,

"Alright, is this better? License, registration and insurance please."

"Shut up. How much you up?"

"About five-grand."

"Cool. Hey I'm gonna meet that Jersey Girl, and grab a bite to eat at that Pharaoh's Garden Café, I'll be back in time for the poker game, she has to study or something tonight."

"Go ahead, I'm good here. I guess you won't be scoring so big tonight Romeo, will you. 'Has to study', sounds like the only action you're going to get tonight is poker."

"Good women, like a fine wine, need to be courted and wooed. With my charm, I'll get lucky on the second or third date." Sam checked his watch, popped Ravi in the arm and headed out toward the Pharaoh Café.

Once outside, he looked around and saw Alyssa standing by the hostess station chatting with the two girls manning the gateway to the Pharaoh Café. Alyssa was holding up a big Louis Voutton bag and showing it to the girls laughing as she looked over and caught his eye. She waved over to him as the other two looked him over and sized him up; making sure he was appropriate material for their girlfriend. Sam made his way over to them and said "Hi" to the three. Alyssa introduced him to her friends and the taller of the two grabbed a couple of menus to get ready to seat them.

"It looks like everyone that works here knows each other. Do you girls always work the same shift?" He asked.

"No, we all go to UNLV, so we see each other a lot, here and on campus."

The girl walked them over to a quiet table that faced the fountain and said,

"Alyssa call me later, maybe we can go to the library and study for the Physics test together." She said, as she took one more critical look at Sam.

The girl left the menus on the table, lit the little candle centerpiece and headed back towards the hostess station to pick up the next group standing in line.

"Are you hungry? They make an awesome Ceaeser salad, and the nachos are really good," said Alyssa.

The server came over, and they ordered drinks and decided to share the salad and nachos. They chatted

168

for a few minutes about school and how Sam had been able to accelerate and graduate early. Alyssa listened in envy thinking that she would not be graduating from the Computer Science Masters Program until May of the following year.

Sam told her all about the Kush program, and she rolled with laughter when he told her how he and Ravi came up with their thesis. Alyssa had followed the Master Kush to Genesis/Kush event, watching and reading everything she could on it. The popularity of Ravi and Sam among the students of universities and youth the world over was high; as if to say, 'see, one of us can do it!' She jabbed him about the South Park and Saturday Night Live appearances. She was so easy to talk to that Sam was able to share his concerns about the fast fame and money that had come their way and how overwhelming it was at times. The food came, and they dug in with gusto.

"So, our buddy at the Goddard Space Flight Center is working with this guy from Kepler, and we should have all the data by the end of next week about the habitability of Kush. If someone could figure out a way to get there, it would be the Shit. I met Elon Musk, you know the guy from Tesla and SpaceX, and he's working like mad on trying to develop a space Mag-Lev drive. He seems to think he's making significant headway. If someone can do it, he could be the one. I just hope it happens in our lifetime. So tell me about what you are doing."

"My girlfriend and I've been working on this cool new App in the computer lab. We're trying to make a Kush-Genesis game. Kind of like an Angry Birds in space App. You know, space ships flying between Earth and Kush, avoiding obstacles and blowing stuff up along the way. We think we can use the touch-screen sensor to read the users body temp and reflex response to personalize the game as they go."

"My girlfriend, Sharon is a psych major, and I'm working on the Java and objective-C game language for Droid and iP products. Sharon is working on a way to tie the camera in so that you play it in real time with up to six people at a time. With the added ability to read eye movement and pupil response, she thinks we can get a fully interactive Virtual Reality portable game that will give us enough human response data to mold play action. What do you think? Does it sound crazy?"

"Wow, it sounds like it could fly! Don't leave Wii, X-box and Playstation platforms out though. There's still a huge market out there for that. You know if you 'mine' the data and analyze it, you could keep the game going in a continual series of updates and make a bundle," said Sam.

The two had been going on so long that neither was watching the time. Their plates had been bussed away long before, when Sam looked down at his watch and said,

"Oh, Shit, look at the time. It's a quarter to nine. I'm supposed to meet Ravi for the poker game! Look, I had an awesome time. I really want to see you again. Give me your email address and let's see if we can get together before we split on Sunday."

"I'd love that!" She put her hand on Sam's knee and looked him in the eye.

Sam felt a bolt of electricity vibrate up his leg and traverse his whole body from her touch. Sam reached for the check, and Alyssa put her hand on top of his.

"Oh, no need. One of the perks to the job and knowing the hostess is no-pay to play!"

They traded emails, and Alyssa got up and gave him a peck on the cheek as she gently held his hand. Sam's pheromone alert went in to high gear, her scent wafted to his nose, hormones started vibrating, in two seconds he was a helpless mess. As she walked towards the door leaving behind a very flustered Sam touched the location of the kiss on his cheek. Sam looked around the room and tried to decide when it would be safe for him to try and stand up without embarrassing himself.

CHAPTER 33

The High Stakes table area of the Luxor had a series of private raised areas devoted to Poker, Baccarat, Blackjack and Pai Gow. Table minimums were set at $1000 dollars, but the players could set their stakes and deal their own cards if four or more were in agreement. The house cut could be managed with a pit boss assigned to each area that tallied chips going in, and chips going out at the end of the game. As far as poker went, the Casino encouraged the flexibility since they got a healthy percentage on each hand with almost no-risk to the house. The poker players at the high stakes tables played against each other and not against the Casino.

Ravi and Sam walked into the restricted area and handed their Luxor Gold Access Cards to two Egyptian Palace Guards, both easily over six foot five in height. The two Man-Towers were dressed in the traditional robes and headgear reserved for Harem Eunuchs, and both had metallic gold body spray applied to their frames for extra effect. Ravi figured they must have been on the UNLV football team since so many of the staff seemed to come from there. He also figured that you couldn't pay him enough to do this job, even if he had been six-five.

Getting their cards scanned and returned by the two gilded and gelded mammoths, Sam nudged Ravi and nodded toward a private poker area where they saw their two new friends. Ravi raised his hand, and S.G. smiled and waived them over.

Sitting with S. G. and Moshe were two younger men of obvious Middle Eastern descent that looked to be in their 40's or 50's. In fact, except for the cut of their beards and a slight auburn tint to the hair on the younger of the men, the boys would have taken them for brothers. They were family for sure, at the minimum.

S.G. said, "Moh and Yeshuah, These are the two new friends that Moshe and I were telling you about. Not only are they our across the hall neighbors, but they seem to play a mean hand of cards! Ravi and Sam, meet Yeshua and Moh."

The four shook hands and invited Ravi and Sam to take a seat at the table. The men chatted and shared some recounting of their session together at the Blackjack table from earlier that evening. The four older men told them that they had recognized them as, 'those Kush guys', which was unavoidable due to the media exposure the two had received. When Ravi and Sam asked their new friends what they did for a living, they stated evasively with a common answer. Yeshua elaborated with;

"Oh a little bit of this and that, but for the most part, we're retired and very active in charitable giving and supporting various causes to better the World. We still do a lot of long distance travel away from home and try to get together as often as possible. I'm the only one still working. I still play around in my cabinet shop at home, sell a piece or two from time to time, just to keep my hand in it, so to speak."

Moh spoke up, "We all worked for the same guy, and we still keep in close touch with him. He's great for support and advice, and we all use it on a regular basis."

"That's Cool. So what's the game?" Said the boys.

"Texas Hold 'Em! Five hundred small blind, one thousand big blind, five hundred minimum -----and no maximum on All-in." said the older players in choreographed rotation as they ticked off the rules.

"We're in!" Said both Ravi and Sam, as they looked at each other feeling like wet fish. Ravi reached in to his top pocket and whipped out the police shades. Sam rolled his eyes as Ravi clipped the aviators to his ears and adjusted them to the ridge of his nose.

Ante and Blinds were placed around the table and S. G. dealt the cards. The men slid the two buried cards close to their bellies, just barely curling the corners up to see their hands. The table was opened for bets.

Tossing a thousand-dollar chip on the table, Moh said,

"I'll open with a grand to get it going."

"A grand it is," said Yeshuah as he tossed a gold chip on the table.

"See your grand and raise you five hundred," said Moshe.

"Fold," said Sam as he looked at the Deuce-Seven in his hand.

"Fifteen- hundred to me," Ravi took a pregnant pause and another look at his cards. "I'll call." He kept his face as expressionless as possible hoping that his police-special RayBans would ensure that nothing 'told' on his Ace-King—both spades, that were resting flat in front of him.

"Dealer Calls," said S G as he tossed fifteen-hundred in chips into the growing pot.

"Pots Right," S G buried a card and then dealt three community cards for the 'flop'.

Ravi tried not to react to the Queen-Ten-Jack of spades lying in the middle of the table. The call to bet was made and each man said in turn.

"Check"

Ravi sighed to himself in relief as no one pushed the hand. Hoping that they all bought in to nothing buried in his hand. S. G. dealt the fourth card, a Queen of Diamonds and the betting heated up.

Tossing five one thousand dollar chip on the table, Moh said,

"Just to keep it interesting."

"If you insist," said Yeshuah as he tossed matching chips on the table.

Sitting in deep contemplation, Moshe said, "see your five thousand and raise you five thousand."

"Ten grand to me," said Ravi, with the straightest of faces. He hesitated for just a beat more.

"I'm all in" he said as he pushed his remaining Ninety thousand dollars in chips to the center. He looked at each man in turn as Sam whispered,

"I sure hope you know what you're doing" Sam looked at his still safe and unused pile of chips with relief.

S. G. looked at the pile and said.

"Fold, I'm out"

Moh slid his hand over and peeked at his cards, gently sliding one past the other two or three times. Having bluffed himself into a corner, he wasn't risking a pair of Queens against a possible flush. He took one more look at the flop and said,

"I'm out."

Yeshua said,

"Too rich for me, I'm out."

"All in," said Moshe with no expression at all as he slid his pile into the middle.

Little beads of sweat were forming on Ravi's forehead as he tried to appear un- concerned and nonchalant about the fact that he had just bet more money than his Dad typically made in a year on a hand of cards.

All eyes shifted on S. G. as he dealt the 'River' card, the Ace of Hearts.

Ravi jumped up and whooped as he rolled over his Ace and King of spades to complete his Royal Flush. Sam slapped him on the back and walked over to the snack table to grab a coke.

Moshe gently rolled over his hand to reveal the Ace of Clubs and Ace of Diamonds in his hand, but sat expressionless, letting Ravi settle back to his seat.

Moshe, said. "So sorry, better luck on the next one," pointing to his trip-Aces.

Ravi looked at him curiously as he looked down at his Ace of Spades and a King that was now displaying --------the black clover of CLUBS! He sputtered,

"BUT----BUT----BUT!" as he looked at the four men accusingly.

"Things are not always as they appear---my young friends, and things are not always as we believe. It's poker—it's just a game."

"This is messed up! Sam did you see that?"

"Uh-Uh, I don't know what the hell I saw; it sure looked like you rolled over the Ace and King of Spades. My eyes were on the pot and the 'River' though."

Ravi said, "This is bullshit, let's get out of here. We came here for an honest game of cards not a magic show. How did you do that anyway?"

S. G. said, "Please, please sit back down. No one is touching the pot. We needed your undivided attention. We'll explain if you give us a moment more."

Way pissed and just as perplexed, Sam and Ravi sat back down at the table. They glared at the four men—whatever these guys had to say—it better be good.

CHAPTER 34

Tension hung in the air around the poker table as the six men faced off. Ravi and Sam with arms crossed across their chests, and the four senior members relaxed and determined. Yeshuah, S.G and Moh looked towards Moshe to indicate he was to take the lead.

"Yes, we did bring you here under false pretenses. For that we humbly ask your forgiveness and patience as we explain ourselves. What you must know is that there are no coincidences here, or rarely anywhere, for that matter.

"We're not here to play cards; we came specifically to meet you two. We came to help you, and, to seek your help as well. We, and you, are desperately short on time, and we hope we can make this clear."

" As much as you two have tried to find meaning and understanding regarding your discovery of Genesis and Kush, that meaning will remain elusive without our help; and, crystal clear if you can open your minds and hearts for a moment. You see we know more about Genesis and Kush than you ever could possibly know without taking this opportunity to talk with us."

"Do, you guys wish to proceed? You are free to pick up the pile of chips and walk out that door, or stay and hear us out. Maybe then you'll truly understand the purpose and meaning of your discovery." Moshe said.

The two scientists looked at each other, not buying it at all and shrugged indifferently. They were curious though and had every intention to snag their chips as soon as they figured out the direction of the discussion.

"Who the heck are you guys, and how could you know more than us about Genesis and Kush?" Are you government agents? Homeland Security? NSA?"

Moshe chuckled, "Agents of a sort, but not for any of the agencies mentioned."

"I asked you to open up your minds and hearts. What we're about to tell you may be difficult to accept. But, what we're about to reveal to you should be no more difficult than accepting that after you two bounced around the festival circuit, having fun and killing brain cells; that in spite of better qualified competition, you were awarded the $250,000 dollar grant and the Hubble time. That consequently, you picked the exact location in all of the heavens containing a new Sun and planet miraculously appearing out of nowhere."

"It shouldn't be more difficult to conceive, it may be something other than coincidence, that the new sun and planet mimic the orbits of the Sun, and the Earth to a tee. Nor, be so difficult to conceive as something other than coincidence, that the new Sun and Planet are stabilized and evolved to the point that they would comfortably support human beings."

"It is all no harder to accept and believe that a Royal Flush becomes a Straight before your eyes. Alternatively, is it that hard to accept that God made Genesis and Kush in six days out of the cosmic plasma of the Crab Nebula? Some things are not explainable by pure science; some things are only explainable if you are given the explanation directly."

They still weren't buying it, only the beginning of attentiveness from Ravi and Sam. Yeshuah reached toward the center of the table and passed his hand over the top of the chips as Moshe talked.

Moh looked over and rolled his eyes.

"Show off." He said.

Hovering over the place where the chips had been, appeared Genesis and Kush in miniature form, and moving in real time. The money was gone. In its place, lighting the green poker table, were perfect, three dimensional, functional images that defied explanation and defied technology. Both boys, now riveted, opened their eyes wide to the limit of the whites, blinked a couple of times and leaned out of their chairs to get closer to the floating orbs---Who are these guys?

"Whoah---are you guys aliens?" Said Ravi.

"Nope, we're Prophets," said Moshe.

"Prophets, like in bible Prophets; like Prophets of God---prophets?" said Sam.

"Yep" they all harmonized.

"Shit! Aliens would have been easier to accept" Said Ravi.

Sam started to lose it right about then---he started sputtering waving his hands around, and, turned a little red, then with veins pumping in his neck—beet red.

"I told you Ravi. I told you in ---Taco—Freakin'---Bell ---that there was more to this! Oh, no Sam; it's like a lottery Sam; it's just luck Sam; stop reading more into it than there is Sam!!!! What say you now, EINSTEIN!!!?"

Ravi started to respond and S.G. put his hand on his shoulder.

"Take deep breaths. That's it, focus and center. I know this is more than a lot to swallow for you guys. Why don't we head up to the Temple Suite and continue this in a more private setting?"

Both Ravi and Sam started to settle as S. G. talked them down. Finally, bewildered but calmer, they agreed to move to the penthouse rooms. As they got up Ravi looked longingly at the rotating pulsating display of Genesis and Kush floating over the card table and offering a clearer than Hubble, three-dimensional view.

"Can we take it with us?" he pleaded.

"Nope, Can't do that; it draws too much attention. Leave it here; I'll do it again for you upstairs." Said, Yeshua.

"What about the chips?"

"If you must," said Yeshua.

The Prophets, flanked by the bewildered Sam and Ravi, walked out of the high-roller area, tipping the two monstrous Eunuchs at the entrance on their way out. Moh hung a little behind to settle up with the

Luxor pit boss, thanking him for the use of the room and providing generous tips to all the staff. Moh picked up his pace to catch up to the five others.

They said very little as they entered the penthouse elevator, leaving the two young men to their thoughts in the hope that it would all soak in and render them open and willing to accept what they all knew, was more than most mortal minds could comprehend. Moshe swiped his gold Luxor Card and activated access to the Penthouse floors. They exited into the opulent hallway and Moshe signaled that Ravi and Sam should join them in the Prophet's suite.

Inside the Temple Suite, sat a large formal dining table that could accommodate them all comfortably. Moh offered to get beverages and went into the kitchenette to get, ice, glasses, sodas and water.

The boys started peppering the Prophets with questions. The two inquisitive scientists tried to pick apart ancient history and gain answers from the four that had eluded factual dissection and irrefutable proof in the past. At every turn, they were shut down with Prophetic evasive tools. The Prophet's answers were as frustrating as listening to a witness defendant pleading the fifth in a US court.

"Did the Red Sea really part." Ravi asked.

"Do you believe it parted? Do you believe that it matters that it parted?" "How might the factual, versus metaphorical parting of the Red Sea, detract or enhance the message of the Exodus event? Please tell me your thoughts," said Moshe, frustrating the boys to the limit.

"Did you really change the water to wine? How about the fish?" asked Ravi.

Yeshua said, "Oh my goodness does it never change! What does it matter? The message wasn't walking on water it was being made lighter than water, free of all weight and restrictions of the flesh through devotion to God." Love your neighbor. Turn the other cheek. Those are the important messages!"

"What is it with you people?" "Why do you get all hung up on whether we can perform like David Copperfield or Chris Angel to make the Word have weight and value?"

"Which religion is right?" queried Sam.

S.G. said, "All of them, and none of them. Religions are just opinions based on limited facts. Spirituality and Faith unfettered is a better path."

"Is there a God?"

"Yes" all said at once.

"Oh, great!" "That's the first definitive answer from the brain trust. Now we're getting there." Said Sam

"Ok. If there's a God, does he hear our prayers? Oh, and is there life on other planets?"

Moshe fielded the question with—

"I don't have to educate you two learned men on the magnitude of the Universe, the number of galaxies, stars and solar systems. So you can do the math. To answer both of your questions, you have to blind yourself to the unique frailties the human body requires to support its physical plant. You must expand your interpretation of 'Life', to be free of human ego and comparison.

"So yes, there are an infinite number of life forms out there, and they do pray. Once you open your mind and free yourself of the confines of comparing all universal life forms in some way to your human condition; you might be able to touch on how many creatures, and voices are out there in the Universe. There are too many beseeching God for individual participation in their affairs. Too many to hear, too many to address."

"As for asking for direct intervention; it makes no more sense than a single member of a colony of Plankton asking that it not be drawn through the baleen of a whale and consumed. Saving that single Plankton, modifying its condition, separating its needs as distinct, important and deserving of God's individual time is nonsensical, is it not? That Plankton best serves God's will by being a good member of its Plankton colony. If its fate is to become a morsel of sustenance for the whale, then so be it. God's will be done. No greater good is served by answering the self-serving needs and desires of a single Plankton. The same holds true for Man. If you pray to God---Pray to know his will and how you can be of service to your fellow Man, a better member of your colony. Anything else is wasted as it has no benefit to the greater good of the Universe."

"It is the Earthlings ego and free will that have gotten him into the trouble that faces him now. Man's ego, his sense that he's unique and special in the world and the Universe, somehow above and better than the lesser creatures of the world is his downfall. Man has never been able to humble himself enough and get right sized against the greatness of the Universe. Man has been narrow and small minded, intolerant and blind to God's plan."

"The evidence of this is defined by how Man mistreats his fellow man. Man's ego allows for prejudice, hate and violence over a one-degree separation in belief structure, one-degree shift in skin pigment or which side of an imaginary line through the real estate of the Earth one calls one's home."

"Hear your prayers. Sure, God hears your prayers. But he can't hear yours over the noise of the prayers praising his Glory as the bomb vest is detonated; the prayers for the guidance mechanism on their warhead to find its mark; prayer taught to slaves to thank God for their masters; prayer taught to children to thank God for making their skin one color, in contrast to the other. God wants you to pray. Not so he can hear you. But in the hopes that you might hear yourself, for once, and actually use free will for the next right thing. Man, hijacked prayer with self-will long ago."

"God has a long-standing policy of not meddling in man's free will. From time to time in his busy schedule he swings his focus back this way to see how you're making out. He makes a tweak here and there; shifts things around; shuffles his feet through the puddles, and then he's off to tend to more fertile ground. God's been waiting on you, and you guys have let him down. As far as sentient beings go in the Universe, God sees Earthlings as an error in the source code."

S.G. said, "Please, please let us get back to Genesis and Kush and the events that have brought us together. There's so much we have to tell you."

Ravi and Sam, said, "Alright but this is way big; we have so much to ask and learn."

"Hey, can you do that thing with the mini-Genesis and Kush"

"If I must," a bored Yeshua said. With a casual pass of his hand over the table top the floating orbs returned.

"Oh, yeah that's awesome," said Sam. The two scientists walked around the floating display in hypnotic focus.

Moh, said. "Can we please get down to business now?"

Moshe said: "Let me start with this. I don't mean to overwhelm you two, but I need to be blunt and cut to the chase here. The world is going to end on December 21, 2012. God plans to destroy mankind, and all that man has created."

"Kush is fully habitable for humans. More habitable, mind you, than the Earth is today, especially so after the damage that mankind has done to this place. God had originally intended to start over from scratch on Kush and shit can Earth as a habitat for humans. Frankly, he thinks the water is tainted here, and that's why Earthlings are such knuckleheads."

"After much begging and pleading by the four of us; God has agreed to two concessions. God has agreed to spare a small percentage of the world's population in two colonies, subject to very specific conditions. One colony can remain here in Tibet to serve as a beachhead for future re-population of the Earth; that is, if the water issue can be resolved to his satisfaction. The second is a colony to be formed on Kush, which is to be populated from those that make the cut and make it to the Tibet colony before December 21, 2012."

"Where you two come in is that we need a boatload of help satisfying God's selection criteria and getting the message out to the world. The right message, that is. We've been given very limiting criteria, little time to get it done and limited disclosure parameters as to what we can say and do. God does not make it an easy undertaking to accomplish."

"So you can see its February, that gives us barely eight months to get the selection process done, the colonies set up and the worst part of all; transportation to Kush resolved. God insists that the knowledge and technology to make the move from Earth to Kush must come from humans. Yeshua thinks he found a loophole to explore in the transportation rule we can take advantage of."

"So to re-cap and simplify the action items:

-Define Prescriptive Criteria for Salvation.

-Produce Salvation Test.

-Apply the test to the broadest number of Earthlings.

-Solve the Transportation Problems.

-Transportation to, and Colonization of, the Tibetan Colony.

-Transportation of Colonials to Kush-Set up Colony.

-God Destroys mankind on Earth.

"We have a tall order and limited time to get it done."

CHAPTER 35

Sam and Ravi sat in dumbfounded silence. The scene in front of them and the information delivered was burning their brains from frontal lobe to the cerebral cortex. They chewed on the words until they could swallow them in little bites. They couldn't quite get past the fact that they actually believed what they were hearing! It was like they had stepped into a script for a science fiction novel.

Their scientific training was less of a barrier than a benefit. Both had little trouble with the concept of God or a power greater than themselves. As scientists they sought to find answers to all they could, but were equally ok with the fact that some things may never be known. As young boys they had stared at the heavens in wonder and embraced the unknown. They got their first telescopes in grade school, ripping off the wrapping paper, opening boxes and counting the minutes until the sun dropped far enough below the horizon to give them that first glimpse of the heavens. They were off to the races without a glance to the rear.

They followed their parent's guidance and had dutifully participated in all the expected traditions and rituals of their respective formal religious education.

As ideological head strong adolescents; they had questioned and rebelled as they sought to secure an identity, an ownership and reconciliation of all that their parents and clergy had given them to ponder. As maturing young men being taught the collective limited knowledge of what man had figured out so far; it wasn't hard to apply science, where facts were available, and spiritual faith to all that had defied explanation. The exquisite order of the cosmos, and whatever forces kept it in motion, were worthy of respect and devotion. With the collective knowledge of what man truly knew and understood about the workings of the Universe, fitting on the head of a pin; it was easy to be humbled and accept that there was a power greater than man.

Sam looked at the group around the table and said,

"This is way scary. I can't believe I'm saying this, but I want to help."

"Scary---- this is heads under the covers, Halloween III, Night of the Living Dead horrifying!," said Ravi.

"Good," said Moh. "Fear is a pretty good motivator for man. If we can just harness it with some faith maybe we can get this job done. Let's go over the action steps and get started."

"Moshe and the Dalai Lama, who is one of us, by the way, have been working on the conditions for testing free will and ego to determine compatibility for Colonial candidates. As a benchmark we've been analyzing the population of the planets that Yeshuah, Moshe and I manage; the followers of the Dalai Lama; and, these Bill Wilson people that God suggested we check in to. We have a good start on qualifying and quantifying the traits required to meet God's criteria as to who may get to go and who may not. The problem is logistics. We can't test enough of them quickly and efficiently in the time we have, using the methods we have. We need you guys to work with us on the criteria and the method to gain the greatest access to the population of the world."

Yeshua said, "Transportation is a big issue, first we have a short time to find candidates for salvation, and then get them to Lhasa, then from Lhasa to Kush. We have no available technology, and we're Prophets not scientists. In fact, we're downright technologically challenged. God tells us where to go and he just makes it happen. We tell God we need to be somewhere, and it happens. We haven't a clue to the process. We asked him once how it works, and I started to fall asleep somewhere after he was talking about "reference points," refraction points, bending time and dimension, folding of space. It's well above my pay grade."

"In this case he won't even help with transportation because he has such a bad attitude about Earth. But, I do have a guy on my planet that I think we can use. I won't be violating God's law---just bending the rules a little if we use his help."

S. G, who had been pretty quiet up until now, said.

"Can I make a suggestion? In the interest of time wouldn't it be best to split up and try to work on the problems concurrently? If one team can work on the testing logistics issue and one team on transportation, then we may get a leg up."

Moshe nodded in agreement.

"Ravi and Sam, taking into account the challenges we laid out, if you two had to tackle the problem who would be the lead on each issue?"

Sam said—well—we're a team and work together on just about every problem. When it comes to straight technology and hardware problems—Ravi is the lead, and when it comes to concept and testing—I typically take the lead. We depend pretty heavily on each other's input though on execution of any plan that comes out of individual efforts."

Moshe said, "Well, I'd like to take you to Tibet with me to meet with the Dalai Lama and get debriefed on what we have accomplished so far. We need your thoughts and efforts on how we can improve on it. What do you think?

"What's not to like? I get to go to a place that I've only dreamed about traveling to, meet one of the greatest minds the world has ever known, and work with him on a project and maybe save humanity. I'm all over this one! Thanks!"

Moshe continued, "Yeshua, this young Gradisian that knows about transportation technology, would he be willing to share it with Ravi? If he will, then I will petition God for special dispensation to get Ravi to Gradis-2 to work with him to overcome the transportation issues."

"Not a problem at all. I think he would be very happy to help. Gradisians get a ten-year market exclusive on new technology and then it all becomes open to the public. I really don't like monopolies."

Ravi said "Gradisians", I don't get it. Where the heck is Gradisia?"

Yeshua and Moshe chuckled as Moshe said,

"Not Gradisia, Gradis-2 is Yeshuah's home planet. It's near the star you call PG-51, in the Constellation

Pegasus. It's about 51 light-years away from Earth. Yeshuah is Planet Manager there."

"No way, I'm going to another world!"

"Space travel! Another planet!" Sam was going through ten stages of envy.

S. G. took one look at Sam and said.

"Don't go there, Sam, envy is a waste. It does nothing for the greater good and will get in the way of your objectivity and inner peace. I will work with you on a great meditation for eliminating it. You will get your chance in time."

Moh said, "Its 3 am. I think that's enough for now. Let's get some rest and make travel plans tomorrow. Moshe you check in with the Big Guy and see if you can get Ravi approved for transport. I have to check on my horse and see about getting back to Jann-1 to pick up the test data that Tenzin had me compile on Jannian ego and free will. So I'm out of here tomorrow."

S. G. Said, "I'll work as 'floater' between the two project teams of Moshe and Sam in Tibet, and Ravi and Yeshua on Gradis-2."

"Sam and Ravi why don't you two go get some shuteye, and we'll hit it early tomorrow."

Sam and Ravi took a long tired look at the floating orbs of Genesis and Kush rotating and lighting the table top.

"Hey, can we take that with us?"

"Not a chance," said Yeshua. "Get some sleep, will you?"

Moshe said, "I'll walk them over to their room."

The two dog-tired docs followed behind Moshe across the hall to their room. Neither had any intention of sleeping as keyed up as they were. They passed their key card over the e-lock and entered, heading over to flop on the two living room couches. They kicked up their feet with hands cradling their heads from behind and started yapping away.

Moshe, walked over to them waved his hand over their heads and said,

"Get some rest; you're going to need it."

Their eyes shut immediately without a word as they went completely out. Moshe smiled at his work and left the room and opened the door to his.

"Are they going to sleep?" said S.G.

"Yah, I cheated a little." said Moshe."

"Look in my eyes----What do you see?----The cult of personality"

—*Living Colour*

CHAPTER 36

Moving quickly through the streets of Washington D.C., two groups of four black Suburbans came from different directions and turned on to Pennsylvania Avenue. The signature black Suburban with tinted windows had become the VIP bus of choice. The mammoth black seven seaters, had become so common and popular in the DC metro area that if it weren't for government and diplomatic license plates, it would be hard to tell the soccer moms from the foreign dignitary, the gang banger from the CEO. In Washington, everyone wanted in the "Game." If you couldn't get in the 'game' they at least wanted to look the part. Power was status in DC.

This convoy, though, was legit. The armored gas guzzlers swung into the auto stacking area at the entrance of 1600 Pennsylvania Avenue and massed single file at the security gate barring entrance to the lower parking garage. Two White House security staffers tapped the driver and passenger-side glass and checked credentials against the information on their clip boards. Three members of the detail, two with bomb sniffing K-9's, one with a mirror on a retractable pole and a rolling creeper, checked each vehicle from stem to stern. Before they were waved forward, one last pass was made over the vehicles by an officer carrying a backpack connected to a long wand; a wand terminated with a butterfly array of wires that scanned for God only knows what. These guys did not play around.

Inside the vehicles were the Prime Minister of England; Chancellor of Germany and Prime Minister of Israel. The vehicles were whisked along and down into the subterranean depths of the protected lower parking garage under the West Wing of the White House. Exiting the vehicles, the visiting heads of state were swept quickly into the hallway that led directly to the 5000 square foot conference room better known as, the Situation Room.

The Situation Room was originally put into service by President John F. Kennedy as a reaction to the communication and information errors that had surrounded the failure of the Bay of Pigs invasion in 1961. Managed by the National Security Council, the Situation Room is chock full of the highest level of intelligence and communication equipment available (to only a limited few) in the world. National and international events are monitored continually from large, wall-mounted monitors, displaying news broadcasts, as well as by, targeted satellite generated views of events on the ground. The satellite imagery is transmitted to the Situation Room at resolutions and magnification levels that would shock the public if they were ever allowed to observe them. Big Brother is definitely watching.

After the events of September 11, 2001, the Situation Room was slated for renovation. As was the case in 1961, communication problems were an issue again in 2001. Complaints about the lack of interagency communication and intelligence sharing abounded. So the Situation Room was put on the 'Fast Tract' for renovations in that way that only Washington can do. 'Fast Tract' Washington style--- the renovations didn't even start until 2006. Three years after the start of the Iraq war and just a couple of months after the Final CIA report that had determined that there were no Weapons of Mass Destruction in Iraq—yet another interagency communication and intelligence sharing problem. Now they got serious about the need to 'Fast Tract'.

The new and improved Situation Room, previously managed only by the NSC, would in addition now house an office for Homeland Security, the White House Chief of Staff, and the Offices of the National Security Advisor to the President. Maybe this would fix the problem. Or not.

The entourage of dignitaries were delivered by the NSC staff to the large conference area and seated at the massive table. A White House food services manager took their orders for beverages and hors d'ourves. The Directors of Homeland Security and NSC along with the White House Chief of Staff made their rounds about the room, making greetings to old colleagues and introductions to new ones. A loud voice came from the hallway as the Vice President and his aid came into the room. Following close behind, came a much harried President of the United States of America.

"Gentlemen and Lady Chancellor, please sit down." The President took a seat at the center of the group.

"Thank you so much for coming and more so, for you and your staff's discretion about this meeting. We're faced with a dilemma far more vexing than the challenges that this world typically throws in our laps.

For all the advance knowledge of domestic and international events that we try to anticipate and adjust for, we find ourselves faced with an event so far from our zone of intelligence capabilities that we're at this moment flying blind."

"The Genesis-Kush presence in the heavens, even if benign in its purpose, has set in motion events and potential threats to governance that we're only just now coming to understand or appreciate. An event that has no explanation attached to it, no threat assigned to it, is serving to tear apart all of our countries represented here today; and, those of our allies and enemies alike. Just for the sake of the unknown, the world responds with fear and violence."

"The worldwide Islamic unrest is just a symptom that makes itself a vocal and easy 'in your face' target. It is not the source, however. We barely keep in check the fringe fanatics who exist in each of our countries; we allow, as any free society should, airtime and freedom to the organized fundamentalists of all beliefs; even those that few of us share in common as to their extremes. We encourage participation in the more conventional practices of worship of your choice. However, at this point even the major religions, the so-called conventional ones, are producing an uncontrollable groundswell of potential unrest."

"Genesis-Kush, and the fear of the unknown that surrounds it, have upset an applecart that was only stable to begin with, to the extent of our own delusions of stability. Folks we have a problem, and very few answers."

"Mr. President, if I may," Said the Lady Chancellor of Germany. "Domestically, we've all been dealing with religious and ethnic blow back events for years. My counterparts in Britain, France, Spain, Denmark as well as Russia; all of us across the face of the globe have had to accept this as a major disruptive force affecting our safety, our financial health and our basic ability to govern our countries. Much of this strife centers around differences in basic religious beliefs. We have to find a way to attack this at its source."

The Israeli Prime Minister said, "The Chancellor has hit the nail on the head. This is the point that we've lived with since long before Israel became a modern nation. This is the point that we've been trying to impress on the global community. This is not a problem of regional conflict where a finger can be pointed at an area on the globe and assign blame. This is not a problem of geography. This is a problem in the underlying fabric of every nation on the planet where man rests his head."

"While things are in control within your borders, it becomes easier to point the finger across the globe at the easy and obvious targets. However, as we see right now, the problem is just below the surface everywhere and requires only a breath of a shift in mans reality, a scratch at the scab that covers his fears, and you are left with a full bleed out with little tools at your disposal to stem the flow."

The British Prime Minister was listening attentively and looked at each of the members sitting at the table. "We built an empire around the globe by colonizing countries and managing cultures that were totally dissimilar to our own. We used a combination of force, treasure and subterfuge to win over and control the minds and hearts of the people. We were not always successful, and in the end we failed and had to make a steady march back to within our own small borders. That being said, we managed long sustained periods of control. I think we need to review those methods and apply them here. Sure, they won't be politically or morally correct as tested against current sentiments---but make no mistake, if we're not at war against these issues now, war stands right around the corner."

"Mr. President may I suggest that we hear from our staff members present as the eyes and ears on the ground, and see if we can try tocome to some plan of action. It is apparent that before we can make any long term conclusions we need to deal with the current events before we can address any long-term solutions," said, the Vice-President.

The Director of Homeland Security drew a breath and started.

"Madame Chancellor and Gentlemen, I am in constant contact with my counterparts in each of your respective nations. The level of cooperation and sharing of information is appreciated. Much of what I am now going to recount is typical to what we're seeing in our respective countries." He continued,

"Fringe fanatic movements of both political and religious ideology are ramping up activities throughout our country and yours. We've seen the incident rate of multi anti-denominational, as well as the typical anti-Semitic/anti-Islamic aggression, triple in the last ninety days. We've seen general anarchist and political agenda groups that typically have been satisfied with internet forums, moving to physical rallies and public displays of their views. These events have usually resulted in some amount of violence."

"We've moved from talking heads on the television and computer screen that we could monitor from a chair, to having to put people on the ground with equipment and arms to control the crowds. My budget cannot support this change in level of threat response! I believe without additional, and substantial, increase in funds that we will be unable to meet this threat."

The Vice President said, "We understand your concerns over the budget issues but let's leave that for internal review and stick to the unrest issues if you please."

"Sorry, I will continue." "On the ground, we're dealing with some amount of violence or destructive vandalism in every major city. The situation is spilling over into the more suburban areas; less so in the rural regions. Where we don't have violence, we have mass demonstrations that try to remain peaceful, but immediately draw out the radical elements with contrarian views that are harder to control. The messages being sent from the pulpits of typically moderate places of worship are becoming reactionary. The shift in the dynamic seems to be in response to individual opinions being formed, and a feeling that their belief structures are being threatened. All of this fueled as conjecture and opinion about the purpose and meaning of Genesis and Kush evolves. Unfortunately, it is evolving into lines being drawn in the sand."

"Monitoring of Internet activity shows a pervasive mention of the Genesis-Kush presence as signifying proof of an 'End of the World' event and a call to the 'faithful', that is, as narrowly defined by each individual group, to rise up as the end is near. I will leave the analysis of specifics on electronic surveillance information gathering to the Director of NSC. That's all I have at this time, thank you."

The Director of the NSC was next to report and shuffled the papers on his desk.

"Please focus your attention to the display monitors, and I will try to walk you through where we are as of today."

Mutiple screens about the room lit up, and the movie and slide show began. Starting with a view of the streets of Detroit, Michigan and a shot of a large gathering of the 99%- Occupy Wall Street movement, the camera panned to the left. He continued,

"This event started as an otherwise peaceful demonstration, pretty typical of one of the Occupy events. I am using this example to show that Genesis and Kush are affecting our stability in the most unlikely forums and where we'd least expect it. As you can see the speaker on the podium is finishing up, and we have the next speaker walking up on the stage. Watch what happens next."

As promised the new speaker approached the mike and said;

"Many of you out there have been following our struggle for social and financial equality. Many of you have seen your opportunities dwindle in your communities and schools as jobs have dried up, student loans become un-available, your dreams, hopes and prospects for your futures dashed. Dashed and thrown at your feet by the 1% 'ers. The imbalance between the 'haves' and 'have- nots', has upset the balance of our nation! " The crowd screamed its ascent.

"Your government says it cares, yet does nothing to right the balance. Your politicians say they care as they stuff their pockets and re-election campaign coffers with the money from the 1%. Meanwhile, day in and day out, conditions are getting worse. In an insult to our democratic right to assembly; our right to free speech, the government has dropped a hammer on our peaceful movement. A modern police state is forming around us in response to our plea. This police state is monitoring our mail, monitoring our internet use, monitoring our cell phone use and keeping tabs on us from above and below! As if that's not enough they are seeking to control what we may know.

Many, if not all of you, are aware of the exciting discovery of Genesis and Kush. In a world with so little hope, I know if you are like me, you embraced the concept of a new world, someplace better than this one; a potential chance for a new start. Yes, it is unlikely and a stretch, but is it too much to ask of this government to even let us have our dreams! Even the hope of a better world was stolen away by the government. They say we can't handle it. I say we take it back! Free Kush! Free Kush! The crowd followed suit and erupted in response with a chant of 'Free Kush" that rocked the City of Detroit. The crowd looked angry.

The Director of the NSC said. "What you just saw is about as gentle an example as I have to show you today. Please sit back as we review the next thirty minutes of data."

The monitors shifted from one scene to the next, each worse than the one before. From Cairo to Cape Town; Kamchatka to Stockholm; Hong Kong to Afghanistan; Tierra del Fuego to Mexico it was frightening to witness. The group listened to sermons from fringe congregations, conspiracy theorists, terrorists, and radical heads of state. All were tying in Genesis and Kush in ways to feed their individual frenzy and raise the fervor of the faithful. As the monitors shut off one by one the President said;

"They are looking for answers, and I think we need to give those answers to them. Somehow we have to gain control of the information. We need to mold it to our goals and get control of the masses. Whether it is a new world as an opportunity; a ray of hope in an unhappy world or a belief that this one is going to end---it doesn't really matter. Maintaining order is our business, and if we want to regain order, we need to control the minds and hearts of the masses. They have questions and they are getting their answers from sources that we cannot accept. We need to create the information, false or not, doesn't matter. We create the answers, we control the flow; and, we control the people. We have to make this happen. Or, the world we know is going to end, whether God's hand is in it or not. We need to get creative here. Let's get to work!"

Heads nodded in affirmation in every direction. The Director of Homeland Security smiled knowing that his job and budget were about to gain a new level of security. The game was on.

CHAPTER 37

"Hey, I was just getting ready to call you!" Alyssa bubbled at Sam on the other end of the line.

"Really. I had to call you 'cause something came up and Ravi and I have to do some traveling. I wanted to see you before I leave but it doesn't look like I'm going to get the chance." Sam replied.

"Well, I am ten steps ahead of you because I already read your check out notice! I'm working the back office computer today for the reservation desk area. It's great 'cause I don't have to dress like an Egyptian harlot for this gig."

"You're here! I'll come down before we pack and check out. When can I see you?"

"I can take a break anytime, so just finish up what you are doing and head down."

"Ok, I'll text you before I head to the elevators."

Sam looked over at Ravi who was rolling his eyes at him and puckering his lips.

"Your level of maturity is amazing." Said Sam.

"Blow me Romeo." Said Ravi.

There was a knock on the door and S.G. poked his shining brown dome into the room.

"You two about ready?"

"Scared and ready." said Ravi

"You have one hour and then we go. Moshe just got clearance on the travel from the Big Guy for Ravi, and, a big break for Sam. Sam won't have to use conventional air to get to Tibet. That should save a lot of time."

"Oh I forgot to tell you. Make sure you don't have any aerosol cans or lighters in your travel bag. For some reason they screw with the navigation. I once got stuck for a week outside Alpha Centauri just because of a can of 'Old Spice'. " said S. G.

"I'm going down to say goodbye to that Alyssa girl I met last night. I know, you don't have to tell me! Even if I told her what's really going on, she would think I'm whacked in the head anyway. I think there may be something here, so I don't want to screw it up right out of the gate." said Sam.

"All right make it quick. We're going to leave right from the rooms so just do an electronic check out. We don't need to go back to the front desk." Said S.G

Ravi was frantically shaking out the contents of his back pack looking for the Bic lighter and muttering to himself, as Sam and S.G. walked out of the room.

Sam strode up to the front desk and saw Alyssa's friend that worked the Pharaoh's Garden Café hostess station, now manning one of the computers at the front desk.

"Hey"

"Hey"

"Alyssa busy?"

"Yep---JK!"

"Yeah, LOL, I'm kinda in a rush."

"K-BBS"

They were conversing in 'Text Speak'. No one under thirty seemed to pronounce anything all the way anymore. They shortened about every affirmative and negative response to either, a letter, symbol, or acronym. The hostess/girl headed toward the front-desk office door.

Alyssa came out with a smile on her face and Sam lit up like a floodlight.

Alyssa smiled at Sam and said, "Lets get out of here for a minute. I can only take ten; we're swamped."

"That's cool. I'm leaving real soon myself."

Alyssa continued.

"The International Computer and Video Game convention starts today and I'm up to my ears in Geeks checking in! I can hardly wait to get over to the convention center and look for new ideas for Sharon and I to try to use."

"Hey, did you hear about that weird weather event before dawn out in the desert? Some guys were camping in the desert and saw this flash of white and then a ball of lighting that looked like it came off the desert floor and flew into the sky. The news said that it was a static electric phenomenon, but the two guys say they saw a white horse and then nothing but a crack of lightening and a fireball."

Sam shook his head in feigned bewilderment.

"Hey can you do Ravi and I favor. I don't know how long we're going to be gone but we have a car out in the parking lot. It's a platinum, Tesla Roadster Sport, and we need someone to take care of it while we're gone. You Interested?"

"Absolutely! Are you sure? What if it gets dinged or stolen?"

"Don't worry about it; we got super insurance on it. The registration is in the glove box. It even has Jersey plates!"

"Sure—I can hardly wait to drive it!"

Sam handed over the keys.

"Why are you guys leaving so soon? I thought you were staying until Monday?"

"Well, we sorta got this job offer for further research and its already behind on schedule. So they asked us if we'd travel to their facility and check it out."

"That's awesome, where are you going?"

"Well, I'm going to Asia and Ravi is going to Uh ------, Gradistan or something, I can't really remember exactly. But, we're coming back here pretty soon. I'll email or text when I can."

"Listen" said Sam. "I really like you and want to keep in touch and spend some more time together. I'm going to try and get back here pretty quick."

"I feel the same way." Said Alyssa as she tippy toed up and gave him a very wet kiss on the lips.

Sam could hardly let go as he hugged her and said a reluctant good-bye. He headed back toward the elevators floating about an inch off the floor on shear pheromone power.

Back in the room, Ravi looked at his flushed friend and shook his head.

"You're whipped already. Hopeless!"

"That girl is going to have my children!" said Sam.

"Yeah, right," said Ravi

Their door opened and Yeshua, Moshe and S. G. came in.

"Ok folks grab your things, it's that time" said S.G.

"Yeshua and Ravi over here, and Sam and Moshe over there." He indicated with a point to either side of the coffee table. Sam and Ravi looking skeptical and scared at the same time, took their positions by the two Prophets.

S. G. made sure all were in their place.

"Ok, Scotty---you know the drill!"

The room was bathed in a warm blue light as if someone had cracked a giant Holloween Cyalume Glow Stick and surrounded the perimeter of the room. In an instant, the room was empty and the light was gone.

CHAPTER 38

Gradis-2

The east side of Lake Tiber had some of the nicest homes in Galil. Stretching up and down its seven mile length were neighborhoods, parks and community landing areas. None of the homes along the gently sloping banks had gone for opulence and grandiose size, but there was a wide varietey of architectural themes represented about the lakefront community. The high level of detail and craftsmanship, and the incredibly efficient use of space, were evident throughout the area surrounding the lake community. Attention to detail and the way the homes were situated on the lots, gave ample views down to the water's edge. Personalized landscaping, blended with natural-looking ponds and carefully tended rock gardens, flowed in a perfect form down to gazebos and docks that obviously got regular use.

Interesting flat-bottom boats hovered within an inch of the surface of the water. Inside the boats, weekend warriors tossed lures and live bait far over the side and jigged their lines back to the edge of the boats. A small commercial boat, about a quarter mile out, drew a net behind it as it trolled its way above the lake surface with a low octave hum emitting from its Mag-Lev drive generator.

The home at 716 East Lake Drive was built in the late craftsman style and sat on five acres of Tiber shoreline. A huge four car garage with two single doors and an expanded double door; was separate from, but directly next to the home. Two men were working in the double garage bay and the blue and white spark of an arc welder crackled in even incremental pulses. Walking along East Lake toward the home were Yeshua and Ravi. Ravi looked like a dollar-store-bobble-head as he tried to keep up with Yeshua, while looking in every direction at the same time.

"Oh my God! I can't believe this. I'm on another planet!! No spacesuit, no oxygen tank. NO WAY!"

"Easy now, easy now the air is just a bit more oxygen rich here so take nice even breaths and relax. OK?"

Yeshua walked in front of Ravi and approached the two men welding the interesting contrapted machine in the double garage bay. The taller of the two men was a handsome looking gentleman of about 40 years of age. He had the almond shaped eyes that were characteristic of Asian people, but the rest of his features defied any placement of what his heritage might be. He smiled as Yeshua, walked up and threw his arms around him in a bear hug.

"Yeshua, Good to see you! And this must be the scientist friend that you said you wanted me to meet. You remember my partner Arto, don't you? He and I are just finishing up on a new project we've been working on. Hi, you can just call me Li," he reached his hand toward Ravi and said "Welcome!"

Yeshua said "Chen Li, It is good to see you again. And to the other man, "Hey, Arto, long time no see." The shop companion smiled and shook his hand.

Chen Li Goldsmith was an interesting man with a quick smile and peaceful way about him. Ravi took an immediate liking to the man's energetic good cheer. After introductions were made, Li walked over to the workbench and passed his hands under a wall hung spout; instantaneously, a blue glow spread across Li's grease stained hands. The grease seemed to evaporate and Li reached into his back pocket and wiped his hands on a blue shop towel. Ravi just stared in amazement trying to draw in the unfamiliar tools and equipment stacked around the workshop.

"Hey Arto, why don't you finish up out here; your welds are neater than mine anyway? I'm going to go catch up with these two."

Arto smiled and waved them all off toward the house as he picked up the welding hood and placed it back on his head. He waited until Ravi had passed out of range and resumed his filet joint weld along the side of the machine.

Ravi followed too far behind, staring at the lake as a group of brightly painted Mag-Lev hydros screamed down one side of the lake in a heated race. Yeshua looked back and beckoned him to hurry. Reluctanty, he picked up the pace.

Li invited them to a seat at his kitchen table. The smooth wood top was mortised and tennoned with a butterfly dovetail along the panels, and, the same unique detail as each leg passed through the top. The complimentary but contrasting colors of the natural wood, coupled with the perfection of the joinery, made for a functional piece of art.

"You're admiring my table I see. Well, the humble artist is sitting to your left. He's quite the craftsman but incredibly slow on delivery. If you want a J.O.N. furniture piece, you better be prepared to wait."

Through an opening at the bottom of the back door facing the lake, came a sound like a cross between a chirp and a bark. A creature like nothing that Ravi had ever seen blew excitedly through the opening. Ravi jumped back and landed on his butt; as the critter started licking, and snuffling his face. It looked like part dog, part goat and part carnival freak--and smelled like three day-old fish; Benny the Gradisian Retreiver of limited intelligence, had found a new friend. Ravi rolled to his right and left trying to avoid the stench of fish and popped up on to his feet to seek the safety of his chair.

The two Gradisian men were laughing as Li coaxed the hound over to his side of the table and admonished him for his exuberant welcome. The retriever settled into his place under the table and stared at the floor at Ravi's feet, in the hopes that some treat might land for him to take advantage of.

"Wow that's one smelly-butt-ugly dog. Six legs, two horns and a smell that could stop a bus," said Ravi

Yeshua said, "If you think he's ugly; you should see the Kazarian version with the extra set of eyes!"

"So, Yeshua said you are interested in Mag-Lev mechanics. Well, I'm happy to share the technology with you. I have all the files here in my office that I think you might need. I believe I should be able to transfer to a format recognizable for your computing and communication device. Yeshua brought me one of your Droid handheld tablet computers a month ago to fool around with, and I believe I have a USB/GSB converter worked out to connect my computer to your tablet or your phone device. I believe that we're going to need some shop and lab time together if we're going to make sure you can replicate a working model."

Yeshua stood and said, "I'm going to leave you two to get acquainted. Ravi, my wife and son are heading down to Li's summer house to stay for two weeks. I want to get home and see Mary and Jimmy before they leave. Li, can Ravi stay here with you? I want him fully up to speed before I take him back to Earth. With our families away anyway, we should be able to focus and get a lot done. We have ten days to work on this, and I need Ravi to leave here fully proficient in Mag-Lev technology and practical applications. We need to be sure he gets enough hands-on knowledge and matching reference support documentation."

"Li, Ravi needs to have the ability to navigate the documentation to a level where he can teach the Mag Lev technology, explain and modify any proprietary tools and produce the equipment as well. He can only leave here with knowledge and reference materials. No product or samples. So you guys have your work cut out for you. I'm going to get out of your hair and walk home.

"We can get it done; Yeshua, the technology is unique but actually pretty simple. I think Ravi is going to be surprised once he sees how it works. As long as they have the alloys and raw materials on Earth, which I believe they do from the computer I took apart, we should be able to get it done."

"Why don't you take Benny with you down to your house, he and Eli like to play, and you can have the girls take him to the summer cottage with the kids? The dogs like the forest hunting and the boys will have a blast with them. Plus I don't feel like trying to wash that stench off of him. Tell Mary and Jimmy, I said hi."

Yeshua whistled and slapped his thigh, and Benny bounded out from under the table as three of his six legs slid on the hardwood floor. In a jumble of legs and fishy aroma he ran after Yeshua and out the door.

Li gave Ravi a tour of the comfortable home and showed him to his room. He showed him how to use the shower and unfamiliar equipment, as well as complete instructions on how to use the paperless and waterless toilet, which was a bit awkward without going through a detailed demonstration. Ravi got the gist and ran through the steps twice, assuring Li he would call him if he couldn't figure it out under actual use.

"Ok, let's head over to the shop and get down to the basics," said Li.

They spent the night working through the computer reference material and trying out the USB/GSB interface cable. Ravi explained the nuances of his imaging and spread-sheet software to Li. By the end of the evening, they could transfer and convert files between the two devices and compress to a workable size for the transfer to Ravi's phone as well.

About one in the morning they decided to turn in and get started again at first light.

CHAPTER 39

Gradis-2, Day 2

"$\mathbf{F}$irst let me walk you through the concept again. Last night we went through all the basic reference materials and the natural raw materials." Chen walked over to a monitor screen on the wall; with a swipe of his finger he activated the screen and began to lecture Ravi on MagLev theory.

"Magnetic materials and systems are able to attract or press each other apart or together with a force dependent on the magnetic field and the area of the magnets, thus a magnetic pressure can then be defined.

The magnetic pressure of a magnetic field on a superconductor can be calculated by:

$$P_{mag} = \frac{B^2}{2\mu_0}$$

where Pmag is the force per unit area in pascals, B is the magnetic field just above the superconductor in teslas, and $\mu 0 = 4\pi \times 10{-}7$ N•A-2 is the permeability of the vacuum.

Now the problem has typically been three fold. Number-one, is getting sufficient power to the magnets, while using a small enough generator. That's were the fusion engine comes in. Number-two, needing a continual opposing force below the source. That's where the dual electron alloy emulsion, I've developed applies. And three, split second modification of both elevation and thrust to provide direction, speed and braking. That's mostly a software management and operating system.

Let me show you how we've solved for each of these."

Li and Ravi rolled up their sleeves and worked well into the wee hours of the morning. Ravi's open mind took in all the information, asking the pertinent questions and digesting the information. The two were moving between the screens of the computer at the workbench, to the working model of the cross section model of the Maglev drive that Li kept in the shop for show. The unusual alloy combination that created the basics for the drive was a unique combination of nickel, cadmium and crushed vanadinite, an iron ore mineral. Mixed in just the right proportions and heated to extremely high temperatures under pressure, an emulsion coating was formed. This emulsion allowed, for a single surface under electric agitation, to excite the electrons on the source and travel surfaces of the Maglev device.

Next they moved to the basics of the Gradisian fusion engine. The technology for this device was so simple, that Ravi was able to mix the alloy for the hydrogen cracking catalyst within hours. Scientists all over Earth had been trying to convert water to power for years and had failed to build a commercially viable product. Ravi learned that they were missing the one stage that allowed for two electrolytic, oppositely charged cores to crack away the hydrogen as fuel, and exhaust away clear water as its byproduct.

On Earth, the problem always became that a large continual power source was needed to produce and maintain the fusion model activity. The negative efficiency burden of the failed Earth models made for interesting experiments, with no reasonable practical application. The Gradisian model, that was explained and demonstrated by Li to Ravi, required nothing larger than a small lithium-ion battery to start the catalytic process and provide the start of the hydrogen combustion.

Ravi and Li then went through an overview of the operating software that controlled the supply of power and the focused directional flow of the magnetic flux to provide, speed, direction and braking control. Ravi worked his way through converting the computer language until he was able to comfortably run it through all of its paces on his tablet computer.

Li lectured Ravi, "Based on what you've told me, your traditional Earth based vehicles are not that different from what we had developed 20 years ago on Gradis-2. When conversion first started here, I just took conventional equipment and coated the underside with the electron alloy emulsion, changed out the drive and connected the steering, braking and acceleration modules to the software. That way, you had a dual-purpose vehicle. Still able to function as a traditional vehicle and utilize the arcane roadway system, but with all the advantage of Maglev. There's just about no limitation as to what you can levitate and transport with this machine.

It was enough for one day, and Ravi and Li called it a night.

CHAPTER 40

The Free Nation of Tibet

By far, the closest place on Earth to Genesis and Kush is Tibet. Tibet is the highest region on earth and closer to the heavens, ok, incrementally not by a lot, but closer none the less. The average elevation of Tibet is 16,000 feet above sea level (4900 meters). That's way up there. Tibet is home to Mount Everest, which towers at 29,030 feet (8848 meters). Most all the life-giving rivers of Asia flow out of the Himalayas and through the Tibetan Plateau. The sources for the Ganges, Mekong, Yangtze, Indus and Yellow Rivers, to name just a few, flow down from Tibet and deliver their life's blood to the lands and people of the most populated areas of the world.

As Sam and Moshe wandered about the streets of Lhasa, Sam became aware of a pervasive and pleasant feeling of peace and tranquility. Whether it was the humbling presence of the Himalayas, the people that seemed to function in complete content, whether working at crafts or driving a team of water buffalo, or the ever-present groups of maroon and saffron clothed monks. Lhasa was orderly, calm and free of the chaos of most cities that Sam had been to in his life. He couldn't quite put his finger on it. He turned to Moshe and said.

"I don't get it. It's just people. Why is there such a difference here? I can't for a moment see one of these people erupting in Road Rage, arguing over a parking spot or pushing in line. I mean the level of activity is high, all the hustle and bustle of a city, but it's like it lacks any tension."

Moshe said, "It's nice isn't it? It's the same on the worlds of Kazaria, Jenn-1, and Gradis-2 as it is here. The people are motivated, peaceful and determined in their very productive daily lives, but the catalyst for their efforts is a desire to focus on tasks that are driven by a communal will, rather than self-will. Self-will powers itself with an ego driven aggressive force, while community will functions on a passive determination to provide for the collective good; which in turn, all benefit individually as part of the whole. Both methods are highly productive, both methods function with determination and get the task at hand accomplished. The aggressive ego, self-will driven path has negative side effects; the passive, common will approach has positive effects. The disparities between the two define the ability of a society to succeed or fail. God has seen this play out throughout the Universe."

"All of God's intelligent life forms, throughout the Universe, have egos and free will at their disposal. How they mold them and grow them as a society and race determine the viability of the species, and often times, their worlds as well. It's not a lack of ego, or an existence devoid of will that succeeds. It is not something that can be governed in to the society by dominance of creed such as Communism, Socialism or Democracy. Nor is it something that can be dogmatically ritualized and bred back in to the populace through religion. It's an individual's innate ability to keep these two key character traits of ego and will in check, right sized, and beneficial to the individual and the group.

With ego and will in check, then tolerance and acceptance of your neighbor can be realized. The fear of those different than you falls away, and peaceful existence becomes possible. Once, both the internal and external fears are gone, and safety is a reality; the society and race can focus on what is important and higher levels of consciousness, and learning can be reached. This is where the majority of Earthlings fall woefully short. This is why we find ourselves faced with the task at hand."

They made their way through the marketplace and entered the terrace and garden area at the entrance to Norbilunkga Palace, the Dalai Lama's home. They greeted the mix of monks and tourists as they milled around the area and accepted the guidance of two ascetics assigned to them as aides of the Dalai Lama. The two monks silently led the way up the steps and through the elegant building. Deep in the recesses, they were brought to two large double doors and bade to enter. The Prophet and his charge entered to see the simple monk, Tenzin Gyatzo, seated on his settee in deep thought as he read from scrolls of computer print outs.

"Ah, Moses welcome back! And this must be Dr. Sam Klein," please come sit down, and I will prepare tea for you." The Dalai Lama went about his ritual of serving his guests.

"Let me tell you where we are. We're charged with the task of selecting individuals for colonization of the new Tibet colony, and then, the Kush colony. We have not been given an upset number of how many we may save, but we've been handed finite criteria for selecting the Colonials. We started with a small sample of qualified testing delivered, via written and oral questionnaire, to the inhabitants of Lhasa, Jenn-1, Kazaria and Gradis-2. Moses, Yeshua and Moh have forwarded the results from their regions to combine with ours, and we've compiled a data-base of comparative common traits. By focusing on areas of thought process and decision-making, and how the individuals applied their self-will and ego in the process; we have the basis to work from. Now that we have the benchmark data compiled, we can test any individual against the control group; the challenge is how we do just that. I'm hoping that young Sam can help. We have a method and a goal, but no way to apply it globally."

"Your Holiness, you mean to tell me that individual interviewers are physically meeting each candidate and then examining them with oral and written testing? Then, you are taking that data and manually entering it into data bases."

"That is correct"

Sam said, "We have to find a way to mechanize this process vertically and horizontally. I guess the advantage of being trained in astro physics and astronomy, is that our palette is so big; we're always looking for ways to compress the information to manageable levels. I have a few ideas about the process, but I believe that the answer lies in the mechanics of it. If we can find a way to reduce the questionnaire data further; to that of reading the human responses that answering the data triggers in the individuals; that's the information we need to process.

To expand on that, if say, a question is provided and during that answer, the respondents body reacts by delivering an exact electric level, a brain synapse in a fixed region of the brain, a pupil response, a nerve response or a change in hormone level; that gives us a different set of data to work with. Those responses can be compared to that of two different control groups, those that meet the criteria and those that don't."

"Taking that data further, once we have the specific positive response data, and opposing negative response data; we can build an electro-mechanical testing device that just measures and reads for the desired scanning results. An ego and will testing device, not so dissimilar in design or concept, to a medical model EKG or EEG machine if you will. If we do it right, we may be able to forego the oral and hard testing completely; just hook them up, read the results and have our match!" Sam stopped and looked at the two men.

Moshe said, "Well Tenzin, I guess that explains why the Boss guided us to this young man."

"Well said, Moses, well said"

"Sam, we have many learned men and woman here at your disposal from Universities around the world. We have a central lab facility that's equipped with the finest computer and medical research products we could procure, and the medical research and technical staff to operate it. We've been diligently at work seeking and testing pharmaceutical products and techniques of both Eastern and Western medicine. We've always believed that the blend between the two would open many doors to better the lives of the sick, and preventing disease in the healthy. They are all at your disposal. Anything you need; just let us know, and Moses and I will respond immediately. Now if you please, I'll have the temple staff guide you to your quarters."

The Dalai Lama reached for Sam's hand and held it gently in his own as he said: " If we can get started after meditation and prayer tomorrow, I will take you personally to the lab facility and let you pick your team. You bring me great hope Sam; maybe we have a chance at getting this done."

The three stood as two young monks entered to take the two visitors to their rooms.

CHAPTER 41

Gradis-2, Day 8

As Ravi's time with Li wore on, the two men built a mutual respect for each other's capabilities. They worked together well, and Ravi was a quick study as he absorbed the progressive physics that Li had at his disposal. He struggled a bit with the advanced metallurgy that Li was familiar with, but for what he could not understand, Li was able to give him reference material that Ravi could study and share with more capable colleagues when he returned to Earth. They hit the shop early, and typically took a siesta style lunch that included fishing excursions on Lake Tiber, and visits to Yeshuah's shop and sheep farm.

Li took Ravi to the commercial production facility for Maglev vehicles. Ravi was amazed at the production equipments technology and advanced efficiency. The sizes and shapes of the transportation equipment mimicked that of rail and tractor trailer, without having the design constraints of traditional surface based containers familiar to Ravi. Without roadway and lane size limitations, more products could be moved longer distances and handled at both ends of the transportation chain with an ease that would revolutionize any industry on Earth.

Ravi envisioned the freedoms that this one simple technology delivered. He envisioned an Earth were all warehousing no longer needed to be along a railway, highway, waterway or airport. An Earth where manufacturing would be free to locate away from its raw source materials had endless possibilities. The application was beyond belief. The concept of a transport the size of the largest shipping container vessel, traveling from port to port at speeds exceeding 350 MPH; rather than the typical 18 to 20 mph those products moved over the oceans on Earth now. Ravi reflected on the benefit of the ability to access any port, regardless of its location or ability to handle the draft and maneuvering limitations of a large ship; the opportunities where endless. And just as quickly he realized that those capabilities would never be tested. Commerce on Earth was just months from ending.

Li came over to Ravi and saw the painedl look in his eye.

"Hey what's up with you? Why so glum today?"

"I was just running through the applications for all of this technology, and then it hit me. It's of no use. Earth is cooked, done, over with. What's the point?"

Yeshua came striding into the shop as Ravi and Li were engaged. Having overheard the exchange, he responded.

"Ravi, Earth as you know it today, is over. I'll give you that. At the same time, this technology is a start at a new beginning. You need to start focusing on where you are going, not where you've been. Focus on right now and the immediate task in front of you, have some faith, and let the events unfold. Think about the benefits of this technology on paving the way for the Tibetan and Kush colonies. Think about how this will ease the transition and lay the path to a better quality of life while the human race re-builds itself. There's a silver lining in your dark cloud."

As was the case, more and more, the Prophet's calming effect took the fear and the pain away in incremental waves of relief. Ravi's face softened and he looked back down at the small fusion reactor and Maglev drive that Li had him welding and bolting together. No bigger than the lid of a coffee can; it was the furniture and appliance moving module so popular on Gradis-2. The device, used in multiple combinations and controlled from a tablet or cell phone, made anything in the home or shop levitate and move about the room to any location desired with little to no effort.

"I get it, said Ravi. It's hard though; this is a lot to take on and digest at times. For all its flaws, Earth is my home and the people on it are my identity. This is so out of my control, but that doesn't stop me from dwelling on it. I'm trying hard to reconcile the end of all that I've ever known to be real."

"Celebrate the beginning Ravi and, mourn for the loss. If you didn't have these feelings, we'd never have come together like this. The Prophets had no hand in the events that led up to your discovery of Genesis and Kush. The Big Guy made you and Sam part of his plan, and then we were given instructions to find the two of you. If there's any comfort to be had, try to take it out of those facts. You and Sam are serving a purpose when so many others float along with none at all."

"Li, how do you feel about Ravi's handle on the Maglev and fusion technologies?"

"He's ready, Yeshua. I'd keep him here if I could. He's equal, or a step ahead of some of my best designers. As long as he can find a manufacturing arm on Earth then he's good to go."

"Ok, Tomorrow is the last day here, and then it's off to Las Vegas! Let's take tomorrow off and all go down to the summer cottage and get some rest in."

CHAPTER 42

Sam and Moshe rose at dawn. After bathing and dressing they were called by the tinkling of wind chimes, a deep gong followed by the low throated bellow of the Tibetan Temple Horns. The call to prayer was made. With light taps on their chamber door, the two young monks of yesterday came to direct them to the great assembly hall of the Temple. They entered along with the steady stream of Temple faithful, just as the Dalai Lama came and took his place among them.

"Welcome to you all. I pray today for the souls of the sick and suffering. I pray today for the freedom of the oppressed. I pray today for peace where strife and violence runs rampant. And I pray today in thanks to our Creator and for the understanding of what his will may be for me today and in the future. Let us all meditate together."

Sam let the quiet surround him as he shut his eyes in collective worship with the group. For the next thirty minutes, Sam found a sense of peace that he had craved without knowing, until he was blessed with it now. Rested and refreshed, all went to begin their day.

As promised, the Dalai Lama personally guided Sam through the state-of-the-art lab facility. Sam was introduced to the team and recognized a name or two from the group. The liberation of Tibet, and the respect for the Dalai Lama and what he stood for, was shared by many in the Academic and Science community. An opportunity to bring that knowledge to Tibet and participate in the new beginning was a dream realized for many in attendance. Sam interviewed from the various disciplines that he felt would be needed to accomplish the task that was expanding and coalescing in his mind. Others would be added based on the mutual input of the team. By late-afternoon Sam was ready to brief them on the task and the goals, and they broke up into groups of three to brainstorm solutions.

The teams worked late into the night; dinner was brought in, and they all took a break to refuel. Sam asked each how they had progressed and was thrilled by the responses. The plan was coming together at a pace that was incredible to fathom. By ten, they called it a night and agreed to start anew in the morning.

Sam looked around the research office that had been loaned to him and started to organize the space to his liking. He took his laptop and some reference material out of his back pack; even though the hour was late he decided he would put in a couple of more hours. As he reached into the bag to remove his spiral notebook, the card with Alyssa's phone number fell on to the desk. He picked it up and smiled, sniffed it and was instantly awash in visions of Alyssa up on her toes giving him his kiss. Ravi was right. He was hopeless. He looked at the bank of international clocks that lined the hallway outside and saw the Mountain Time clock reading 10am and figured what the heck.

"Hey, Alyssa how are you!"

"Hi Sam! How's Tibet?

"It is beautiful, the mountains, the people; I even met the Dalai Lama today!"

"No Way! You met the Dalai Lama!"

"I did, I'm working on a project that he's personally overseeing. I really wish you were here."

"I wish you were back in Las Vegas. The car is without a doubt the coolest thing I've ever driven. I had to talk my way out of two tickets already. Successfully both times, I might add."

Sam laughed and said, "Ok racer, just be careful."

Sam said, "Let me tell you about this project. It is so big, and on such a short string for time that I'm a little overwhelmed. They put me up in a super lab facility, and I have a team that's incredibly trained, but I don't know if I can get it done quickly enough. We have to convert raw human mental response data generated from a questionnaire, to electronic data, and then to measured electro mechanical transmission. Sort of like an EKG or EEG machine."

Alyssa said, "Come on Sam, we're working on just about the same thing. The gamer platform that Sharon and I are developing is a step ahead of what you are talking about. We're already measuring all the physical and neural responses in our study. You're just doing it off of a questionnaire, and we're doing it from game play. We know what gaming reflexes and responses we need to data mine for, and just test for those. If you have a different set of responses to read, all you have to do is provide us with the ability to sensor and read them. Once we have that, we can gather them and write them into the code of our software. How cool would it be if we collaborated?"

"You know you may be on to something. If I can get my team here working on breaking the data down to make the test machine, maybe we can combine the two technologies and shorten the time. I'm so glad I called you; let me check in with the guys who contracted us and see if I can get you and Sharon clearance."

"So enough business, tell me what you've been up to otherwise."

The two spoke on the phone for over and hour talking about everything and nothing. Finally, with Alyssa needing to go to work at the Luxor, they had to sign off. Sam put the phone down and tried to find any way to place 'coincidence' on what was going on, and failing that, decided to head back to the Palace and get a little sleep before it all started again tomorrow.

By the end of meditation the next morning, Sam had a plan in mind. At mid-morning, he asked Moshe and his Holiness if they had time to talk for a minute or two.

The two Prophets and Sam retired to the office of the Dalai Lama.

"We made a huge amount of progress with the research lab team yesterday. We believe we can model after technology that's already available once we isolate the ego and self-will response parameters. I believe that if I have three or four more days, we should be able to leave it in the hands of the technicians. We should be able to produce a working model pretty quickly thereafter. But what we don't have, is the mass exposure to the populations we need to test--or a test delivery system."

"Moshe, you remember the girl I met at the Luxor." Moshe nodded. "She's working on a game and individual response software program with a partner, and from what I could gather, it may be the answer to our problems. If I can get the two projects working in tandem, we could skip a step and really ramp this up. But, I can't see any way to get the full benefits of the collaboration if I don't bring them in, and tell them our true purpose. The data we're mining is borderline invasion of privacy. And when I tell them how I think we need to get it out into the public domain, we'll be flat out breaking the laws of many countries."

Moshe said, "I have to trust your judgment on this Sam, you are the one with the task. Tenzin and I are just your humble facilitators. How can we help?"

"I need to get back to Las Vegas and meet face-to-face with these two woman and convince them of the urgency----and hope they don't think I'm nuts! What I have to ask them to do would put them at risk for prosecution, and only we know that none of that matters anymore. They need to know that as well, and put all of their efforts in to getting the testing system out to the public; regardless of the consequences."

"I need a working test model of the scanning device, and a chance to take that to Las Vegas and win these two gals over to the cause."

"Moshe will have to arrange travel. I will work with you to facilitate all lab efforts to be at your disposal," said the Dalai Lama.

Moshe said,

"This all may work out well. Ravi is finishing up on Gradis-2 and having the two of you together might help get the message across to the two computer programmers in Las Vegas. Ravi is only going to have a day or two to rest, and then he has a good bit of travel and work to accomplish with his transportation task."

The trio sat for a moment more while Sam told them more specifics about the process and how he saw it tying together. The Prophets nodded in satisfaction and wonder as they realized how much of what was going on was out of their control; all events were being manipulated and molded in the usual mysterious and convoluted way that their Boss brought events to be. They had seen this method before, and much of what they had to offer was just being along for the ride, pushing the cart from time to time until the Big hand came and moved it his way.

"I sell the things you need to be----I'm the smiling face on your TV----Oh, I'm the cult of personality"

-Living Colour

CHAPTER 43

Washington DC

"Call it what you want!" said the President. Propaganda, misinformation, disinformation! I really don't give a damn what your call it! We have to take a position and take one quickly. I see the Presidential Daily Brief, every day I get the crap scared out of me by the CIA, NSC and Homeland Security. You guys are scary! We have to do whatever it takes, and leave the consequences for later. We're going to have to control what the media is getting and now! Look out there on the sidewalk and look at what's happening on the Mall. The crazies are out in full force. The world is smoking and about to catch on fire."

"Let's redirect the focus. Let's give them hope and a reason to behave themselves. I think the best approach is telling the public that we've made an astounding discovery and have developed the ability to travel to Kush. We tell them we've made the first test shot, and it was successful. We are now four years away from a manned mission, and we intend to colonize the planet along with our allies."

"But Mr. President, that's utter bullshit!" said the Vice President. We're talking about mounting the biggest conspiracy since Area 51. They won't buy it."

"They'll buy it if we get all of our major allies to sign on. How can you not believe they'll buy it? The whole world bought that Saddam had Weapons of Mass Destruction. The WMD fake-out bought eight years of budget increases and two wars. If it only comes from the United States alone, no one is going to bite. If the Allies sign on; we're just a step away from convincing the Chinese and Russians that NATO has the technology. They'll want to do a joint program, in fact they'll insist."

"We can hold negotiations over three or four years. Have them fall apart a couple times. It will be like the SALT II talks all over again. Everyone will focus on the talks, do nothing, and without paying attention to whether we're any closer to delivering and landing on Kush. Every time we're supposed to deliver we blame technology, the weather, solar flux! We can buy all the time we need. It doesn't matter, because if we don't, we're going to be fighting a war on five international fronts and at home."

If the Russians and the Chinese buy in, even for a minute, they'll start throwing billions at a race to the finish line. They'll spend all over the world to get ahead of us. They'll create jobs that we won't have to. It'll be a new space race but well be building a boat that won't float. Another Howard Hughes Spruce Goose. The potential is huge. Once the Ruskies and Chinese kick in to gear we can squeeze whatever we want out of the Senate and Congress. The Republicans don't want to spend a nickel on social services, but if you give them a chance to fight a good war, or beat the

Commies out of something, they'll spend. Oh, will they spend.

In the States, we'll pump billions into education, industry, create jobs and get the 99% working, or at least interviewing. That should get them off the street. We'll have jobs popping up all over the place in no time, when private industry starts looking for ways to cash in on the program. This is big! We're at 15% unemployment in most industries, and the economy hasn't produced any significant number of jobs in four years. Come on, this is a winner."

"The religious fanatics will get pushed back into the background. Instead of worrying about the end of days, people will have hope for greener grass on the other side of the fence. All we have to do is make them think they can get across that fence. Heck by the time the wheels come off the bus, maybe some genius will really come up with the technology to really pull it off."

The Vice President said, "I don't like it! It could backfire."

"It might just get us re-elected. I'm really on to something here. Don't fight it," said the President.

"OK. I will reach out and broach the subject with London first. Once they are on board we'll decide on a unified front and hit the rest of the Euro Zone. We'll wait to tell the French last."

Everybody in the room stood and said, "Good meeting."

CHAPTER 44

Las Vegas Nevada

In 1931 with the whole nation rocked by the Great Depression and out of work, President Herbert Hoover pushed hard for the construction of the dam that would eventually bear his name. The unemployed descended on the tiny town of Las Vegas which had a population of about 5,000 at the time. By 1931, over 20,000 unemployed men had set up camp in and around the area of Las Vegas and Lake Meade, hoping for a chance to feed their families and be productive. We need jobs, jobs, jobs was the buzzword mantra of politicians of the day, not unlike the current economic situation. There's nothing like a good infrastructure project to put the hungry back to work, get some decent press, and help a couple of politicians get re-elected in the process. Oh-- and we got a cool dam for the greater good, in the process.

Using government money funded first by the Bureau of Reclamation under President Hoover, and finished with funding from the Work Progress Administration of Franklin Roosevelt. The Hoover dam made living a little easier for some very hard up and out of work disgruntled Americans. First, they built Boulder City, Nevada to house the homeless, and then they spent the next six years building the dam. Now why can't they do that kind of thing nowadays?

Standing on the observation deck and looking down into the blue waters of Lake Meade, Ravi turned to Sam and said,

"You can't believe what it's like, Sam. The whole Gradis-2/Maglev thing! The planet is gorgeous, the people are awesome, and the creatures some of the coolest I've ever seen. I mean come on, a six-legged dog with a head like a goat! I can't wait to get back to the hotel and show you the rest of the pictures I took on my cell."

"Ravi, I'm still rocking from you and me materializing out of thin air in the mechanical room of the Hoover dam. Get out! One minute you are on another planet, I'm in Tibet, and the next we're standing ten feet apart in front of the biggest freakin' turbines in the world. Did you see that maintenance guys face?!"

'You guys can't be in here. I'm callin' security!'

"Yeah, right buddy and we'll sick our Prophet buddies on you and fry your butt to hell! "Well maybe not, but it would have been fun anyway."

"Hey, let's go---there's the hotel shuttle bus back to the Strip!"

The men grabbed their back packs and headed toward the bus and got in line with the rest of the tourists. With hands stuffing Hoover-brochures into purses and back pockets, and cameras swinging from neck and wrist straps, the line of Vegas tourists pushed their way on to the bus. Pushing back into the seats enjoying the sweet smell of bus diesel, the two young scientists felt good to be back home—one of them, just to be on Earth.

After four stops to let off some travelers at the MGM, Stardust, Mirage and Bellagio, the bus made its trip through the legs of the Giant Sphinx at the Luxor and delivered Ravi and Sam to their destination. Sam felt his heart thump a single flip and a flop as he thought about seeing Alyssa again. They gathered their bags and made their way through the doors to the hotel lobby and up to the front desk.

A beaming Alyssa said, "I got your text---and, I got your rooms!"

"I can't wait to get off work and see you! Sharon is coming at six, so we can meet and have you guys fill us in. I parked the Tesla in the employee parking lot—here's the key."

Sam fought an urge to jump over the granite counter and hug his Egyptian Princess. Thought the better of it, and decided to just be a little cool in front of Ravi.

"Awesome, Thanks—same floor and same rooms, you hooked us up, for sure."

Ravi said, "We're beat. I think we're going to go up and bag any Casino time until we get some rest. It's one pm now, so we'll try to be rested up by the time you and your friend get here."

Sam looked at Alyssa a bit longingly and said,

"I'll see you at six."

She said, "Forgot to tell you, but two of those guys that were here when you stayed the last time are on the same floor as you two. The chubby guy and the curly haired dark one."

The two left the front desk and walked over to the elevators to the Penthouse floor. They wondered what the Prophets were up to.

They walked down the now-familiar hallway to room 3618 and went in. Ravi had not stopped talking from the moment they had met.

"So, the Maglev drive is simplistic in its design, easy to adapt to about any size or shape container or physical form. It's only limited to the extent that you need to follow within about two feet of an opposing surface area. After two feet separation, it slows way down and then drops back to level right above the contact surface. As long as the propelled object is structurally capable of supporting itself and its contents without a surface support, then you can just about fly it anywhere."

"Wow, think of the applications, Ravi." Sam was excited. "If it wasn't the end of the world, we'd be rich. Instead, we have the most awesome technology, and we get to try and save what is left of mankind with it. I'm not so sure I am feeling so grateful for this opportunity. I go from being into the pace of the effort and the fascination over the new information; to being depressed about the reason we're involved in the first place"

"Yeh, I have the same feelings. Yeshua helped some with it---you know—'focus on the future and what it might bring' yaddi yaddi adda! I get it at times, but I'm struggling the same as you."

Sam said, "So I have this team   that's un-believable in Tibet, it's like a staff that walked out of the pages of Science Today, American Journal of

Medicine and C-Net. I think they can do about anything. On the good side when the dust settles we have a heck of a core of great minds to fall back on for the new colonies. Let me show you what we developed."

Sam reached into his bag and pulled out a black box about the size of a Television Set-Top-Box. Its face, except for a grouping of small knobs, was almost an all black glass digital screen. There were two white labels attached with 'Prototype' stamped and taped at angles on the surface. Across the screen were the letters EGG/FWG.

"Ravi, meet the EGG/FWG—The Genesis-Kush project Ego and Will graph meters. When connected to an individual, we can get pheromone, hormone, brain synapse and neural reflex response that we can instantly compare to our target goal population. Other words, if we plug them in and get the proper number of positive colonial traits as we defined, you win and get a ticket to life in Tibet and Kush. If not, you fry with the masses. It's pretty powerful and pretty scary."

"The good thing is we got all the result side and comparative bugs worked out. But we can't plug into seven billion people. We need a delivery system. So I have a couple of ideas, and that's were Alyssa and Sharon come in."

Sam went through his ideas on how it might work to combine the hardware and software conceptually together. He pointed out that he didn't know enough yet to determine whether it would work, but figured they were soon to find out when the girls got there. Ravi switched over to his challenges,

"So, I have the Maglev technology, and the downloaded design and theory documentation. I know how to manipulate the raw materials. I know how to handle transitional modifications. I don't have any manufacturing resource yet. Where do you think we should start with that?"

Sam thought for a minute and said, "It's the same situation as I was in. If you have to take this to the next level it means including others at the risk of them thinking we're absolutely off our rockers."

"Hey Ravi, what about Musk? He has tech, transportation, and hell, even space transportation! He has full manufacturing capabilities, and you can't get much more of an open mind and forward thinking group than who he's surrounded himself with! I mean between Tesla and SpaceX if anyone can get it done they could!"

"That's it. He's our guy!" said Ravi.

The two brainstormed on how to approach Elon Musk with the problem and felt relieved that they had a direction to go in. Sam asked about the pictures from Gradis-2 and Ravi pulled out his tablet computer and loaded up his picture gallery.

"This is Benny the Space Dog. Smells like fish, but other than that, just your typical K-9. Except for the nubby horns and two extra legs that is."

"Check out this bird, looks like a mini-peacock, but they can hover like a hummingbird."

"Ok, take a look at the Maglev boats; I took this right in Li's back yard."

He ran through the pictures with Sam riveted to the screen in wonder.

A knock came at the door, and Ravi popped up and took a peek through the viewer. Smiling he opened up, and S. G. and Moh stepped in. The two Prophets warmly welcomed the two and Moh said,

"So Sam were you able to use the survey data from the Jann-1 population?"

"Oh yeah, they were easy to qualify. They are very simple people and completely malleable on both ego and self-will. They were perfect for a control group. We had a little harder time with the Kazarians. They fall all over the place. All are within parameters, but with the ten unique tribes we had to sift through a lot of variable swings. If Moshe isn't careful, that group could get a little out of control."

S.G. said, "Ravi, I understand you are now the Maglev transportation expert. Do you have any better handle on where you go from here?"

Ravi brought them up to speed on their discussion and brainstorming process about Tesla and SpaceX. Both Prophets nodded in satisfaction that maybe they were on the right tract. Both Prophets committed to provide their full support, and that of their two counterparts to the effort.

Sam said, "We may need some convincing to seal these up. I don't know what you two can do, but it may take more than just talk to swing these people to accept that the world is going to end in eight months. Not easy to gain buy in on that one."

Ravi said. "Maybe you two should stick around for when the girls get here and help pave the way for us."

Both Prophets nodded their agreement.

Sam, turned on the TV and Al Jazeera blared on to the screen.

"……..Israel denied it had any knowledge of the fully armed predator drone that crashed outside of an Iranian Nuclear Research facility in the Dasht-et-Kavir desert. A spokesman for the Iranian government said that the failed attack against their peaceful nuclear-power facility by the criminal Zionist occupiers would be dealt with a swiftly……….." Sam flipped the channel to CNN.

"………...In the Free Nation of Tibet today, it was announced that the Tibetan and Indian Governments had signed a trade treaty. The Tibetan Government announced it was planning to mount a massive immigration and relocation program within its borders. Fueled by massive donations from the fund raising efforts of the Dalai Lama, the flow of food, medical supplies and building materials for temporary housing were pouring into Calcutta, India. Calcutta is the closest deep water port serving Lhasa. Special arrangements have been made for a restricted air space area between Calcutta and Lhasa, as well as a rural ground passage, to allow free movement through the two border areas of the large quantity of goods."

Except for the positive news on Tibet, Sam clicked through the news channels with the same general results. Things were deteriorating pretty quickly here on planet Earth. There was no solace to being 'in the know' as to where it all was heading and were it would all end. His phone dinged a temple bell chime, and he looked at his text messages----the girls were on their way up.

CHAPTER 45

Sam went to the door to answer the knock. He opened it up and was met with a hug and a kiss from Alyssa that swooned him upon contact.

Her girlfriend Sharon stood a step behind and gazed just a bit warily at the occupants standing behind Sam and Alyssa. Sharon was tiny, with porcelain skin; she had eyes that twinkled with a bright intensity and burned with intelligence.

Sam released Alyssa and said,

"Come on into our humble abode!"

"You must be Sharon. We've heard quite a bit about you and your gaming project." Sharon smiled as she extended her tiny hand and sized Sam up.

"Sharon and Alyssa meet our friends Moh and S.G.---they help head up the team that Ravi and I are working for, and Sharon this is Ravi my partner. Alyssa you already know Ravi." Handshakes and salutations were passed between them.

"Why don't we go take a seat at the dining room table? We have some pretty heavy stuff to lie out. Can I get anybody something to drink?"

"Water, Water would be fine?" Said the girls.

"Same for us." Said the rest.

Sam said, "Well here goes, Alyssa and Sharon. I know what I'm about to say is going to be hard to accept. It was for me and Ravi. Alyssa, you and I talked about how crazy and unexplainable the discovery of Genesis and Kush is. You and I listed the facts that there's no reasonable explanation in any scientific discipline---astronomy, astro-physics, quantum mechanics---nothing. There was no science for us to hang on to in our search for answers. You and I came to the same conclusions that Ravi and I had. It's baffling, more miracle than science, and it's more than a bit frightening.

On our last trip to Las Vegas, Ravi and I got our answer and it isn't an easy one to accept.

Genesis and Kush are God's work----I don't mean the metaphorical, Sunday school, lesson from the pulpit kind---I mean its six Earth days of Gods work—strap on the tool belt version! Please, don't get up---don't leave. Hear me out. It gets better----no, I mean worse."

The girls had made a half attempt to start to rise out of their seats. They reluctantly sat back down keeping an eye on the door for a quick exit if one was required. Sharon thought about the 'pepper spray' on her key chain and looked over at her purse. Sam continued.

"On December 21 2012, God is going to wipe the Earth clean of all human life and human imprint on Earth. We cease to exist. God built Genesis and Kush to start over. Actually, he kind of likes Earth as a template but thinks the water here has messed with his original plan. I'll get in to that later. We know this all to be true because we've seen with our own eyes and touched with our own hands the unexplainable! The four men that you checked in last week and the two seated in front of you are Prophets. No Shit, for real Prophets."

Sharon said, "Right, and I'm the Good Witch Glinda and on alternate Thursdays, butterflies and unicorns fly out of my skirt!"

"Lyss, let's get out of here these guys are fruitcakes!"

Sharon made to leave, and Moh turned his head and waved over toward the coffee table in the living room. A very dense miniature thundercloud formed, the mini-heavens opened up and poured rain from about 6 feet up on to the table and sofas as a bolt of mini-lightening arced out of the cloud and split the table in two.

The girls both shrieked and eyed the door.

S.G shrugged at Moh and said, "Don't you think that's a little overkill, I mean really"

S. G. Passed his hand over the dining table, and the Kush-Genesis orbs formed in a hover over one end of the table. Across the center, and stretched along the remaining length, was a 3-D real time portrayal of the Himalayas and Lhasa. The "bird's-eye-view', produced a panorama created vantage-point hovering above the Tibetan Plateau.

Both girls started to stammer; sputtering in disbelief at what they saw before them, they sat back down. With wide eyes staring they shifted between the split coffee table to what was in front of them, as if hypnotized by the unexplainable display. Both girls' eyes rotated between the doors to the suite while keeping an eye on the two older men. Sharon put her hand on her purse and started to squeeze around the outside, feeling for her pepper-spray gas weapon.

Alyssa said,

"Prophets—like in bible Prophets; like Prophets of God---prophets?

"Yep" said both elder gentlemen.

"This is just too hard! This is hallucination, voices in your head material."

"Sam and I, went through the same process as you guys. Take a minute, try to open your minds. Your both scientists—you both have accepted the unexplainable as an element of fact. Please open up to this because without your help, we lose any chance to save a little piece of humanity. God has given us a crumb. We can save just a small portion of mankind. But he's made it really hard to make the cut."

"We need you two sane and on board for what we have to tell your next. This is no hallucination. It's mind boggling real," said Sam.

The two lady academics started talking----fast. The questions poured out in similar fashion to the night that Ravi and Sam had been delivered the same message. Sam and Ravi did their best to keep up with their part, and S.G. and Moh fielded theirs with the same level of evasiveness that kept forcing the conclusions back on to the two women. Not totally convinced but coming around, the questions slowed and skeptical acceptance started to form.

Alyssa said, "But end the world, get rid of mankind? Its too harsh."

"Really" Said S.G. "Mankind thinks much too much of themselves and were they fit into the grand scheme of things. The Big Guy views man like an out of control mold; a mold, that's eating away at the canvas and palette of one of his great artistic efforts. We've always been just parasites on Earth. We had all of the tools given to us to be beneficial ones; instead we've become a flesh eating plague that ignores treatment when offered or applied. He's no longer placing the care of Earth in your hands. He's doing something proactive about it."

"Great, HE! There's part of the problem. I think I can start to accept this." said Sharon.

"It's so much to take, so many concepts, beliefs and expectations about what's real or not. I'm really trying here and I'd like to help."

"Alyssa, if this is real, if we deny it and walk away. With what we've heard tonight it would be infinitely worse than trying to accept this and help them with our efforts. If we walk, if the world were to end, as they say; we'll have made a contribution to the end of man, when we could have saved a chance for our race to survive."

"Shar, if you're in, I am in. I can't bear to think of the repercussions in either direction. If we walk away without trying, we're doomed. If we help we're committing masses of people to their end. It's hard to get happy in either direction with this. I guess, though, that we have to chose here, and at the risk of making the biggest mistake of our lives, I say let's do it."

Sam said, Ok, here is what we need to do and how I think you two can help.

Sam pulled out the EGG/FWG scanner and began to explain the working prototype to the girls. Sharon, with her med-school and psych back round took the lead and was quickly up to speed. Alyssa took notes as she built a chart for Input-in/Data- out results that would be required to meld the processes together.

Sharon took a breath and said.

"I think we can get this a step better. I think if you give us a chance we can get this to a point that just from keyboard, a cell or tablet activity, we can match viable candidates to obvious rejections. We can run the scanner source code through our program platform and deliver the information back to our database the same way we track gamer preferences and activity. We're already most of the way there. We just need to include source code that mimics in full the scan data produced by the EGG/FWG."

"I can make the software work," said Alyssa. If we can patch the prototype in line while we do our calibration on test subjects; I should be able to tweak it to work."

Sam said, "We have to go way beyond game platforms though. Way beyond. We have to touch seven billion out there if we can, and that's going to take a bit more."

Sam, Ravi, and the Prophets breathed sighs of relief. The challenge was still there but they were at least back in business.

CHAPTER 46

Ravi made the trip from Las Vegas to Palo Alto, California in record time. Seated next to him and strapped in for dear life, sat a more green than nut-brown complexioned S.G.. They pulled into the entrance of the salmon colored building with TESLA printed across its face.

"I'll find my own way back when we're done," said S. G. "That was horrible. I will never drive with you again!"

"Come on, that was some serious fun," said Ravi. "We made great time!"

"Always in a rush, you people are always in a rush. Maybe if you had slowed down a little and thought about a consequence or two, you wouldn't have invited this mess."

"What a buzz kill. Let's go and meet, Elon. I called and he was excited we're coming. I told him you were my Asian investor so try to play the part please. I hinted it was Chinese money."

The two men entered the building and walked up to the receptionist.

"Hi, Ravi Najir and S. G. Shakya to see Elon Musk, we have a 1 o'clock."

"Please have a seat over there, and I will buzz his personal assistant. Can I get you gentlemen anything? Coffee, tea, mineral water?"

"Just water would be good. Thank you." Ravi answered for both of them.

"Here you are, Mr. Musk's personal assistant will be down to get you in just a minute." The men gratefully took the water bottles.

Instead of the personal assistant, from down the hall came Elon Musk himself. Sporting his relaxed and charismatic smile, he waved towards them.

"Ravi, my Kush man! How the heck are you? How do you like the Roadster? And this must be your associate. Mr. Shakya was it. Pleasure to make your acquaintance sir. Welcome to Tesla Motors?" Elon put out his hand and placed it into S.G.'s.

"Pleasure is all mine, S.G is fine."

"S.G. it is then. Ravi, the Roadster?"

"Oh, man, Elon. Sam and I've been having a blast with it! Did you see our unofficial test results? I sent you an email with the radar results from the ticket. Did you get it?"

"Oh I got it allright. I took the whole package and then emailed it to the BBC just to rub it in a little. I don't think they got the humor and my attorney yelled at me. But it was worth it. So, what is this exciting news you have to share with me?"

"Well, is there somewhere we can go that has a computer and a more than two monitors I can access. I have a little presentation for you on Maglev."

"Maglev, Hmmm. That's a step away from stargazing. I'm intrigued. Come right this way, if there's anything we're not short on, its computers."

Musk brought them to medium-sized conference room with a bank of multiple wall mounted monitors, and a computer terminal built into the surface of the large oval table at the center of the room. Ravi took out his back pack and unloaded his tablet computer and sat down.

"Elon I just need to be able to access your secure web so I can connect and download this. Can you type in the password for me? Thanks. Ok, Here goes." On one monitor appeared a rotating image of the Gradisian Maglev drive, and a Hydrogen fusion reactor, cut away, to show the interior mechanisms. On the neighboring monitor appeared a step by step Power Point display.

Sam said,

"I'm going to walk you through this step by step. What you are looking at is a working Maglev drive fueled by a hydrogen fusion reactor engine. I've built a couple. I've driven equipment powered with it. And I am here to show you how it is done."

Elon blew softly through his lips, looked up to the screen at what he was sure looked like the real deal.

"Ravi, my man, I am all ears."

Elon Musk was going to be very easy to convince.

"Don't surround yourself with yourself--Move on back two squares--Send an instant karma to me--Initial it with loving care"   *-Yes*

CHAPTER 47

UNLV Computer testing lab

Alyssa and Sharon were focused at the work table in the computer lab at UNLV. They had burned the midnight oil for three days and were feeling fried. The fifteen test subjects were in the control group waiting area, milling around as they pounded back sodas and snacks from the bank of vending machines. Some of the subjects were walking around with their head gear sensors still attached. With wires wrapped around their shoulders and necks like a bad hair weave; they tried to keep them out of the way while munching Doritos and tossing back energy drinks.

As they made their final adjustments, Alyssa and Sharon tried to tune out the laughter and noisy conversation that seeped under the door and through the walls,

Looking at the data from the EGG/FGG, Alyssa typed in to her keyboard as she adjusted the software code. With painstaking precision she modified first in Objective-C for the iP platform, and then to Java for the Droid products to shift her results. After each adjustment, she would hit 'save'—then 'calculate'—then 'send, as her results downloaded on to Sharon's display.

"That's it!" Sharon said. "I think you got it," Lyss.

"That last set of code matches the pheromone response to pupil contraction about 99.4%, so we are there."

Sharon locked the information and adjusted the frequency and squelch on the EGG side of the device as Alyssa hit the 'save to file' command on her desktop.

"Ok, let's try the same set on the FWG and see if it matches."

Alyssa maximized the window for the FWG software and looked at the notes she had scribbled during the last adjustment session. She brought up the Java and Ojective-C files and started to enter code as she referred back to her notes.

"Ok I got it to run on everything so far except Blackberry and Sprint. I'll work on those next, but they're buggy."

After about a minute of typing she said, "Ready"

Sharon said, "Ok let's load it in and see what it does."

Alyssa turned to the monitor attached to the EGG/FWG device and checked the leads from the command module to the CPU. There were groups of monitors set up across the table. Displayed on the monitors were Angry Birds-Kush; Call of Duty, Words with Friends, The New York Times Crossword Puzzle

On-Line and the log in pages for Facebook, Linkedin, Google and Twitter.

Sharon checked her monitor and said,

"Ok, give it a simulated finger swipe and a double thumb press. Ok—Ok, that's it. Now hit the "Like" button on Facebook—Ok, good!" Sharon leaned over and worked the amplitude increase bar on the face of the prototype unit. She leaned back in her chair and said.

"Girlfreind, we did it. We're over 99% accurate across the board. You can call up the next test group to come back in."

Alyssa hit the save and manual backup on her computer and leaned into the mike on the table.

"Hey guys, listen up! Can we have group numbers 5,7,3, 11, and 15 in here, please? Be sure to Purell your hands before you come in, 'cause the oil messes up the electrode sensors. Those of you we didn't call yet, we need the rest of you on deck, so go get with the technicians and get your sensor kits put on; you're next. We should have all of you out of here by 11:30 and $10 bucks richer!"

The test group filed into the room; Sharon and Alyssa sat them at their booths. Head and hand sensor units were affixed and adjusted. A single eye response sensor projected out from each head unit on an adjustable tentacle. The girls bent and molded them into place to gain the perfect alignment. Making one last check of the lead connections back to the hub; the girls walked back over to the equipment. Sharon looked down at her test booklet and said:

"Ok, you guys know the drill by now. We're going to start with a couple of pre-calibration questions, and then you just start using the game and information Apps the way you normally would. Try and surf through as many different functions as you can, and be sure to change screens at least twice during the session. If you have a computer or tablet at your booth, for the calibration questions use the "pop up box" at the bottom left of your screens. For the two of you on iPhones and Droid platforms use the forward and back keys. For the X-Box use the toggle left for 'no' and right for 'yes'. Ok, you guys ready?"

"Here's the questions,

-Have you ever worked for the DMV?

-Do you like cats?

-Have you experienced Road Rage this year?

-Are you a Lawyer or considering Law School?

-Have you ever run for office in an election environment?

-Do you like to take suggestions?

-Are you currently in, or have you ever considered a career in Law Enforcement?

-Have you ever been a member of, or given money to the Tea Party?

While Sharon ticked off the questions, Alyssa made adjustments on the various pieces of equipment arrayed in front of the two girls.

"Ok, that's it Shar, were ready."

Sharon said, "Ok, folks you can begin anytime you're ready."

The test group went to work, mouses clicked and fingers swiped across screens. Keyboards were pounded and punctuated while controllers rotated in the air; toggles were bent left and right, buttons 'a' and 'b' selected by second nature. The test was in full swing.

The girls settled back and watched the read outs coming across their screens. They had done it. In less than 30 days they had software that once downloaded on to any computer or gaming platform, cell phone or tablet, could accurately measure the level of one's ego and the malleability of self will. Each finger touch, each key stroke, each pupil response sent a group of data to the software. The control group information was collated and compared to the individual responses in the data-base generated by the initial testing and surveys done on the Gradisians, Jannians, Kazarians, Lhasa monks and Wilsons. Now they just had to figure out how to get it out into the public domain without being arrested in the process. The only way any of them had come up with, was going to require the biggest and most coordinated hacking effort since the invention of the first computer virus.

Alyssa picked up her phone and dialed Sam's number; she waited for the extended connection time to Tibet. Boy she sure wished he was here. Sam picked up on the second ring.

"Hey Sam...We did it!"

"I know you did it---I have a room full of techs here looking at the monitors. We're getting full download as fast as you pick up and transmit the data. We're ready for a test run. You girls rock!"

"Every day you'll see the dust-As I drive my baby in my Magic Bus"

-The Who

CHAPTER 48

Ravi was cruising down the 101 heading back to Palo Alto from San Francisco. It was Friday afternoon and he and Elon Musk had put in a hard week. Ravi had the XM tuned to JAM ON and was listening to Moe's the Pit at maximum volume. On a whim, he reached over to the radio dial and tuned to NPR's Science Friday.

"…….This is Ira Flatow, and you are listening to Science Friday. My guest today is Col. William Nussim head of the manned Space Flight Program at NASA. Col. Nussim thanks for being here."

"Your Welcome Ira, and thanks for having me."

"So Col., Please tell us about the reasons behind the Government's decision to take the Genesis Kush-Hubble project away from private research and bring it under the direction of NASA? Even more so, why was it so critical to do so?"

"Well Ira, the answer is complicated. There has been a lot of Space Science research that has been going on for some time that's directly related to the opportunity that the Genesis-Kush discovery has allowed for us. Much of this research has been handled jointly with our allies. And, much of this research could have military applications if it got into the wrong hands. The Office of Homeland Security picked up a heightened amount of chatter that occurred around the time of the broadcasting of the initial Genesis and Kush observations while they were under the direction of Humoldt and Goddard. At the risk of losing whatever edge we have, a joint decision was made to halt the program and properly protect the information and the public."

"Really Col.!, Do you folks have any direct knowledge of the nature of the chatter and how it might have put us at risk?"

"Well Ira if I did, I wouldn't be free to discuss it on National Radio." He chuckled.

"Tell me Col. Can you expand on the research for our listeners."

"That, I can do Ira. NASA and the Military, along with our allies in England and Germany, have been working for some time on expanding our manned Space Program. One of the biggest difficulties has been a drive system and life support facility that could give us the ability to travel outside of our own Solar System. We've been hard at work on tackling these two issues to open opportunities for all free peoples to eventually have access to what may be out there."

"Today I can tell you that we've recently tested, successfully I might add, an experimental drive system that will allow for moving a large manned transport through space. That, coupled with the technology that we've developed for life support during the period of space travel----when complete and fully operational---would allow us to colonize a planet such as Kush."

"Wow, Col. I am ---completely taken off guard here. I mean Col., myself and my colleagues, are pretty tuned into the research and advances being made in the manned space programs. This is the first time I've heard of an advance of this kind! I really don't know where to start, but I'll give it a shot anyway. So tell me how did this come about?"

"Ira most of this is highly classified, but I'll try to tell you what I'm authorized to release………."

Ravi, screeched the tires and grabbed for his phone.

"Elon Musk, Please---it's Ravi Najir---yes I'll hold."

"Ravi…I heard it to!!"

"Elon, what the hell is going on! What are they up to and where the heck is this coming from?"

"I'm as much in the dark as you are. I got a call about an hour ago from the head of the Presidents Chief of Staff and the Director of NASA basically asking me not to comment and not to make waves. They said they would brief me in full in two weeks; also made it pretty damn clear that if Space X valued its NASA contract that I better play along. At their request, I submitted a form comment to NASA to get approved. I'm not supposed to say anything until they clear it. They wanted something to the effect of Space X working on many research programs on behalf of the Government, but not being at liberty to discuss the nature of potentially classified programs. Something is weird here. I got at least fifteen calls on my desk from science and news reporters wanting my comments."

"This is bizarre," said Ravi.

"Agreed."

"Where are you now"

"Just outside Palo Alto on the 101, sitting on the side of the road talking to you, I can be there in fifteen minutes."

"I'll see you then."

Ravi, checked his rear and side view mirrors and pulled back on to the highway. He jammed on it all the way to Tesla. Pulling into the employee parking lot, he did a quick step to the building entrance. Barely acknowledging the receptionist, Ravi headed back towards Elon's office.

The door was open with Elon on the phone. Ravi tapped and walked in, slumping into one of the cushy chairs across from Elon.

"Hey, can I call you back? Something just came up I have to deal with. Remember, 'No Comment' and refer them to the contact at NASA."

"That was my guy at Space X. He said he has a group of reporters at the door wanting to know whether the 'so-called successful test' was the Space Maglev drive. Shit Ravi, the Space X Maglev is still a piece of paper and a drawing on the computer. It's a lab test at this point. A concept only. The Washington event was the 'roll out party' not the 'Oh, we tested it and sent a freak'n monkey into space party'.

And, the 'life-support system' what the hell! The best they have that I know of, is Tang, dried shrimp in a tube, and a way to suck your excrement out and shoot it out into space. As far as I know that's the extent of 'life support system'."

"Elon, we have to set this aside for now if we can, we've got bigger fish to fry and we need to go over the REAL Maglev conversion issues. If we get drawn in to this fiasco, it's going to steal time we don't have to spare. Let's try and focus and go over where we stand. Maybe you can divert this NASA thing to some senior Space X executive on staff? You and I need to stay on the task of saving some people, instead of feeding NASA's media machine."

"Ok, I think I know of just the guy to put on it. He's good and can spin with the best of them. I'll get with him tonight when you and I get done with the update."

"Here's where we are:"

"We have a small fleet of six converted buses and four smaller transports that can be moved by air or sea cargo; and, we'll start moving them into Lhasa next week. We bought the shells at the auto auction out in Oakland; they aren't real pretty, but they do the job.

The technology is the best part; it's so simple once we got the hang of it, the retooling was a no brainer. The fusion drives take about 1/8th of the time it takes us to do a Tesla motor, the Maglev drive, just a little more. You can try one of the smaller operational units with me out in the desert tonight if you want."

"We've bought four mid-sized passenger cruise ships and six multi-hull tankers, as discreetly as possible, through various corporate entities. We've been funneling the Lhasa relief funds through dummy accounts and then to the acquisition entity; so it should be tough for anyone trying to determine the true chain of title back to us.

We're buying the ships out of dry dock storage stocks, which is making it easier. One, they are

264

already out of service, so we have no crew issues to deal with; and two, we can readily access them. Without the distractions we can easily re-out fit them, either for cargo or passengers. We're running nighttime crews during off hours at the dry dock storage facilities. In addition, we have six more targeted for acquisition that are still in negotiation. Of the ten, four are already Maglev alloy emulsion coated, and that crew is going to the third facility in Greece tomorrow. By Tuesday next week, I should have another crew set up in Stockholm. We have enough emulsion run for two more mid-sized tankers, and I am making emulsion as fast as we can get the Vanadanite in from Colorado. I can't tell you how happy that iron ore mine is to get rid of it!"

Ravi was making notes as fast as he could while Elon went on.

"Based on your schematics, we have to place a large fore and aft engine and drive units into the hulls of each ship, plus two smaller units, port and starboard, for maneuvering. We built a one eighth scale mock up in the big hanger facility out back here, and it seems to prove out ok at that scale. We figure that we can make the trip from any major U.S. or European port to Calcutta in less than two or three days. We're taking in to account that until we go public, we'll be dropping into shipping lanes outside ports, and then steaming in under conventional power. We'll high speed Maglev the new UN designated relief routes, that will keep us out of traditional international shipping lanes at all other times."

"I have a team working on a hacking program that should rotate the names of the ships to modify port records. That should avoid confusion as to how the hell they got from port to port so fast! At some point, we're going to be found out, so we'd better be prepared for that eventual event. The good thing is that a leak out of Tesla or SpaceX is pretty unlikely. My guys don't even tell their wives or girlfriends what they're working on!"

"If you guys are ready to begin transport, I think I can have you two up and running passenger vessels that can handle up to 4000 persons each by the fifteenth of April and three cargo ships at the same time. We'll be at seventy-five percent capacity by end of May; and, I can be fully operational with everything on-line and ready for orders and passengers by June. That's about it. So far, so good. How are you guys doing on selection and travel logistics to the ports?"

Ravi put down his pen and looked up.

"Elon we're doing pretty damn good here on schedule. You and your staff have really stepped up. Sam and Alyssa have the first market driven prototype of the selection APP running on Angry Birds-Kush. We priced it low and Rovio bought the rights immediately; they made it an instant downloadable update to the original series. 'Call of Duty' goes out tomorrow so we'll see how the game platform module works. We're going to give it two weeks to run and de-bug, review the output, and then we go global."

Ravi paused in thought as he closed his spiral notebook.

"Let's get out of here and tour the plant for a few minutes, and then I'm game for that test drive of the working unit. What is it anyway?

"It's a Mercedes Benz mini tour bus with cushy seats and an awesome stereo."

They toured the plant, which was running on a twenty-four-hour schedule. Musk had broken the manufacturing phases into parts, with hydrogen fusion reactors in one area, Maglev components in another. The metallurgy section that had been previously devoted to aluminum casting for Teslas was now converted to making vats of Maglev alloy emulsion coating. The controller and software modules were being made at the Space X facility down in the Los Angeles area.

"Elon, it's incredible how quickly you turned this around. I'm blown away! Let's try the Benz out and see if it handles like the Gradisian models."

They went out to the rear parking and test track arena. Musk tossed Ravi the keys to the van, which had Korean Script on the side, and Kim Chi Tours, written below it. Ravi hopped in and started the engine conventionally and hit the door lock release so that Musk could get in. Ravi futzed around with the stereo and Elon pulled out an iPod and plugged it into the port.

"What's your pleasure?"

"How about 'Stairway to Heaven' that sounds appropriate" said Ravi.

They cranked up the tunes and headed out west towards the desert. Once the city lights were faded away, Ravi looked for the first available dirt road cut off from the highway. They pulled off to the side and Elon pointed out the controls which Ravi was already very familiar with as they were straight from the Gradisian design manual. Flipping on the fusion reactor and warming up the Maglev interface to the control module took all of thirty-seconds. Ravi turned to Elon and gave him the 'thumbs up'. The Benz lifted with a barely perceptible cushioned response. Now hovering about nine-inches above the bottom of the tires over the rocky desert floor,

Ravi turned to Elon and said—

"Strap in---here goes!"

Pressing on the accelerator and holding the wheel tight in his hands, Ravi took off and cruised off the roadway quickly gaining speed. As obstructions, scattered across the desert floor came up, the van anticipated them well in advance as the surface analyzer kept perfect pace with the speed of the vehicle. The van gently rose and fell with the grace of a porpoise jetting through the water, maintaining its near-perfect clearance over the rise and fall of the desert floor. Ravi kicked it up a notch and banked left, then right, and then braking suddenly as both he and Elon knocked around inside the cab. Starting back up to speed, he ran the van up to 263 MPH before the wind dynamics on the frame sounded like they might lose some body parts. Ravi finished the test with a 360, then dropped the unit back down on the road surface and switched off the drive. Elon turned in his seat with a grin from ear to ear.

"So, what do you think?"

"I think, you got it!"

"I've seen all good people turn their heads each day- So satisfied, I'm on my way" -Yes

CHAPTER 49

Alyssa and Sharon were seated at their workstations in the UNLV computer test lab. Skyped in on the monitors were Sam and two Lhasa techs that were stationed in Tibet. Sam was holding out a computer graph on a piece of 8-1/2 x 11 paper and pushing it up to the screen.

"Can you see the 'delta' error line? It's down to .0041%. I know its people. I know you feel bad, but its less than 1 person in 100 of error. We have to live with that. The number of potential 'problem' colonists will be so low, and we'll lose so few to the 'end', that our consciences can be reasonably clear.

The girls were nodding, but they were not on board.

"Sam, it's not a graph of whether someone is or isn't going to buy a game. It's a graph of who gets to live, and who dies!" said Alyssa.

"Ladies, we have to draw the line somewhere and pull the trigger. I say we run with it and get as many as we can. Every day we delay is just that critical.

Keep in mind we have to notify them, motivate them, get them to a serviceable port and get them to Lhasa."

Sharon broke in "But look at the qualifying numbers. We're getting less than 900 qualified out of a 1,000,000 hits! We are talking at best a remaining population of six million people!"

"Look girls, we keep going around and around with this. It's rough. It's cold. I get it. But we aren't the arbiters of man's fate here. We're nothing more than the damage control and cleanup crew. The numbers aren't lying. God seems to have already figured out that percentage wise, there just wasn't that much good raw material left to work with down here."

"Let's vote again—How many in favor? Slowly, four hands followed behind Sam's into the air. Sharon's and Alyssa's arms were bent low at the elbows signifying their protest.

"Ok that settles it---we go global across all networks tomorrow."

Sam turned to the two technicians sitting at his table. Both were computer geeks, a far cut above the rest. Both were named Tyler. The name thing was a challenge for everyone on staff, so they had taken to just calling the two by their last names. Unfortunately, both young men were saddled with last names that were so long and so un-pronounceable that their colleagues had resorted to either referring to them collectively as "The Tylers" or just B.E. and K.; the starting initials of their impossible to pronounce last names. Both, B.E. and K. had found themselves, from time to time, in trouble with the authorities over their favorite hobbies and pastimes. Both, enjoyed the challenge of hacking into the networks of corporations, government agencies and organizations that held information that they felt might be better used if out in the public or, for their own personal gain. Being that none of their unfortunate targets felt the same way, the two boys had been continually running to stay one step ahead of the law.

Whether it was encryption technology, multiple firewalls or daily virus scanning hunting for security breaches, the two Tylers had a way around it. Virtually nothing was safe from these two. The opportunity to move to Tibet had been part heartfelt identification with the Dalai Lama's philosophy, as well as a desire to hide from the cyber police that were hot on their trail. Seemed like a perfect fit for them. Sam had quickly snatched them up and offered them both jobs working for the cause, figuring it might keep them out of trouble.

Sam said, "So, B.E., bring me up to speed on how far you and K. have gotten. How soon can we be fully operational and online?"

"Well, K. has been focusing on TV, radio and cell networks. I've been sticking with the electronic gaming companies and government networks. So far, we've pretty much hacked into everyone. While inside, we placed a 'worm' that preps them to let us download and embed the EGG/FWG software as soon as you say 'Go'."

K. stepped in, "I just got the bug worked out that kept having Blackberry and Sprint drop the imbed. Sharon and Alyssa sent over their version, and I found a way to bypass the problem. So we're good to go, even on the slower technology front."

"Give us the green light and within four days if a device runs Apple-OS, Microsoft, Linux, Unix, Android or, in any way accesses Cloud, WIFI or 4G, we have 'em!" said B. E.. If they finger swipe a screen, toggle a controller, use their phone cam or, for that matter, just have one. We get them."

"Green light---Go!" said Sam as he looked at his watch.

The two techs slapped a high-five in the air and bounded from the room.

Sam went into the data control room and looked at the twenty colonists assembled around their workstations.

"O.K. folks I hope you are ready. It's about to get really busy around here. We go live starting tomorrow!"

Over the course of the next two days, the EGG/FWG software gently inserted itself across the globe. Pushing and probing its way into the servers of every cell phone network and remote storage provider. Government and private, independent closed secure (or so they thought) network firewalls, melted like butter under the hacking barrage of the two Tylers. The boys were in their element, kicking butt and taking names as one after another, the resistance was pushed aside.

The network connected world went about its daily routine tapping keyboards, merrily clicking mice and swiping screens. They played games, they Tweeted and texted and updated their 'Walls;" and all the while, unwittingly broadcasting to Tibet a window into the depths of their character that was being crunched, dissected and compared against benchmark data that would determine their fate.

Out of the giga-bytes of individual personal data flowing into the Lhasa facility, for only a few----an email, a text and a form letter went out. But, only to a very few.

By the time Ravi and his passengers arrived in Lhasa driving a 2003 Mercedes Benz twenty-passenger tour conversion van complete with Korean characters emblazoned on the side; selection was already in full swing.

"I know your anger, I know your dreams--I've been everything you want to be.

Oh, I'm the cult of personality"

-Living Colour

CHAPTER 50

Washington D. C.

The White House Situation Room was buzzing with activity. Added to the usual list of characters, were the Director of NASA and the Presidents Media Advisor. The Chancellor of Germany, British Prime Minister and Israeli Prime Minister were already seated at the table with the Director of Homeland Security. As the group was milling around and getting re-acquainted, the monitors were tuned to CNN and the BBC with the sound off; as the continual ticker tape headline banners annoyingly rolled across the bottom of the screens. Both monitors picked up in tandem;

"SPECIAL REPORT.....UN Security Council passes Free Nation of Tibet's request for dedicated shipping lanes and Airway Flight paths for the transportation of international relief to affected areas around the world. The UN Secretary General thanked the Tibetan Delegates and praised Tibet for their tireless efforts and good works."

The Vice President and the NSC Director had just taken their seats when the President of the United States entered the room.

"No need to get up---please stay seated we have a lot to cover."

"At great risk to all of our reputations, credibility---and our abilities to hold office or ever get elected again; we made a joint decision here last month to take a big chance. Well, I am happy to inform all of you that our risk is paying off! Today we're going to run through some of the successes, and review the remaining challenges, of our efforts to disarm the negative Genesis-Kush impact to national security and global unrest. I would like to hear from the Media Advisors office first and then NSC and Homeland Security departments------Gentlemen?"

"Mr. President, esteemed guests and colleagues, the following is a brief breakdown of the information, and information flow, that we've been feeding to the media and the public in our respective countries. Starting with the initial introduction through the NASA interview on National Public Radio; we've continued to leak tidbits of information across the broadcast news network. Frankly, it doesn't take much; the networks are so hungry for news, that all seem capable of taking a single news story and multiplying it like rabbits in to four days of media created commentary. They 'make' more news than we ever give them to start with. They make our job much easier."

"We've built off of the original NPR platform and have a steady stream of leaks going out that seek to support the efficacy of the space drive being operational in the near future. At the same time that we've been feeding out technical tidbits, we've been promoting discussions on the social networks. By participating in various 'blogs', discussion groups and religious forums that have wide internet exposure, we're slowly but surely guiding the tone of the discussions."

"Our message is one of 'hope'. First we're dangling the carrot of the reality of space travel being accessible to the masses-----in the near future—not some dream; and then pushing out into the media the individual social benefit of having an opportunity to better ones condition as a colonist, or even better, on a population reduced Earth. With all the natural resources and land area available by having two worlds at man's disposal, much of the innate fears of how much there is to go around starts to go away. A little misinformation is going a long way. We plant a seed and the media runs with it, only to be picked up by the social networks, then it's global in days. And, it seems to be having the desired effect."

"I will now turn it over to my colleagues at NSC and Homeland Security to map some of the results." With that, the President's Media Advisor took his seat as the Director of Homeland Security stood up.

"The positive media campaign seems to have taken some of the steam out of the doomsday promoters. It's not immediate and it is not, by any means, swaying the full blown fanatics, but it is having a progressive positive effect. '

"The 'hope' message has gained popularity over the doomsday message. As a direct result, we're seeing a reduction in incidents that normally have led to violent confrontations between disparate ideological groups. The mainstream religions have backed off of some of their initial knee jerk-jump on the bandwagon,

Genesis-Kush -time to repent programs. The fanatic faith-based initiatives have shifted moderately in their positions, but we're not seeing the same support for their views via mass membership increases, or large sums of money flowing in at the rates that we saw prior to our efforts. The threat is not gone, but we are gaining some amount of relief and quieting of the insanity."

"Unfortunately, we're not getting the same positive results with the extremist groups that operate within and outside our borders. They are looking for ways to promote their agendas and exploit for their own benefit the shift in sentiment. They seem to be attacking from every direction by fomenting fear about the original Genesis-Kush doomsday promotions that gained them ground; now coupling it with fresh suspicion and conspiracy theories. They are still pushing an agenda about a Western driven plot to exclude them from any potential benefits that might be denied them through Western control. I will stay behind to deal with any individual questions after the Director of NSC's and other agency reports. Thank you."

The Director of the NSC rose to begin his report.

"I concur with the report just tendered by Homeland Security and have both domestic and International data to support it. If you would, please direct your attention to the monitors around the room. I will begin in the Middle East and move through Western and Eastern Europe. We have some Asian data but there has been a real crackdown on media access and sharing of information that far exceeds the limited access we were already challenged with........"

After an hour of visual and technical stimulation eyelids were drooping, and the attendees were hyper fidgeting with the Presidential pens and notepads provided at each seat. The reports droned on in continual support that there was a consensus. Their measures were working, and the world was returning to the level of chaos that had previously been deemed acceptable. The last report finished; the Vice-President moved to close the meeting. There were no dissenting opinions on the suggestion, and all rose to leave, stuffing ample White House office supplies into their briefcases and purses as souvenirs.

BOOK II

"I don't care if it rains or freezes--'Long as I got
my plastic Jesus--Riding on the dashboard of my car"

-George Cromarty and Ed Rush

CHAPTER 51

San Francisco California

The four men were creating their own traffic jam in the aisles at the Walmart Superstore on Dubuque Avenue in San Francisco. The rotund, nut brown complexioned man pushing the cart, kept clipping the heels of his three companions walking in front of him. The slow-moving trio in front of the cart kept halting in staccato steps as they stopped to admire the wares on the shelves. Skilled and determined Walmart shoppers careened around the quartet as they tried to avoid an aisle pile up that might delay their getting into the perfect check- out line in time.

"That's ridiculous!" said Yeshua.

"I think they're pretty funny said S.G. After all, I've been adorning back yard gardens, fish ponds and the occasional door stoop for years."

They were standing in front of the Bible Story Action Figure display not quite knowing what to make of it. Yeshua reached in and picked up a 'Bobble-Head' Jesus and flicked the head into action.

"Its just plain disrespectful. The least they could try and do is get the skin and hair right for once. My mother, God rest her soul, was not a blue-eyed Scandinavian you know!"

Moshe had picked up a 14" replica of himself holding his staff high in the air with his fist raised towards the heaven with the other.

"Angry, very angry looking. Why is it that they always try to show me at my worst?"

Moh was looking up and down the shelves, moving Samson and Delilah out of the way, pushing John the Baptist into Pope Pius the X. Figures tumbled over as he worked his way across the shelves; all the way over to where Yoda and Chewbacca announced the start of the Star Wars figures. He stepped back scratching his head.

"Well, I don't see anything that looks like me. Maybe they are sold out."

Moshe, S.G. and Yeshuah looked at each other.

"You tell him"

"No, you tell him"

"Oh alright," said S.G."

"Moh, if they stuck one of you up on the shelf, there'd be a four day riot that would make the Watts riots look like a Kumbaya camp fire."

"Yeh, OK, maybe your right." Moh said dejectedly.

Into the cart went one Bobble Head Jesus and the 14" Angry Moses. S.G. moved aside the four Memory Foam cushions, and his new blue 'yoga-mat', as they moved to the checkout lanes.

The men paid and headed out to the parking lot to wait for Ravi to pick them up.

S.G. said, "I know I agreed to this, but I have to warn you guys. I rode with this kid in that Tesla thing from Las Vegas to Palo Alto and just about lost my lunch."

"How bad can it be?" said Moshe. I rode on one of these things with Yeshua the last time I was his guest on Gradis-2 and it wasn't so bad."

As they were pushing toward the rows of parked cars, a deep base sub-woofer thump came from their left, as the Korean Tours van headed toward them with a friendly beep of its horn and a waving Ravi smiling at the Prophets through the windshield. The thump of the base started to vibrate their bodies the closer the van bore down on them. As it rolled to a stop right outside the parking lot shopping cart pavilion, the doors opened up to blast the four with the full force and effect of L'il Wayne.

The four men stepped back with no intention of coming any closer to the din coming out of the van. Ravi capitulated reluctantly and turned the volume down all the way.

"Oh come on guys, we won't blast it he whole way to Lhasa, promise."

Inside the van sat Sharon and Alyssa, who waved at the four Prophets. Ravi jumped down and helped them stow their purchases in the luggage rack and said.

"Ok, who wants to ride on the dash and keep us safe----just kidding, just kidding!"

"Seat belts everyone first Maglev bus to Lhasa is ready for its maiden voyage. We're heading up the coast toward Muir Beach and then making a hard left out to sea. We're going to stop at the Mountain Thunder Coffee Plantation, Kona the Big Island tonight, and after that a bit of a haul on to Calcutta tomorrow at day break. Elon re-fit the window and doors seals and we have air deflection shields that give us a push to a maximum cruising speed of 325mph. Our cruising altitude will be at a constant 18" above the surface of whatever is below us. Any questions of your captain?"

"Ravi you sure you know what you are doing?" said Alyssa

"Pretty sure, I had the best training available on Gradis-2 . I've run this baby through its paces a few times out in the desert and off the coast at night. It might get squirrely over near the China Sea, but we can out run anything on the water and we're too low to be picked up by radar. I think we can swing it—no sweat."

Moshe said, "Just keep the music low please, I'm going to take a nap."

S.G. handed the other three Prophets their Memory Foam cushions, which were gratefully placed under their behinds. Yeshua reached into his bag and handed Ravi the 'Bobble-Head Jesus.'

"Just pull off the plastic strip on the bottom. The directions say it'll stick to any clean surface."

Ravi took the figurine out of his hand; pulled the strip, and pushed the figure down on to the center of the dash. Looking back at his passengers he gave the thumbs-up sign and headed north on the 101 towards Highway 1. Ravi intended to sneak off the highway and hit the Maglev for a shortcut to the coast, one that only Maglev made possible.

CHAPTER 52

Dr. E. J. Camlala walked into his office on the campus of Humboldt State University. He tossed the pile of mail on to his desk where it joined about five months of debris. He walked around the messy surface that rarely showed the exposed wooden desktop to the occasional guest to his office, and settled into his chair. Camlala started to leaf through the messages that the department administrative assistant had slipped under the corner of his phone. He smiled when he saw the two from "Dr. Najir and Dr. Klein. Camlala was rested and relaxed after a three day rafting and camping trip on the Smith River. He had started at the head waters with two old college buddy's and they had rafted, fished and camped their way down from Oregon to California. Every evening was spent pitching tents in private and remote groves of magnificent redwood glens. The experience had humbled the trio in to a sense of relaxation and calm. He was sorry to see it end, but well reinforced to face the neglected work on his desk.

Out of the corner of his eye, a splash of golden yellow and maroon peeked out from the splayed stack of mail that he casually launched onto his desk. With a curious squint, Camlala reached over and released the single envelope and pulled it free of the pile. The envelope was of fine handcrafted paper and dyed in an unusually vibrant swirl of gold and maroon designs. Flipping it over in his hand, he saw the senders address: "Nation of Free Tibet -----Bureau of Special Offers and Promotions"

With a shrug that gave a resigned 'what the heck', he popped the seal on the letter and removed the sharp looking paper and opened it up.

Dr. E J Camlala, You have been randomly selected, and we are pleased to announce that you E J CAMLALA are:

Certified Prize Winner Number: CZ318B11JT26

You have won an all expenses paid, two-week vacation to the New Free Nation of Tibet!! Plus, $5,000 dollars in Resort Dollars spending money! No hitches, no gimmicks! All you have to do to qualify is register and report on one of the below dates to the Port of San Francisco---Tibetan Office of Tourism---New Tibet:

Your personal Cruise Dates are:

April 15, 2012---April 21, 2012----May 15,2012----June 15,2012

Your trip includes an all expenses paid four-day cruise on our luxury high speed Tibetan Princess, Tibetan Paradise, Himalayan Wind, or Garhuda Wings cruise ship.

Attendance at a four-day resort seminar once you arrive in Tibet is required where you will be presented with a seminar on Tibetan Life and a potential purchase opportunity. The trip and the $5,000.00 are yours to keep without any requirement that participants commit to, or make a purchase at this time. No purchase is necessary.

To activate your award and schedule your departure date please do one of the following within 5 days of receipt of this letter. Please have your Certified Prize Winner Number handy as you will need this to register.

To Register by Phone:

1-888-TIBETTRIP (842-8747)

To Register online:

Go to www.tibettripawards.com

And follow the prompts for registration.

Peace be with you

Kale Shoo,

Dolma Sherap—Tibetan Rewards Events Director--The Nation of Free Tibet Bureau of Special Offers and Promotions

Camlala put the letter down on the desk and tapped a drum roll in celebration. His good fortune just wouldn't let up! What a year it was, first the $250K score for the Hubble grant; then the Genesis-Kush discovery. A little fame and glory and now this! An all expenses paid trip to Tibet! He grabbed his cell and picked up the phone message slip with Sam Klein's number on it. He saw the message light blinking red on his cell and took a look at the texts. A new message was listed:

YOU WON CALL TIBETAN REWARDS FOR DETAILS- 888-842-8747

He chuckled as he dialed Sam's cell number. Sam picked up on the third ring.

"E. J. How the hell are you? I left a message for you the other day and hadn't heard back. What's going on?"

"Hey, check it out, I just won an all expenses paid trip to---get this---TIBET! Can you believe that shit! How lucky am I, or what!"

"No way, well how about this E. J., I'm already in Tibet and thinking of staying. I have an apartment in Lhasa and a job at a research facility; all in the last thirty days. I've been trying to call you to tell you about it but you don't answer your freakin' phone or return your messages!"

"Oh man, I haven't been around. I just came back from a two week camping trip that was superior! Fresh caught trout and salmon out of the Smith and a little class II rafting. Not a soul around but us and the Giant Sequoias. Awesome ten days. Sorry I wasn't around to get the messages."

"So you are in Tibet. Where is Ravi?"

"Ravi's on his way here. He's in Palo Alto working on a job with Space X and some research that they have going. Pretty cool stuff from what Ravi has shared with me. So tell me about the dates that you are coming. I've heard a little bit about this promotion thing through the grapevine here in Lhasa."

"Well they gave me four alternate dates; the first one is April 15th. I have so many unused sick and vacation days left that I'm tempted just to pack up and do the 15th and the hell to getting back to work. I'm only teaching one class and you guys graduated early, so I don't have any doctoral students on my sponsor program. I'm free and good to go."

"Cool, E. J., Listen I'll email you all the contact information and directions to my house here. When you get to Calcutta text or call me, and I'll meet you when you get into Tibet."

"Yeh, I don't know what it's all about but I think I have to do like a time-share seminar to get the vacation bucks, but I'll let you know when I find out more. Tell Ravi I said hey and will call him soon."

"Alright, see ya later."

Sam put down the phone and gave little thanks that E. J. had made the cut.

All across the Earth in multiple languages, the maroon and saffron gold handcrafted sweepstakes letters were going out. Each letter followed up with text and email notices that would keep prompting the qualified recipients to respond until the last transport date occurred. None of them knew just how important it really was for them to register. Tossing the pretty handcrafted award notice in the circular file or deleting the text or email, an accidental hitting of the junk mail/spam file, was as good as signing their own death warrant.

Sam wrapped up his day in the office, said hello and good-bye to the rotating day and evening shift data collection and selection staff that were entering and leaving the facility, as he made for the door. It had been a long day and he was whipped. His cell phone chimed temple bells announcing a text, he looked and he fished his cell from his pocket.

There was a text from Ravi saying,

"We're here and I have a little surprise for you!" Sam looked forward to seeing his partner and stepped up the pace out the door.

CHAPTER 53

Lhasa Tibet

Sam pulled his Tesla Model S Signature four door into the Tourist Parking area at Norbilunkga Palace. Two spaces over was a Korean Tours van that looked like it had been through a dust storm and then some. The van logo was barely readable through the grime covering the sides; it was encrusted with a collection of salt spray mixed with the red dust of the desert; it needed more than a bath to remedy the situation. Sam walked through the courtyard and made his way toward the monastery; he was looking forward to a quiet night catching up with Ravi. He wondered what kind of surprise his friend had for him as he mounted the steps and entered through the large doors being opened by the saffron and maroon robed monks tending the entrance.

"Surprise!"

Alyssa jumped into his arms and gave him a big hug and a kiss as Ravi and Sharon stood in the back ground waiting their turn to greet him. All five Prophets were standing patiently by.

The Dalai Lama said, "Let's retire to my private quarters so that we can meet and talk freely, shall we."

The entourage made its way toward the back of the palace with Sam and Alyssa holding hands and whispering as they kept in step with the others. Ravi and Sharon looked a bit red-eyed and bedraggled from the ordeal of the marathon two-day trip across the Pacific. They had much to tell about their travels that had been less than a walk in the park for all. Only the Prophets seemed to be able to shrug it all off as uneventful.

"I can't believe you are here," Sam said with relief. "I didn't think you were going to come until the end. I had every intention of having to travel back to Las Vegas to see you."

"I couldn't stay away; this whole process is so fraught with emotion. If I am not immersed in the project, then I'm left with too much time to think of the enormity of the 'end'. While we worked on the program, I guess I was able to put it away, but as soon as it was done, I was lost. My first thought was to get to Tibet. Get to you, and try and find a place within the Colony to put my mind and skills to use.

Sam looked Alyssa up and down smiling at his good fortune, "Best idea you could have had. I was finding it hard to have a Skype relationship. That was not working at all for me. As far as help being needed here, it's a no brainer. There's so much to do and such little time that you have no idea what a contribution you can make. The selection teams started running three shifts with 24-7 coverage as soon as the EGG/FWG software went global. We need all the hands we can get over there."

Alyssa kissed him on the cheek and said, "I think the only way for me to get through this is to be busy non-stop. And, if you and I are doing it together, then it all seems right. Sharon figured that she could put her counseling skills to use with all of the stress and pressures of people relocating and leaving loved ones behind, she figured she had plenty to offer as well. You can't really say there was a future for us in Vegas, now can you? The only futures I know of right now are here at Tibet Colony and up there on Kush."

Sam looked over at Sharon and said, "We have a small mental health center being set up at a building near the research labs. The director over there's a guy who used to work at the Menninger Clinic. Maybe you can go see him tomorrow and find out how you can help."

Sharon glowed her porcelain smile and said, "I'd like that. I feel the same way as Alyssa, the day we finished up the download, and the distribution and program maintenance went into your team's hands; we were like two fish out of water. I tried to go to class and just sat there in a fog wondering what the hell was I doing there. I mean, I was sitting in a class that was a pre-requisite for a lecture program that isn't even going to exist in seven months, being taught by a Professor that's going to be dead. Hell, the school isn't even going to exist. It didn't make much sense to stick around. Coming here was the logical choice. Driving with Captain Ravi at the helm------ maybe not so logical."

"So tell me about the trip getting here. What's the Maglev like?"

"The Maglev is awesome. The speeds we were going were easier to handle at night. As soon as day broke, and we had a reference point to gauge speed and really see our movement over the water; it was downright scary." Said Alyssa.

Sharon stepped in, "Then we got just past the Philippines and we blew past a Chinese naval patrol. That got really hairy, they scrambled some aircraft and we set down on Bancalan Island, south of the Philippines but, still in the China Sea, and hid on the beach. Ravi backed into a grove of breadfruit trees, and we sat it out for about two hours until we stopped hearing jets and helicopters. I thought we were done for."

S.G. said, "That's my second and last trip with that young man. I'm done with mechanized travel. If the Boss isn't transporting me, then I'm doing it on foot from now on."

"I'm with you, S.G." said Moshe. "Its loud, it's uncomfortable, and unstable."

"I like it!" said Yeshuah. "Granted the conversion vehicles are a little rough compared to Maglevs that are engineered and designed for the drive, but the movement and speed is pretty much the same as the Gradis-2 model. The main difference is the conversion models sound like they're going to rattle apart at high speeds."

"Oh, come on. It wasn't that bad. Other than the adjustment over the high seas and the one airfoil blowing off I got everyone here safe. The Chinese navy never had a chance of finding us. We had our plastic Jesus on the dash!"

The Dalai Lama put his hands together and said. "Let us discuss where we are right now, and were we need to get to in preparing for the first waves of Colonists. I have some concerns that are offset by great faith in all of your efforts. I'd like to air those concerns though and be comfortable that we're all following in the proper direction."

His Holiness continued, "Transportation of building materials and stores of food are going very well both from Calcutta to here, and then again, from here to the construction sites of the colonial villages. As far as colonial candidates go, we have enough EGG/FWG facilities in place to test them on entry. If we get a positive hit, we're sending them to orientation for settlement. If we get a negative hit, we offer them a seven-day visa and then pay for their transit back to their native land."

"Through a series of United Nation sponsored and diplomatic efforts, we've secured a very open visa program with all nations. Tibet is such a non-threat, that basically registering for the Travel and Rewards program is all that's required to get a visa. By the time the sending countries start to realize that the travelers are overstaying, we'll be so close to the end that it really won't matter anymore."

"Since we're currently dealing mostly with people that are gravitating to Tibet as part of a prior devotional connection, and a desire to be part of the rebuilding of our free nation, we're enjoying a high level of positive hits. The amazing thing is the high level of education and valuable skills that they are bringing to the effort. Unfortunately, the volume of people and materials is unwieldy with the resources we currently have at our disposal."

Sam raised his hand to interject. "Your Holiness if I may. The logistics get much more complicated as the number of Colonist increases when the first cruise ships start running on April 15th. Ravi, what we need is to set up the Maglev production and research program here in Tibet. Is there a chance that Elon would come here?"

"I don't know. His presence in the States is so instrumental to what we've accomplished so far I don't know if we can afford to have the management hic cup it would cause for him to pull up shop. The first group of Maglev conversions is coming in tomorrow by air transport; so you will have a small operational fleet at your disposal for speeding things up between Calcutta and here. I know its not much, but it's a start." said Ravi.

"Why don't you assess what it would take to put in place a Tibet Maglev program and work on that with Musk, and we'll circle back in three days to see what it entails? Meanwhile, I'll work on getting task team placements for Sharon and Alyssa tomorrow, and then help you with our logistical issues. The Prophets will focus on the big picture and keep our butts out of trouble------I hope!"

The Dalai Lama said, "Let's retire to the dining area and feast our good fortune and futures. Come my friends, we can't be all business all the time. Both the soul and the stomach need planning and care as well."

They all followed along to the dining hall. Entering the room, the tables were set with steaming platters overflowing with exotic dishes. Each culinary wonder was giving off aromas that spiked everyone's appetites. The food blended the cuisines native to China and India with the unique cultural essence of the Tibetan people. The result was like nothing the American crew had ever experienced, and they ate heartily without being quite sure exactly what they were eating. Keeping it a mystery was probably a benefit for the pickiest members of the group.

The guests enjoyed themselves late in to the evening and then bade each other good night. The well-fed group was individually led from the room by Temple monks assigned to each as guides while guests of the Dalai Lama. As the two monks led Sam and Alyssa down the maze of hallways to the sleeping quarters, Sam turned to Alyssa and said.

"Remember, 'Dharma Suite', South hall, fourth door on the left." He said with a wink and a nod as he squeezed her hand and headed in the opposite direction. Sam kept glancing back as they were led away, catching Alyssa's eye as she did the same. They had much to talk about.

"The magical mystery tour is dying to take you away, Dying to take you away, take you today".

-Beatles

CHAPTER 54

Tibetan Colonies—June 21 2012

As promised, on April 15th 2012, the first four cruise lines arrived at the port of Calcutta.

Utilizing the dedicated and secure Land and Sea shipping lanes that the UN had granted Tibet, the three and four-day trips had gone off without a hitch. Leaving out of London, Stockholm, San Francisco and New York; the voyages brought in 16,583 previously qualified Colonials to Lhasa. On schedule and according to plan, by June, the full-scale transportation program was up and running.

People from every nation were making their way to Tibet with their registration packages in hand. By any means available, the excited winners traveled overland, by commercial air, and by way of the weekly Tibetan Cruise Line tours. All were ferried to Lhasa to begin orientation.

The Tibetan Cruise passengers were tired upon arrival, and a bit confused by the requirement that they be secured below deck by nine-pm each evening. All hatches were buttoned down at night before the full speed Maglev kicked in; blowing them across the globe at 383 MPH.

The lock-down policy ensured that Tibetan Cruises would avoid the embarrassment of an untimely accident; such as having passengers sucked off the deck at cyclone wind speeds, and dumped into the sea. While locked below deck without access to the outside, no one felt the impact of the Maglev drive, nor really was able to appreciate the uniqueness of the new mode of speedy travel.

The onboard cruise accommodations were comfortable, yet sparse, with most of the amenities geared toward living room type relaxation activities. Tibetan Cruise Lines did not offer the typical high level entertainment of the opulently appointed commercial cruise lines that most were familiar with. To keep everyone happy, half-day excursion stops had been made in the Azores, Madagascar, Hawaii and Sri Lanka along the way. Dropping in just outside territorial waters with the Maglev off, they steamed into port under conventional power. The half-day break seemed to refuel the passengers and allow for a smattering of remote, pre-qualified colonist pickups to add to the group. That being said, all were safe and looking forward to their continued all expenses paid Tibet experience.

Upon arrival the Tibetan guests, as promised, were given orientation seminars that progressed through various stages. Ultimately, the attendee's attention was skillfully guided to the fact: that purchasing a Tibetan 'Time-Share' was not the product being sold here in Lhasa. With multi-linqual translator's headsets handed out at the door to each seminar; the attendees entered the auditoriums anticipating a sales pitch, and receiving something very different indeed.

Orientation Seminar-one, 'The State of Your World', was the first stop. Attendees were segregated by geographic region; then broken down into smaller groups. The seminars were customized to focus regionally on their particular portion of the globe. Though each of the seminars started with a world wide overview of the issues, the subject matter then ratcheted down to a subjective and familiar regional focus, catered to the group. Heart strings were tugged at hard, and stark realities were driven home.

The seminar started with a global overview of each area of the world, and broke down the blatant gathered evidence proving how deeply the quality of life had deteriorated over time in a region. Stressing how damaged and unsustainable the natural resources had been rendered, and how violence and strife were destroying the moral fabric of society, the heads were reeling on their necks. A question and answer session was offered at the end of each seminar hosted by guest panels. The panels always had two or three notable regional celebrities from the entertainment, media and political world, to help drive home the credibility with the particular group.

Once the Tibetan Rewards winners were finished with Seminar-one, with its tragic presentation on global and regional distress, the groups were combined once again and moved to a massive IMAX auditorium. Seminar-two, 'Welcome to New Tibet', was an incredibly moving panoramic display in full IMAX formatted surround view that captured the senses of the audience.

Narrated by the Dalai Lama himself, his quiet sonorous voice drifting from the speakers, calmed the audience into a state of serene attentiveness. Crisp aromas of Tibetan spring and summer were strategically atomized and dispersed through the ventilation system in the room; all timed in concert with the subject matter being displayed. Starting with a dynamic display on the natural beauty and wonders of the Himalayas and surrounding area, the guests were washed down rushing rivers, floated across the tops of the Himalayan Mountain Range and guided through smokey valley forests of old growth timber. As if they had strapped on their rappelling gear, put on their skis, or jumped into their speedos for a white water adventure; the IMAX participants were given an electronic eco-tour that was un-paralleled in experience. The sense of being in, and one with the picture was felt by all.

Moving from the natural wonders to the nascent village life of the New Tibet communities establishing themselves throughout the Tibetan country side; the benefits of being a part of this new approach to a Colonial society were driven home. Stressing the quality of the diversity of the population's education and skills, coupled with the broad scope of the relocation and settlement support program; something for everyone was identified by the Dalai Lama.

The Dalai Lama's voice trailed away, and the narration process was picked up by international celebrities and notables from industry, medicine, science and education; each narrator in turn, gave the attendees sensory enhanced mini-tours of their new state of the art facilities and centers, springing up over the Tibetan landscape. Whether one was a ditch-digger or physicist, housewife or PhD, the narrators kept stressing their welcome invitation to all of the attendees. There were jobs aplenty in Tibet, and unique opportunities to participate in. What could be more exciting than creating a new society? All levels of skill were needed and all were invited to participate. This new world was offered up as their golden opportunity.

The audience was beside itself with excitement as the technological breakthroughs of the Maglev and hydrogen fusion power supplies were explained. Step by step, the positive impacts on transportation, convenience and the inherent ecological windfall that Maglev brought to the human condition, was presented on the IMAX screen. When the screen showed them how they were to travel around the Tibetan landscape for the remainder of their stay, moving from place to place Maglev style, the murmurs of excitement rose in anticipation.

The IMAX presentation closed with an announcement that following the production, each member of the audience would be able to pick from a list of villages and areas of interest to customize their tour of Tibet. As the lights came back on, the excited audience was guided to the individual booths lining the interior walls of the auditorium. Each booth was manned by proud Tibetan villagers and professionals wishing to share their piece of the New Tibet experience with their potential fellow Colonials. Attendees gravitated towards the Agrarian Resource Village, East Miami, Genesis City and South Kiev, among others, to meet with the representatives and schedule their stays.

Once selected, the visitors were given a breakdown of the next day's activities. In the morning, the attendees would have two hours of elective personalized seminars based on their area of interest. In addition to the electives, there would be a mandatory presentation that was entitled 'Why Me?', which would be their final seminar, and complete their obligatory requirements to gain their $5000.00 dollars in Tibetan vacation bucks. The Tibetan dollars were non transferable but were legal currency anywhere within the borders of New Tibet, or when traveling on Tibetan Cruise Lines. All of the attendess were anxious to be on their way with pockets laden heavy with free money to spend. All were looking forward to a start to their tours of the Tibetan sites and scenes; all, previously dangled like carrots on sticks during their orientation process.

Tired and overwhelmed with new information to process, and just as many questions left unanswered; it was time for the travelers to call it a day and retire to their hotel rooms for the night.

The next morning, the Tibetan Rewards groups were roused early and Maglev shuttled to the Tibet Orientation Center. It was a cool morning that was blossoming into a bright sunny Lahsa summer day. Once exiting the MagLev shuttles, the various groups milled around meeting new friends and trading notes about their experience so far. At 7 am sharp, a gong sounded to announce the start of the first morning seminars.

A large group of visitors originating out of the Port of Miami was making its way to the Colonial Life seminar. The tour director had them wait while he went looking for a Spanish interpreter to work with the group.

A boisterous contingent of Russians disembarked from one of the transports talking loudly, and heading over to the Ballet and Orchestral Arts Village line. The men were all wearing track and warm-up suits and sporting oversized designer sunglasses; the woman had teased hair, and inspite of the heat, were still trying to get the last days of wear out of their fur coats. Mornings were cool in Lhasa, but it warmed up quickly in the early summer months as the day moved on.

Tibetan villagers, both native and new colonials, moved around and socialized with the groups making them welcome, showing some local wares, and offering drinks and refreshments to those entering and leaving the seminars. The whole atmosphere was pleasant and had the feeling of a large central quad at a major University. People gathered and exchanged notes on this seminar and that, passing suggestions to others along the way as they made their way down their list of elective presentations.

At the far end of the quad, was a separate pavilion much bigger in size than the IMAX Theater. The wide bank of 'Entrance Only' marked doors, had an electronic marquee above with--'Why Me?' in massive letters over the top of a flickering rolling digital sign that stated----- 'next showing---9am.'. The 'Why Me?' pavilion exited on the rear of the building and right into the waiting line of Maglev shuttles. The Maglev's were painted a wide range of colors and adorned with the names and symbols that had been adopted by the various Tibetan Colonial villages. The participants looked longingly at the waiting transports knowing that once they made it to the entrance doors, only three hours of final obligatory participation stood between them and the rear exit to freedom. The promise of an escape out the back, a hop onto a transport and into the Tibetan wilderness, was all that kept them going.

This sunny Lhasa afternoon found the Dalai Lama and Moses deep in thought as they took a break between the one-pm and start of the two-pm 'Why Me?' seminars.

"I can't believe that lady from Dobrovnik, it's just a cat. What a whiner. Is she really willing to die over a---a---cat?" said Moses.

"Moses, you are lost in the fact that it is 'just a cat'. You're applying the same intolerance of thinking that got us here in the first place. Though God has chosen to deny the cat salvation, the representative symbolic message is being lost on the people. The cat represents the self centered will and ego issues that when applied to man, deny access to colonial salvation. Conversely, the people see the cat as just another one of the innocents that they unconditionally love. The love they are expressing for that animal is part and parcel of why they made the cut to begin with; it's why they are a colonial candidate. It's part of the whole that triggered their positive EGG/FWG hit in the first place."

Moses continued emphatically punctuating with his finger. "Look Tenzin, I hear your logic, but I don't think in his present state of mind, that God is going to start granting special dispensations for cats. He doesn't like them, and that's that." Moses's mood shifted more positive and a smile broadly lit his face.

"How about the nine to eleven seminar this morning? That was my highpoint of the day! Did you see Jimmy and Rosalyn Carter come around once Yeshua came into say hello! I was about out of tricks, and they were still hemming and hawing back and forth. Yeshua walks into the room and pulls them aside for two minutes; the next thing you know, they're asking if they can sponsor and run a village! Then they grabbed Sam, wanting to know who they could talk to in the agriculture village about peanut propagation in Tibetan soil. Great turn aound."

"We have about ten minutes and then the next group is heading into the orientation pavilion. Let's grab a cup of tea and get ready."

"...And during the few moments that we have left, we want to have just an off-the-cuff chat between you and me -- us. We want to talk right down to earth in a language that everybody here can easily understand."

-Malcom X

CHAPTER 55

The line of anxious Tibetan Rewards winners was already queued up and creating a stacking problem at the 'Why Me?' auditorium. Moshe and Tenzin slipped in the back entrance cradling paper cups filled with steaming tea. The two Prophets paused to take a quick drink through the sippy tops, before settling into their seats at the raised forward platform in the room. Sam, Yeshua and Moh came in through the back entrance as well, and greeted the two as they found their seats.

A group of traditionally robed palace monks opened the entrance doors; scanning each person's ticket as they walked through the turnstiles. The last monk in the path of each entrance aisle, ink stamped the back of each entrant's hand with a pattern in the shape of a lotus flower. Ushers guided the participants to their seats with pen light flashlights piercing the subdued interior lighting like lightning bugs swirling from all directions in the building.

The interior of the auditorium was domed and had a capacity to seat twenty-five thousand participants at a time. The seating was set up in a similar fashion to a Planetarium. The mechanical reclining benches could have just as easily fit in at Walt Disney World on a high tech ride. The ceiling was painted black and there was a system of IMAX screens around the perimeter of the dome. The screens were massive; starting at the dome springline, and shedding down the vertical face of the auditorium walls.

As the last of the guests were trickling in, the lights dimmed further; a spot played over the raised platform at the forward area of the room. The seating adjusted mechanically to provide the best view from each direction as Sam stepped up on to the center of the stage.

"Good afternoon and welcome to the New Free Nation of Tibet. For those of you that don't know me or recognize me, I'm Dr. Samuel Klein, one of the astronomers that discovered Genesis and Kush. On behalf of His Holiness the Dalai Lama, I wish to welcome all of you to Tibet, and begin the last seminar before you start the land tour portion of your free vacation to our exciting nation!" The room erupted in applause. "Please, please the quicker we can get started, the faster I can get you good folks on your way!" The room settled to silent in record time.

"For the next three hours, we're going to answer the question that I am sure has been on all of your minds. From the minute you opened your gold and maroon envelopes. Right after you answered your emails and texts from Tibetan Rewards, I'm sure that in addition to celebrating your good luck, you wondered, 'Why Me?' Please buckle your seatbelts provided on your benches, and give myself and our esteemed group of speakers your undivided attention. Sit back, relax and listen, as we present to you what I'm sure will be a life changing learning experience for all of you today."

With the advent of a deep gong and lowing of Temple horns, the lights went out. Just as the room darkened, at the apex of the dome, a star appeared and exploded in a burst of color. The mass of light, in a three-dimensional display that filled the upper area below the ceiling of the dome, appeared to move downward toward the viewer's up-turned faces. As the mass swirled, it began to form and take shape into the once familiar vision of the Crab Nebula. The iridescent mass took form, and continued to drop closer and closer to the reclining observers. The brilliant display hovered above, appearing as if one could reach up and touch the multi-colored bands of scintillating cosmic dust.

Suddenly, as if drawn into a vacuum, the Crab Nebula display drew upward toward the ceiling and exploded in a bang of light. In its place, rotating in a massive form was the spinning orb of Kush lit by the gentle sunlight of Genesis. The object filled the capacity of space within the underside of the dome, and appeared as solid as the terra firma below the crowd's feet.

The oohs and aahhs emitting from the patrons, sounded like a gathering at a fourth of July pyrotechnics display; resonating in timed response, as each thump of the mortar built to the crescendo of a finale. With each change of Kush's position, the surface features blended in the light of Genesis. At each showing of Kush's magnificent natural features; the crowd moaned its approval and emotional participation. Sam knew he had hooked them. Now he and the prophets just needed to reel them in.

"What you are looking at is an actual physical view of Kush. This incredible display is being brought to you for your viewing pleasure, through technology provided by a power much greater than ourselves. What you are gazing at is not computer generated, is not a holographic display or some fabulous new 3-D technology. The fact that you are witnessing what you are seeing, and about to hear what is being offered to you is only possible through direct divine intervention. This is not technology-- it's a miracle."

The room began a low murmur, but all were so mesmerized by the impact of the display, that they remained transfixed and motionless as Sam continued.

"Why Me?" is a question that Dr. Ravi Najir and I asked ourselves daily upon our happenstance discovery of Genesis and Kush. 'Why Me?' is the question that you folks have on your minds as well. The answer to the question is that all of us, myself included, have been selected by God to participate in populating this wonderful new world, Kush." Sam paused as the first bold participant shouted out---"Yeah, Right" . Sam continued. "We'll answer all of your questions at the end of the presentation. Please let me continue."

The man seated next to the vocal skeptic, gently shushed his neighbor, who then settled back into his seat shaking his head.

"Each time one of you has accessed one of your personal electronic devices over the course of the last few months, starting in March and April of this year; individual data unique to each of you, was downloaded and analyzed. The criteria for this analysis were defined by God and you have all met the parameters of that search. You all share a common group of character traits that fit God's plan for the ultimate base population to inhabit this new world. You have the qualities of, being open minded, tolerant of others to a fault. Your egos are kept easily in check. Each of you is responsible and uses your ability to seek spiritual guidance from whatever source at your disposal, before applying your free or self will to your next action. These qualities are so rare in the population of Earth, that only about .01 percent of the population meets the full compliment of traits as a package."

"All of these things, these traits that you share, the devine intervention that freed Tibet, the unique technology that you see powering travel in this country----and that brought you here; all these things, including the tangible display that's rotating over your heads in effigy, and in the heavens in reality, are part of the answer to 'Why Me?'."

"As an astronomer I've always believed that mankind is not alone in the Universe; and now, I've been introduced to facts that prove my belief without a doubt. For an introduction to those facts, I will now turn over the mike to Yeshua, the Planet Manager of Gradis-2, Moh, the Planet Manager of Jann-1 and Moshe, the Planet Manager of Kazaria; three planets within our galaxy that are not only habitable, but are currently inhabited by beings like ourselves. Inhabited by beings who share these same unique selective traits in common, with each of you."

As Sam finished and sat down, Yeshua stood and walked to the front edge of the stage. As he came forward, he held his right hand outward towards the Kush display and with a wave of his hand the image was replaced in kind with Gradis-2. As the planetarium erupted in excited murmurs, the IMAX screens surrounding the room lit each in turn. Lifelike scenes of daily life on Gradis-2, moved and alternated in slow transition around the perimeter of the room. He paused for a moment for effect, and then went in to a lengthy description of the planet, the lifestyle and the technology enjoyed on Gradis-2. The IMAX movie portrayed in clear lifelike detail, each activity, event and feature, in perfect concert with Yeshuas presentation, and when finished, Yeshua sat down.

Each Prophet in turn, followed suit and in kind; until a complete picture was painted on the minds of the attendees. A picture driving home, that they were experiencing the unbelievable. And yet, the unbelievable had become reality. Mankind not only was'nt alone in the Universe, but there were some damn fine places to visit out there.

The seminar wore on and not a soul was watching the clock and looking for the exits. Gone was the impatience and obsession to finish up the obligatory strings attached to theTibetan Rewards program, grab their 5k in resort dollars, and hit the road. They were glued to their seats, drinking in the opportunity of gaining at least some of the answers to the Universe that had baffled mankind for all times.

As the planetary presentations winded down, the Dalai Lama and S. G., replaced Moh finishing up on the stage. The IMAX screens once again filled with scenes of man's insults to his fellow man, scenes of his physical progressive destruction of the Earth, and the progressive deterioration of its natural wonders.

The Dalai Lama started his presentation.

"Peace be upon all of you and all that you hold dear." He continued, "I am a simple monk of the Tibetan Buddhist practice. I'm merely a man, a human being, just as you seated all around me. But, I have been blessed with special knowledge and granted special gifts by our Creator. As with the three men who have shared the stories of their planets with you today, and as is the case with the man who stands next to me today, we've all been blessed and touched in a special way by the hand of God."

Pausing and taking a deep breath, the Dalai Lama continued.

"Our creator has seen fit, from time to time throughout the history of man on Earth, and on other worlds in the Universe; to send enlightened messengers to help guide the way for his beings. These messengers-teachers and leaders, have touched the world and become a part of our history and our religions. However, they are just men. Special men yes—capable of great and wonderful acts that may defy explanation; but men none the less. The messages they have brought to man, the roles that they have played throughout history, have often been misunderstood. More often ignored and taken for granted. And worse, the message has been manipulated by man; misused and abused for his own personal gain and control of his fellow man."

"The end result of that abuse is the destruction that you see portrayed on the screens throughout the room now as we speak. The insults to the world that in your hearts, you know are real. The beauty that you were experiencing, during the prior presentations, is now replaced with the contrast to the death and destruction of our species and our planet."

"These are desperate times, and as a responsible creator, God has called for drastic measures to fix the world that man has broken. I ask you to open your minds to the messengers of God. Put away your resistance to accept what is being said here today, and what you've seen with your own eyes. It is much to take in, much to accept without skepticism. Standing in front of you today and giving this message to you, are the wise adopted son of a Pharaoh-Moses of Israel, a simple carpenter and rabbi- Jesus of Nazareth, a strong and moral general of Arabia-Mohammed, a philosopher of man-Siddharta Guatama Buddha and, a simple Buddhist Monk of Tibet."

"Shake away your skepticism! Look past the powers and miracles bestowed by God."

"The message was meant to be given from one man to another. Shared and presented for the benefit of all. God has sent you these Prophets-these teachers— these divinely influenced and enlightened men, to tell you that God is going to destroy all of mankind on Earth and all his affects on December 21, 2012---that is except for you and your neighbors, that choose to settle here in Tibet.

"You good people are the chosen few to colonize the planet of Kush and eventually repopulate the Earth. Make no mistake this is your destiny and your fate, just as it is mine."

"Just as Abraham beseeched God to allow him just ten righteous souls to save before Soddam and Gomorah were destroyed. The Prophets before you today, beseeched God to spare each and every one of you."

"Please don't take the responsibility lightly. I know that I have not."

With that the Dalai Lama sat down. The Free Nation of Tibet grew by some eighteen thousand new fully invested Colonists.

Each week the process was repeated as the .001 percent found their way to Tibet. With the help of the Prophets adding color commentary and dynamic displays to the seminars, the people didn't require that much more convincing than what was offered in the first round.

Some, only a few, required re-booking on a future cruise transport to tie up affairs in their native lands. In actuality though, when the realization set in that there was no future that included Earth as they knew it to prepare for, much of the loose ends to tie, became nonsense to worry about. Immediate family, kids and pets (other than cats) were all welcome to return to Tibet.

CHAPTER 56

Palo Alto California-Lhasa Tibet
July 21

"Where do I start?" said Elon. "I can't come to Tibet yet. I need to stay at the Space X facility until I finish the research I'm working on."

"Why, what could possibly be more important? We're already in full production here in Lhasa building new Maglev transports. We're popping them out as fast as we can get steel and aluminum out of China and into Tibet!" said Sam.

"That's one of the reasons." You and Ravi have six of my best design engineers and shop managers in Lhasa already. We still have a lot to get done here before we can pull up stakes!" said Elon, continuing.

"We're running two maintenance crews at each location in twelve countries, that's just keeping the passenger and cargo ships tuned up and operational. We're running eighteen passenger ships continually at three to four thousand heads per run. It's the only way we can handle the people. Just cleaning, stocking and rotating crews is a logistical nightmare, forgetting the mechanical maintenance on them."

"Elon, that's just it---its working—we did it. At the pace you are running passengers we'll make it. Almost two million are rolling in over land, sea and air on their own. Your Cruise Line and heavy transport program looks like it can handle about four million more. That's about the extent of what the actuarials have seen for potential candidates anyway. If we go over 6.5 million qualified colonials, we'll all be shocked. Can't you get away and leave it in your staff's hands? You've accomplished the job. We need you here!"

"Look Sam, I'm so close on what I'm working on. I'm trying to keep a lid on my progress while dealing with having a bunch of NASA goons up my behind. The government over site people are complaining that I'm putting too much of my time into my Tibetan charitable efforts, as they call it. If they only knew! I have to fly to Washington D.C. next week and give the NASA and PCAST director an update on the Space Maglev Drive---you know the one that doesn't work! The one they have decided to blow smoke up everyone's ass about. They are pushing out another one of their bogus media press releases and want me to add credibility to their BS."

"I'm juggling balls in the air and just waiting for one to fall on my head!" Elon said in exasperation.

"Listen, give me ninety days; I believe I can have a working Maglev Space Drive! If I come to Lhasa now, I'll lose thirty days just getting set up. It doesn't make sense to pull me right now."

Sam paused and leaned forward in his chair with feet flush to the floor,

"Did you say a real working Maglev Space Drive?"

"I did, with the technology Ravi brought back from Gradis-2, I was able to overcome the roadblock we kept hitting on the Space X/NASA version in two weeks. This changes the whole picture for us if I can get it up and running. We can't risk NASA getting it!"

"Ok, you have sixty days. And----you get Ravi back to help you get there on time. How is that?"

"Perfect. He and I should be able to knock it out. Tell Ravi to meet me in L A at Space X and to bring his original notes on the emulsion technology. That's the key to this."

"You got it.", said Sam. Sam hung up the phone with Musk and hit Ravi's number in his contact list.

"Hey, I just got off the phone with Elon. I wasn't real successful in convincing him to come to Lhasa right now. I hope you don't get pissed, but I offered up your services to him."

"Sam, I am up to my elbows here as it is. What does he want me for?"

"He says he thinks he's just a couple of steps away from an operational Space Maglev Drive. Says he needs your handwritten notes on the alloy emulsion thing. This is way beyond my technical level. Why don't you call him?"

"Damn right, I'll call him. If we can build a true Space Maglev then we'd be ahead of the Gradisians and ten steps closer to getting set up on Kush! I'll pack tomorrow and take the next Tibet Cruise Lines transport out of Calcutta!"

Ravi and Sam signed off and Ravi immediately reached out to Elon. Things were moving, and moving fast.

"As of now, I am in control here of the White House"

-*General Alexander Haig*

CHAPTER 57

The Director of NASA and Homeland security were sitting in the Situation Room deep in thought, eyes glued to the wall. The White House Media director was on the phone talking to the Vice-President. On the wall-mounted monitors were infra-red, nighttime satellite shots of two large Tibetan Cruise Ships, moving at amazing speeds across the face of the screen.

"How the hell are they doing that," said the NASA Director.

"I haven't a clue. But we're going to find out.

The Media Director placed the phone in its cradle and turned to the other men.

"We can't do it. All they'll let us do is put extreme pressure on Musk. No wire taps, no electronic suvellience domestically whatsoever. Musk and Tibet are media darlings, and the White House thinks it could blow up in our faces."

The Director of Homeland Security fumed. He slammed his pen on the table and sputtered.

"I have the Patriot Act behind me. This guy is withholding technology that has military implications! You guys are tying my hands behind my back and sending me out to fight. Come on!"

"They said no way. Hands off. Bring him in; gently coerce him, lightly threaten. But you can't touch him or his facilities. The ships are under Tibetan registry, the work he does for the Tibetan Charitable Services- U.S., is all above board and all of their i's are dotted and t's crossed. The downside of a negative reaction by the media to our meddling could set us back from the media gains we've made with our Genesis-Kush propaganda program. The President says back off.

The NASA director said, "We already tried the 'soft hammer' approach. We had him in here this week and practicaly begged him to come clean. He keeps sticking to his story that it's a Hydro-foil technology that even he doesn't have access to. He insists it's just his job to facilitate for the Tibetan Government."

"But you did get him to do the press conference. He did state publicly that the NASA Maglev Space Drive program was progressing. A statement that we all know is complete bullshit. That press conference concession is all it took to satisfy the President to leave the guy alone."

The Homeland Security director said, "What about the overstay visa issue. Every one of my counterparts in every country is having the same crap going on?"

The media director said, "Tibet is a non threat. There's no indication that anyone is making permanent moves. No one is putting their homes up for sale. No one is emptying bank accounts. All of them are filing thirty and ninety-day visa extensions before expiration, through the appropriate channels. We can't figure it out, but none of it falls in to a chargeable offense."

"Just keep doing what you are doing and let's kick the can down the road. The Presidential election is coming up, and we don't want the boat rocked. Tread lightly here gentlemen; you guys do anything that reflects poorly in the poles, threatens or changes the President's popularity, and we have a bigger problem than a group of tree huggers and left wing liberals traveling to Tibet and overstaying their visas."

Pissed and with their wings fully clipped, the NASA and Homeland directors, having gained no ground, grabbed their files and walked from the room.

As they walked to their limos, the Homeland Security Director turned to his aide and said. "I have no intention of letting this drop. Someone in this administration has to grow some balls. Make arrangements to fly out to L. A., I want a full advance team in place with surveillance and mobile strike capabilities. I'm going to fix this situation before it gets out of hand."

The aid stopped making notes and was already dialing his cell by the time they got to the car.

"Come one. Come all. Come to this place------All recent disciples and tired saints"

-Reid Genauer and Assembly of Dust

CHAPTER 58

Port of Calcutta, India

Ravi was standing in the visitor waiting area to the left of the Tibetan Cruise Line Customs and Immigration counter. He was watching the passengers streaming in from the 1pm Tibetan Princess coming in from New York City. From the back of the line came a whoop and a wave from Perry Stanton. Ravi, waved to his friend and leaned over to the Tibetan customs officer and said,

"There he is, can I go get him out of line?"

"Yes, sure Dr. Ravi. Just sign here and I can release him into your responsibility."

Ravi quickly signed the immigration and customs documents and ran over and grabbed Perry and gave him a hug.

Perry was fully aware of the true nature of the Genesis-Kush and Tibetan relocation plan from very early on. Perry had been instrumental by adding his support by remaining behind as an extra set of eyes and ears. For the past months, he had been feeding information to the cause on NASA, and the events of the manned space program. Perry mined the internet and monitored the government computers, aided with a couple of programs written by the Tylers.

"Wow, nice shirt!" What Hawaiin did you have to chase down and tackle to get that thing?" said Ravi.

"Hey, it's my summer vacation, fun in the sun shirt. What, you don't like it?"

"It's a little loud dude. At least I won't lose you in the crowd. Come on, I'll show you around; my ship doesn't leave for two hours so we can catch up. I'm booked on the Himalayan Wind bound for Los Angeles, leaving at three o'clock."

Ravi steered Perry out of the building toward the cargo area and away from the throngs of people milling around.

"So tell me what you've been up to. What's going on at Hubble?"

"Oh, man. I am so glad to be out of there. I talked to Sam last week after the last board meeting with NASA. We can't touch a knob, dial, or a computer there without some NASA or Homeland Security geek up our ass. It has been a miserable environment. Brisbane Brown quit last month, and they put some ex-Jarhead engineer in charge in his place. I couldn't work for the guy. I gave them my two-week notice and walked out a week later."

"Well we're lucky to have you here." Said Ravi.

"Hey, I have to check on some cargo transport manifests that the transition team asked me to look in to. Want to come?"said Ravi.

"Sure, just don't let me miss the Calcutta-Lhasa bus."

The two friends headed over to the main cargo terminal, and Ravi sought out the terminal transport manager.

"Hageye! How's it hanging?"

"Dr. Ravi, glad to see you. I just wanted to check on a couple of things with you. I have a couple of containers that came in over the last few days and have a chance to push things around for priority. Come on in my office."

Hageye was a sixtyish Israeli that had a colorful past. He had been a former IDF Special Op's officer that had made several incursions into the Iranian countryside to identify progress on their efforts to produce weapons grade plutonium. His ability to move freely in Iran had embarrassed and frustrated the Iranians to no end. The Iranians had breathed a sigh of relief when he retired.

One of the earliest colonists, Hageye had been recruited away from a Kibbutz outside of Jerusalem where he was managing the fruit shipping warehouse with near perfect military execution.

After introductions, the trio followed Hageye into his office, which was covered in maps of the world with multi-colored lines criss-crossing the face of the maps like strands of food dyed spaghetti in a game of pasta 52 pick-up. One wall was singularly devoted to an eight by ten blow-up of Tibet, and the Calcutta-Tibet trade routes. The Tibetan map had numerous stickeys applied over the face where it was hard to keep up with the names and locations of the re-settlement villages that were popping up all over the countryside. Names like New Jerusalem, Little New York, and Eastern Miami were peppering the Tibetan Plateau region. Perry walked from wall to wall taking note of the names and marveling at the extent of the growing expansion of the Tibet colonization.

"Ok, here's what I have. We got a large shipment of what I guess are Maglev parts from Tesla in San Francisco. I know you were waiting on that one. There's another container that came from Space X in Los Angeles on the same manifest. That one I don't know where you want it to go."

Ravi said, "Send the Tesla container to the Little Detroit Village plant. I guess the other one should probably go to the Genesis- Kush Space Research Center in Genesis City."

Hageye said, "I have just two others I'm not sure about. I have two with lost manifests. One is a full container of water samples that has been bounced around on every transport picking up additional boxes in each port. I don't know where that one goes. The other one is packed full of high-quality coffee beans, cartons of cigarettes and packs of Oreos and Chips Ahoy cookies. Those two have me baffled."

"Well Hageye today is your lucky day. Those are no brainers. The water samples go to EKEV, the Earth- Kush Ecological Science Village in Qinghai, they've been waiting on those. It's right here." Ravi went over to the big wall map and showed Hageye the location high up on the Tibetan Plateau.

"The coffee, cigarettes and cookies go to Wilson Village about five miles east of Lhasa. The Wilsons go through those stores at an alarming rate."

"Hey, thanks for the help," said Hageye continuing,

"I'll get the two Maglev parts transports out first, and then focus on the rest."

Ravi and Perry said their good-byes and walked around reading the manifest labels off of some of the containers, making their way back towards the passenger area. They milled around the market that had grown up around the Calcutta-Lhasa staging area, looking at the collection of exotic foods and wares from around the world. The merchants were always keeping their eyes out for the random unclaimed freight container that could be cannibalized for additional inventory.

Perry reflected, "I'm really excited to get started at the Kush Research Center. There're two guys I've worked with before already settled in there. Remember my buddy over at Kepler? He's there, and a guy I roomed with in college that worked at the Houston NASA facility."

Ravi said, "I'm going to see Elon at Space X in about four days. From what he tells me it sounds like we may be bringing back some pretty interesting technology to play with here. I bet that container he sent is part of the first round of supplies he has slated for the next phase of research."

"Hey, it's about time for your bus up to Lhasa. I'll walk you over and then get a little work done on the computer before the Himalayan Wind leaves."

The two walked over to the bus loading area and said good-bye. Ravi watched his pal get on the bus and then headed over to the Tibetan Cruise Lines pavilion to get a little down time in before he left for L.A.

CHAPTER 59

August

Working out of the converted offices and warehouse storage facilities of a now decommissioned hydro electric plant on the Yangtze River; the Earth-Kush Ecological Science Research Center, or for short, EKEV, was charged with a huge task. Don't repeat the same mistakes on Kush that man had sullied the eco-systems of Earth with.

With the massive immigration and resettlement program going on in Tibet, there was much to do in applying new technologies. Key among these, were the generation and distribution of energy for powering the new settlements; as well as, the collection and distribution systems for handling the inevetible waste that came with human occupation of a planet. The hydrogen fusion reactor and Maglev transportation systems gave them a leg up from the start. In fact, the hydro-electric plant they were currently housed in, had recently been converted to hydrogen fusion power. The conversion, which allowed for the restrictive flow of water previously strangled by the water turbines, to be free to be released in controlled, increased flow downstream for irrigation and potable water supplies to the new colonists.

Experts on global warming, bio-fuel management, energy, air quality and water, to name just a few, were busy at work applying their disciplines in advance. The goal was to have new technologies in place, long before the first Earthling stepped foot on Kush and started the insult to its surface, water and air.

In addition to the immediate Tibet and Kush efforts, the hydro studies group was working on Moh and Yeshua's pet project; a complete analysis of the drinking water on planet Earth. Moh and Yeshuah had provided ample water samples from the aquifers, lakes and rivers of Jann-1, Gradis-2 and Kazaria, for control group comparison.

Coming from the south at a high rate of speed, was the weekly supply transport for the village and research center. Moving with the now familiar undulating motion that made the line of transports look like the cars on a Six Flags Great Adventure roller coaster, the transport train moved swiftly foward. All that could be heard was the low-frequency hum of the Maglev drive and the whistling of the wind off the vehicles.

Two large container carriers' veared off and headed to the research center; coming to a hovering rest at the rear doors to the storage warehouse. The staff opened the hangar doors, and the transports hummed their way into the facility. Maglev material handling equipment was floated over to the large containers to unload the transport. Looking similar to floating pallet fork-floor jacks, the Maglev material handlers latched on and floated the containers into their resting positions for off-loading.

Two scientists in full length white lab coats, came out and clapped the side of he container.

"Ok this one is all us!" said one. "We were wondering were this got off to."

They opened the container and walked in moving boxes aside and opening a sampling from the stored contents. Inside each box were cushioned egg-crated vials of water. Each vile was marked with the country of origin, and the water-supply source that the sample came from.

"Ok, let's get these into the lab. The control samples are already done."

The two scientists assisted the warehouse staff with loading and hauling the samples into the lab area. In the hydro studies department the technicians and scientists were anxiously awaiting the arrival of their samples. Sorting the samples by geographic hemisphere, country, drainage basin and source aquifer; it took over the course of the rest of the week to get the samples in place to start the analytical process.

Over the course of the next two weeks, each sample was tested, categorized, vaporized, boiled, evaporated, mass spectrographed and mixed with a multitude of chemical reagents, then spun in centrifuges.

When the physical sample testing was done, the work turned to computer data base analysis and cross comparison to each sample. By the end of August, the first reports were ready to review.

The Director of the Hydro project called Lhasa and asked for Sam.

"Hey Sam, It's Vladmir Leibov up at the EKEV center. Can you get in touch with the Prophets? We're ready to review the first set of hydro analysis reports. It's pretty interesting results, you might want to attend."

"Hey, Vladmir—Yah, I'm supposed to meet with three of them tonight and give a report on village life. I'll ask them then and get back to you with a date. Can you give me a hint?"

"Yep, we found a direct correlation to some mass human behaviors that compare to unique variations in water chemistry."

"Ok, that gets my attention. Let me get back to you tomorrow. I'll talk to you then Vlad, see you."

The next day, Sam called the EKEV center and asked for Vladmir in the Hydro Studies Department. Vlad picked right up and said, "Hey Sam, thanks for getting back to me. Do we have a date?"

"How does tomorrow at 2 pm sound? We can Maglev in and meet you then."

"Perfect, I'll get everything set up here in the conference center."

CHAPTER 60

At 1:45 pm the next day, Moh, Yeshua, Moshe, Sam and the Dalai Lama came hovering into EKEV Center in a new Maglev hover van. Comfortably seating twelve passengers, the hover van looked like a cross between a stretch Suburban and a Gulfstream V. Sleak and painted maroon and yellow, it cut quite the image of Tibetan technology---and art.

Vlad Leibov met everyone at the receiving area, and after a quick lab tour of the Hydro lab, he handed the group off to his other department head colleagues. The group of scientists waited impatiently for their opportunity to show the visiting group the various recent advances that the Center had made.

The troup finally made its arrival to the conference center at 2:30pm and settled into their seats.

"Welcome to all of you, and thank you for indulging myself and the rest of the Hydro staff. I asked you here today, because it appears that we've made some significant findings. If you will, I'd like to walk you through the process that has led to these discoveries."

The group nodded their heads in anticipation of keeping things moving.

"We started with a benchmark target sampling utilizing the native water samples that Yeshua and Moh brought us from Jann-1, Kazaria and Gradis-2. We then focused on collecting samples from Earth regions that had historically low incidence of aggression in the overall populations. We concentrated on populations with low violent crime rates, and little or no history of bellicose activity toward their neighbor nations. You won't be surprised to know that the Earth control sample group was very small. The greatest sources were mostly island nations that had long periods of limited contact with the outside world. The Polynesian Island nations—Tahiti, Hawaii and remote atoll societies were a good source. We used Tibet, Nepal and a few other continental based societies, but we were limited."

"We then used the same methods to study areas that had typically violent historical experiences. For obvious reasons, we had a lot to choose from."

"What we found is a direct correlation between two factors. One is dissolved radon gas; the other is the presence of dissolved hydrocarbons in the water. Radon is a radioactive gas created by the decay of uranium in the Earth's crust. There is some level of radon in almost all of the fresh water sources on the Earth. We found no evidence of radon in the samples from the three host planets of the Prophets."

"It gets even more interesting when we took the study to the next level. The influence of dissolved hydrocarbons in interaction with radon, delivers some significant results. In most regions, radon exits the public water supply by dissipating in the atmosphere.

Highest levels are found in direct aquifer contact wells. Lowest levels, in rainwater supplied cistern systems. In regional areas with high levels of hydrocarbon deposits, ie, coal, oil, natural gas; the radon seems to bond with the hydrocarbons in the water supply, and, form a compound that is unique to those water supplies."

"In almost every instance in the study; where there are high levels of radon and high levels of hydrocarbons, we have our most indicative violent societies."

"Please turn to the map and graph on the monitors. As we walk through the areas that have experienced the most violence in their history, and continue on to those areas that have the lowest levels, we can see the pattern."

"Look at the area of the oil-producing nations of the Middle East. You can see in this region the greatest level of an exemplar corrollary. This is by far the most concentrated area. You get a similar effect in the history of the Native American tribes that were situated over the larges deposits of coal and oil deposits such as Texas, Ohio, Pennsylvania, Oklahoma and the Appalachian regions. Over to China, the greatest dynastic warrior tribes came from the areas over the largest coal deposits. Then to Ireland, were lignite and peat areas held the highest concentrations in those regions."

"We've found a connection. We have no idea how the physiology works and how it manifests the behaviors in the subjects; but the evidence is there. We suspect that once an individual is exposed, modifications to the genetic code come from the exposure to the compound. We believe that the likelihood of reversal of symptoms is low. The best we can work towards is a preventative solution. There does not appear to be an opportunity to cure."

"We then took the study one further step and made direct comparisons to geographic success rates of the EGG/FWG screening. The graph on the monitor is an overlay of passing to fail ratios, by region and family origin, for candidates screened by the embedded software progam. You can see the direct results. With a two generational separation, those candidates having a direct connection to high Radon-High Hydrocarbon water supplies; fail horribly as candidates for reduced ego, will and aggression quotients as tested by the EGG/FWG parameters."

"We believe that there's a problem in the water on Earth. We have no idea how to remedy it, but we've identified the problem. It seems that our Earth is a nice place to visit, but don't drink the water. If there are any questions I will try and field them for you one at a time."

Yeshua said, "We should all be grateful for this discovery. With the problem identified we're that much closer to a solution."

"If only we could have found this out sooner. Maybe we could have headed this off!" Moh lamented.

The mood was somber and reflective. It was not hard to dwell on the past and what might have been. Some limited solace was found in Yeshua's words. Maybe if the issue could be addressed successfully, and a way to remove the threat through filtration or chemical intervention was found, then future re-colonization of Earth may be possible. None saw any path that would stop the clock ticking down to December 21 2012.

"Welcome to the Hotel California......You can check out anytime but you can never leave."

-The Eagles

CHAPTER 61

Ravi landed in LA late on Wednesday. He was rested and relaxed after having slept more over the three day trip from Calcutta to L.A., than he had in the prior thirty days. To clear his head, he had hiked for half a day in Hawaii, reporting back at the ship just minutes before it was ready to steam out of Honolulu Harbor.

Ravi grabbed his gear and headed to the US customs gate at the Tibetan Cruise Lines gate. He submitted his passport and tossed his two back packs up on to the counter. Looking over to the visitor area, he saw Elon wave to him but looking like he had aged significanty in the six short months since they had met.

"Anything to declare?" the customs officer said

"Nope"

"Business or pleasure?"

"Oh, a little of both",said Ravi.

As the exchange was going on a senior customs officer came over and peered over his subordinates shoulder. The senior officer remained there while the younger man started to unzip Ravi's first bag.

Holding his hand to his earpiece, the senior officer looked up to the administrative area of the customs clearing area. He nodded in the direction of a mirrored glass enclosure along the back wall. After pausing for a moment, he put his hand on Ravi's bag and said,

"Sir, could you please bring your bags and come this way with me?"

Ravi asked, "Do I have a choice? Is there a problem?"

"No, no problem we just need to ask you some questions."

Ravi glanced over at Elon, who was looking concerned and a little frightened. Ravi hefted his bags and followed the customs officer to the door next to the large glass mirrored panel; a buzzer sounded and the officer stepped aside with his hand on the knob and indicated that Ravi should enter in front of him. The two entered the room as he door clicked and electronically bolted close behind them. Seated at the table was a man that Ravi thought looked familiar but couldn't exactly place.

"Dr. Najr, I am Roland Gerber---Director of the Office of Homeland Security for the United States of America. I believe you are the same Dr. Ravi Najir that discovered the Genesis-Kush system utilizing the Hubble Space Telescope."

The statement was not offered in a tone that indicated a friendly introduction; no handshake was offered. The man just sat silently assessing Ravi with his small piercing eyes, like a python looking at a rat dropped in its cage. Ravi was not feeling that this was going to be a welcome homecoming to the States.

The Director continued.

" I have some questions for you if you would take a seat. "Is that Mr. Elon Musk out in the waiting area?"

"Yes"

"And, can I assume that He's here to pick you up."

"You can."

"And what is the nature of your relationship with Mr. Musk."

"We're both active in various charitable efforts that are related to the Free Nation of Tibet. Why do you ask?"

"Mr. Najir I am questioning you, not the contrary. Please just answer my questions without responding with one of your own."

Asshole, Ravi thought. He offered no response, now starting to get more pissed than scared.

"Charitable efforts---hmmmm. Do those charitable efforts include sharing classified US technology with members of nations that are unfriendly to the United States?"

"I have no idea what you are talking about, sir. I am a simple scientist that has a backround in astronomy and astrophysics. To my knowledge I have not been working on anything that's classified, nor have I associated with anyone that I know of as being 'unfriendly' to the United States."

"Did you realize that Mr. Musk has access to classified military data through his association with Space X and NASA?"

"No I have no idea what Mr. Musk has access to. Our relationship is limited to a mutual interest in science, and a mutual interest in promoting the charitable and global relief efforts of the Free Nation of Tibet."

"Dr. Najir, how long do you plan to be in the States for this trip?"

"Well sir, If I'm not mistaken, that is a passport issued by the United States of America---and, I'm a U.S. citizen working abroad. I believe my travel and work visas are in order, and unless you intend to charge me with some specific crime, I'd like to go meet my friend and get the hell out of here."

"Dr. Najir, I'll tell you when this interview is over. We have significant leeway in the Homeland Security office, powers given to us by way of the Patriot Act legislation. If I wanted to, I could haul your ass off for ten days without anymore cause than I don't like you. I don't tell you these things because that's my current intention. I tell you these things because we're watching your activities and those of Mr. Musk. We have'nt yet decided how we wish to proceed. How we proceed, will be at our will and decision, not based on whether you are dissatisfied with the inconvenience. You're free to go."

The man flipped Ravi's passport to him and watched as Ravi shaking in anger, checked his bags and zipped them tight. Ravi suppressed the urge to flip the guy the finger as he headed for the door.

Barging through the door and storming his way toward a frowning Elon Musk, Ravi breathed under his breath, "Let's get the hell out of here. I was just interrogated by the fucking head of the U.S. Gestapo."

Elon grabbed one of Ravi's bags and guided him out to the parking lot. Ravi was looking around for the latest iteration of some Tesla product line as Elon walked them over to a white chevy impala and opened the door. Elon looked at Ravi's confused facial expression and said.

"Don't ask, I'll explain in the car."

They loaded in and Elon put the keys in the ingnition, reached across Ravi, and opened the glove box. Inside was an electronic device that was about the size of a small compact disk player. Elon pressed the power on switch and a red and a blue light came on. He closed the glove compartment and navigated out of the parking lot.

Looking very obvious in their attempt at being inconspicuous, two black Suburbans slowly turned out in the traffic behind the Chevy, staying about three cars behind.

"Ok, Elon what gives?"

"It started about ten days ago. Right after I spoke to Sam and then you."

"My own security noticed it first and we stepped up security at the plant. Typically we sweep the phones twice a week. Now I'm doing them twice a day. We've had two positive hits. I downloaded all the Maglev files, both conventional and space drive data, on to the Tibet servers and had K. and B.E. start monitoring all activity on our local U.S. servers. They sent my local IT guys a stripping program to remove all mirror images of the data and clean our drives. The two goon squads behind us are running high tech scanning equipment and we're scrambling their signal with the unit in the glove box. The Chevy gives me a chance now and then to lose them. The Teslas, no way, they are on them like white on rice. The Chevy is a Maglev conversion though. I haven't kicked it in yet to blow them away, but I'm looking for just the right opportunity," Elon flashed the first smile that Ravi had seen since his arrival.

"Elon lets get our work done here and get the hell out. This is a disaster waiting to happen. You may need to step up the clock. I think your days are numbered here."

"I'm beginning to believe that now," said Elon.

They pulled the Chevy into the parking lot at Space X and watched as the two Suburbans motored pass as if that would matter. They exited the car and walked together to the entrance of the building. Elon motioned Ravi to follow him to the lab and 'clean room' area connected to the large double hangar assembly room.

"Ok let me tell you about the Space Maglev. Originally the NASA research model we were working on was a sub space propulsion system that we were trying to develop. The concept was to have a twin hull with a magnetic flux between the inner and outer hull. The thrust was basically generated by the differential in energy between the two. At best, in the vacuum of space, the lack of friction would allow us to set a body in motion and eventually, maybe achieve mach speeds. Not real conducive to intergalactic travel. Maybe it would be ok for individual solar system exploration."

"Ok, I get it, so what's different now?"

"A lot. We began to have progress after we started to analyze the reaction of the Gradis-2 Maglev in relation to what happens when the two surfaces under excitement move apart. We studied the effects as the magnetic flux starts to deteriorate. Another example we used was when the Maglev ships travel continually over the crests of waves and inertia is maximized. The object continues to travel at a balanced speed in spite of the fact that the vehicle is only gaining thrust at the crest of each wave and no thrust with the valleys. Conceptually those conditions were the basis for how we address continual thrust to gain Hyper Space velocities. To really achieve hyper space intergalactic travel we need to warp lightspeed.

"Ok, I'm with you but not quite getting it. Enlighten me."

"Ok, to get a Maglev that can achieve warping the speed of light; the answer lies in the atomic and molecular make up of the particulates that fill the void of Space. Call it Space Dust or Cosmic Dust, intergalactic dust---its all just particulate organic matter. It's simple in concept. Concentrate the particulate matter into a platform for the Maglev, a wave crest if you will, to thrust off of, and in a frictionless environment such as space, eventually we can achieve ever increasing velocities. So, the first step was to build a hydrogen fusion directional condenser that could attract and consolidate the particulate matter; then focus it in a mirrored position to the emulsion surface of the Maglev object to be propelled.

"Wow, Elon this is phenomenal. I get the concept all the way. Where are you with it now?"

"Well we got a small vacuum enclosed model to work but it's glitchy. It worked well enough to prove the concept, but I need to focus on the difference in the ratio of specific thrust platform to magnetic flux emulsion materials; that's were your hand written notes come in.

I remembered in your written notes that there were a set of formulas for utilizing dissimilar contact and emulsion materials. You and I didn't need the list because we just checked off the known composites that we knew were on Earth. Our current drives are tuned to Earth based molecular compounds found in water and land ---more specifically—water and land on Earth. I need your notes so we can build a universal drive. One that's capable of exciting electrons in compounds that you would not find on Earth, but are in concentration in space. Get it!"

"Oh yah, I get it! It's pure freakin' magic. Let me grab my notes and let's roll our sleeves up.

Rolling the sleeves up turned in to days of eating and sleeping in cat naps at the lab. The two only ventured out to make short excursions out to Musk's residence or, to field collect samples minerals from a couple of rock shops and jewelers. In addition to their target minerals they purchased a host of 'red herrings', ever aware of the two black Suburbans that were following them. The Homeland Security Goons would enter each establishment after they left to badger the proprietors in to divulging the purchases' of the duo. They finally found the key in the wee hours of the following Tuesday after Ravi's arrival.

Using a pulverized mix of Cohenite, Feldspar and Olivine as part of the alloy emulsion mix, they hit the key to the space highway. When drawn into the fusion condenser, and also used as a constituent of the emulsion coating; the thrust platform remained stable each time they pulsed the machine.

That night they downloaded the data to the two Tylers and then wiped the server and resident memories clean on the Space X mainframes.

Tired and relieved that they had succeeded, the two men walked out to the Chevy and decided to go back to Elon's to get some well earned sleep. Looking back at the other side of the parking lot, their two shadows were parked with engines running.

Going through the routine, Elon opened the glove box and turned on the scrambler; they buckled up and headed out of the parking lot.

They had not driven more than a mile when one of the Suburbans pulled in front of the Chevy and the other pulled tight to the tailgate. Elon took one look front and rear and signaled to the shoulder.

"What could these assholes possibly want now?" he said.

"I don't know, but it can't be good."

Sitting on the shoulder they waited patiently while the door of the rear Suburban opened. A black suited walking tank stepped out of the truck. A matching version of him stepped from the rear passenger seat of the forward vehicle. One of the Man Mountains walked to the drive side of the Chevy and the other, to the passenger side. Elon hit the locks and lowered the window all of an inch.

"Can I help you two?"

"Yes, Mr. Musk, could you please step outside and ask your passenger to do the same?"

"Not a chance my friend. I am placing a call to my lawyer right now and we will not move one step outside of this vehicle until he arrives and advises me on how to proceed. While he's coming, my next call is to Station KLM's news desk to ask them to get down here and cover this fiasco. How does that sound?"

"Mr. Musk, we don't want any trouble, but we'd like your guest to come with us for questioning."

"Not a chance of that. Same goes for him as for me." said Musk. He looked over at Ravi who shook his head.

"Don't push it Elon, we're so close."

Elon picked up his phone as the driver side goon said to his partner. "Hey, go call Gerber and find out what he wants us to do." The passenger side goon headed back to the Suburban and leaned on the hood while dialing his cell.

Elon looked over at Ravi and flipped the Maglev drive switch at the base of the ignition. Elon started to make conversation into his cell while Ravi looked down as the ready indicator signified that the Maglev was active. Ravi looked over at Elon and said.

"Don't do it, Elon."

Elon continued his mock phone call and just as the driver side goon looked over at his buddy leaning on the Suburban's hood, Elon dropped the phone and screamed to Ravi:

"Hold on!"

He pushed the side control hard to the right. The Chevy, in two instantaneous moves, lifted nine inches off the road surface and moved ten feet to the right, over the far side of the shoulder. Then, with just a hint of a pause, shot straight forward, leaving the two bewildered Homeland Security Officers scrambling for the doors of their vehicle.

"Now you did it, Elon. I hope you have a plan."

The Chevy was cruising at about 255 mph over the desert floor west of L.A., there was not even a hint of a chance that the Homeland guys had any idea where they were, or what direction they had gone.

"Well, I'd say the plan is we better find our way to the nearest port and get both of our butts to Tibet."

"Well I'd suggest that you turn west and head out to sea. The only chance we have is getting to Hawaii ahead of the Wednesday Himalayan Wind out of L. A. That's if they let it leave port tomorrow, after your little side show tonight."

"Hawaii it is, crank up the tunes."

The two men leaned into the banked turn as the Chevy headed across the north side of L.A, away from the lights of the city and out to sea.

"To everything there is a season, and a time to every purpose under the heaven"

-Pete Seeger- and guy that wrote Ecclesiastes

CHAPTER 62

As the summer months wound down and autumn started its steady march toward the inevitable countdown to winter, the Tibetan Colonial experience started to mature and take shape. With so much to do and so much to prepare for, it was the transitional task at hand that prevailed over dwelling on the future. The Tibetan colonials found that staying fully grounded in the moment was the best preparation for the event that was about to reshape everyone's reality. It took great effort to push the imminent end of the world out of one's mind. When thoughts of pending death and destruction welled to the surface, they could be replaced with additional effort of throwing oneself in to the work of nation building for the greater community good.

The diversity of the population had its challenges as the populace melded together in its common goals. More copies of the Rosetta Stone software progam were sold in the ninety day period from April thru June than any prior period in the history of the company. The stock was soaring, profits grew; the massive annual bonus checks were prepared for corporate officers and shareholders that would never have a chance to spend a dime. The people of Tibet, both original inhabitants and their new guests, walked the streets and went about their days with headphones attached and mouthing words in all of the global languages as they struggled to bridge the communication gap generated by settling in the worlds new ultimate cultural melting pot.

Sharon had settled into an office at the Lhasa Mental Health Center and was proactively setting up a Grief Counseling program in anticipation of dealing with the inevitable social fallout that would occur in the days leading up to, and the months to follow after December 21.

Alyssa was actively focused on the computer language architecture for creating children's programs and games that would help kids, fourteen and under, transition into the new world experience. To bridge the gap between the various cultures; she had aligned efforts with a team of child development psychologists and educators that were as multi-national as the General Assembly of the United Nations. There was much to overcome, molding and building the young minds that would be the future of the Colonies. There was so much new information that was foreign from what they had been traditionally exposed to attending schools in their native lands.

For Sam, there wasn't a moments rest. He had become the 'go to man' for the colonists and the transition administration of the Colonies. He was forced to mature at a rate that left him little time to reflect on how his life had unfolded, and how that deviated so immensely from any expectations that he had. The resources he had in his team of advisors, kept him sane and helped to lighten he load. He had the benefit of experienced and educated diplomats and prior government officials from all over the face of the Earth. He sought their council, and the business of the Tibetan colonization was functioning at a reasonably high level.

The one solace and relief from the daily pressure for Sam, was that when the day quieted and Norbilungka Palace settled in for the night; he and Alyssa had each other to hold and caress. In the quiet of their chambers, they shared their challenges of the day and their hopes and dreams for the unfolding future. The nights spent together in their quarters made it all possible to get up the next day and face whatever obstacle awaited them.

Sam opened his eyes and nudged Alyssa. "Hey, you asleep?"

"Mmmmm. What is it?"

"I can't sleep."

"Mmmmmm. Try counting water buffalo and yaks"

"No, seriously I can't sleep! Let's talk."

Now completely denied a shot at a full eight hours, Alyssa sat up and pulled the covers close. "Ok, what's bugging you? Its three in the morning and both of us have huge days tomorrow. I have to head out to the Indian/Nepal Border villages to deliver books and reading software to the new schools out there. "

"I keep thinking that I haven't done enough, experienced enough, and now I will never have the chance again." Sam sighed

"Sam, what the hell are you talking about?"

"One more walk in Central Park with skaters and musicians, R.C. boats on the lake and falafels under a tree." Sam said.

"Oh honey, I just want one more trip to Saks and Cartier," Alyssa wistfully moaned. "Rest assured YOU won't be denied, there will be parks, boats and falafels again; but shopping, fashion and jewelry are surely going to die in my New Colonial lifetime! I mean really, Sam, Sharon and I are going to miss the last Black Friday ever-----Ever! Now that's something to really be depressed about."

"What about Carnival in Sao Palo, Mardis Gras and the running of the bulls in Pamploma? No Super Bowl, no World Cup Soccer match." Sam was really getting worked up now. "I mean, I'm not even going to bother to turn on the first NFL game 'cause these guys haven't got a clue how much of a short season they are going to have. I don't know if I can embrace a new world so different from what I've identified with in the past."

"I think you are putting way too much importance on what the loss of the familiar is going to mean," said Alyssa. "Maybe the importance of all of our diversions was made so; only because the need to escape from our existence was so high." "Maybe we focused on all of these diversions to kill the pain of a sick world that surrounded us. Maybe for once we'll be able to live in the moment---truly live in the moment and experience and embrace it for what it is.

A present and future that are completely unfettered by the ball and chain from the past will be a whole new unique experience. This opportunity holds so much hope and promise that all the diversion we'll need or want will be at our finger tips. Don't worry, we'll find someway to keep you occupied on Sundays from 1 to 11- pm other than football." Alyssa gave Sam a kiss on the lips and rolled over. "Now get some sleep, would you? You have a country to run in the morning."

Sam threw himself down into the depths of the mattress and stared at the ceiling. Whether she made sense or not, the death of the NFL was not something to trifle with. He had every intention of scouting for talent among the Colonials and starting a team. He was sure that there would be plenty of support from others in the Colonies. Visions of a KFL/TFL inter-galactic conference championship played between the worlds, had great appeal to him. Hell, maybe even enlist the three Prophet Planets in the mix.

Better than counting Yak, Sam slipped quietly into a peaceful slumber.

CHAPTER 63

As the kids were donning Darth Vader costumes and Jason style hockey masks; as pumpkins and corn stalks sprouted around the cities and towns announcing the seasonal close to the Harvest months; the news of the date of December 21, 2012 as the date of the world's destruction was widely talked about the world over.

The predictions of the Mayan astronomers were getting more than their usual media treatment as the citizens of the world pondered, without truly believing---What if? With renewed interest and fervor, the media jumped on the 'End Days' bandwagon realizing that it was a golden opportunity to sell just one more rag at the grocery market checkout lane. Screaming 'Buy Me!' from the magazine rack, were glossy newspapers and periodicals emblazoned with pictures of Kentucky trailer park baby aliens born to virgin mothers, and stories of alien abductions from the creatures of Kush. 'Oprah leaves Graham to relocate to Tibet' and 'Brad and Angelina' call it quits as the Mayan end date nears, spurring them to end the marriage for good. It was great marketing, and they were all taking advantage of the short window of opportunity. As tired a tag line as it was, even ---- 'Nostradamus Predicts' threw a few extra coins to the bottom line as long as Genesis, Kush or Mayan end of Days was coupled with it.

Bitter returning Tibetan colonial rejects that had missed the cut, only getting as far as testing and orientation centers, brought back the news. Incensed over the rumors that they heard while taking their consolation tours of Tibet, they returned to their native lands and fueled the fire. Enough were believed that the rumor mill was churning and giving each of them their requisite fifteen minutes of fame. Loose lips, doing their best, to sink the ship. Most folks, however, did not jump on to the doomsday bandwagon, choosing not to drink the kool aid, they wrote it off to another crackpot conspiracy theory as they had in the past. It was business as usual as the unrest and chaos in the world kicked up a few more notches.

As far as the activities in Tibet went, they did not go unnoticed. It became widely accepted that something was going on there. The media hyped the mass transportation effort; the overstayed visas and cultish activities. The world however, found it hard to see the Dalai Lama and his minions as a credible threat to upsetting the balance of the world. The increasingly violent character of the real threats to world safety, offered enough ammunition to keep the CNN's of the world, and the viewers busy. While Tibet, as weird as it may be, just seemed like a silly op-ed tool to fill page three, or offer a late night editorial comment from a journalist with a camera crew and mike. Tibet wasn't scary enough to sell advertising time. The assumption was, that after the initial wave of relocation and colonization excitement wore off, people would trickle back to their homes, disillusioned by ideologic dreams unmet and unfulfilled.

Social and political unrest the world over, had in the last sixty days risen back to the levels experienced prior to the unified propaganda campaign mounted by the western governments. In Washington, the group of Usual Suspects was gathered in their think tank chambers, looking for a new and innovative way to spin the story and regain the lost ground. The pending Presidential election still controlled all decisions being made. It was the silly season in Washington, and all were complying with expectations.

As Halloween transitioned to Thanksgiving and the street decorations were rolled out for the Christmas Holiday season, the world settled into complacent ignorance to what fate was about to deliver.

"Ashes to ashes; dust to dust--May soul encounter soul-- on the cross-town bus--Ashes to ahshes; smoke to flame--May soul encounter soul on the sideways train"

-Reid Genauer and Assembly of Dust

CHAPTER 64

Dec 1, 2012

The American contingents of Colonists were returning to their respective villages after having spent Thanksgiving week in Lhasa. The Tibetan capital had a full party calendar as the city had become a destination for the multi-cultural holiday celebrations of the Tibetan population. There was always a cultural holiday somewhere, and as each one rolled around, the city population ebbed and flowed. Tibetan colonists of common heritage from scattered villages around the nation, sought a connection, or re-connection to their prior lives. The simple act of celebrating together the familiar holidays of their respective countries and cultures, seemed to ease the fears of what was quickly coming to a head.

Regular Tibetan passenger transports from the major ports slowed to a mere trickle, as first the U.S., in September, and then following suit, Great Britain, China, Germany and Russia in October; stopped access to their ports for Tibetan Cruise Lines. Though not buying in to Tibet as a world trouble spot, the example needed to be set. Travel rules applied to all, and Tibet was breaking the rules. A proper spanking was in order, and it was being delivered.

The Governments of the world were warned to make the spanking a light one though. The parade of lobbyists and CEOs, finance ministers and White House financial advisors pleaded their warnings---- tread lightly—Tibet is damn good business. While the rest of the world's economy was in the recession doldrums, Tibet was booming. The warning was a literal 'don't rock the boat' with no pun intended. Tibetan orders for durable goods, commodities and consumer discretionary products were fueling growth. Tibet was single handedly bolstering the Gross National Product of nations the world over. Tread lightly they did. Tibetan Passenger transportation was out, but industrial transports continued and were increased. It was an election year after all.

Those individuals' still holding Tibetan Rewards promotions, had to find their way to the only three remaining active ports of Athens Greece, Stockholm Sweden or Sidney Australia. Those ports stayed operational until October, after that, Tibetan Cruise shut down and port entry was closed.

Unlike the rest of the complacent world, the Tibetan colonists knew what was coming. In Lhasa and the village communities, the 5.8 million Tibetan colonists somberly began the countdown.

Ravi and Elon were working at a frantic pace on the Space Maglev drive. Alyssa was shipping out the first iteration of the scholastic series of interactive educational programs to the village community youth learning centers in each region. Sharon and the Mental

Health Center had set up fully staffed grief counseling centers in easily accessible groupings to serve multiple villages. They could barely keep up with the load.

EKEV Center was furiously working on 24-hour shifts looking for a solution to cleansing the Earth's water supply by releasing the Radon-Hydrocarbon bond and then filtering the offending molecules away.

And Sam was busy just barely keeping his head above water as he tried to keep up with the various committees and liaisons from each village administration. Sam had come to rely heavily on the council of the Prophets as they made governance suggestions based on their own experiences on their respective planets. The Dalai Lama and Sam were working with staff, compiling and writing a charter that utilized elements from those on Jann-1, Kazaria and Gradis-2, to try to refine a guide for living that would apply both on Earth, as well as Kush, when the time came to start colonizing the new planet.

As December 21 2012 ticked closer; such was the state of the Earth and the Tibetan Colony.

CHAPTER 65

Sharon and Alyssa had the day off! Whoo Hooo! It had been a grueling schedule for both girls as they had jumped into the business of the Tibetan colonies. Today though was all theirs, and they were going to make the most of it. Getting up early they started at Norbilunkgka Palace with the ultimate meditation and yoga session. Having the Dalai Lama as your meditative guide, along with yoga masters from all the corners of Asia at your daily disposal; all made for some serious healthy living. Mentally, spiritually and physically fit, they blew through the palace doors to the waiting Maglev transport in the courtyard.

"Ok girlfriend, where to first?" said Alyssa.

"I have it all worked out." Sharon was the consummate girl with a plan.

"First Viet Village for Mani-Pedis and then over to the Wilson Village to try their new coffee shop and internet café, 'As Bill Brews It'."

"Sounds like a plan to me," trilled Alyssa.

The girls fastened their seat belts—big rule followers that they were---and settled in for a rapid g-force ride to Viet Village. They fished in their oversized bags making sure that they had their

Havianas and toe socks. As the girls compared soon to be exfoliated dead skin and bunions, they relaxed and put aside the pending impact of the looming countdown.

"We're here!" they both exclaimed as the Maglev settled on to the grass.

Viet Village was alive with activity. The people of the village took great pride in bringing the best of Vietnamese culture with them to Tibet. French and Aussie expats had settled in a great number among the inhabitants, re-kindling a cultural affinity that unfortunately hadn't ended well in the 1970's. A chance to right old wrongs and build on positive co-existence was offered under the wing of the New Free Nation of Tibet, and all were taking advantage of it.

The girls headed to Saigon Sally's nail emporium and bowed reverently to Sally as she welcomed them in. Sally brought the two over to the wall rack display of nail colors that practically took up one whole side of the room.

"Lotus Lilly—I love that color!" said Alyssa

"Rotus Rirry" said Sally with a smile as she nodded her approval of the shade.

The girls settled into their seats as a chorus of girls soaked, scraped and massaged their feet and hands back in to suitable shape. The nail technicians chatted in Vietnamese while Sharon and Alyssa talked about everything and nothing. It was just the medicine they needed.

Buffed and polished they slipped into their flip-flops. Once ready to make their exit, they paid their bill and tipped the girls and Sally heavily, waved a good-bye and bowed affectionately to the room as they headed back out the door to their next stop. Wilson Village.

Wilson Village was the most eclectic cultural mish mash that had risen out of the Tibetan country side. Settled just five miles outside of the borders of Lhasa it was one of the first settlements to open its doors. The residents came from every socio economic back round, every color and creed. No defining cultural, educational or regional reference was defined. Even more unique was that age did not seem to define the depth of association between villagers in any way. It was not unusual to see eighteen-year olds colorfully tattooed and dangling in piercings, dining with little grey haired men and woman without any familial connection attached. Talking animatedly as they were enjoying a slice of pizza and a cup of coffee, it was a bizarre social experiment that appeared to function seamelessly without rules.

Except for the extreme tobacco use, the residents were about as healthy in their lifestyles as anyone could hope for. Where other villages advertised heavily to promote their community's benefits and encourage new residents; Wilson village seemed to just continually attract newcomers without having to raise a finger. It had become a favorite spot for Tibetan villagers to relax, have a cup of coffee, grab a bite to eat, away from the hustle and bustle of Lhasa.

Sharon and Alyssa walked up the multiple steps to the entrance to 'As Bill Brews It', and stepped up to the counter.

"I'll have a Vente double shot latte with caramel, please." said Alyssa.

"And can I have a Grande cappuccino with a twist," said Sharon.

The girl behind the counter smiled and said.

"Wow ladies, I'm sorry but we don't do that here. I have fresh brewed Folgers Mountain Grown, and our special flavor of the day is Dunkin' Donuts. I might have a little Chock Full of Nuts decaf left, but I think I have to brew some more. Milk, sugar and free Oreos and Chips A'Hoys are on the counter over there." She said, pointing to a serving station against the back wall.

Sharon and Alyssa shrugged their shoulders' and looked at each other quizzically. As a compromise both picked the Dunkin Donuts to go and decided maybe they would head back to Lhasa and hit the Palace Starbucks for more familiar fare. Grabbing their to-go cups they headed back to the waiting Maglev. Alyssa said,

"Well you know Wilson Village can't be for all Earthlings."

When they returned to Norbulungka Palace, Sharon and Alyssa dumped their DD coffees and went over to the Palace Starbuck's. With relief they ordered their traditional coffee drinks of choice. The two girls settled into the comfortable community room that served as a gathering and living room for both guests and residents alike. Pulling out their laptops they settled into the silk upholstered Memory Foam cushions strewn about the room and began to internet shop with determination. Each girl had a full open poker hand of credit cards laid out in front of them as they began the session.

"Oh, would you look at this dress at Nordstrom's!" said Alyssa reaching for a card. Sharon leaned over and nodded approvingly.

"I've been waiting for these boots to go on sale for three months!" said Sharon as she clicked her way down the Zappos page.

Both girls were busily typing in card numbers and shipping addresses. Being sure that they hit "Expedited Shipping", ensuring delivery in three to five business days; they completed their initial transactions. Insistent internet retailer warnings of 'Order now for guaranteed delivery by Christmas', had a subtle sobering effect.

Christmas wasn't coming this year. Thankfully, neither was the monthly statement for the array of credit cards strewn on the hand-woven carpet in front of them. Debt forgiveness was about to take on a new meaning. With just two weeks before the end of the world, Alyssa and Sharon did just what they should have done. If the world was going to end they made sure that their hair and nails were tuned up, and they had new outfits.

UPS, FED-EX, DHL and the international parcel post of every nation were shipping massive orders to Tibet as the last chance shopping spree to end all, was entering its final big swing. Air-traffic control in Lhasa could barely keep up with the stacking of cargo jets as they swooped in and out of Lhasa and Calcutta. Tibet was doing its part and then some for the world economy. Too little, too late was only an awareness that Tibetan residents held the ticket to.

CHAPTER 66

When Genesis City first formed, at the beginning of the Colonization of Tibet, a traveler asking the way would have been told: "Take the north fork of Kiber Road out of Lhasa, and it's about twenty- minutes up on the right." Since the wide application of Maglev travel, Genesis City was a five-minute as- the- crow-fly's hop from Lhasa.

In keeping with the new Tibetan tradition, the city was founded on a common theme; industrial manufacturing technologies, and the research for better means and methods to accomplish them. Research and technology were the driving focus of the town's efforts.

All the heavy lifting that made the Tibetan colonial rapid growth and expansion possible was the result of the Genesis City efforts. Without the limitations of rubber tired transport ,and the freedom to move men materials and equipment Maglev style, the response time and ability to provide near instant infrastructure to an area was amazing. The Genesis City technicians got the job done quickly and on budget. The technology moved so fast that each subsequent project was just done better than the last.

Whether it was a system of breeding and holding ponds for the Aquaculture Village in Yangtze province; or, the ninety-day construction and fit out of the Hotel, Auditorium and Conference Center that housed the Tibet Orientation Pavilions; these guys were a well-oiled machine that delivered near flawless results. As the Tibetan Colonial expansion progressed, the Genesis City crews laid so many pipes and installed so many pre-packaged Hydrogen Fusion power plants, that as quick as the last temporary village tents went up and were staked into the ground, the first few permanent resident structures were being readied for occupancy-----with toilets that flushed. There were no long-term contracts for temporary toilet facilities needed.

Genesis City is where Elon Musk, Sam and Ravi chose to set up the Genesis Space Research Center and manufacturing plant. And when Elon fled the States, this is where he chose to make his home.

From the beginning of the Colonial effort, the Prophets had instilled in Sam, Ravi and Elon that making a Kush based colony a reality was a necessity. With no guarantee, that Man was going to be able to spread beyond the Tibetan borders on Earth in the near future; Kush was a goal that offered species sustainability. All you had to do was get there.

"How's it going, Elon," Ravi said walking on to the production floor.

"Still a lot of tweaking to do, but I'll meet the initial launch date."

Ravi walked around the various equipment staging areas and stood in front of each one as Elon explained their individual function.

"This is a two-man Maglev submarine. Two men can navigate to a depth of about fifteen-hundred meters based on the relative pressures on Kush. We should be able to get a pretty darn good picture of the sea bed and have the ability to take a full complement of samples along the way. The whole unit fits inside here." Elon walked over to a large cigar-shaped transport sitting on supports in the center of the hangar. He opened a hydraulic side panel of the fuselage with a whisper of solenoids, pistons and escaped air. Patting the side of the space stogie he walked over with Ravi to the next piece of equipment.

"This is a typical Maglev drone that's outfitted with every kind of camera you can think of. You have your infra-red; your ultra-violet; your wide spectrum and detail lens. This baby will photograph, map and air quality test from surface to mountaintop the whole damn planet in a matter of weeks. What's good about this one is that it'll live feed all the data back to here for real time analysis, while the Kush side landing teams can focus on hard surface and air samples in the field."

"Ravi, we just need to be sure that all the ICBM's are gone. The last thing we need is an un-manned land based missile being left behind that tries to intercept us. As long as that risk is gone, we could launch on December 22nd and come back as soon on February 25th. The advance team is training daily; they are anxious and ready as they'll ever be."

"How are you coming with the first group of large passenger Space Cigars?"

"Well, I know the shape isn't pretty but the physics is kind of based on the technology of an eggshell. Ever try to wrap your hand around an egg and crush it. It's damn hard to do because the force is so perfectly distributed. That's what we have with the Space Stogie shape. We figured function over beauty was the path to take. This shape is the least likely to deform under Hyper Space Maglev thrust. We have four under construction that can handle about eighteen-hundred passengers and enough ground based supplies and equipment to support them. We're good and ready."

They both went outside and stood in the chill of the Tibetan winter. It was mostly clear, and they could just about see the peaks of the Himalayas.

"Doesn't look any different—does it?"

"Nope."

"Clear blue skies sure don't hold an ominous feeling do they?"

"Nope."

"So, you think he really is going to do it?"

"Yep"

They both looked at the ground and walked away without another word back into the hanger.

*'Woke up this morning, put on my slippers;
walked in the kitchen and died. And oh what a feeling
as my soul went through the ceiling, and on up in to
heaven I did ride!'*

-John Prine

CHAPTER 67

End of the World

It was December 20th 2012, and God hovered
gracefully over the Earth. Gone was any semblance of
his Earthly body and "hovering" over Earth was not
meant to imply that God the Almighty was fixed above
any definable point of reference. God's presence and
power enveloped the Earth in total. God is many
things and all things and tomorrow, as promised, God
was vengeance. God gazed down on the small human
colony of Tibet reaching high above the other cities of
the world and saw hope. He looked toward his newest
fine piece of handiwork spinning about Genesis and
smiled in the warmth of new beginnings. He rested for
tomorrow his work would be methodical and swift. He
had a plan, and he intended to follow it to a tee.

It was the Winter Solstice, and Earth was quietly
turning on its axis. In New York City, it was 7 am and
the day was starting in full swing. Lines were already
starting to form at Starbucks all over town, and the
number of horn honks increased in density as each

minute of the clock ticked forward. The first large groups of passengers were exiting the metro stations and heading up the escalators and stairs in Downtown as the initial wave of the throng headed for offices on Wall Street. The ferries from Red Bank and Hoboken dumped off their fares on to the docks as the Jersey commute was pouring in from all directions. Suits, skirts and pant suits were on the march like lemmings to the sea.

Traffic was already backing up on the Cross Bronx and BQE. All three tunnels were packed to full capacity, and the Verrazano and George Washington bridges strained under their loads of cars, trucks and busses. Traffic snaked up and down the Jersey turnpike, I-95 and the Garden State Parkway like some kind of undulating serpent. From the West 287, 78 and 80 fed into the mess that supplied the teeming masses to the Big Apple.

God smiled, Garden State—Big Apple, How appropriate.

At 9 am sharp, at the very peak of the start of the day, every cell phone, iPad, computer monitor and TV blinked once and displayed:

So sorry to inform you but your position has been terminated. Good-bye-----GOD.

Across every cell phone screen, tablet, computer monitor and television, a thirty second countdown meter appeared and began its monotonous reduction.

No amount of button pressing, ctl/alt/del, pulling of plugs or removing of batteries eliminated the message.

Starting with four, the New York Stock Exchange, Citi bank, Bank of America and Goldman Sachs a brilliant light seemed to highlight the structures. The light was neither shining on the building nor reflecting off of them. The light consumed the buildings as if all the elements of the structure were imbued with the transformational glow. The inhabitants looked at each other in wonder as each started to be -----blue. A low-frequency hum filled the air; and in an instant, it was all gone---everything---gone.

No conflagration, no smoke, no ash, no screams; just gone. It was quite a tidy affair and incredibly efficient. It lacked all the elements of drama. With just the breath of a pause in the sequence between the initial four structures; the cleansing blue energy consumed everything from the Mississippi East, from pole to pole 9 am was the hour, and the longitudinal time frames were the guidelines. God had a plan and was sticking to it. Ok, he had to accept that there was a touch of a message in his first choices of buildings and inhabitants, but only a touch and for only an instant.

At 9:02 all that remained on the Island of Manhattan were the untouched Guggenheim, the Museum of Modern history, MoMa and the Libraries at Columbia and New York Public. All else were gone.

In Washington, the eerie blue glow started at Capitol Hill and moved westward to the White House just as in New York. They were just simply gone. Along the Washington Mall, the Smithsonian and a small grouping of museums remained. The only other structure to remain was the Lincoln Memorial.

From the Mason-Dixon Line south, other than a couple of buildings in New Orleans, one at Tulane University, and the other the Desire Oyster House all were simply----gone.

In Boston, Miami, Philadelphia all the same. A museum here, a library there. No people, cars, boats trains or the ability to transport them. Just the Earth below that they had sat on. It had started at nine am EST. on December 21 2012, and that would be the gauge for all that was to come. Even God had to start somewhere. There had to be an 'In the beginning' to get to an 'In the end'.

Between the longitudinal borders of the Mountain Zone and Halifax, from the Northern Hemisphere to the Southern Hemisphere, the blue destruction cleansed its way marching east and west over the face of the globe. Lima Peru which did not recognize multiple time zones or Daylight Savings Time paid the price for its choice. Peru would have enjoyed about fifty additional minutes of Earth time but was summarily dispatched along with its Eastern neighbors sharing the same time zone.

Commercial air craft radioed back to towers their confusion as they entered the airspace of cleansed areas, only to find their destinations no longer in existence. Turning backward and heading west or east, they bought a few hours of time as the only witnesses to the unfolding events. The blue fire marched west, time zone by time zone as the hour of nine in the morning rolled over and found its mark.

It took 24 hours before the blue cleanser made its way around the time and datelines to Greenland; and man ceased to exist on Earth ------that is, except for 5.8 million souls living within the borders of the Free Nation of Tibet.

In the blink of an eye, mankind and all of his structure's machines and filth were wiped away from the face of planet earth, an eerie silence fell until broken by a unified display of a large pod of blue whales alternating between acrobatic breaching, barrel rolls and the pounding of flukes on the surface of the oceans.

"Gaia's jigsaw earth is free-Early in the morning, rise and shine, and the world is callin'-Gaia's actuality-Sky, the ground, and a place to roam-Circus in a bubble, a place called home."

-Disco Biscuits

CHAPTER 68

First Kush Colony

It was early morning, and the activity at the Tibetan-Kush transit staging area was jam-packed with people. As the colonists assembled at the shuttle area, the steady train of boxes, luggage and multi-stickered steamer trunks made its way over to the massive transport ship. The luggage carriers floated effortlessly, hovering nine inches off the ground as they were Maglev lifted across the natural grass paver tarmac staging area. While the luggage was lifted into one side of the ship's hull a continuous stack of large shipping containers was elevated into huge hull storage areas at the lower level of the ship. The ship was shaped more like a Zeppelin than a sleek futuristic --- made for Hollywood ----space vehicle. Pretty was not the goal. It was all about function. Painted across the side was 'Enterprise II'. It was less than six months since Ravi and Elon's capable engineering and research team had perfected the Maglev Space drive. And only three months since the return of the first advance Kush research team.

The Space Maglev Drive's incredible ability to concentrate and convert into a magnetic resistance platform, the inert matter in space that permeated the cosmos; warp hyper space travel became available to bring the colonization of Kush to a reality. Today was a big day.

The first group of Colonists was ready. In groups of eighteen-hundred, they would be ferried to Kush. By the end of the next ninety-days, a tent community of seventy-two-hundred was planned to be in place. Moshe offered his services in managing the tent encampment organization. It made good sense with the similarity to the Kazarian way of life being built around temporary structured communities.

The majority of this wave of Colonials was made up of engineering and construction crews that hailed from Genesis City. The experienced team was charged with the task of building the initial settlement village, and the infrastructure required to support the next stage of immigration. The prospects for a successful colonization looked good; the testing and advance team experience had gone well. First, the unmanned probes to Kush, and then the advance team mission had established water, soil and air quality. The testing determined that the water was sweet and free of Radon or Hydrocarbons; the soil, fertile arable land, and the air, oxygen/nitrogen rich with no un-natural pollutants. The goal was to try to keep it that way.

Ravi was going to Kush to oversee the Maglev and Hydrogen Fusion installations for power and transportation, as these would be required immediately to get the village off the ground. Elon's hands were full with the responsibilities of the space transportation program and keeping up with the building of sufficient passenger and cargo ships.

Sam and Alyssa looked on and felt hope for the future. As the ship rose and prepared to move out to the launch zone; Sam and Alyssa walked back toward the path leading to Norbilunkga Palace and their home. Alyssa smiled up at Sam as she took his hand and placed it on the 'baby-bump' just starting to show. It was a different world. It was a good world.

EPILOGUE I-EARTH

The wind blew off the African Veldt with a warm dry breath as it pushed the waves of grass down announcing its path to where the grassland met the edge of the forest, then, climbing its way upward and into the verdant hillside. The grassland and forests were alive with a renewed bustling activity that was surprisingly relaxed since the exit of man from the mix. Such was the case across the face of planet Earth.

God smiled as he watched the two primates moving warily towards each other. The mass of the large silver backed male mountain gorilla shimmered in the African sun. The female chimpanzee stepped forward hesitantly and offered a stick coated from top to bottom with termites to the large male gorilla. The gorilla grunted his satisfaction at the offering and gently took the stick from the chimp. Swiping the stick through his broad lips, he heartedly munched the tasty treats as they burst with flavor over his palate. Dropping with a thump on to his behind in a passive show of trust, he offered the stick back to the chimp. The female feeling no threat, came over and began slowly and lovingly grooming the gorilla while making soft cooing sounds.

Just a beginning; it was Creative-Evolution in process.

EPILOGUE II-KUSH

The villages were set up along similar lines to the successful pattern that had worked so well in Tibet. If it wasn't broken, no one saw a reason to fix it. Travel time between Kush and Earth had been reduced to a two-week time period, which had greatly increased the passage of people and goods between the two planets. Land Maglev speeds allowed for no more than a day's travel between even the remotest of Kush villages and its neighbors.

The small Wilson colony decided to set up in a mountainous rain forest region with a climate similar to Costa Rica. They lobbied hard for the area saying that it was very important that they be close to the source of the best coffee producing regions of the planet. They hoped to be able to increase production above the levels of local consumption by next year and allow for some export.

In New Lhasa, the reassembly of the Dharmasala Palace was just about complete. The plan was to have the welcome center, hotel and conference pavilion done by December 21, 2014---the date of the first Kush-Earth-Jann-1-Gradis-2-Kazarian Jubilee music festival.

But that's a whole story in itself. Stay tuned.

THE END

ACKNOWLEDGEMENTS

The novel you just read was only made possible through the collaborative effort that went in to the process. Needless to say, my editing skills leave much to be desired—and leave an equal amount of errors in the body of the copy.

My lovely spouse had given me a budget of zero to work with for outside editing—so that left me no choice other than to enlist friends and family. Enlist I did, and with great response—coupled with a healthy dose of humility. Content critique and suggestions came from many directions. David Dafilou, Al Brothers, Alyssa, Mom, your comments were incredibly helpful, your honesty treasured. Thank you for your guidance and suggestions.

Now to the staff copy editors: Jefferson Link and Leah Ellenbogen. I can't thank my two copy and content editors enough. Not only were they un-compensated for their efforts, but they were harried by me to deliver the goods. Jefferson's attention to detail, punctuation, posessives—etc... gave me the beneft of a set of grammatical eyes and a tool belt of rules that I either didn't have at my disposal— or had lost on the way. Leah Ellenbogen, your copy editing was fabulous and complimentary—you caught much of what Jefferson did and then all that he might have missed. Your content editing, story line suggestions and attention to past, present and what voice to use were a lesson in themselves. I tried to apply what you suggested, learn from the common mistakes that you pointed out and to push myself beyond where my laziness told me to stop. I could have done more. Nothing you pushed me to do was wasted effort or anything but an enhancement. Your margin notes and comments of "UGHH!!!, Passive voice is the Devil!!!"; "Dad, I'm falling asleep" "Is that English"?"Now you're mixing tense!!" Only served to bring a smile to my face and make me think and strive to do better.

The errors that remain in the copy of this book are mine to own. The fact that they are still here should not reflect as detraction from the skills and efforts of the gracious and cost affective editing staff; however, they represent a laziness and lack of skill on the author's side.

Thanks to all for taking the time to read this book.

TURN THE PAGE FOR A PREVIEW OF THE
SECOND BOOK IN THE EXCITING KUSH
GENESIS SERIES

COMING IN JANUARY 2013

ENDANGERED SPECIES

ANOTHER NOVEL BY

MARK ELLENBOGEN

Endangered Species

Book 2 of the Genesis-Kush Trilogy

Chapter 1

Earth- Former Islamorada-Florida Keys

The huge tarpon rolled over slowly in the heat of the morning sun. The hog of a fish was the first to push up on the flats since the boat had anchored up. Fat with a stomach full of herring, all lulled lazy by the warming gulf waters; the monster fish looked to be a prize catch. Sam shushed Ravi as he polled the hovering Maglev skiff quietly forward across the flat. A flock of Flamingos squawked over head in a blaze of pink feathers, a small bonnet head shark cut the surface of the shallow water feeding its way back to the deep channel. Both men cringed as the shadow of the birds blended with a ripple from the shark, crossing the nose of the huge fish. The minor distractions were all it took; the combination spooked the big boy into a swirling exploding whirlpool of foam as the fish darted back to the deeper waters of the Gulf.

"Shit, he was easily a hundred and fifteen pounds!" Ravi moaned.

"Did you see what a pig that fish was? He looked like a fat torpedo coming up onto the flat." Sam put his fly-rod down and looked up at the sky; he shook his fist after the Flamingos merrily banking towards a small mangrove island to their left. In the distance, the bonnet-head cut a serpentine path across the flats with its dorsal pushed high out of the water. With a twitch of its tail, the shark blew across the duck grass waving in the current only inches below its belly.

The fishing day was just getting going; the two young anglers were ready for a very big day. It had been a short sixteen months since the end of the global occupation of Earth by humankind and the changes were striking. As was the case all over planet Earth, the wildlife in Florida Bay had responded quickly and positively to being free of their human companions. Not having a glut of humans bugging them constantly while soiling their habitat was a welcome change. In a little less than a year and a half, with no motors running on the water, no seines dipping tons of fish and feed out of the oceans, and no angling pressure from any direction, the Earth was healing itself as fast as it could.

Gazing around the calm blue shallow waters of the Florida Keys it was eerily quiet. The typical fishing day out on the flats, before the end of man's tenure, was continually interrupted by the noise of flat's skiffs and the stink of exhaust. Back in the day, powerful outboard driven boats, cris-crossed the channels and flats; throwing up a wake, scaring the fish off the shallows to shoot back to deeper water. The frightened fish high tailed it back into the depths at every pass, sometimes hours before they would return. Even more annoying, were the errant idiots on personal watercrafts blasting across the flats, traveling where they had no business going and too far offshore. The obnoxious jet-skis poured out from whatever resort had been stupid or greedy enough to rent the inconsiderate fools the noisy machines; they could ruin the best fishing day.

No, today none of that noise was going on, Drs. Ravi Najir and Sam Klein were about to have the Grand Slam fishing day to beat all times. The water was calm, the air crisp and smelling clean. The two had looked forward to transporting to the Keys in anticipation of the start of the annual tarpon migration that occurred every year. The tarpon, depending on conditions, started their migratory move in May or June of each year. Beginning their annual trek out of the Gulf of Mexico and Caribbean, the giant silver herrings made their way to the coast of Florida. Arriving first at the lower Keys, the fish made a circuit over the summer months that moved northward before completing its circuit. The fish started the season in Key West, Marathon and Islamorada, then on to Flamingo, Naples and Marco Island to the north and west. As the summer progressed they focused in greatest numbers, favoring the Gulf side of the state. They swam up to Tarpon Springs, Homosassa, on their way to Apalachicola and Sopchoppy, before heading back to their deep Gulf and Caribbean waters for the winter.

The two astronomers, formerly of Humboldt California (which no longer existed with any trace), and now of Tibet and the planet Kush, respectively;

were hovering silently, nine inches above the surface of the water. The only disturbance on the bay was the quiet swish of the push-pole as it moved the Maglev skiff towards their targets, and the gentle plop of a fly being perfectly placed by the anglers. Maglev fishing was going to open up a whole new opportunity for sight fishing, and Ravi and Sam intended to take advantage of the possibilities it brought to the table. The fish didn't have a chance!

Ravi looked back west towards the Gulf of Mexico pointing to the where the deep water met the edge of the flat.

"Hey Sam, there they are. It's a big school and they're moving this way. Whoa! Check it out, their Daisy-Chaining!" The school of tarpon formed a neat circle swimming in a perfect circumference, rolling right and left in the unique instinctive manner that was definitive of the species. As each fish rolled over in sequence, the bright morning light flashed a silver, gray and black shimmer that reflected off of the fish, flashing the water's surface.

"Point the nose their way Ravi. I can't reach them from here across the bow."

Ravi pushed away with the pole on the side of the boat and then switched the Maglev on. With a foot peddle operator configured from a salvaged Minn Kota trolling motor kit, he swung the boat slowly towards the school of fish positioned still well out of Sam's casting range. With only the low resonant hum of the hydrogen-fusion Maglev motor making a sound, he inched above the water and towards the school of tarpon.

As the great Silver Kings got closer to the shallow water, they stopped their circling antics and floated in groups of three. Each pod in turn, floated up on to the flat and into crystal-clear water barely twelve-inches deep. The fish took up position in two groups of three with a large lead fish at the center of each. Gliding slowly, like birds in formation, the triangle of tarpon started to drift towards the anxious fishermen.

Sam checked his Sage ten-weight-ten fly rod making sure the line was free and loose in the glides. He rolled out some line, holding it in his left hand squinting through his Maui Jims at the advancing fish. The polarized green lenses enhanced his visible range to well below the surface of the calm water, cutting through the glare and reflection of the Florida Sun like butter. Sam flicked the fast-action head of the rod, and the 'Tarpon Bunny' fly pattern, a flat's favorite, landed in his hand. He smoothed out the feathers checking his fly, knot, hook and barb. The pattern was banded and buff colored, mimicking a tasty flats shrimp when jigged through the water.

"OK Ravi, that's it; keep the bow to the left of their noses, I'm going for the big sucker in front. Look at the size of that hog; he's bigger than the one we put you on to yesterday. My turn! Come to Papa! I won't hurt ya, just want to catch-ya!" Sam said in a horse, hushed whisper of anticipation.

With two distance-increasing false casts, and a perfect loop back-cast behind him, Sam laid out sixty feet of line and plopped the fly and tippet silently down in the water; the perfectly presented fly, barely four-feet in front of the lead fish. The fly and the fish were clearly visible in the sparkling shallow waters of the flat. As the fish turned his head toward the fly, Sam gave two rapid strips of the line and stopped, holding his breath, he waited. The fly hung suspended in the water as the Tarpon's platy mouth opened wide and engulfed the Tarpon Bunny. Sam counted to three, pausing to let the fish commit to the bait. Then with a sharp pull back on the loose fly line—he banged the fly hard; once, then a second time lifting his rod tight.

"Hit him! Hit-'em again!" screamed Ravi. "He's gonna spit it! Hit 'emmm!

Sam pulled twice more, firmly setting the hook into the monster's bony jaw. In a shower of salt spray and sheer power, the angry fish took off. The line screaming off his reel, Sam held on for dear life as the one-hundred and fifty pound fish started to strip his reel deep into the Dacron backing line. The tarpon shot across the flat like a bullet as the pressure on Sam's line whipped the boat around to face the ass-end of the retreating fish. Sam kept palming the face of the reel trying to slow down the fish.

"Sam, you better try and turn him or he's going to snap you off," Ravi coached.

Sam started to apply pressure gaining a few yards that he quickly rolled back on the reel. As he tried to horse the tarpon his way, in a splash of silver, the fish erupted out of the water dancing on its tail trying to toss the hook. With a slam of its full broad side against the water, the fish landed with a loud 'smack' that cracked across the flats echoing off the nearby mangroves.

"Get a picture! Grab the camera!" screamed Sam. Sam started furiously reeling up the slack unintentionally created by the fish dancing on its tail toward the boat.

Ravi jumped off of the poling platform and started digging around the well of the boat looking for his camera. Finally succeeding he got off two good shots as the silver beauty breeched the surface for a second time. Sam kept the line taught, trying like hell to avoid being broken off, while stealing some more precious yardage yielded by the brute.

"Did you get it?" asked an anxious Sam more concerned about photo-documenting the event while gaining on his catch.

"Yep, two good ones. You better get the job done though; look over at the channel marker." Ravi nodded his head to his left.

Whipping around in an erratic pattern was a dorsal fin sticking a good twelve inches out of the water. Attached to the fin was a very excited nine-foot bull shark sensing distress, and a meal, courtesy of the two anglers. The shark was heading determinately their way. Ravi shifted his foot over to the pedal controller and started backing the boat down on the tarpon as

Sam did his best to keep up with the pace. While they fought the fish, both men kept their eyes on the shark as it twitched in anticipation and adjusted its path toward the humongous tarpon.

"Come, on we're almost to the leader. Just let me touch it and I'll snap him off."

"Uh-Oh, here comes the big set of swimming teeth!" said Ravi. He jumped back down off the platform grabbing the fourteen-foot graphite push-pole. Ravi raised the pole high and slammed it down hard on the water in front of the shark. The behemoth shot off like a rocket but immediately adjusted, turning back toward the boat to make an approach from the other direction.

"Do it now Sam! This guy isn't going to keep being fooled by the pole."

"Oh, all right. What a waste."

Sam reeled down tight to the surface of the water as the tarpon resisted and started to make another screaming run. The hooked beast was no more than twenty-feet off the bow of the boat and began turning to shoot back across the flat. Pulling the rod tip back and up at the same time, with a loud retort, Sam broke the leader away from the tippet. Like a rocket, the freed tarpon flew off of the flat and out into the deep waters of the Gulf. The pissed shark shot around the opposite side of the boat in pursuit. Luckily for the tarpon, the toothy predator was outclassed by the faster fish's speed and Ravi's diversion tactics.

"Nice fish!" said Sam. Stupid shark almost ruined the day.

"Nice fish." agreed Ravi. "At least we got pictures. Who boated their tarpon yesterday---that would be me, Ravi." taunted the captain for the day.

Ravi lowered the boat from its nine inch floating hover above the water and switched off the Maglev. The skiff settled down with barely a splash onto the calm surface of Florida Bay.

"Ok, Ahab. That counted as a catch. I touched the leader. It just wasn't still connected to the fish. I get special treatment for natural interference and being a socially conscious angler. It would've been poor sport to keep him on the line or tire him out for shark bait. We did the right thing. How about we pull over to those mangroves; regroup, fix our tackle and have a snack? We'll get rigged up for bonefish and see if we can't complete the Slam before dark. One big bone plus a snook, permit or redfish equals a Grand-Slam for Sam! Then we can call it a day."

The satisfied fishermen stowed their tackle, wiped down the goo on the deck and gunwales. Done with the scrub down, they leaned over to wash their hands in the briny liquid. Once again ready to roll, Ravi flipped the hydrogen fusion generator back on and sat down at the controls.

"Hold on, this won't take long."

With a quiet hum, the Maglev skiff lifted free of the water's surface and shot over to the largest of three mangrove islands. In less than a minute, they were parked on the sand of the small sandy beach on Upper Arsnicker Key.

Sam, opened the cooler and grabbed two large bottles filled with iced green tea, he popped the tops and handed one to Ravi. The boys kicked back sipping their tea and recounting the morning excitement from the beginning. As was the custom, telling of the 'fish-tail' after the catch, was as important as the catch itself. The audience didn't matter. All you needed was a set of ears in the vicinity.

As the two relaxed between fishing sessions, Sam held out his arm to Ravi and with a curious frown said:

"Hey Ravi, take a look at my arm. What's missing here?"

"I don't know I have a better tan?"

"No. Come on what's the one thing you can count on sitting next to a mangrove in the Keys?"

"Mosquitoes! That's it! There's no mosquitoes, no chiggers!" I didn't even realize it. They're gone!"

"Where'd the little blood-sucking bastards go?" said Ravi.

"Now, that's literally a gift from God," said Sam. "Need I say more?"

Chapter 2

The flavorful and anti-oxidant rich Tibetan green tea, had become the new beverage of choice since Power Aide, Gatorade, Monster and Red-Bull were no longer available. The manufacturing facilities for the famous beverage brands, and all of their workers, vaporized sixteen months prior on December 21, 2012. Coca-cola was still being manufactured in Tibet, but production could barely keep up with local consumption. There was no allocation to allow for traveling with it out of the border area for recreational purposes. Tea was in ample supply in Tibet, and every one of the surviving humans carried a large store of the high quality tannic leaves with them wherever they traveled.

Coca-Cola wasn't the only thing no longer available, there were a lot of things in short supply these days. The shortages were to be expected when one took in to account that the face of the Earth was wiped clean of approximately 6, 994,000,000 human inhabitants along with almost everything they had ever built, modified, used or placed, above below or upon the surface of the Earth.

Mankind finally paid the ultimate price for his folly. After years of abusing the planet, its air, its waters and each other; God had set the table right. In a brief twenty-four-hour period, he wiped the Earth's slate clean in anticipation of a do-over to end all. Ravi and Sam, along with about six-million others were the only Earthlings that remained alive and well. It seems that the mosquito had also missed the cut.

God (that's right, for real,-God), had produced in six short days a new solar system and planet out of the Cosmic Goo of the Crab Nebula. The Crab Nebula, originally formed in 1054 AD, contained the perfect mix of particulate matter and energy that God liked to work with. Strapping on his tools in December of 2011, God set the stage for his cleansing of Earth. Starting with a sparkling new sun and then molding an Earthlike planet to orbit around it, God built a new platform in the sky. God planned to begin anew with what he hoped would be a better product than his last results on Earth. Mankind had become more trouble than he was worth. Rather than trying to fix humans with limited results; God decided to start over and get it right from the start.

Ravi Najir and Sam Klein, while still PhD students at Humboldt State University, had been the two unlikely souls that discovered God's recent handiwork in the heavens. With the help of the Hubble Space Telescope, they had rocked the world, reset reality and fattened their bank-accounts overnight with their discovery of God's new solar system. Their discovery and subsequent naming of the two new celestial bodies, Genesis for the star/sun, and Kush for the Earthlike planet; had shifted the world paradigm. The result of that shift was that their lives became intertwined in incredible events leading up to the end of the world as it was; and the ultimate fishing opportunity they were enjoying this day.

Of the six-million Earthlings that had made the cut and were enjoying salvation, about four-million lived within the borders of Tibet and the remainder had colonized the new world of Kush.

But seriously, if I have to tell you all this stuff and burn a whole chapter in the process; then you didn't read the first book in this series. THIS IS THE SECOND BOOK. Don't you think it would make sense to do them in order? If you haven't read the first book then close this one—go buy the first one and catch up. OK.

Chapter 3

Planet Kush-State of New Tibet-Max Yasgur Village

Over by the Festival Pavilion the last transport to Gradis-2 was lifting off. New found friends stood on the platform and whooped and waved good-by to the final group of folks heading back to their home planets. It had been three days of music, arts and fun in the Genesis sun. The close of the First Annual Interplanetary Jubilee Festival had arrived sooner than the participants wished. In the last three days the first broad social interaction had occurred between the remaining earthlings and the inhabitants of Kazaria, Jann-1 and Gradis-2, the sister planets that had played a role saving the few remaining earthlings that were now colonizing Earth and Kush.

The sound stage was still in place, littered with the tools and equipment of the crew dismantling the two speaker towers on either side. Perched on top of rolling scaffolds, the men were working from the top down sequentially disconnecting and lowering the sound units to the waiting workers below. Banners and concert posters were being rolled up and stowed away in anticipation of the next event. In the open field in front of the stage, clean-up crews were gathering up the litter left behind by the festival participants.

Walking along pushing a floating platform that looked like a cross between a garbage can buggy and a wheelbarrow (sans wheel), the hovering pushcarts were transportable low-energy, clean emission incinerators. There was no longer need for the requisite black garbage bag. No longer any multiple truck laden runs to the landfill on Kush. As each piece of detritus was encountered, the tech just tossed it with a flip into one of the barrels on his cart. A sneaker here, plastic water bottle there, with a flick of the wrist they landed in the mouth of one of the barrels, disappearing in a flash of blue glow. A few stragglers were still breaking down their campsites as the clean-up crews came their way. The bedraggled music goers helped the trash removal effort by trying to see just how big a chunk of garbage the vaporizing barrels could handle. It was a great fun to drop a sizeable load of junk, watching it dissolve in stages from bottom to top as it dropped below the rim of the barrel and was engulfed in a blue vaporizing zap. New technology was always cool to play with.

With remarkable efficiency, the clean-up process commenced. Barely leaving an ash behind to deal with, the new technology developed by the Earth-Kush Ecology Village Research Center (EKEV), in Quinlan Province, Tibet, was making its mark on keeping Kush green and clean. Making a mark, by leaving no mark behind, was the goal. All that remained at the bottom of the barrels was a fine film of carbon dust that was totally contaminant neutral. The miniature hydrogen fusion engines ran the propulsion and incinerator process with only a puff of water vapor as emissions. With good old H2O, and a small compact high-capacity lithium-ion battery the only fuel required to run the machines, the technology was as planet friendly as one could get.

Dr. E.J. Camlala, former professor and chairman of the Humboldt State University Astronomy and Space Science program, was busy breaking down his campsite and cleaning up the mess he and his buddies had produced over the last three days. With a look of excited anticipation, he saw the incinerator buggy heading his way. Looking around he tried to make as big a pile of garbage he could muster, not wanting to miss the opportunity of making the mound of crap evaporate. As the clean-up tech made his way over toward Camlala, he waved the guy over and grabbing his pile of refuse. Camlala walked over, ignoring the tech's offered reach to relieve him of the trash. Leaning over the top of the barrel, he dropped the load. In a flash of blue hue the stack began to disintegrate, suddenly the machine coughed twice and erupted. Blowing out of the mouth of the barrel popped half of a barely cooked, partially eaten burger, a beetle and a pile of ants. The entire barrel rejects spewing up and away from the barrel's mouth and landed on the lawn. Camlala jumped back while the tech chuckled.

"Yeah, pretty neat, huh! New safety modification came out last month. Now they can differentiate living flesh from inert material. A lot safer to operate and we don't fry anything we shouldn't. The Tibetan's were so appalled at the first commercial test models after they saw a couple of mice get dumped into a high-volume unit, wasn't real P.C.. The Western design team needed to be more sympathetic and sensitive toward their Buddhist and Hindu co-designers."

"Wow, that thing is great," said Camlala. I wish I had one at home before the end; would have made one hell of a difference during spring cleaning." Camlala continued,

"Were you here for the concert?"

"Just the last two nights; I got to see the Marley brothers and the Umphrey's show. I saw what was left of the Dave Matthew's band last night. How great is it that so many bands made the cut to salvation, mostly still together?"

"Yah, we lost a lot of artists, kept some great ones though. I'm thankful that the 'arts' are strongly represented among the surviving inhabitants. It could have been worse. I almost lost it when the Stones walked out Saturday night. How the hell did Mick Jagger ever make the cut with that overblown ego? I could see Keith Richards maybe, his ego has taken a beating over the years, most of it from the bottle or at Mick's hands!"

"Yeah, they rocked, 'Sympathy for the Devil' was quite the jam. As far as Jagger goes, I have a friend that worked on the selection software. He says that there was a .00043 percent error factor that would produce false negatives or false positive. They didn't have time so they couldn't de-bug it, not even sure if they could. The result is some were lost, some saved without truly passing the ego and self-will tests. Mick Jagger's presence is an example of source code error."

"I really got into the music from Kazaria. The string arrangements were like nothing I have ever heard. Sort of like a combination of a Celtic rock band and a Kleizmer Polka. It had a dissonant quality but unique and captivating. That lead violinist with the wa-wa attachment blew me away. I didn't care for the Jann-1 music though, all that out-of -tune harp stuff and the vocals sounded like they were crying in pain. The Gradis-2 bands were hot though. Good rock and roll and awesome light show."

"Talk about hot, did you see the women from Jann-1! They were like freaking goddesses! Eyes like saucers, exotic pale blue and green ones, with olive skin and brown hair. I thought I died and went to heaven. Oh—that's right this is pretty damn close to that reality, now isn't it." Camlala looked dreamily off into the sky then turned back to his fellow Kushen (they all liked the newly penned moniker).

"Well, I'm going to finish cleaning and pack up. I teach a class tomorrow in astro-physics at Kush-U. I have some review to do and need to get some sleep so I'm on my toes in the morning. Thanks for the help and the incinerator demonstration."

"No problem. Maybe I will see you around the campus. I'm a first year med- student at KU myself."

Camlala, looked at him with a twinkle and a smile and said, "So did you have any trouble getting in?"

"Nah, ninety-nine percent of the competition is dead. Most of them probably ego-fried in 2012. I think it will be a long while before anyone has trouble getting into med school, or for any major at that!"

The two did a fist bump and went about their tasks. Camlala, back to wrapping up his tent and pulling stakes out of the ground. The clean-up tech/med-student back to tossing left-over festival mess into the barrels.

The huge Festival Pavilion was a temporary structure with a polymer-canvas skin stretched over a light-weight metallic frame. The combined frame and body were stretched in a parabolic shape that maximized the interior volume while minimizing any wind or snow load from having an impact on the structure. Until yesterday, the pavilion had housed about a thousand vendors and artists from the five worlds participating in the three-day event. Crews from Genesis City--Tibet, flew in from Earth on a large hyper-space transport two-weeks prior. In the middle of Yasgur field they had unloaded the frame, skin and mechanical plant and assembled the whole kit and caboodle in three short days. The self-contained structure was outfitted with its own hydrogen-fusion power plant that ran all heating, ventilation and air conditioning, as well as the general power for the lighting and electric. The building came with portable bathroom facilities that used no water at all, depending instead on the efficient systems provided by the blue evaporator technology similar to the garbage incinerators. Potable water was provided by way of a collector pipe that ran from the pure mountain stream that snaked its way through the open meadow. The stream started high in the Dharmasalla range of mountains to the East and gushed pristine waters down through the countryside. No commercial industry, hydrocarbon spill or human insult of any kind had ever touched the water on Kush. No Kush native ever thought twice about dipping a container or a hand into the river to get a drink. The Pavilion could be dismantled and stored, barely leaving behind a blemish on the surface of the planet.

Camlala walked by the Pavilion and watched the workers as he made his way over to the last Maglev transport back to Kush City. He tossed his back-pack and tent on to the storage rack at the rear and hopped on board. He hooked up his iPod and headphones and flipped around the dial looking for some traveling tunes for the high-speed ride back to the city center. Settling on U2's 'It's a Beautiful Day' he settled in and waved to the driver. The pilot motioned to a couple of slow pokes stopping to take one last look at the concert grounds to hurry them along. Picking up the pace they double-timed it to the waiting ride, not wanting to have to wait for the next one. Everyone on board, the Maglev jockey flipped the power switch, made sure everyone was harnessed in and jammed on the pedal. The trip from Yasgur Village to Kush City was just under three-hundred miles door-to-door.

They would make it in fifteen-minutes. Maglev was the only way to travel.

www.ingramcontent.com/pod-product-compliance
Lightning Source LLC
Chambersburg PA
CBHW071643260626
47170CB00001B/219